Falling for Her

A yellow ladder lay on its side on the ground. Judging from the marks it had left, Nolie had set it up in soft soil and then, because it was only six feet tall and the roof was at least seven, she'd disregarded all the warning labels and stood on the very top to make it onto the roof. Unstable footing plus a shaky transfer of weight equaled a ladder on its side.

"*Micahlyn!* Come out right now!"

"She's abandoned you," Chase said, surprising her.

She let out a shriek, lost her grip, and started to fall. Reacting instinctively, Chase grabbed her around the hips, planted his bare feet in the dirt, then slowly lowered her to the ground.

God, he'd forgotten how different women were from men. How nice *soft* could be. How stimulated a man could get.

But it didn't mean a thing. Was purely involuntary.

Like the widening of her eyes when she felt it too.

The instant her feet touched ground, she scrambled back a few yards, tugged her T-shirt down past her hips, then folded her arms across her chest. Her cheeks were flushed bright red. . . .

CABIN FEVER

Marilyn Pappano

A DELL BOOK

CABIN FEVER
A Dell Book / July 2003

Published by
Bantam Dell
A Division of Random House, Inc.
New York, New York

Dell is a registered trademark of Random House, Inc., and the
colophon is a trademark of Random House, Inc.

ISBN 0-440-24118-9

Manufactured in the United States of America
Published simultaneously in Canada

OPM   10 9 8 7 6 5 4 3 2 1

A List of Characters

Nathan and Emilie Dalton Bishop,
New York City detective turned small-town cop and assistant manager at the local inn
Michael, *son*
Alanna, Josie, and Brendan Dalton,
Emilie's nieces and nephew

Berry Dalton,
the Dalton children's drug-addicted mother

Corinna Winchester Humphries & Agatha
Winchester Grayson, *Bethlehem's grand dames and matchmakers extraordinaire*

Ross and Maggie McKinney,
CEO of McKinney Industries and wife/mother
Rachel, *daughter*

J. D. and Kelsey Grayson,
psychiatrist and social worker
Trey, *J.D.'s son*
Caleb, Jacob, Noah, and Gracie Brown-Grayson,
adopted children

Bud, *J.D.'s father and newly wed to Agatha Winchester Grayson*

Gabe and Noelle Rawlins,
engineer at McKinney Industries and angel-turned human

Sophy, Gloria and Norma,
guardian angels; Noelle's replacements

Tom and Holly McBride Flynn,
second in charge at McKinney Industries and owner of McBride Inn

Ben and Lynda Barone Foster,
carpenter and top executive at McKinney Industries

Alanna Dalton,
Ben's daughter

Melina Dimitris,
private investigator from Buffalo

Sebastian Knight, *carpenter*
Chrissy, *daughter*

Julie Bujold,
Alanna's homeless friend and caretaker

Bree Aiken,
Holly McBride Flynn's half sister

Alex and Melissa Thomas,
lawyer and plant nursery owner

Mitch and Shelly Walker,
chief of police and wife/mother

Harry Winslow and Maeve Carter,
owner and waitress at Harry's Diner

Chapter One

"AND THEN THE PRINCESS KISSED THE FROG—"

"Ewww!"

"—and do you know what happened then?" Though she'd heard the story a hundred times or more, five-year-old Micahlyn Harper solemnly shook her head.

"Nothing!" Nolie said. "He just sat there in her hands, still an ugly old frog, and then he jumped into the water with a splash and— Oh, blast." Seeing a faded yellow mailbox a few yards ahead, she reached for the directions tucked beneath the visor and scanned for the reference to the mailbox. The sudden blare of an approaching car horn made her drop the paper, steer back into her own lane, then grip the steering wheel with both hands as they sailed past their turn.

They were almost there . . . and it wasn't dread but anticipation that had her stomach tied in knots, she lied to herself. For the first time in her twenty-five years, she was on her own, solely responsible for herself and Micahlyn. They were making a new start in a new town far from the wide spot in an Arkansas road where they'd both lived their entire lives. They were beginning an adventure.

One that, according to her in-laws, was certain to end in disaster.

So far, they'd been more right than wrong. Nolie and Micahlyn's great journey to Bethlehem, New York, had begun three days ago with a flat tire outside Little Rock and been livened up by a speeding ticket outside Memphis, a dead battery in the middle of Pennsylvania, and a second flat in New York. As if that wasn't enough, the farther they'd gotten from Whiskey Creek, the more resistant Micahlyn had gotten. She'd whined each night she'd had to sleep in a motel room and each morning she'd had to eat a breakfast that wasn't lovingly prepared to her specifications by her grandma. She'd fussed about the long hours in the car and had marked their crossing the New York state line by throwing up a Happy Meal, two jelly doughnuts, and a carton of chocolate milk in the backseat. Instead of asking, "Are we there yet?" she'd been satisfied with frequent repetitions of, "Can we go home now?" She'd heard her grandpa declare she would hate Bethlehem, and, by God, she was determined to prove him right.

Fortunately, Nolie was more determined to prove him wrong.

She turned around at the first chance, then headed back up the mountain. When she saw the yellow mailbox up ahead, she slowed and put on her left-turn signal. After an eighteen-wheeler blasted by fast enough to rock her car, she turned into the narrow dirt lane, then drew a deep breath.

The lawyer who'd settled her great-grandfather's estate had warned her that the two houses she'd inherited weren't anything fancy. They'd been built at a time when money was tight, and the old man had never seen reason to improve on them when his cash flow improved. The smaller of the two cabins had been rented, though, nearly a month ago, to a woman from Boston, so at least they were livable and providing a little income. And as far as fancy . . . heavens, her best friend back home in Whiskey Creek hadn't gotten indoor plumbing until they were in third grade, so sleepovers had meant middle-of-the-night trips to the outhouse. She didn't require fancy.

All she wanted was a place that was clean and in good repair, that provided a sense of security as well as shelter from the cold and rain, with running water and windows to open for cooling breezes in the heat. Oh, and this was important—it had to be hers. No more living like a guest in someone else's house, barely able to make a move without advice or interference. She needed her own home for her own little family.

Follow the dirt road to its end, the lawyer had told her. They would come to the unoccupied cabin first, then fifty yards farther down the road was their Boston neighbor. Nolie hadn't thought to ask whether the woman used the cabin for a weekend getaway, or if she'd taken a year's sabbatical from her job in Massachusetts. Maybe the woman had kicked the city's dust from her heels for the slower pace of small-town living. She supposed she would soon find out, since being neighborly was something everyone did well in Whiskey Creek.

The road was narrow, wide enough for only one vehicle in most places, and wound through dense woods. Twice the car bumped over rough-hewn bridges that spanned a pretty little creek, and several of the curves could challenge any hairpin in the Ozark Mountain roads she knew so well for sharpness. After what seemed like a mile and a half, maybe two miles, they chugged up a rather steep incline and then they were there.

The cabin stood on the left side of the road, set back about twenty-five feet. Trees shorn of their branches and laid end to end marked off a double-wide parking space, but otherwise it was difficult to tell the difference between parking space, yard, and road. All three were dirt and liberally covered with pine needless, and all three sprouted hardy weeds here and there, along with a few ferns, vines, and other shade-loving plants.

Nolie parked between the tree trunks, shut off the engine, then went back to gripping the steering wheel tightly. Her dominating impression of the cabin was simple and immediate—it was very brown. Brown planks, brown shingles, brown porch, brown paint on the trim. Even the window screens, in bad need of scrubbing, appeared a murky rust-brown.

Her second impression was that Great-Grandfather Legare must have liked the rustic look. The posts that supported the porch roof were slender tree trunks, stripped of their limbs and bark. The railing was more trunks, turned horizontally and supported every eight feet by fatter naked trunks. The bench pushed against the wall was a tree trunk split in half, bark still intact, supported by sturdy branches lashed together in an X shape. The front door was massive, the axe marks visible even from a distance, and a pair of antlers hung crookedly above it.

After a steadying breath, she forced her fingers to release the steering wheel, then looked at Micahlyn. Her daughter was listlessly toying with the hair of her favorite Barbie and paying zero attention to the fact that they'd arrived. It was as if she believed if she ignored it, it wasn't real. She wanted so much to be home with Grandma and Grandpa, and why shouldn't she? It was the only home she'd ever known, and she had no clue that it was the most suffocating, restrictive place on earth. Of course, Obie and Marlene had treated her differently than they had treated Nolie. Micahlyn was the grandbaby they loved more than life itself, while Nolie had been the daughter-in-law foolish enough to not curl up and die when their son had. She'd been selfish enough to want a life, to want some say in raising her own daughter, to—God forbid—have a relationship with a man sometime.

"We're here, Micahlyn."

Her daughter ignored her.

"Come on, babe. Let's start unpacking the car, and then we can have a look around our new home."

At that, Micahlyn gave her a narrow-eyed look. "*My* home is in Arkansas."

"No, honey, your home is with me, right here in Bethlehem. Come on. Once we get the car unloaded, we'll go into town and see if we can find a place that serves ice cream for lunch."

Once again the kid ignored her. With a sigh, Nolie got out of the car, took a box of cleaning supplies from the backseat, and climbed the five steps to the porch. There she was stopped in her tracks by the sight of a heart, pierced by Cupid's arrow, carved into the post on the left. Shifting the box to her right hip, she drew her fingers over the outline. Long ago someone had carved initials in its center, but all that remained now were scars and gouges. The result of a broken heart? Impossible. According to her grandmother, her great-grandfather hadn't had a heart.

Shaking her head wryly, she crossed to the door. The lawyer had changed the lock as she'd requested, adding a shiny brass dead bolt to the old knob. She fished the key off her ring, propped back the screen door with one foot, and opened the door.

The air that drifted out to greet her smelled musty. Fair enough, she supposed, since the place had been closed up for a year. Once she stepped inside and put the box down on a dustcloth-covered lump, she took a deeper breath and identified the faint aroma of tobacco underlying the must.

In the one photograph she'd seen of Hiram Legare, he'd been clenching a stogie between his teeth. A nasty habit, her grandmother had said, fitting to a nasty and heartless man. That was the one and only time she'd ever talked about him to Nolie.

The living room was paneled—brown again—with a mostly brown rug covering a plank floor the same color. A rock fireplace filled one wall, with built-in shelves on either side, and the furniture was better than she expected. Peeks under the cloths revealed a leather sofa—brown, of course—and an easy chair in a heavy floral print, as well as a recliner and a rocker. The drapes at the windows were past saving, but out here in the woods, with no neighbor but the woman from Boston, what need did she really have for draperies?

Pausing in front of the picture window, she watched her daughter play. Micahlyn had gotten her looks about equally from her mother and father. She had Nolie's red hair and fair skin, poor thing, and her stubborn jaw and blue eyes, and Jeff's ears, nose, mouth, and eyesight. Her glasses' lenses were thick and magnified her eyes, giving her the look of a solemn little owl. A *sad* little owl at the moment.

Panic seized Nolie, tightening her chest. What if her child was right in her insistence that their home was in Arkansas? What if taking her away from Obie and Marlene and forcing her to live in New York caused irreparable harm to her still-developing psyche? What if Nolie *was* simply being selfish, thinking only of herself and to hell with everyone else, even her own baby, as her in-laws insisted?

She wheezed a couple of times before she was finally able to take a full breath. She *wasn't* being selfish. She'd made this move for Micahlyn as much as, if not more than, for herself. Micahlyn could only benefit from having a healthier, happier mother, and the past three years had been a painful lesson that Nolie was happiest away from the Harpers. She wasn't cutting them out of their lives completely. She'd stressed to them repeatedly that they could call anytime they wanted, and they were welcome to visit as often as they liked . . . within reason, of course.

She just needed some freedom. Needed to have friends other than her in-laws. Needed to be able to smile at a man without their acting as if she'd desecrated Jeff's memory. Needed to be treated like an intelligent, capable adult—like a person.

She needed to be Noile McVie Harper once in a while. Not Micahlyn's mother. Not Jeff's widow.

Of course, she couldn't tell Micahlyn any of that, and her daughter wouldn't understand if she did. But she would come out of this blue mood. As soon as they were settled in and she'd made some friends, she would be fine.

Repeating that mantra to herself, Nolie set to work. She removed the heavy, dust-coated cloths, opened the few windows that weren't painted shut, lit scented candles, and swept, vacuumed, and dusted. She made frequent trips to the porch and to the car, and each time Micahlyn remained in the front seat, still buckled in, pretending she was someplace else. Nolie tried a couple of times to coax her out, then decided to leave her be.

She was in the kitchen, laying new shelf liner in the cabinets she'd scrubbed earlier, when a bloodcurdling scream sent chills down her spine. She dropped the ivy-patterned paper she'd just finished cutting and rushed to the front door. Micahlyn reached it a few seconds before she did and leaped into her arms, shrieking and clutching Nolie in a choke hold.

"Mama, Mama, the bogeyman's outside!" she wailed.

"He's big and scary, and he was gonna drag me off to his cave!"

"Shh, baby, it's all right," Nolie said, patting and bouncing her the way she had when Micahlyn was a baby with teething pains. "It's okay, sweetheart. You know there's no such thing as bogeymen. It's all right, baby, calm dow—"

She wasn't sure what made her look outside just then—the hair on her neck standing on end or the goose bumps racing down her arms—but for an instant she understood her daughter's mistake all too well. Maybe it was no bogeyman that had frightened Micahlyn, but it was definitely a man, and from her vantage point, he looked pretty damn scary.

He stood several inches over six feet, and when he was eating regularly, she imagined he was broad-shouldered and muscular. As it was, he was lean, almost painfully so, and looked meaner and scruffier than a hungry coyote that had cornered its prey. His hair was black and hung, lank and tangled, past his shoulders. His eyes were dark, his jaw was stubbled with a heavy growth of beard, and his skin—like everything else—was also dark, except where the broad pale line of a scar slashed across his ribs. He wore jeans that were faded practically white and slid down his narrow hips, and tennis shoes that should have been relegated to the trash a long time ago.

He looked more like the bogeyman than anyone she'd ever met.

Still shushing Micahlyn, she moved to the screen door and not so subtly secured the hook. He saw her do it, and the corner of his mouth lifted in what she imagined passed for a smile. Of course, they both knew the flimsy screen wouldn't keep out much more than a gnat, and not even that if it was determined to get in. She figured one thrust of his large, powerful hand, and he could reach through the screen and snatch both her and Micahlyn outside.

"C-c-can I help you?"

Some folks might have taken that as an invitation to come closer, but he remained where he was, motionless at the bottom of the steps. "What are you doing here?" His voice was little more than a growl, as rough as everything else about him, and made her want to quake the way Micahlyn was.

Somewhere deep inside her cowered the urge to inform him that *she* got to ask the questions on *her* property, but she'd been timid far too long to change now. "We're m-moving in."

"You can't do that. The real estate agent said this place wasn't for rent."

Her back was starting to ache from the strain of holding her daughter, on top of the heavy cleaning and three days' driving, but when she tried to lower Micahlyn to the floor, the girl hung on for all she was worth. Gritting her teeth, Nolie resettled her on her hip. "It's not for rent. I own it." Just so he didn't miss the significance, she nodded toward the other cabin. "I own that one, too."

For a long moment he stared at her, then he uttered an obscenity. She'd thought she was accustomed to swearing— after all, her father had had a colorful vocabulary, and Jeff had had a pretty good grasp of all the bad words by the time he was twelve, though he'd watched his mouth in front of her—but this wild-looking stranger's obscenity was truly obscene and made her clap her hand over Micahlyn's ear. It didn't matter, though, since her sweet daughter was still muttering about the bogeyman.

"I-I'm Nolie Harper," she said, making an effort to sound neighborly. "This is my daughter, Micahlyn. And you are? . . ."

He swore again, one succinct word, then dragged his fingers through his hair. It did nothing to restore order to it. Then he sourly, reluctantly, gave his name. "Chase."

At least, she thought it was his name. For one regretful, wasted moment, Nolie wished she'd been more on the ball when the lawyer had mentioned her tenant. He'd told her that a real estate agent in Howland, forty-some miles from Bethlehem, had rented the cabin to a woman in Boston for a year, and nothing else. And she hadn't asked any questions. Not "What is this woman's name?" or "Does she live alone?" or "Does a very scary, menacing, dangerous man live with her?" She hadn't even asked how much rent the woman was paying.

She needed to get a handle on this property-owner business before some hustler figured out she was ripe for the pickin'.

"Do you . . . uh, do you live over there?" she finally asked.

"Yeah."

"Alone?"

His gaze narrowed and sent a shiver down her spine. "Until today."

"I–I was told the-the person who rented that cabin was a woman. From Boston. In Massachusetts." She clamped her jaw shut to keep from blurting out anything else she might think of in short fragments, as his gaze narrowed even more.

"Lorraine," he said grudgingly, as if he resented every bit of information he had to give her. "She leased it for me."

Nolie didn't mean to let her gaze slide over him again, from that unkempt black hair all the way down to the wretched shoes, and she didn't mean to think that this Lorraine, whoever she was, must be one desperate woman

if she was interested in this man. Maybe it was just preju-
dice because he was so spooky, but Nolie swore he didn't
look too sane. And as a breeze blew up from behind him,
she noticed he didn't smell too sweet, either. Stale cigarette
smoke, sour booze, and a general disregard for daily
baths—eau de neighbor from hell.

Maybe she could break Lorraine's lease on the grounds
that . . . what? Her friend-boyfriend-relative was too scary
to have for a neighbor in such isolation? He'd made her
daughter cry? Made her want to keep a sturdy door barred
between them?

"Well . . ." She couldn't think of anything else to say, so
she tightened her grip on Micahlyn and said it again.
"Well . . . I-I have things to-to do. If you'll excuse us . . ."

He stared at her, and she stared back. When a moment
passed and he still hadn't moved, she did, closing the door
and locking it securely. Sidling up to the window, she
peeked out as he muttered something—most likely
another vulgarity—then spun on his heel and headed back
to the second cabin. He never looked back and didn't slow
his steps when he reached his own porch. He took the
steps two at a time, went inside the cabin, and slammed the
door. She imagined she heard it even from a distance . . .
but in reality, it was merely the thudding of her own heart.

C HASE WILSON PACED FROM THE LIVING ROOM TO
the kitchen, a cold beer in hand, muttering every foul
word he knew—and considering that he'd spent twenty-
two of the past twenty-three months in prison, he knew
'em all. He'd come back to Bethlehem to be left alone. He
didn't want to see or talk to anyone—didn't want to feel
their stares or hear their whispers. He didn't want to face
their accusations or his own feelings of guilt.

And he damn well didn't want some woman and her kid living fifty yards down the road—especially when the kid had a scream that could raise the dead and she wasn't afraid to use it. He didn't like kids in general and homely little red-haired ones in particular.

Truth was, he didn't like *people*, not anymore. He wasn't fit to be around them. The kid's scream had proved that.

He thought about packing up and getting the hell out—was on his way to pull a suitcase from the closet when he stopped. Where would he go? If he got anywhere near the house he'd bought in Boston, his ex-wife would have him hauled off to jail in handcuffs while his ex-partner, her new husband, stood by and laughed. Ditto on the beach house. There was no way he could go to his parents' house in town. It had been a hell of a long time since he was welcome there . . . if ever.

And he had no place else. New places required energy, stamina, courage—things he'd been missing for a long time. He didn't have the nerve to face a new place.

That admission brought a bitter smile to his mouth. He was a loser and a fool. He'd screwed up his career, his marriage, and his life. He'd lost everything he'd ever had, and he'd brought shame on the family name.

And now, to that list of sins and shortcomings, he could add one more—he was a coward.

If his father could see him now. . . .

He drained the last of the beer and tossed the bottle in the trash can that held nothing but empty beer and liquor bottles. When was the last time he'd eaten, not counting stale cereal straight from the box?

He couldn't remember. That was pathetic.

He was pathetic.

If his father could see him now, he would claim he'd always known Chase would never amount to anything.

Hell, the old man had done his best to guarantee that outcome, riding Chase all the time because he wasn't smart enough, popular enough, talented enough on the football or baseball fields. Earl Wilson had wanted a son who would be just like him, and he'd been damned displeased with the one he got instead. He'd once declared Chase would be dead or in jail by the time he was twenty.

Actually, he'd been thirty-one when he'd gone to prison.

Dear old Dad's opinion notwithstanding, Chase *had* amounted to something . . . for a time, at least. Unwilling to stay in Bethlehem after high school and face more of the same censure and conflict, he'd moved to Syracuse, where he'd busted his butt to get into college and to stay there—with no help from Earl. There he'd found out he was smarter than anyone had given him credit for, even himself. He'd gone deep into debt to attend law school and had worked long hours for little pay, making a name for himself in criminal law before snagging the job that made it all worthwhile. Before long he'd been earning a mid-six-figure salary and been engaged to the most beautiful woman he'd ever known. He'd had it made.

Until he'd lost it all.

Lost so much that there was nothing left for him but to go back home.

With a snort, he took a Healthy Choice dinner, the name mocking him, from the freezer in the laundry room, then set it in the microwave. He didn't *have* a home . . . or a family, friends, a career, a reputation, or even self-respect. What he had was a used SUV, black all over except for one primer-gray fender, some secondhand furniture, some third-time-around appliances, and eleven months left on the cabin lease. What he had was not much better than nothing, and a lot of people who thought even that was more than he deserved.

Most of the time he agreed with them.

Oh, and neighbors. He couldn't forget that. Now he had neighbors.

Maybe they wouldn't be a problem. Maybe they wouldn't stick around or, at the very least, would keep their distance. Considering the way the kid had reacted, no doubt she'd stay as far away as she could. He figured the same for her mother. Though she'd tried to hide it, she'd been afraid, too—her blue eyes had been alive with it.

As long as she stayed at her cabin, he would have no problem keeping to his. Like he said, he didn't like kids, and the mother was about as far from his type as a woman could be. He liked beautiful, delicate, ultrafeminine women. *Not* redheads with freckles who stood closer to six feet tall than five. Certainly not chubby redheads who looked as if they had a fine appreciation for food in all its fattening forms.

He liked women like his ex-wife, Fiona, who was five feet four, as fragile as a china doll, with the softest skin and the sweetest voice. She'd had a fine appreciation, too, for four-star hotels and the best restaurants, for designer clothing and flawless diamonds and A-list parties, and—for a time—for him. Prison had been easy compared to learning to live without Fiona.

Not that he'd had any choice.

The microwave stopped and beeped three times. He pulled the plastic plate out, thought of all the two-hundred-dollar meals he and Fiona had shared over the years, then dropped the plate, food and all, in the trash and opted for another beer instead. He wanted it. Needed it.

In the five weeks since he'd been released from prison, he'd learned two lessons.

On a good day he only wished he was dead.

On a bad day he might make his wish come true.

And this day was turning out about as bad as they came.

COMPARED TO WHISKEY CREEK, BETHLEHEM WAS practically the big city. Where Nolie's hometown had one grocery store, one combined gas station/restaurant, and fewer residents every year, Bethlehem had every convenience she could think of—clothing stores, restaurants, gift shops, a bookstore, and even a library and a movie theater.

As soon as she was settled in, they would have back a business they lost when old Hiram passed away—the feed store. Her great-grandfather had left that to her, too, along with the two cabins and about forty acres of heavily wooded land. There was a trail through the woods that led from the back of her cabin to the back of the store, according to the lawyer, but she hadn't walked it yet.

Frankly, after meeting her neighbor two days ago, she was a little afraid to be walking through the woods alone or with Micahlyn. Not that she'd caught so much as a glimpse of him since then. Once, when she'd walked around her cabin, she'd seen just the back end of a black truck pulled around the far side of his cabin. Other than that, the place could be abandoned for all the life it showed. There was no loud music, no slamming doors, not even any lights on at night. Maybe he couldn't afford to pay the electric bill, or maybe he was just one of those people who went to bed when the sun set. She'd known plenty of both types back home in Arkansas.

"What do you think of this, babe?" She held up a bolt of fabric—pale yellow with a subtle leaf pattern a few shades lighter.

Micahlyn shook her head and patted the bolt she was carrying in both arms. "I like this."

"I mean for the living-room curtains"

With a grin, Micahlyn patted the pink-hearts-and-flowers fabric again. "So do I."

Nolie rolled her eyes and added the yellow leaf fabric to the bolts she was already carrying. After meeting Chase, she'd decided curtains were definitely called for on every window. Truth was, she wouldn't object to iron bars on every window, either. For all her talk about a new life, she hadn't been prepared for one major aspect—living alone. She'd gone straight from her parents' house to the trailer she'd shared with Jeff, and from there to the Harpers' house. Now that she was in a house all her own, she'd discovered what comfort there was in knowing someone else was just down the hall.

There had been *such* comfort in knowing Jeff was right beside her. Feeling his warmth. Hearing his soft little snores. Knowing that if she moved against him, he would automatically snuggle her close. Three years he'd been gone, and she still wondered how she'd ever learned to sleep without him.

She wondered how she would ever learn to sleep in this strange new place without him.

Curtains would help, would make the cabin cheerier and homier. There were yellow-and-white stripes for the kitchen and dining room, pink-hearts-and-flowers for Micahlyn's room, a swirl of pastels for her own room, and white eyelet for the bathrooms. As soon as she got home, she would hang the miniblinds she'd bought earlier and install the additional window locks she'd picked up at the hardware store down the street. Then she would haul out her sewing machine and whip up the curtains so she could take down the sheets that currently covered every pane of glass.

And then she would feel safer. More at home.

Once the fabrics were measured and cut and she'd matched thread to each of them, she paid for her purchases, then followed Micahlyn out the door. "Now I have to meet with Mr. Thomas, the lawyer," she said as they carried their bags to the car. "But when we're finished, want to have lunch at the café over there?"

Micahlyn looked across the street at Harry's Diner, then lifted one shoulder in a negligible shrug. "I s'pose," she replied, using one of her grandmother's favorite phrases in a disinterested tone. "Mama, when we get back to that house, can I call Grandma? I wanna tell her 'bout my new curtains."

"Why don't you wait until this evening, so you can talk to Grandpa, too?" Nolie kept her tone mild and even managed a smile, though it felt more like a grimace. They'd been in Bethlehem only three days, and Micahlyn had called Grandma and Grandpa three times. The first time she'd told them all about the bogeyman, and Obie had gotten Nolie on the phone and demanded that she bring his granddaughter home right away. When she'd refused, Marlene had taken the phone and cried, and that had made Micahlyn cry and left Nolie so frustrated that she'd wanted to cry.

Micahlyn stared at her through smudges on her glasses, then gave a long-suffering sigh. "I s'pose."

Alex Thomas's office was on the second floor of a two-story stone building a few feet down the sidewalk. They went inside to find the receptionist, a grandmotherly type, chatting with a dark-haired woman about Nolie's age. When Nolie gave the receptionist her name, the woman beamed. "Welcome to Bethlehem! I'm Eleanor Perkins, and this is Leanne Wilson. Leanne, Nolie is Hiram Legare's great-granddaughter, and she's come to take over his business. Isn't that great?"

Leanne's smile was only a fraction the wattage of Eleanor's, but it was warm and friendly and encouraged Nolie to smile back. "It *is*," she agreed. "I bet you'll like it here. I've lived here all my life and can't imagine moving anywhere else."

That had been true of Whiskey Creek for Nolie . . . but here she was.

Shifting her gaze, Leanne bent and extended her hand. "Hi. I'm Leanne."

Micahlyn slowly eased out from behind Nolie and laid her hand in Leanne's. "I'm Micahlyn. I'm gettin' curtains with pink hearts on 'em."

"Oh, that'll be so pretty. I love pink hearts, but you know what? My little boy won't let me put them in his room."

"Well, of course not," Micahlyn said with a giggle. "They're for *girls*."

"Yeah, that's what he keeps saying."

Eleanor spoke again. "Nolie, you can go on in. If you'd like to let Micahlyn wait here, I'd be happy to show her the toy box."

"Great. Nice meeting you, Leanne." With another smile, Nolie moved to tap on the inner office door. The knock was answered almost immediately.

"Mrs. Harper, come in, please." Alex Thomas was tall, handsome, and reminded her of her favorite TV lawyer. He shook hands with her, offered her a seat, then sat in the second of the two chairs rather than behind the desk. "How was your trip?"

"Long," she said with a faint smile. "Moving with a five-year-old who doesn't want to move, isn't a lot of fun."

"I bet she'll be fine once you get settled. Bethlehem's a great place for kids. Whenever you're ready, give me a call and I'll ask my wife to arrange a picnic or something so your daughter can get acquainted with some of the kids around here."

Of course he was married. All the gorgeous ones were. "I would appreciate that."

"Is everything okay with the house?"

She thought of Chase and managed to smile again. "It's fine."

He grinned. "Old Hiram lived a rather drab existence, don't you think?"

"He must have gotten an exceptionally good deal on brown paint. If he was anything like my grandmother, he pinched his pennies until they squealed."

"Sounds about right. I take it you never met him?"

She shook her head. "My grandmother left home when she was sixteen, and she never saw him again. Did you know him?"

"Just to say hello to. He wasn't the friendliest soul in town. Is your grandmother still living?"

Nolie shook her head. She'd never had much family, and except for Micahlyn, they were all gone. She'd been pretty much alone in the world since she was eighteen, which helped explain why she'd been married and pregnant at nineteen.

Rising from the chair, Mr. Thomas circled the desk and pulled a file from the stack on the corner. "I've got some papers here for you to sign, as well as a set of keys to the feed store. People will be glad to see you open it up again. They've been having to drive to Howland, which can be more than a little inconvenient when you're trying to get some work done. Do you know anything about feed stores?"

She accepted the ink pen and the papers he offered. "Not a thing," she said, then offered what she hoped was a confident smile. "But I'm a quick learner." Which wasn't entirely true. She was a quick study on subjects that interested her—things as common as cooking, sewing, and crafts, and as unusual as astronomy, herbology, and Egyptology. What could she say? She liked knowing that the constellation Cassiopeia had shone down as brightly on Ramses II all those hundreds of years ago as it did on her and Micahlyn today.

He explained each document she was signing, separated her copies from his, then picked up the conversation where they'd left off. "Don't worry about the store. The place practically ran itself when Hiram was alive, and there's no reason it can't do the same now. And if you run into any problems, give me a call. I'm sure we can find someone who can solve them for you." Tapping the folder against the desk, he asked, "Do you have any questions?"

"Nothing I can think of." Then curiosity forced her to change that. "Actually . . . I was wondering about the people who rented the other cabin. Do you know anything about them?"

"Not much. The name on the lease is Lorraine Giardello, she lives in Boston, and she paid a year's rent in advance. At the time Mr. Harper gave the okay for the lease, I wasn't aware that you and your daughter would be moving here. It seemed a good idea for the property to be earning a little money. Of course, if I'd known you would change your mind . . ."

She brushed off the apology in his voice. It hadn't been a matter of changing her mind, exactly, but a flash of temper at finding out that, at Marlene's direction, Obie had been running her business behind her back. He had okayed renting the cabin. He had put the feed store up for sale. He'd been in the process of arranging for the disposal of Hiram's personal property when she'd found out and put a stop to it. Marlene had even had the nerve to claim they only had her best interests at heart.

That was bull, and she'd told them so in language that had made Marlene turn purple. Right then and there, Nolie had decided to take back her life and move to New York.

She hoped she didn't live to regret it.

"Is anyone staying at the cabin now?" Mr. Thomas asked.

"Yes, a—" She'd been about to say *gentleman*—one thing Chase definitely was not. "A man by the name of Chase."

His brow wrinkled. "Is that his first or last name?"

"I don't know."

"Is there a problem with this man?"

His concern made Nolie feel foolish. What answer could she possibly give? *He looks scary?* There were certain times of the month when she could match him in the scary department—times when even easygoing Jeff had been quick to duck and happy to keep his distance. Even at her best, she was no great beauty. Red hair, freckles, and forty extra pounds of lusciousness didn't rank high on most men's ideal-woman list.

"No, no problem. I was just curious."

"If you'd like me to find out who he is and check into his background, I can do that."

Nolie considered it, then shook her head. He'd paid his rent—or, at least, Lorraine Giardello had—and he'd done nothing wrong. Scaring her daughter was hardly deserving of being investigated, especially when Micahlyn was scared by lots of things, like bugs, thunder, and that talking Chihuahua on the old Taco Bell commercials.

"No, thanks," she said as she stood up. "I was just curious. I know in most small towns everyone knows all there is to know about everyone else, so I thought I might learn something."

"Well, that's true in Bethlehem, too, but the power of our grapevine doesn't extend all the way to Boston. We'll have to find out about this man the old-fashioned way—asking him."

She thought about sitting down for a get-acquainted chat with her neighbor and mentally shuddered. There were only two questions she wanted to ask him: *Would you cut your hair, shave, and take a bath?* followed by *If I return Lorraine's money, will you go back to Boston?*

Switching the papers to her left hand, she stood up and walked to the door with him, then extended her right hand. "Thank you for your time, Mr. Thomas."

"Anytime. And, please, call me Alex. Mr. Thomas is my Uncle Herbert. And let me know when you're ready to get your little girl together with some of the other kids in town. You can call here, or my home number's in the phone book."

"I will. Thanks. Micahlyn, let's go."

With all the toys to choose from, her daughter had picked a book she couldn't yet read. Heaving a long-suffering sigh, she put it away, said good-bye to the receptionist, then dragged herself down the stairs in front of Nolie.

After three days of waffling, Nolie was just almost certain that she'd made the right choice in leaving Whiskey Creek. She was the owner of a business that could practically run itself. For the first time in her life she had money in the bank. The more she saw of Bethlehem, the more she liked it, and if the other folks in town were half as nice as Alex Thomas, living there was going to be a delightful change from life in Obie and Marlene's world.

And if only one of those other folks was male and single and as nice as Alex, if he wasn't prejudiced against kids, and if he could see past her size-sixteen exterior to the perfect ten hiding inside, she would be downright ecstatic.

The improbability of it all made her laugh out loud, which earned her a scowl from Micahlyn. Forget Obie and Marlene's world. She had now entered Nolie's Fantasyland.

Welcome and enjoy the visit.

Chapter Two

CHASE WAS FEELING DAMN SORRY FOR HIM-self when he finally had to admit he was awake on Thursday. Truth was, the sound of car doors had awakened him half an hour earlier, but he'd kept his eyes closed and pretended he was about to fall asleep again. But he wasn't, and finally he quit pretending otherwise.

Turning onto his side, he reached for the cigarettes he usually kept on the night table, but found only an empty pack. He'd smoked the last one on the porch the night before, he remembered with a grimace, kicked back in a wooden chair, with nothing but the darkness, the tree frogs, and a bottle of Jack Daniel's for company.

And his neighbors. Not that he'd seen them. No doubt, Miz Nolie Harper and her prissy little girl were staying inside with the windows barred and the doors bolted. But he didn't have to see them, or their car, or the lights in their windows, to know they were there. Their mere presence had changed everything. His private hideout no longer was.

The sun was high in the sky, shining brightly enough to hurt his eyes as he sat up. Catching his reflection in the dresser mirror, he grimaced. He'd slept in his jeans again—

the same jeans he'd worn the day before, and the day before that—and the sharp light showed stains on the denim and a torn place on the knee where a hole was trying to start. He hadn't shaved in a week or more, and he smelled of stale tobacco and sweat. No wonder the screamer had mistaken him for the bogeyman the other day.

He eased out of bed carefully, then combed his hair with his fingers as he went into the kitchen to look for food. A liquid lunch would be easiest, but he already had so much booze in him, his blood was probably 180 proof. There was stale cereal in the cabinet but no milk in the refrigerator, and the freezer in the utility room was packed with frozen dinners. He thought about walking the extra twenty feet to the freezer, then waiting five to six minutes for the microwave, and instead he took the cereal box from the cabinet. He didn't bother with a bowl, but ate straight from the box as he walked through the cabin and outside onto the porch.

It was a warm day in spite of the trees that towered over the cabin. It was April, though his best guess for the date would be exactly that. It was funny how things like days and dates no longer mattered when you'd lost your job and your obligations. No one cared whether he got up at five-thirty, as he'd done for years, or slept in until the middle of the afternoon, least of all him. After all, the things that filled his time—watching television, drowning his sorrows, a whole lot of nothing—could be done in the middle of the night as easily as during the day.

No one cared.

Hand in the cereal box, he eased down onto the top step, then automatically looked toward his neighbors' place. The station wagon was parked out front—he'd heard it leave that morning, then return—and the screamer was standing near it, but there was no sign of her mother. No doubt she was around, though. No way the kid would have ventured outside alone, where she might run into *him*.

As he munched the cereal, he wondered what kind of name Nolie was, and whether there was a Mr. Nolie Harper, and why they'd left Arkansas in the first place. Not that he cared about any of it. After a month of no one's company but his own, he was just so damn bored.

The kid tilted her head back, then raised both hands to shade her eyes. She was dressed in pink shorts and a T-shirt—not the best color with her long red hair—and appeared to be paler than anyone he'd ever known with blood pumping through their veins. Even Fiona, who religiously protected her delicate Irish complexion from the sun, wasn't that white.

For a moment he wondered when the kid would get started in school, if she was old enough, and whether the other kids would give her a hard time because she wasn't cute and apparently couldn't see without those thick glasses. Probably. They sure would have when he was her age. Hell, back then, he would have been the ringleader in the tormenting.

God, that was another lifetime. Another person.

Not wanting to remember, he shifted his gaze in the direction the little girl looked. Pine trees blocked the best view, but . . . yeah, he could just make out a flash of white on the cabin's roof. Miz Nolie, he presumed.

He polished off the cereal, tossed the box aside, and calculated the odds that if he went inside to the refrigerator, he would come back with water or pop instead of beer. Since they weren't in his favor, he more or less stayed put—not on the step but on the hammock that hung at one end of the porch.

Settling in, he folded his arms under his head and contemplated a nap to make the day pass more quickly.

Freedom—at least, his freedom—wasn't really so different from being in prison. Both inside and out, all he was doing was passing time. He had no goals, no plans, no future. He just wanted to make it through one day at a time.

But instead of closing his eyes and willing himself to sleep, he looked over at the Harper cabin again. How had Nolie gotten on the roof? There was no ladder propped against the porch, and no way she could have climbed up without one. She'd probably gone out one of the upstairs windows, though *why* was anyone's guess and none of his concern.

His view of her became clearer as she scooted near the edge of the roof to talk to her kid, but whatever she had to say wasn't going over well. The kid— What had Nolie called her? Something unusual, a guy's name . . . Michael Ann, Michael Lyn—no, *Micahlyn*. Micahlyn stood there, hands clasped in front of her, shaking her head adamantly enough to make her hair fly. Nolie argued. Micahlyn refused. Making an exasperated gesture, Nolie turned onto her hands and knees and hesitantly backed to the edge of the roof, then extended one leg into space.

She was actually going to try to climb down from the roof to the porch railing. It would be a miracle if she didn't fall and break her fool leg—or, worse, her fool neck. The only thing he needed less than a neighbor was a neighbor who couldn't take care of herself and her banshee-voiced child because she'd fallen off her damn roof.

He rolled out of the hammock—a task easier drunk than sober—and took the steps in one stride. By the time he'd covered half the distance to the cabin, her other leg was dangling in thin air, too, her feet searching for the railing and missing it by a good twelve inches.

"Micahlyn, you *have* to go get our neighbor," she was saying, her tone sharp. "I don't know how much longer I can hang on. Come on, baby, he's not gonna hurt you. *Please*, just run over and knock on his door—"

"*Nooo,* Mama! I'll get you a chair, and you can stand on it!" She started toward the steps, then turned as Chase rounded the station wagon. Her eyes opening wide, she let out a squeal and ran inside, slamming and locking the door. So much for family loyalty.

"Micahlyn!"

A yellow ladder lay on its side on the ground. Judging from the marks it had left, Nolie had set it up in soft soil and then, because it was only six feet tall and the roof was at least seven, she'd disregarded all the warning labels and stood on the very top to make it onto the roof. Unstable footing plus a shaky transfer of weight equaled a ladder on its side.

"*Micahlyn!* Come out here right now!"

"She's abandoned you," Chase said.

She let out a pretty good imitation of her daughter's shriek, lost her grip, and started to fall. Reacting instinctively, he grabbed her around the hips, planted his bare feet in the dirt, then slowly lowered her to the ground. Slowly because, books and movies aside, anything over a hundred pounds was a lot for the average guy to support, especially when he was off balance.

Not because he hadn't held a woman in more than three years. Certainly not because she smelled sweet and clean and . . . jeez, innocent or something. For damn sure not because her skin, when his hands slid under her T-shirt, was soft, warm, smooth.

God, he'd forgotten how different women were. How nice *soft* could be. How stimulated a man could get.

That last was brought home to him with a vengeance as his body reacted to the contact with hers, but it didn't mean a thing. Was purely involuntary.

Like the widening of her eyes when she felt it, too.

The instant her feet touched ground, she scrambled back a few yards, tugged her T-shirt down past her hips, then folded her arms across her chest. Her cheeks were flushed bright red, and her gaze never quite reached his as she shifted uneasily. She looked as if she wanted to rush inside and cower someplace safe with her daughter, but she didn't flee.

"I, uh, I'm sorry. I mean, thanks. I–I didn't expect the ladder to–to fall and strand me up there. I, uh, really do appreciate . . ."

When her voice trailed off, he waited a moment, breathing deeply, replacing sweet, clean, and innocent with the scents of pine and richly decaying vegetation, and he willed errant parts of his body to behave. Feeling steadier at last, he said, "Get a taller ladder. A ten- or twelve-foot extension ladder should do it." That way she wouldn't need rescuing again.

"I'll do that." She freed one hand long enough to anchor a strand of thick coppery hair behind her ear, then immediately tucked her long, slender fingers between her body and her other arm again. "I, uh, haven't seen you since—since we moved in."

"I'm not a neighborly person."

She tried to laugh, but it sounded as phony as it was. Her skin, where it wasn't colored by the blush, was as fair as her daughter's, with freckles scattered across her cheeks and one right in the fullest part of her upper lip. He could tell because she wasn't wearing makeup.

He'd been married to Fiona for more than eighteen months before he'd seen her without makeup. It had been quite a revelation, not that he'd cared. It was just that Fiona without makeup bore little resemblance to Fiona with.

One was incredibly beautiful, glamorous, damn near perfect, and the other was . . . average.

How much Fiona Kelly Wilson Kennedy would have hated being described as average.

Nolie Harper was average, too, he decided, though in a healthy, fresh-faced Midwestern farm girl sort of way. He doubted all the cosmetics in the world could come close to making her beautiful, glamorous, or anywhere near perfect, but she was *real*. He'd discovered in the past few years that that counted for a lot.

She was shuffling awkwardly, at a loss for words, and he didn't have anything to say, either. He should tell her bluntly that this was his first and last rescue, that she wouldn't be seeing him again except at a distance, then make good on it by leaving. But his feet seemed rooted in the warm soil, his gaze locked against his will on her.

"Well . . ." The word sounded more cheerful than it deserved, the cheer as phony as the smile that fluttered across her lips. "I-I really do appreciate your help. I, uh, was going to remove the window screens. They're so dirty I can hardly see out, and I-I like that. Looking out, I mean. At the stars. I like stars. Astronomy is kind of an interest of-of mine."

She tucked her hair back again, this time with her left hand, and this time he noticed what he'd missed earlier—a slender gold band. So there *was* a Mr. Harper. That was relief he felt inside, he told himself, though for some odd reason, it felt more like . . . disappointment. Which it obviously wasn't. He wanted to be left alone, and no husband worthy of a family would let them have any contact with the ex-con down the road.

"Let your husband take them down," he said at last. "When will he be here?"

She lowered her gaze to the wedding ring, looking at it

as if she wasn't quite sure how it had gotten there. Then she glanced up again. Her expression was distant and colored with emotions he had no desire to identify. "My husband's dead. It's just Micahlyn and me."

"I'm sorry."

"So am I." A breeze rustled around them, and her nose did a delicate little twitch. As if to cover it, she forced another fake smile. "Micahlyn and I baked a cake earlier. Would you like a piece? It's pineapple upside-down cake."

When a grateful neighbor trying hard to be friendly couldn't hide her aversion to the fact that he reeked—and worse, he was only vaguely aware of it himself—it was way past time for a bath. His own face grew warm as he backed away. "No."

"It's a good cake," she said. "You don't have to take my word for it. The judges gave it a blue ribbon at the last county fair. And it's still warm from the oven, so it's—"

He made it past the station wagon before she finally shut up. Hopefully, she got the message that he wasn't interested—not in cake or blue ribbons or county fairs in Arkansas.

And he damn sure wasn't interested in her.

B Y SATURDAY AFTERNOON, NOLIE HAD CLEANED the cabin from top to bottom. She'd found places for everything she'd brought with them in the station wagon and had called her best friend back in Arkansas and told her to ship the few things that hadn't fit. She'd also whipped up curtains for every window in the place, and had endured two more phone calls with Marlene, followed by two more temper tantrums from Micahlyn.

And she hadn't seen Chase again.

He'd made it clear that he wasn't the neighborly sort,

and she intended to respect that. He'd made something else very clear that day, she remembered, heat flooding her face again. Of course, it hadn't meant anything. That sort of thing happened a lot, and men just happened to be equipped where they couldn't hide it. He certainly wasn't attracted to her in particular. It had just been coincidence.

A coincidence that hadn't happened to her in a long time, and one that reminded her how lonely it was, being widowed at the age of twenty-two. She missed the intimacies she and Jeff had shared—the little things like hugs and holding hands, and the big things like toe-curling kisses, making love, and snuggling in bed together afterward. She missed talking to him in the dark and watching him doctor the cattle as if the thousand-pound beasts were nothing more than oversized puppies. She missed doing his laundry and listening to him laugh and watching him with Micahlyn.

Lord, she missed *him*.

Giving a sigh, she folded the last of the laundry, then went to stand in the living-room doorway. Micahlyn was sitting in the easy chair with one of her dozen dolls, carrying on a conversation that no one else could share. Nolie watched her a moment before moving into the room. "Hey, babe, get your shoes on. We're going for a walk."

"Don't wanna."

"That wasn't a question." She dropped Micahlyn's shoes on the floor in front of her, then sat down to lace her own sneakers. "We've both spent too much time cooped up inside. We're going exploring."

"No, thank you."

"Micahlyn." There had been a time when she'd never had to speak to her daughter in that warning tone, but in the past few months she'd found it necessary all too often. When she'd realized her daughter was looking to Marlene for guidance before obeying her, she'd known something had to change.

And it had been a good change. She felt happier and freer than in years. And Micahlyn would come around soon.

Once her daughter had grudgingly fastened the Velcro straps on her sneakers, Nolie herded her out the door, locked it, then headed for the woods. She was aware Micahlyn didn't follow immediately, but she didn't wait or turn back. She knew, given a choice between walking with her mother or staying alone at the cabin just down the road from the bogeyman, Micahlyn would come running.

By the time Nolie passed the first pine, little footsteps were thudding behind her.

The trail leading into the woods was so faint that Nolie had had to look twice to find it. Old Hiram had been dead more than a year, and presumably no one had used the trail since then. But fifty years of his tramping back and forth every day had left marks that needed much more than mere months to disappear.

It was a beautiful day for a walk—sunny, not too warm, a nice breeze cooling the air. Everything smelled so fresh after the stuffiness that was slowly disappearing from the cabin, and the birds' songs were comfortably familiar. It was too perfect a moment for pouting, which was exactly what Micahlyn was doing.

When they reached the stream that she'd seen so far only from the car, Nolie slowed to a stop. A footbridge stretched in a low arc from one side to the other and appeared far sturdier than many of the bridges she'd crossed back in Arkansas. Instead of crossing, though, she knelt in the middle, then stretched out on her stomach with little more than a grimace. The tenderness that had come from hanging off the roof a few days earlier was almost gone now.

So was the hypersensitivity where Chase's hands had settled.

Pillowing her chin on her folded arms, she gazed into the water. "When I was a kid, every time my dad drove across a bridge, he'd tell me to lick my fingertip, hold it up, and make a wish. Do you ever do that?"

"No." Micahlyn sat down beside her, then rolled over, and let her chin hang off the side.

"Don't let your glasses fall in," Nolie warned, pushing them back up on her nose. "You want to make a wish now?"

"No."

"Oh, come on." Nolie gently elbowed her, then moistened her index finger, raised it in the air, and closed her eyes. "I wish . . ."

When she opened her eyes again, Micahlyn was watching her. "What'd you wish for?"

"I can't tell you, or it might not come true. You want to try?"

With a sulky sigh, Micahlyn mimicked her actions and whispered, "I wish I could go back home to Grandma and Grandpa"—opening one eye, she peeked to make sure Nolie was listening—"*where I belong.*"

Clenching her teeth, Nolie ignored her words. "Look at that fish. Do you think he'll get big enough for us to catch and cook him?"

"I don't eat fish."

"You do, too." There wasn't much Micahlyn liked more than fried catfish with hush puppies and her grandmother's special tartar sauce.

"I don't eat *that* fish. *I* only eat Grandpa's fish."

Trying to ignore a sense of failure, Nolie got to her feet

and dusted her clothes. "Come on, kiddo. We're gonna see the store that used to belong to your great-great-grandpa."

"I only have one grandpa, and he's great enough for me," Micahlyn said, her bottom lip poked out, but she stood up and crossed the bridge at Nolie's side.

Hiram's feed store was located another five minutes down the trail. They came out of the woods behind the store and circled around to the front.

The gravel parking lot provided a home for weeds and assorted trash thrown from car windows. Nolie and Micahlyn stood in the middle of it and looked at the store. The building had once been painted red, though it probably hadn't seen fresh paint in Nolie's lifetime. One of the two plate-glass windows was boarded over, broken by vandals, according to the lawyer. The other was coated with grime and flaking paint.

It didn't look like much, but that was to be expected after standing empty for months. It was dilapidated, a little lonely, but it had once been a prosperous business. She intended to make it so again.

Not that she knew anything about stores. Or feed. Or, as far as that went, being prosperous.

Movement at her side drew her attention to Micahlyn, who was waving hesitantly. "Who are you waving at, babe?"

"The ladies."

Nolie glanced at the store, then back again. "What ladies?"

"Them."

Nolie looked back at the store as the door opened and two women came out. They reached her and Micahlyn before she had time to voice any of several questions dancing in her brain. *Who are you?* and *What are you doing in my store?* and *Who else has keys?* and *Why wasn't I told?*

"I told you it was them," the older woman said to the younger. "Nola Harper and her daughter, Michael Lyn. Welcome to Bethlehem, and welcome to Hiram's Feed Store. You know, you don't look much like a Hiram. You might want to consider changing the name."

"Of course she's not a Hiram, and she's not a Nola, either," the younger woman said. "Her name is *Nolie,* and the little one is Micahlyn."

"Well, of course she is. That's what I said." The woman beamed at Nolie and extended her hand. "I'm Gloria, and this is Sophy. We were just doing some cleaning inside. The place is a mite dusty."

Which would explain the smudges of dirt across her cheek and the cobweb in her brown-and-gray hair. She was about Marlene's age—late forties, early fifties—and had the sort of smile that involved her whole face. She was plump and, as Nolie's father used to say about her mother, built for comfort.

Her friend, Sophy, was the type Nolie had always envied—slender, pretty, with golden skin, blond curls, and not a freckle in sight. She wore a white T-shirt and short faded denim overalls, and looked about fifteen, though in reality Nolie would put her age closer to twenty-five. There wasn't an ounce of extra fat on her hips, or anywhere else, for that matter, and she seemed genuinely happy to meet them. Beautiful, blond, thin, *and* nice. The worst kind. Nolie couldn't even properly dislike her.

"Are you two the welcoming committee?" Nolie asked.

"Sure are," Gloria replied at the same time Sophy said, "Not exactly."

Nolie looked from one to the other, and so did they, then Gloria laughed. "We're not *officially* the welcoming committee. In fact, I wouldn't say there was one officially—well, unless you count Miss Agatha and Miss Corinna. But we make it our business to look out for everyone."

"That's a nice business to be in." Taking Micahlyn's hand, Nolie started toward the store. The two women fell into step beside them.

"It keeps us busy," Sophy replied. "When do you think you'll be ready to reopen the feed store?"

"I don't know." Nolie hadn't thought to ask Alex Thomas what had happened to the store's inventory. If it had been disposed of, she would be starting from scratch. If it hadn't . . . The thought of eighteen-month-old feed made her nose twitch. If it was still around, she would have to get rid of it, and then start from scratch.

A cement slab extended ten feet from the front of the store, with one step running the length of it. Spidery cracks rambled across the surface, and a dandelion bloomed near the door. As Micahlyn bent to pick it, Nolie released her hand and stepped inside.

The place smelled worse than the cabin had—of must and dust, various animal feeds, and fifty years' of cigar smoke. If she had to guess, she would say old Hiram had spent most of his time on a tall stool behind the counter, where a sooty trail wound its way around a post to the ceiling.

The steel shelving was bare, and nothing remained on the walls but some old calendars and a clock, its hands permanently stopped on 3:17. The old-fashioned cash register still sat on the counter that stretched practically across the store two-thirds of the way back, and a dull brass bell sat beside it. Everything seemed original to the store—translating to *old,* but at least she could clean up that bell and make it shine.

"We did some sweeping," Sophy said, "and started

washing the windows. And we found some old catalogs from Hiram's suppliers while we were dusting. We figured you might want to do business with them, too, so we left them on the desk for you."

Gloria picked up where she left off. "Trust me, if Ham did business with them, you won't get a better deal anywhere. The man was a stickler for getting his money's worth."

While she'd spoken, Nolie had started toward the counter. At that, she turned back. "Did you know him?"

"Oh, honey, we know *everyone*."

"What was he like?"

"That's right—you never met him. Well, let's see . . ." Gloria tapped one finger against her chin. "He was really quite—no, forget that. I remember a time when he— Hmm. Forget that one, too. He was—"

"Ill-tempered," Sophy supplied. "Unforgiving. Hard. And just plain mean."

Gloria's eyes opened wide, and so did her mouth. "Why, Sophy, you can't be saying things like that! Poor Mr. Legrand had some major disappointments in his life that were beyond his control. That's what made him the way he was."

"Which was ill-tempered, unforgiving, hard, and mean. You wouldn't want me to lie, would you?"

"Well, of course not! But—but—"

"And his name wasn't Legrand. It was Legare. Like Simon Legree."

Micahlyn chose that moment to wander inside, the ragged dandelion clutched in her hand, and gaze up at Gloria. "My daddy's dead," she remarked as evenly as if she were commenting on the blue sky. "That means he's living in heaven."

Gloria knelt in front of her. "Why, that's exactly right,

Micahlyn. Your daddy's in heaven, and he's watching over you and your mama."

Unbidden, an image of their neighbor flashed into Nolie's mind—his strength when he'd caught her the other day, especially impressive since she was no lightweight. His hands, so large and warm when they'd touched her skin. His arousal for that moment when they'd touched practically from head to toe. She fervently hoped, if Micahlyn and Gloria were right, that Jeff's attention had been elsewhere at that moment.

Not that he would have begrudged her feeling, wanting, or remembering. He never would have expected her to live the rest of her life alone. He'd been too sweet, too generous for that . . . even if his parents weren't.

"There's really not much else to do here," Sophy said, drawing Nolie's attention back to her. "Why don't you take those catalogs home with you and get some idea of what you need to reopen? And there's a list inside the top one of phone numbers you'll need—the power company, the water company, the best glass man in town."

"Yes," Gloria chimed in. "Sit out on the porch and enjoy the beautiful weather. It'll make the catalogs seem less like work. And since it's going to be a lovely evening, too, when you're done, you can fire up that new grill you bought and invite your neighbor over for hamburgers or steaks."

"How did you know I bought? . . ." Nolie let the question trail off. Compared to Whiskey Creek, Bethlehem seemed like a bustling city, but in reality it was still a small town, and she was the newest outsider in town. No doubt there'd been plenty of talk and speculation about her and Micahlyn.

"Here you go." Gloria handed her a plastic shopping

bag, loaded down with catalogs, then walked them out the door.

Nolie stopped long enough to lock the door, then slid her keys back into her pocket. "I really appreciate all the work you did."

"Oh, it was nothing. Was it, Sophy?" Gloria bent to solemnly shake hands with Micahlyn. "It was a pleasure to meet you, Martha Lyn. And you, too, Nola."

"Nice to meet you, too. I hope we see you around."

Sophy smiled. "You will."

The two women headed across the parking lot as Nolie and Micahlyn started off in the opposite direction. They'd just turned the corner when Nolie remembered the bell. Leading her daughter by the hand, she went back around the corner and came to a sudden stop.

The parking lot was empty. She could see both shoulders of the road all the way into town, but there was no sign of the two women. Maybe there was a path hidden in the weeds and they'd taken that, she told herself, even as she searched for and didn't find any evidence of it. After a moment, a soft flapping in the breeze drew her attention skyward, where a vinyl banner stretched from one corner of the roof to the other. REOPENING SOON, bold gold letters proclaimed on a red background.

"That wasn't there . . ." But of course it had been. It couldn't have just appeared out of thin air.

But how could she have missed it? She'd stood in the middle of the parking lot and studied the building carefully. She couldn't have overlooked such a large, brightly colored banner.

But she must have. She hated to repeat herself, but it couldn't have just appeared. Either Gloria and Sophy had had helpers outside who hung it while they talked inside, or Nolie just hadn't noticed it. Those were the only two choices.

"Mama, let's go home," Micahlyn whined, tugging her hand. "I wanna dry my flower so I can send it to Grandma. Come on."

"Okay." But Nolie didn't move until Micahlyn tugged hard enough to pull her off balance. Giving a shake of her head to clear it, she stumbled after her daughter.

Micahlyn made a beeline for the path, charging up the hill with much more energy than she'd shown coming down. When they crossed the footbridge, she licked one fingertip, raised it in the air, and clomped across the bridge in time to her singsong words. "I wish I could go back home to Grandma and Grandpa, where I belong."

Nolie was about to make a face at her back when Micahlyn spun around. "I liked Gloria." She continued spinning until she was facing forward again, then marched along the trail.

Well, that was *something,* Nolie consoled herself. Not the wholehearted acceptance she was looking for, but quite possibly the only thing Micahlyn had liked since they'd left Arkansas. It was a step in the right direction. Raising her gaze to the pale blue sky that showed in patches through the pines, she mouthed, "Thank you."

And for one fanciful instant, she would have sworn she'd heard the words, "You're welcome," in a whisper as soft and as distant as a memory.

But surely it was just the wind.

L IPS PURSED, AGATHA WINCHESTER GRAYSON STUD-ied the basket on the table. She and her sister, Corinna, had begun packing it that morning, before Sunday church services, with a foil pan of their famous cinnamon rolls, bags of cookies in five different varieties, and a tin of brownies. After Sunday dinner with their usual crowd of children, grandchildren, and good-as-family, they'd added some of the leftovers—thick slices of ham, creamy potato salad, a low-fat pasta salad, and a fluffy fruit salad, as well as two loaves of fresh-baked bread.

"Do you think it's adequate?" Corinna asked dryly. "There are only two of them, you know."

"I know." Going to the counter, Agatha took a loaf of banana nut bread from the rack where it had cooled and wrapped it tightly in foil before adding it to the basket. Like the pasta salad, it was low-fat. She had never thought she would see the day when anything low-fat would come from *her* kitchen, but she was a married woman now. She had good reason to watch her figure.

When she started back to the counter, Corinna stopped her, then firmly closed the lid on the basket. "That's plenty. We're just welcoming the Harpers to town, not feeding a horde. Come on now. Let's go."

"I was just going to fix a jar of lemonade . . ." Agatha's explanation trailed off as her sister picked up the basket and headed for the door. With a sigh, she hurried after her.

Agatha's husband, Bud, was playing football with the younger of their grandchildren. With squeals of delight, the children tackled him, then they all rolled together on the ground, laughing and gasping for breath, until they realized she stood over them.

"There's my girl," Bud said, disentangling himself from the boys and getting to his feet quite easily for a man of his years. "Where are you off to?"

"Hiram Legare's great-granddaughter has come to town to take over the feed store, and Corinna and I are going to visit her."

"Be careful, and come back to me soon." He kissed her

soundly, not on the cheek as he usually did when they had company, but on the lips. They'd been married almost a year, but he still had the power to make her blush with no more than a kiss.

"Young love," Corinna said when Agatha joined her in the car.

Though Agatha gave an unrefined snort, secretly she smiled. She'd found love once when she was a girl, only to lose it when war claimed her young man's life. She had mourned Sam so long that eventually she'd despaired of ever finding someone else. She had resigned herself to being an old maid, to doting on her nieces and nephews and the children of friends, and never truly having a family of her own.

Then, when she'd least expected it, along had come Bud. He'd fallen in love with her—an act that she still considered nothing less than a miracle—and he'd given her a family. His son, J.D., called her Mom, and J.D.'s kids called her Grandma. That, she'd discovered, was one of the sweetest words in the world.

She and Corinna talked of little things as they drove the short distance outside town, to the lane that led to old Hiram's cabin. It was a lovely day, so they'd rolled down the windows. The forest scents carried into the car on the breeze were sweet and fresh, and made her breathe deeply more than once.

"The last time I came out here, Hiram said if I ever came back again, he'd call Sheriff Ingles to haul me away," Corinna remarked as the cabin came into sight.

"I'm sure his great-granddaughter is much friendlier." Under her breath, Agatha added, "Of course, a polecat would be much friendlier."

Naturally Corinna heard her. Though she tried not to smile, the corners of her mouth twitched anyway.

There was a station wagon parked in front of the cabin, and a pair of redheads on the porch. The woman looked up from her magazine, the girl from her dolls, and watched as they parked, then got out.

"Good afternoon," Corinna called. "I'm Corinna Humphries, and this is my sister, Agatha Grayson. We wanted to stop by and say hello and welcome you to Bethlehem."

The woman set aside the magazine and stood up from the rocker to meet them at the top of the steps. "Hi. I'm Nolie Harper, and this is my daughter, Micahlyn."

Agatha hefted the basket from the rear seat, then opened the lid for Nolie's inspection when she reached the porch. "We brought some goodies—cookies and brownies and a few things to make this evening's dinner easier." She beamed at the little girl standing shyly half-behind her mother. "Do you like cookies?"

Micahlyn nodded.

"What's your favorite kind?"

"Peanut butter."

"Well, you're in luck. That's my favorite kind, too, so I included two bags of them. If it's all right with your mother, would you like one now?"

Micahlyn peered up at her mother, who nodded.

"Why don't you show me to the kitchen, Micahlyn, so I can put these things in the refrigerator, and then we'll dig out those peanut-butter cookies."

"It's inside." Releasing her grip on her mother's skirt, Micahlyn held the screen door open for Agatha, then skipped ahead of her through the living room and into the kitchen.

"You have the prettiest red hair," Agatha remarked as she set the basket on the counter, then unpacked it. The perishable food went into the refrigerator. The rest she left on the counter for Nolie to put where she wanted, except for the peanut-butter cookies. Those she handed to Micahlyn, who took one, then carefully rezipped the plastic bag.

"Do you know I had hair that color when I was young?"

Micahlyn's gaze darted upward, and her eyes widened. "What happened?" she asked around a mouthful of cookie.

Agatha laughed. "I got old." Her hair color had faded, her eyesight had dimmed, and her hearing wasn't what it used to be. But she wouldn't trade this time in her life for youth or anything else. She was too happy.

With Micahlyn leading the way, Agatha returned to the porch, where Corinna had taken a seat in one of the two rockers and Nolie had moved to the rough-hewn bench. Agatha seated herself in the second rocker and turned her attention to the conversation.

Corinna was telling Nolie about old Hiram, not that there was much to tell. His early years in Bethlehem had been fairly unremarkable, until his wife had run off, and with another man, no less—something simply not done fifty years ago. She'd left their daughter, Betty Lou, behind, to be raised by her angry, bitter father. First chance Betty Lou had gotten, she had run off, too. She'd been sixteen at the time.

She must have found happiness elsewhere, Agatha reflected with some measure of satisfaction, for Nolie spoke fondly of her.

After visiting for well over an hour, Agatha and Corinna were saying their good-byes when the sound of a slamming door drifted down from the distant cabin. Agatha shaded her eyes against the afternoon sun and just made out the back end of a vehicle parked on the far side. "You have a neighbor."

The surprise was so evident in her voice that both Corinna and Nolie laughed. "Agatha's convinced nothing goes on in Bethlehem without our knowing it," Corinna said. "However, I must admit, I'm also surprised. We hadn't heard a word about anyone moving into that cabin."

Nolie gazed that way a moment, her arms folded across her chest. She seemed to choose her words carefully when she responded. "The opportunity to rent it to a man from Boston came up before I'd decided to move here myself. It seemed a good idea at the time."

Agatha looked at her sister. "Perhaps we should drop in and say hello."

"It would probably be best if you didn't," Nolie replied rather quickly. "He's a very private man. He prefers to be left alone."

Agatha raised her brows. "Sounds mysterious."

"He's the bogeyman," Micahlyn piped in. "He's big and scary and tried to drag me off to his cave, but I ran fast and got away."

Her mother looked faintly embarrassed. "He has long hair and a beard, and he frightened her the first time they met. But he's *not* the bogeyman, Micahlyn, and you've got to stop saying so."

Corinna looked from the cabin to Micahlyn to Nolie. In the careful manner that meant she was treading lightly, she asked, "Are you comfortable with him for a neighbor?"

"Oh, sure. Like I said, he prefers to be alone."

Nolie's words were confident, but Agatha thought her smile and shrug lacked the same assurance. She didn't seem frightened, but rather . . . uncertain. Presumably, the man from Boston lived alone down the road. Could it be he was young and perhaps handsome in addition to single?

When she mentioned as much to Corinna as they began the trip back into town, her sister gave her a wry look. "Let's not go playing matchmaker for someone we just met, Agatha."

"But why not?" Agatha smiled her sweetest and most innocent smile. "After all, Corinna . . . we do it so well."

Chapter Three

AFTER WRAPPING A TOWEL AROUND HIS WAIST, Chase left the bathroom for the bedroom, a steamy fog following him. He'd just discarded the towel across the bed and pulled on a pair of faded old jeans when movement outside the uncurtained window caught his attention.

He was about to have company. Nolie Harper was walking down the dirt road straight to his cabin, and trailing twenty feet behind her was Micahlyn. The kid dragged her feet, obviously tagging along against her will. In contrast, the mother moved easily, her skirt swinging with every sway of her hips. Her hair was pulled up on top of her head in a style that should have looked messy but instead just looked soft, and her feet were bare beneath the long skirt, and somehow *that* managed to look ... intimate.

Grimacing at the thought, he started to fasten the button-fly of his jeans, and found to his annoyance that the denim was stretched tighter now than it had been two minutes ago. It didn't mean anything, he reminded himself. She wasn't his type. He'd just been alone too damn long. Any woman would have that effect on him.

His best bet would be to stay out of sight and wait for her to go back where she belonged. So his truck was parked at the side of the cabin. So the front door was standing open. He wasn't sure of much in life, but he'd bet next month's rent that she wouldn't invite herself inside when her knock went unanswered.

Then she walked past his bedroom window, and the wind chose that instant to blow through the screen, bringing with it the smell of flowers and spices—of *woman*. Maybe it wouldn't hurt to see what she wanted. It didn't mean he had to be friendly, or invite her in.

By the time she walked up onto the porch, Chase was standing half in the hallway, half in the living room, pulling a T-shirt over his head. With the lights off and the shades pulled to block the evening sun, the room was gloomy enough that she couldn't see much without pressing her face right up to the screen. She didn't.

Her first knock was tentative. Micahlyn's whine, coming from somewhere in the distance, wasn't. "He's not home. Let's go, Mama."

"In a minute, babe." Her second knock was louder, and made the screen door rattle on its hinges.

He stood motionless, debating between stepping forward into the living room and retreating into the hallway. Indecision was a new thing for him. From the time he'd started college, he'd known what he wanted, and he'd done what it took to get it. He'd been single-minded and driven . . . and now he couldn't decide whether to answer a knock at the door.

"Come on, Mama, it's gettin' dark. Let's go home."

"Micahlyn, it's nowhere near dark. You know who you're starting to sound like? Laura, from your Sunday school class in Whiskey Creek."

"Huh–uh! Laura's a crybaby, and nobody likes her 'cause all she does is whine."

"And lately that's all you've done."

Their voices were so different from what he was accustomed to—soft, Southern—and their rate of speech was slower than the rapid clip prevalent in Boston. Nolie, with her woman's voice, talked the way she walked. Easily. Lazily. Comfortably.

She knocked one last time, and was turning to leave when the weaker side of him won the debate. He crossed the living room in silent strides, braced one hand on the doorjamb, and bluntly said, "What?"

She'd pasted on a smile when she turned back to face him. "I was willing to pretend you weren't home and go away."

When he offered no response, she lifted the shopping bag she carried. "I'm doing my Little Red Riding Hood impersonation, carrying a bag of goodies through the woods to Grandma's house." The smile wavered uncertainly. "That's this cabin. My great-grandfather built it for my grandmother to live in when she got married. Unfortunately, she ran away from home when she was sixteen and wound up in Arkansas."

For a moment he simply looked at her through the screen—soft hair, pale skin, bare feet—then grudgingly he asked, "Which is the unfortunate part? That she ran away or that she wound up in Arkansas?"

"Hey, that's my home state you're criticizing."

He'd never felt sentimental about home. All he'd wanted from Bethlehem was to be away from it. And now he'd gone from prison back to Bethlehem again. It was hard to say whether that was an improvement. "If it means so much to you, why aren't you there?"

"Because this is my new home. Have you eaten supper?"

Warily he shook his head.

"We got a welcome visit today from two ladies in town, Miss Agatha and Miss Corinna. They brought us more goodies than we could possibly eat, so . . ." She held up the bag again, this time offering it to him.

He hadn't noticed the car parked beside hers that afternoon until he'd already stepped outside, and then he'd made a hasty retreat, not only closing but locking the door behind him. At the time, he hadn't had a clue who was visiting. Now that he knew it was the Winchester sisters, he was glad he'd hidden like a coward. They were the next-to-the-last people he wanted to know he was back. They knew everyone and everything, and what they knew, others soon found out.

When Nolie rattled the bag, he opened the screen door with a squeak and took it without coming anywhere near touching her—not on purpose. Not because he wanted to avoid touching her. Just because that was the way it happened.

As soon as he unfolded the top of the bag, the aromas of cinnamon rolls and cookies made his mouth water. Over the years, between church, school, and holidays, he'd eaten probably a couple hundred of the Winchester sisters' rolls and double that number of their cookies. They were the best.

"The sweets are on top," Nolie said. "Underneath, there's some great salads and ham and bread, warm from the microwave. I-I included utensils."

Because she hadn't been sure he was civilized enough to have his own?

Now all he had to do was thank her, step back a few

feet, and close the door in her face. He could eat alone. Could spend the rest of the evening alone.

Instead he stepped out, letting the screen door bang behind him, and sat down on the top step. After a moment, Nolie sat at the opposite end, as if she wasn't sure of her welcome. Fair enough. *He* wasn't sure she was welcome, either.

He fished out the ham and bread, made a sandwich, and took a bite before speaking. "If you're Little Red Riding Hood, I guess that makes me the Big Bad Wolf."

She smiled, chasing away the uncertainty and looking so damn . . . feminine, but Micahlyn didn't give her a chance to respond. From fifteen feet away, with a couple of Barbie dolls clutched to her chest, she fixed a scowl on him that reeked of hostility. "The Big Bad Wolf eated Little Red Riding Hood."

The temptation to bare his teeth at the kid was strong, but he managed to resist by taking another bite of sandwich. His silence seemed to encourage her.

"And then the hunter came and *killed* him."

Tough luck, kid. No hunters around here. And the only thing he wanted to devour at the moment was his sandwich and, maybe, a cinnamon roll.

"Micahlyn, why don't you go play, babe?" Nolie suggested.

Micahlyn looked around, then wrinkled her nose, making her glasses bob precariously. "In the *dirt*? With *bugs*?" She sniffed haughtily. "I'd rather go home."

"Then go. Stay on the porch, so I can see you from here."

"That's *not* home. Home is with Grandma and Grandpa." Giving another of those sniffs, she took another look around, then marched off to sit on a log laid out at the edge of the road.

Nolie lowered her voice. "Sorry about her. She's usually much more pleasant than this."

"When she gets her way?" The comment was out before he could think better of it, and he could actually see the defensive-mother stiffness spreading through Nolie.

After a moment, though, it faded, and she smiled ruefully. "Yeah, I guess so." Then she gave a sigh that seemed to come from way down inside. "She was only two when her father died and we moved in with his parents. He was an only child, so she's the only grandchild. They spoiled and coddled and babied us both, which was just fine with her, but . . . I couldn't take it anymore."

Moving her feet to the second step, she rested her elbows on her knees and her chin on her hands. "I don't mean to sound ungrateful. My in-laws are wonderful people and they were there for me when I needed them most after Jeff died, but . . ." With a shake of her head, she let the words trail off.

In the silence that followed, he finished the sandwich, dug into the bag again, and came up with a bag of cookies. He took a chocolate chip for himself, then offered the bag to Nolie. She looked at it a moment before shaking her head. The movement renewed the scent of flowers and spices that stirred a hunger in his gut as if he hadn't just eaten.

But didn't he know better than most that not all hunger was for food?

As he munched the cookie, he watched Micahlyn, still sitting on the log, hugging her dolls, and looking angry and . . . pitiable. He knew from experience how hard it was to have your life turned upside down. He was still having trouble dealing with it, and he was a grown man. *She* was only five years old.

Peripherally he saw Nolie tilt her head to the side, then

he felt her gaze on him. "It occurs to me that we've been neighbors for nearly a week, and I don't even know your last name. I don't know anything about you."

"Is that so."

"I come from a place where everyone knows everyone else."

"I come from a place where everyone minds their own business."

His flat tone didn't discourage her. "Okay. You *are* renting my house. That qualifies as business."

"I'm not. Lorraine is."

By sheer will Nolie kept her expression relatively open and unthreatening, while inside she was annoyed . . . and curious. Technically, he was right—the lease *was* in Lorraine Giardello's name, and there was nothing in it prohibiting her from letting someone else live in the cabin. Still . . . "Is Lorraine your wife?"

He continued to stare off in Micahlyn's direction. "Nope."

"Girlfriend?"

He gave the slightest shake of his head.

"Mother? Sister? Aunt? Fourth-grade teacher?"

That earned a snort. "Miss Agatha was my fourth-grade teacher." Then abruptly he looked at her, his face flushed a dull crimson. "Forget I said that."

Oh, yeah, that was likely. So Chase Whatever was from Bethlehem. How interesting . . . and how odd, that he was hiding out only a few miles from town. Obviously he *was* hiding, or else the Winchester sisters would have known he was living there. That, even more than his general reclusiveness, would explain why he'd done such a quick U-turn when he'd come out of the cabin that afternoon and seen that she had company.

There were a dozen questions she wanted to ask, starting with, *Do you have family in town?* But he looked irritated, angry, even a bit anxious, so she pushed them all aside. "How long did you live in Boston?"

She got the feeling he didn't want to say another word, but after a time, he replied in short, clipped tones. "About eight years."

"I've never been there. Until we came here, I'd never been anywhere. Maybe when Micahlyn's a little older and can appreciate it more, I can take her. I'd like to see the USS *Constitution* and Paul Revere's house and the Old North Church." Without missing a beat, she went on. "Is there really a Lorraine, or did you invent her so no one would know you were here?"

"Lorraine's very real."

Something about the way he said it made the muscles in Nolie's stomach tighten—maybe the slight emphasis he put on *very,* or the increase in warmth in his voice. Whatever it was, she had little doubt that the woman *was* real, and was important to him.

So why was she in Boston when he was here?

A breeze drifted in from the west, tickling loose strands of hair across her neck, carrying the combined fragrances of soap, detergent, and fabric softener. She'd noticed as soon as she'd seen him that he'd apparently just gotten out of the shower. His wet hair was slicked straight back, and frankly, it was impossible to miss that the offensive odors were gone. Now if he would shave and cut his hair—she'd always preferred the clean-cut look—even Micahlyn would forget his derelict look when they'd met.

Even unshaven and with hair as long as hers, he was sort of handsome, especially when he wasn't scowling or intimidating the heck out of her.

As if her opinion made a bit of difference to him.

Beside her the paper bag rattled again. This time he

took out a dish of potato salad and a fork. Considering how thin he was, the calories in the rich, creamy salad would do him as much good as the harm they'd done her. She loved potato salad—and pasta salad, fruit salad, and even garden salad as long as it was buried under blue cheese dressing—and she'd eaten too much of it before packing up the rest to share. Too bad she couldn't just give him the forty extra pounds she carried. Then they would both be perfect.

"What did you do in Boston?" She asked the question because she was curious, of course, but also because the silence had gone on too long. If she couldn't think of anything to say, there was no reason for her to stay. After spending the past week with little human contact aside from Micahlyn, she really wanted to stay, just a little bit longer.

"Time."

The muttered answer made her look sharply at him. He shrugged. "I made money, paid taxes, worked eighteen-hour-days six and seven days a week, and then . . ."

Nolie waited, filling in her own answers while waiting for his. *And then I got tired of it. I realized that was no way to live. I lost my job, my health, my wife, my self.*

But his answer was simpler and told her nothing. "I got out."

"And came here."

He shrugged again.

Too simple. A workaholic didn't exile himself to a solitary life in a cabin in the woods without experiencing some kind of life-changing event. But who was she to push for that information? Neighbors or not, they were little more than strangers. Acquaintances of a sort, who'd spoken a few times. Just because she would like to be more didn't mean that he wanted the same.

"Are you going back to Boston?"

"No."

"You're staying here?"

"No." He polished off the potato salad, then started on the fruit salad. It was her favorite kind—mandarin oranges, nuts, coconut, and fruit cocktail, all stirred into a creamy dressing. Her mom had made it for every holiday meal, and after she'd died, Marlene had taken up the tradition. Nolie had eaten too much of it for dinner, too. But wasn't that the story of her life?

Chase's voice startled her from her thoughts. She'd thought *no* was all he'd intended to say on the subject, but she'd been wrong.

"First chance I had to get out of here, I did, and I'll leave again the first chance I get."

What constituted *the first chance*? Was it a matter of money or something else?

The sun had disappeared behind the trees to the west, turning the sky faint pinks and purples, and leaving them in the lingering, dim light of dusk. But it wouldn't matter if it was high noon or the dead of the darkest night. His expression was so blank that looking at him told her absolutely nothing.

"If you feel that way, why did you come here?"

The blankness didn't waver, but the plastic container that held the salad crinkled under the tightening of his grip. "It seemed a good idea at the time."

From the log, Micahlyn chose that moment to peevishly wail, "Ma-maaa! I wanna go hom—back. It's gettin' dark and I don't like it here."

"All right, babe." Standing up, she dusted her bottom, then faced Chase. She suddenly felt awkward again. "Well . . ."

"Thanks for dinner."

"You're welcome. I, uh . . . we'll see you."

He didn't run screaming into the house and lock the door, which she took as a good sign. In fact, he didn't say anything at all, which maybe wasn't a good sign.

When she reached the log, Micahlyn was on her feet and practically dancing with her impatience to be gone. She tucked her hand into Nolie's and hurried her along at a pace that was far beyond leisurely until they'd covered more than half the distance between cabins.

"Okay, Mama, we gave him some of our food. Now we don't never have to see him again, do we?"

"Honey, he's our neighbor."

"So?"

"Remember our neighbors back at Grandma's? Tiffany's family and the Beckers across the road and Brother and Sister Thomas from church on the other side? Chase is no different from them."

"Uh-huh. Tiffany's dad is just a dad, and Mr. Becker always has candy for me, and Brother Thomas is somebody's grandpa, like my grandpa. *He's* scary." To emphasize her point, Micahlyn looked over her shoulder, then picked up the pace again.

"So if he gave you candy like Mr. Becker, you wouldn't be afraid?"

"He pro'bly don't even like candy, and he pro'bly don't like little girls, neither."

Since Nolie wasn't sure about that last part herself, she didn't try to argue the point with Micahlyn.

By the time they reached the cabin porch, darkness was settling around them. Nolie locked the dead bolt behind them, then followed Micahlyn upstairs. She filled the tub with bubbles that smelled of bubble gum, washed her own feet first, then sat on the floor to supervise Micahlyn's bath.

Now that they were safely locked away from their

neighbor, her daughter was chatty and in the first good mood in too long. Nolie said a quick prayer that she would see more cheeriness and less brattiness in her daughter from then on out, then felt guilty for even asking. She'd uprooted her little girl from the only life, family, and home she'd ever known, and it was going to take time for Micahlyn to get over that. Rather than hoping her daughter would behave better, she should be asking that Micahlyn's adjustment go smoother.

Which would give the same result.

They went through their evening routine—bedtime story, making a wish on a star that had just started to twinkle in the night sky, tucking in, a bedtime prayer, and trading kisses. Nolie sat on the edge of the bed, gazing down at Micahlyn, and felt a lump form in her throat. "I love you, babe."

"I love you, too. And I love Grandma and Grandpa and home and Whiskey Creek."

Oh, well. It was good while it lasted.

She gave Micahlyn one last kiss, then shut off the lamp and went to her own bedroom down the hall. She wasn't sure what drew her to the window, or so she insisted until she stood there, curtains pushed back with one hand, and gazed up the road to the other cabin. Without lights, it was nothing more than a shadow, until the clouds shifted and the moonlight filtered through.

Chase still sat on the porch, the paper bag beside him, but he wasn't eating or relaxing or, apparently, even enjoying the cool evening. His feet were planted a few steps below where he sat, and he leaned forward, shoulders hunched, head bowed. He looked so lost. So alone.

She watched him even though she felt as if she was intruding on his private sorrow, watched until the moon disappeared behind the clouds again, until it reappeared a few long moments later.

When it did, he was gone.

For eight years, Leanne Wilson's children's boutique, Small Wonders, had occupied the same space, the first floor of a hundred-year-old two-story building that faced the back of the Bethlehem courthouse. In all that time, until the past month, she'd ventured onto the second floor only once—before she'd signed the lease. She'd looked at the apartment up there, decided she couldn't possibly want to live above where she worked, and had more or less forgotten about it.

Funny how things changed.

On a cloudy Tuesday morning, she stood under the gaily-striped awning that fronted the building, key in hand, and with some trepidation unlocked the door that led upstairs. Last night a half-dozen friends had finished moving her into the apartment, and this morning she'd finally told her parents. If it was already a done deal, her mother couldn't complain too much, right?

She stifled the contemptuous snort trying to escape. If Phyllis Wilson someday found herself in heaven with the good Lord himself, she would find fault with *something*.

"Hurry up, please. It's going to start raining any moment now, and I'd rather not get wet. I came here from the salon, you know."

Leanne glanced over her shoulder at her mother, who looked as if she'd been sucking on a lemon. Behind Phyllis, her father appeared put out, as if spending a few minutes looking at her new apartment was such a burden.

In truth, Leanne knew, the burden for Earl was spending time with Phyllis. She had a few vague memories of them in happier times, when she was a kid, but for most of her life, they'd been at each other's throats. She couldn't understand why one of them hadn't divorced the other years ago. They'd had separate bedrooms for ages. Why not separate lives? Why settle for such misery when life was so short?

With a mental shrug, she opened the door and started up the stairs. "Come on. I want to show you what I've done."

"I don't know about these stairs, Leanne," Phyllis groused. "You know, you're not so young anymore. And what about Danny? It's so dark and gloomy in here. He could fall and break something."

Earl's voice boomed in the stairwell. "For God's sake, Phyllis, the girl's twenty-eight years old. She can handle stairs, and so can Danny. And any fool can see there are lightbulbs up there that she just didn't bother turning on since it's the middle of the morning."

At the top of the stairs, Leanne turned to wait. "Thank you for shaving a few years off my age, Dad, but I'm thirty-two."

Much of the hostility left his voice. "How can you be thirty-two when I'm not much past that myself?"

Phyllis harrumphed disdainfully, then stepped into the apartment's entry. It was tiny, opening into the kitchen and living room on the right, and with a coat closet on the left. Leanne preferred the antique coat rack in the corner, though. She'd picked it up for a few bucks at a yard sale, cleaned it, and polished the brass hooks until they gleamed. It looked perfect there.

Of course, her mother didn't share her opinion. "What are you doing with that old thing? And you *are* going to put rugs in here, aren't you?"

"A few. I like the wood floors."

"You won't like taking care of them, trust me. That's why I carpeted over the ones in our house. They were nothing but work." Followed by Earl, Phyllis walked around the counter into the kitchen, silently taking in the blue walls and white cabinets, the intricately patterned tile backsplash Leanne had knocked herself out with, the vinyl floor, and her nose wrinkled just a bit. When she moved on to the living room, painted a deeper blue and sporting a wicker dinette and sofa, along with vivid tropical-print fabrics, the wrinkle turned into severe disapproval. "Why on earth did you buy wicker? You know how it creaks with every move."

"Not the good stuff."

Phyllis sniffed. "These walls are too dark for this room. You should have painted them a nice neutral, like our living room. You'll be tired of this in no time."

Leanne shoved her hands behind her back before knotting them into fists, gritted her teeth, and said nothing in her defense. Instead, she looked to her father for his opinion. Years of experience told her it would be 180 degrees opposite her mother's.

He proved her right with a shrug. "I like the blue. And the wicker. It looks vacationy."

Phyllis's jaw tightened as she turned, hands on her hips. "Well, where are the bedrooms? There *are* bedrooms, aren't there?"

"Of course." As if she would rent an apartment for herself and her four-year-old son that didn't have a place to sleep? Leanne led the way back through the kitchen to the small alcove at the end of the hallway. The door on the right led into the bathroom, the one in the center into Danny's room, and the one on the left into her own room.

Phyllis inspected her room and the bathroom without comment. When she saw Danny's room, though, her tongue loosened. "For God's sake, Leanne, *red* walls? What were you thinking—or were you even thinking? This is *awful*. Danny will have nightmares for sure in this—this dreadful place. *Red!*"

Not just red, but fire-engine red, bright, cheery. Leanne smiled as she recalled Danny's delight with the finished product. "It's what he wanted."

"You don't let a four-year-old decide what color to paint his walls."

"Why not?" Earl countered. "It's his room."

"Oh, please. As if you have any taste whatsoever." Phyllis turned to stare out the window that looked out on the courthouse and, to the west, the town square. "This is a ridiculous idea, Leanne, living downtown above your shop. If you're tired of your old apartment, fine. Move in with us. We'll fix up the garage apartment for you. Then you can find someone to fix the mess you've made here, and maybe your landlord can rent it to someone else."

Leanne flinched at the idea of moving back into the house where she'd grown up. Even the apartment over the garage out back was way closer to her parents than she wanted to be—or wanted her son to be.

Earl slid his arm around her shoulders. "I think it's a great idea. That Knight boy's wife has an office in their house. And that lawyer—what's her name?—lives above her office. And they're both just across the square."

"Jillian Freeman," Leanne supplied.

"Yeah. And just look what a short commute you'll have to work." He grinned and pressed a kiss to her forehead. "I think you made a wise choice."

Phyllis turned a scathing look on both of them. "You would. Since I have better things to do than waste my breath on someone who obviously cares nothing for my opinion, I'm leaving. Don't bother to see me out."

When the door at the bottom of the stairs closed with a thud, Earl broke the silence. "Doesn't it feel nicer in here already?" Releasing Leanne, he wandered back into her bedroom. With its pale peach walls and antique oak furniture, Phyllis had found it the least offensive room and given it little more than a glance before moving on.

"What do you think, Dad?" Leanne leaned against the doorjamb and watched him walk around the room, touching things here and there, looking at knickknacks and photos.

"I told you."

"You and I both know that was for Mom's benefit. What do you *really* think?"

He stopped in front of a window, gazing at the photographs she'd arranged on the sill, picking up one, then replacing it for another. "I think you did a great job. I admit, I don't think I'd want a blue living room or a red bedroom, but I'm not living here. If you and Danny like it—" He'd been reaching for the last frame when he froze, his hand motionless in midair. After a moment, he drew back and turned to face her, his jaw tight, his eyes shadowy. "If you and Danny like what you've done, more power to you. I've got to go, princess. I've got an appointment in fifteen minutes. Give my grandson a kiss for me, and tell him we'll go fishing Saturday."

Leanne murmured a response and accepted his kiss, but didn't move until the distant closing of the door signaled he was gone, too. Then, with a heavy sigh, she crossed to the window and picked up the picture that had caused such a change in him.

It was about twenty-five years old, the colors faded. Her mother truly looked happy, and so did her father. Leanne was grinning bigger than usual to show off the two front teeth she'd lost when she'd tripped over the sandbox at the park, and her brother, who'd made her trip, was smiling, too, in spite of the punishment he'd gotten.

Had they really been that happy then, or was it just an illusion—a moment of let's-pretend captured for eternity by the camera? She couldn't remember. There was certainly no illusion about their family now. Her parents lived to make each other miserable, her brother had broken off contact with all of them right after high school, and she . . . she felt like an orphan half the time and wished she was the other half.

Movement outside drew her attention from the past and across the street. The real estate sign was gone from the yard of old Mrs. Miller's house, and a silver Lexus was pulled into the driveway. She wondered who'd bought the place. Certainly no one local, or she would have already heard. Bethlehem's grapevine was extraordinarily efficient.

As she watched, a man came out of the house and stood at the top of the porch steps, gazing about. He was tall, blond, tanned, and wore khaki trousers and a white dress shirt. His sleeves were rolled up, his tie loosened. It was impossible to tell at this distance if he wore a wedding band—as if that mattered to most men—but surely he had a wife and kids somewhere. Surely he hadn't bought the Miller mansion just for himself.

His gaze scanned the block, slowing, then coming back to her window. Abruptly she took a step back, then glanced at the bedside clock. It was 9:32, two minutes past opening time for Small Wonders. Tossing the old family photo on the bed, she spun around and hurried toward the stairs, and to work.

M AMA. I GOTTA GO TO THE BATHROOM."
        Her shoulders and back aching, Nolie looked

down at Micahlyn from her perch on the ladder, six feet above the concrete floor of Hiram's Feed Store. She swiped the back of one hand across her forehead, where she felt a headache trying to start, then wiped the paint she'd just smeared on her sleeve. "So go, babe. You know where it is."

"I'm scared to go alone."

"You've gone alone a half-dozen times today."

"But that was today. This is tonight, and I'm scared."

Resting her roller in the paint pan, Nolie bent to glance out the small bit of window glass that wasn't taped over with newspaper. She wasn't a careless painter by intent. Splatters just seemed to happen every time she picked up a brush. "It's not night yet." Truthfully, though, it was coming close. There was still a good amount of light to the west, but dusk was approaching rapidly from the east.

Micahlyn crossed her legs and bounced in place. "I really have to pee, Mama. Please . . ."

"The bathroom's right through the storeroom. Just turn on the light inside the door, then—"

"Mamaaa!"

With a sigh, Nolie climbed down from the ladder. It was time to quit anyway. They still had to walk home, and those woods were bound to be darker than either of them would like. Moving stiffly, she walked into the storeroom, flipped on the lights that did a sorry job of illuminating it, then crossed to the tiny bathroom and turned that light on, too. Micahlyn went inside and primly closed the door on her.

After getting the power and water turned on and the plate-glass window fixed, scrubbing the bathroom had been Nolie's first job at the store. Maybe Hiram had had a different notion of what constituted clean, or maybe men just didn't care about such things the way women did, but the tiny room had been a disgrace. She hadn't let Micahlyn set foot inside until it had been Chloroxed from top to bottom. Twice.

Then she'd started on the paint job. Cleaning. Spackling. Sanding. Cleaning again. Taping. Painting. Painting. And painting. She'd spent the past four days standing or kneeling on unforgiving concrete and climbing up and down the ladder until every joint in her body ached. Her reward was that the room looked a million times better. The bright white paint covered fifty years' worth of stains, and transformed the store from a grimy, dirty place to a place filled with light and possibilities. This weekend she intended to drag the steel shelving outside and give it a fresh coat of gray, and to slap a few gallons on the trim, and by the middle of next week, she would be ready for her first delivery.

Then she could open.

Trying to ignore the anxiety bubbling inside her, Nolie picked at spots of paint dried on her hands. What if Hiram's customers didn't come back? What if they'd gotten used to driving to the next town, if they'd developed some loyalty to the store that had been there for them when this one had shut down? What if she couldn't make a go of this place?

She could always sell it to someone more capable than she, then she could get a job in town. She didn't have many skills, but she could wait tables or make beds at the hospital or the motel. And no matter what, she still had Jeff's insurance money safe and sound in the bank to pay for Micahlyn's education.

She took a deep breath that made her vertebrae protest. It would be all right. Everything would work out just fine. Even if she failed miserably with the feed store, she and Micahlyn would always have a home—and it *wouldn't* be Obie and Marlene's.

After a time, the bathroom door opened and Micahlyn

came out, drying her hands on a paper towel. "I'm ready to go home now, Mama."

Nolie was about to bargain for just a little more time when she walked back into the main room and saw how much darker it had gotten outside. She should have paid closer attention to the time, or driven the car down after lunch. "Okay, babe, just let me put everything up."

Within five minutes, they were searching out the path behind the store. Micahlyn clung tightly to Nolie's hand, darting anxious glances about. "I don't want to walk in the woods at dark."

"It's not completely dark. You can see the path easily enough, can't you?" Nolie's reassuring words were for herself as much as her daughter. It was no surprise Micahlyn was timid about this darkness business, since her mother was a weenie about it herself. Logically, she knew they were likely as safe in the woods as they were in their own backyard. Rationally, she was 99 percent sure those rustling noises off in the shadows were just little forest creatures going about their business.

Realistically, the hairs on the back of her neck were standing on end, her heart was beating faster and it had nothing to do with the exertion of climbing the uphill path, and she was getting jumpier with every passing moment.

"Sing a song, Mama," Micahlyn requested, her voice quavering.

" 'In a cabin in the woods—' " Nolie sang, then asked, "Do you think I sing badly enough to scare away all the little field mice?"

Micahlyn huddled closer. "I don't like mice!"

"Honey, they're more scared of you than you are of them." At least, that was what Nolie's mother used to tell her. She'd never believed it, though.

The deeper they hiked into the woods, the less light penetrated the heavy canopy of leaves overhead. Nolie's feet and knees hurt, her back throbbed, and she was working on a stitch in her side, but still they scurried together along the path. She wished she had a flashlight, the high-intensity kind with a beam that could penetrate any darkness. And her dad's old hunting rifle would be nice. She'd learned to shoot it when she was ten, though she'd never used it against anything deadlier than tin cans.

Forget all that. She wished they were in her car, driving with locked doors up the winding lane to their cabin. *Then* they would be safe and secure and—

Before she could finish the comforting thought, they rounded a boulder and crashed into a tall, solid shadow on the other side. Micahlyn's scream pierced through the woods, echoed by Nolie's frightened shriek and, deeper, more subdued, a grunt from whatever—whoever—they'd impacted. Micahlyn leaped into Nolie's arms, trembling and whimpering, and Nolie would have spun away and torn off back down the path if the shadow hadn't grabbed both her arms.

"Jesus, the two of you make a lot of racket," it said, and Nolie's heart slowed its gallop. It was Chase, and instead of running away as if the Devil himself were after her, she would much rather throw herself into his arms.

She didn't, of course. Instead, she opted for action almost as embarrassing—babbling. "Oh, my God! You scared— I didn't expect— We thought you were—"

"The bogeyman?" he supplied dryly. Apparently convinced she was going to neither fall nor flee, he released her and stepped back into a narrow shaft of dappled light that had worked its way through the trees.

"N-no, not—" He had shaved, Nolie noticed numbly,

and cut his hair, and he was much more handsome than she'd given him credit for.

Determinedly, she shook the thought away and tried to set Micahlyn on her feet, but her daughter was having none of it. She clung, arms around Nolie's neck, legs twined around her hips. Leaning against the boulder for support, Nolie patted her. "It's okay, babe. It's just our neighbor, see?"

Micahlyn refused to raise her head. "I wanna go home. I wanna go home. I wanna go home," she whispered in a tiny voice.

"What are you doing out here this late?" Chase asked.

"I was working at the store. I didn't notice how late it had gotten." Then, curiosity stirring, Nolie turned the question back on him. "What are *you* doing out here?"

"I, uh . . . I just . . ." He shifted, took a few steps back, then gestured toward the path.

Clearly he was waiting for her to go first, but she didn't move. After the long day's work and the scare he'd given her, to say nothing of her general out-of-shape condition, she needed a moment's more rest. And an answer. "This trail doesn't go anywhere but to the store."

"I know."

"So where were you going?"

Though he'd moved back into the shadows, hiding his expression, she knew he was scowling. She could feel it in the tension in the air between them. She half-expected him to turn around and stalk off without answering, but after a moment he gave a grudging reply.

"To see where you were."

"Where we? . . ."

More grudging words. "When you walk, you're always home well before dark. I thought . . ."

He had come looking for them to make sure they were

all right. Warmth flowed through Nolie, easing her myriad aches, renewing the energy she'd thought gone for good.

"Thank you. That was very neighborly of you," she said softly.

"No, it wasn't. It was just . . . curiosity."

"Uh-huh." She untangled Micahlyn and set her down. Immediately, her daughter tried to climb back up her body. "I can't carry you, sweetie. You're too heavy."

"But, Mamaaa—"

"I'll carry you," Chase said, surprising Micahlyn into silence and catching Nolie off guard, too.

Micahlyn's tears dried instantly, and she raised her head to send a haughty gaze in his direction. "I'll walk."

Of course, he'd known that would be her response when he offered, Nolie realized.

Grasping Nolie's hand—the one away from Chase—Micahlyn began marching up the path. Nolie dragged along behind, and partly behind, partly to the side, Chase brought up the rear. Once she stumbled over an exposed root, and he reached out to steady her just as she caught her balance. Too bad.

"Why don't you have a flashlight?" His voice was quiet, a deep rumble in the night, so different from her own and Micahlyn's. It sounded like strength, security. Like a protector, she thought with a faint, foolish smile.

"Because I didn't plan to be out after dark," she replied cheerfully. "But I'll take one from now on."

"Look, Mama!" Micahlyn cried, pointing to the lights shining through the trees twenty yards ahead. "We're home! We're safe!"

Nolie had to admit the lights she'd left burning in the cabin were a welcome sight, glowing through the kitchen window—not because she was scared. She wasn't, not now. But she *was* tired and thinking longingly about a comfortable chair with her bare feet propped up.

When they reached the front corner of the cabin, Chase angled to the left, toward his own cabin. Before he'd taken more than a few steps, she blurted out, "Would you like to stay for dinner?"

This time the pale light from the front-porch bulb allowed her to see his face, marked with indecision. When it appeared he was going to turn her down, she headed him off. "My grandmother always said never trust a skinny cook." Holding her arms out to her sides to indicate her lushness, she smiled. "Obviously, you can trust me."

His gaze shifted from her to Micahlyn, who'd run ahead to the porch and was leaning on the railing, watching them. Her alternately hostile and whiny behavior would probably scare him away . . . but no sooner had Nolie finished the thought, he spoke.

"Okay. Do you need time to clean up?"

She looked down at her paint-splattered clothes, then ran a hand through her hair, falling loose from its ponytail, and came across a chunk of dried paint. Embarrassment turned her face hot. "Yes, please. Why don't you come over in half an hour?"

He glanced at Micahlyn again, then nodded, turned, and walked away.

"Good riddance," Micahlyn muttered from the porch.

But he was coming back soon, Nolie thought.

And the prospect pleased her far more than was wise.

Chapter Four

HE SHOULD HAVE TURNED HER DOWN. HELL, he never should have gone looking for them in the first place. Nolie was a grown woman, perfectly capable of taking care of herself, and his tramping through the woods in the dark just because they were late had given her the idea that he was . . . What had she said? *Neighborly.* Such a lousy thing to say.

Chase scowled as he took the steps two at a time, hesitated at the door, then knocked. After a moment, the door swung open as if by magic, then Micahlyn peeked out from behind it. "You can come in."

He pulled at the screen-door handle, but it didn't budge. With a put-upon sigh, she eased closer, unhooked it, then darted back again. As he stepped inside, then closed the door behind him, she raced up the stairs, bellowing, "Mamaaa!"

No surprise, the cabin was homier than his. All the furnishings were beyond old, except for the curtains at the windows and the matching pillows tossed on the sofa and the easy chair. The bookcases on either side of the fireplace were filled with books—adult titles on top, brightly colored children's books on the lower shelves. Hanging on the brown paneled walls were photographs—of Micahlyn from birth until sometime recently, Nolie in her wedding gown with a very young man at her side, and mother, father, and daughter together. They were a perfect little family, with no clue that disaster was going to strike before long. How much happier Micahlyn would have been if fate had spared her father's life.

How much happier would Nolie have been?

As he crossed the wood floor to the sofa, he caught the faint hint of ancient cigar smoke overwhelmed by the cinnamon and spice candles burning wherever a flat surface offered support. It reminded him that he hadn't had a cigarette since noon, when he'd had a smoke and a handful of dry cereal for lunch. He was trying to cut back, and not finding it so hard, but at the moment, he'd give a lot to have a pack in one hand and a lighter in the other.

Creaks on the stairs drew his attention that way. Nolie had showered and changed into an outfit identical, though cleaner, to the clothes she'd worn earlier—jeans that fitted probably a little more snugly than she'd like and a T-shirt that looked at least two sizes too big. Her hair was pulled back again, red where it was dry, deep copper where it wasn't, and her face once again was free of makeup. Her feet were bare, and she looked young and fresh and smelled sweet. Feminine. Sensual.

Oh, hell.

"Hi," she greeted him as she reached the bottom step, then continued toward the kitchen. "I probably should have warned you that in the Harper house, Friday night is hot-dog night. Is that okay?"

"That's fine." The best he could recall, he hadn't had a hot dog since high school. They'd never been one of his favorite foods, and they certainly weren't on the menu of the restaurants he'd frequented with Fiona in Boston.

But this wasn't Boston, and Nolie damn sure wasn't Fiona.

Aware of the kid hanging on the stair railing and watching him warily, Chase followed Nolie into the kitchen. It was larger than the kitchen in his cabin—cleaner, too— and smelled of sweets and spices. Though the walls were the same ugly brown as his, the yellow-and-white striped curtains at the windows brightened it, along with the lights overhead.

"When I moved into the cabin," he said, half-surprised by his desire for conversation, "every single lightbulb there was forty watts."

Nolie, chopping onions at the counter, smiled. "Here, too, and in the back room at the store. My great-grandfather was apparently quite thrifty. Did you know him—Hiram Legare?"

He'd heard the name, of course, and had passed Hiram's Feed Store a thousand times on his way someplace else, but he'd never met the old man. He shook his head.

"Me, neither. So far, the nicest thing anyone's had to say about him was that he was ill tempered, hard, and mean. Not much of an epitaph, is it?"

"Unless it was the impression he was striving for." He leaned against the counter a good eight or ten feet from where she worked. It occurred to him to offer to help, not that he was qualified to do anything in a kitchen besides open the refrigerator. Give him a knife and fire, and he was a disaster waiting to happen.

"If it was, then he succeeded admirably." Setting the onions aside, she emptied a can of sauerkraut into a pan and set it on the stove, then scraped a can of chili into a second pan. After doctoring it with mustard, hot sauce, onions, and cheese, she put it on the stove, too, then glanced around. "Do you mind lighting the grill for me?"

Chase glanced out the window behind her, where a yellow patio light shone on a gas grill. He'd never gotten any closer than this to a gas grill in his life. His father had sworn by charcoal, and in Boston, when he'd wanted something grilled, he'd gone out for it.

Reading his reluctance, she started toward the back door. "Keep an eye on the chili and kraut, would you?"

He moved to the stove, where he had a clear view out the window over the sink as she bent to turn on the gas, pressed a button, then turned a couple knobs. Seemed easy enough. Even he could have figured it out . . . eventually.

"You haven't cooked out much, have you?" she asked when she returned. Her tone was mild, curious, not at all critical.

"Never."

"Ever? Don't you eat hamburgers, steaks, chicken, and ribs?"

"Of course. At steakhouses and barbecue joints, where someone else cooks and all I have to do is enjoy—and pay."

She made a *tsk*ing sound. "My burgers were the best in Whiskey Creek, and my ribs are darn good, too. Aren't they, Micahlyn?"

Chase looked over his shoulder and caught a flash of red hair and pale skin disappearing around the doorway where she'd been peeking. Strange child.

Nolie didn't ask him to do anything else except sit down after she'd set the small corner table. She cooked the hot dogs, dished up the chili and sauerkraut, and poured their drinks, then called Micahlyn to the table.

Still looking at him as if he might grow horns and fangs at any moment, Micahlyn dragged into the room and studied the table before choosing the seat farthest from him.

That left her mother sitting closest to him.

"Would you say the blessing, please, Micahlyn?" Nolie

asked as she settled in her chair. She automatically bowed her head. So did her daughter and, after a moment, so did Chase. But neither he nor the kid closed their eyes.

"God is great, God is good, let us thank him for our food," Micahlyn intoned. Then, her gaze narrowing on him, she added, "And please, *please,* let him take us back to Grandma and Grandpa, *where we belong.*"

Chase shifted his gaze in time to see the tightening of Nolie's jaw, but after she murmured, "Amen," and raised her head, she didn't comment on the request.

The hot dogs were better than Chase expected. So was the company—at least, part of it. Nolie seemed satisfied to keep the conversation going, while Micahlyn did little but eat and watch him. He didn't have to offer much, which was good, since he didn't have much to offer.

"Did you get enough to eat?" Nolie asked once Micahlyn had disappeared upstairs to take a bath.

"More than enough." That was the best meal he'd eaten since leaving Massachusetts, though he didn't tell her so. It would only lead to questions he wasn't about to answer, such as, *What were you doing before you left?*

Using a fork, she pushed a few chili-coated onions around her plate. "I hope to have the store open in a week or so."

"What do you know about running a feed store?"

"More today than when I came here." Then she smiled. "Not much more than nothing."

"Then why don't you sell the place?"

She laid the fork down, gathered their plates, and carried them to the sink. He followed with the rest of the dishes. After she'd rinsed the dishes and put away the leftovers, she faced him. "If I can make a go of it, the store will provide for us forever."

"That's a big 'if.' Small businesses go under every day.

If you sell it, you can invest the money so it will provide for you."

"Investments go south every day."

"You're a single woman with a child to consider."

"I *am* considering my child. Every day, everything I do—it's all for Micahlyn."

"She doesn't seem to appreciate it much."

A wry expression slid across her face. "Not at the moment. But she'll come around. Today she referred to the cabin as 'home.' That's a start."

A small one. But Chase didn't say it out loud. He didn't need to.

And so ended that thread of conversation. In the silence that followed, she leaned against the counter, hands resting on the curved aluminum strip that edged it, ankles crossed. She should have looked relaxed, comfortable, but telltale signs disputed that. Her fingers held tightly to the aluminum, her toes pressed hard against the linoleum, and her mouth twitched as if the smile she wanted wouldn't come. After a moment, she freed one hand to gesture to the half-full glasses he'd left on the table. "Would you like more to drink?"

"No, thanks." She'd served iced tea, already sweetened with enough sugar to send his system into shock. If he hadn't already known she was a Southerner, the tea would have been a dead giveaway.

"Why don't we go into the living room and sit down?"

What he really should do was thank her for dinner, then go home. But when he pushed away from the counter, it was with the intention of going no farther than the living room for the time being.

She curled up in the armchair, feet tucked into the seat. He sat stiffly at one end of the sofa.

With long fingers, she gracefully tucked a strand of hair

behind her ear, then gestured toward him. "The shave and the haircut . . . they look good."

Chase wasn't sure why he'd made the changes. All he knew was he'd gotten up that morning, showered, and shaved—automatically, as he'd done practically every morning of his adult life. Then he'd driven to Howland, stopped at the first barbershop he came to, and got his hair cut. When he'd gotten home again, he'd stood in front of the bathroom mirror and stared at a reflection that looked very much like the man he used to be. That man had been thirty pounds heavier, had worn custom-tailored suits and paid two hundred bucks for his haircuts, but clearly they were the same guy. *Before* his life had gotten shot all to hell, and *after.*

With a shrug, he carelessly remarked, "The disreputable look wasn't working."

"I don't know. It certainly put the fear into Micahlyn."

"Scaring small children wasn't the goal."

"No, keeping people away was. Though I suspect it'll be a long while before she completely forgets the disreputable you."

He didn't bother to correct her. Yes, he wanted to be left alone. That was the purpose of having Lorraine rent the cabin. But the not shaving, bathing, cutting his hair, changing his clothes, or eating, all the smoking and drinking and brooding about . . . that was about defeat. Acceptance that the life he'd worked so hard for was over.

Did the small changes he'd made mean he was ready to at least consider what kind of life was left for him?

Or was he just tired of looking, smelling, and living like a bum?

"Do you have any children?"

Nolie's question drew him out of his thoughts. "No."

"An ex-wife somewhere?"

He thought of Fiona, beautiful, elegant, sophisticated,

and costly, and for the first time since he'd found out about her affair with Darren Kennedy, his former partner, he wondered if he wasn't lucky to be free of her. It sure hadn't felt that way when he'd first found out about the affair, or when he'd found himself divorced, damn near bankrupt, and serving a thirty-six-month prison sentence, or even when he'd been released after only twenty-two months. Did he feel lucky now?

It was hard to say. Maybe. Not much. But a little.

Nolie took his silence as a refusal to answer. Her smile was tinged with weariness. "Okay. You don't want to talk about Bethlehem, and you don't want to talk about Boston, and personal things, like your last name and whether you've been married, are off-limits. So what's left that we can—"

"Yes, I have an ex-wife."

Her smile became sunnier, lighter, and added a certain prettiness to her features. "That wasn't so hard, was it?"

"Her name is Fiona. We were married three years. We've been divorced three years."

"You must have been more outgoing when you met her."

That was a mild way of putting it. Aggressive, brash, ambitious, and determined were descriptions he was more familiar with. He'd gone after Fiona with as much zeal as he applied to his court cases. And he'd won—both her and the cases. For a time. "Why do you say that?"

"Because getting conversation out of you now is like pulling teeth. I bet you were the most sullen teenager Bethlehem ever produced."

"I admit to being a bit of a hell-raiser." *A bit?* Most folks in Bethlehem would say that was the understatement of the year. "I bet you were the most goody-two-shoes teenager Whiskey Creek ever produced."

"I *was* a little prim and proper in school," she admitted with a modest smile. "My parents had certain expectations of me, and I always did my best to live up to them."

"My parents had no expectations of me, and I did my best to live down to them."

Too late he realized how personal that information was, and he scowled as he got to his feet. "I've got to go. Thanks for dinner."

"But— Wait—"

He reached the door before her feet touched the floor. Once outside, he ignored the steps and jumped to the ground, then set off through the night toward his cabin.

What the hell had gotten into him? Was Nolie just the type who invited confidences—open, friendly, comforting in a mother-hen sort of way—or was he tired of keeping to himself? Whatever the answer, he had to watch out, or he'd find himself telling her everything. *Trusting* her with everything.

That he was an ex-con.

That he'd failed at his job. Failed miserably at his marriage.

That he was the loser his father had always predicted he would be.

And she would tell someone else, who would tell someone else, and before long everyone in Bethlehem would know, including his father.

Damned if Chase would give the old man the satisfaction of knowing just how right he'd been.

CHASE MIGHT HAVE GIVEN UP THE DISREPUTABLE look, but Nolie had taken it up for work the next morning. She'd dressed in her oldest torn and faded jeans, a T-shirt that was permanently stained, and a pair of tennis shoes with soles that were determined to stay behind on the ground, the sooner, the better. Her hair was pulled back into a ponytail, with an old Case Tractor cap crammed over it, and every bit of exposed skin was spotted with white paint and oversprayed with dark blue.

So naturally she had visitors at the store.

The minivan that pulled into the parking lot was painted on the sides with a lovely garden scene underneath the name, Melissa's Garden. The woman who climbed out of the driver's seat was young, pretty, and had the sort of smile that made a person feel like her new best friend. "Hi," she called as she went to the back of the van. "Beautiful day, isn't it?"

"Yes, it is." It was perfect weather for the job Nolie had tackled that morning—spray-painting the store's metal display racks. Initially she'd planned to duplicate their original battleship-gray color, but when she'd stopped at the hardware store two hours ago to buy supplies, she'd chosen deep blue instead. She'd matched it for the trim inside and the long counter that served as both desk and checkout, and was already envisioning a few bright yellow accents to bring out the best of both colors.

The driver returned from the back of the van, carrying a basket filled with brightly colored spring flowers and followed by three children. "You must be Nolie," she said, smiling that amazing smile again. "I'm Melissa Thomas. My husband, Alex, is your lawyer."

Self-consciously, Nolie straightened the brim of her cap, then tugged the hem of her shirt over her hips. "Oh, yes. He's been very helpful." She glanced at the basket. "Beautiful flowers."

"Thanks. They're a slightly late welcome-to-Bethlehem gift from my shop."

Bending, Nolie breathed deeply of their fragrance. "Thank you. That's so kind of you."

Melissa handed the basket to the middle of the three children and instructed her to take them inside. As the girl raced off, the woman directed her attention behind Nolie. "And you must be Micahlyn. My husband told me about you. I'm Melissa."

Micahlyn slowly rose from her place on the concrete stoop, three Barbie dolls clutched to her chest, and sidled closer to Nolie before ducking her head. "Nice to meet you," she mumbled, the way her grandmother had taught her to.

"It's very nice to meet you, Micahlyn." Melissa slid her arm around the blond girl to her left. "These are my friends, Alanna Dalton, her brother, Brendan"—she hugged the young boy with her free arm—"and their sister, Josie. Guys, this is Miss Nolie, and her daughter, Micahlyn."

Josie, who'd taken the flowers inside, skidded to a stop with a spray of gravel and a grin. "Lannie used to play with dolls, but not me. I'm gonna be a cop someday, like my Uncle Nathan."

"I like dolls," Micahlyn replied, her lower lip stuck out.

"That's okay. So do Gracie and Chrissy. That's part of who we're goin' to see. They're bigger 'n you, but they'll play dolls with you anyway. And cats. They play with the cats 'til they run and hide from 'em. You like cats?"

Micahlyn slowly nodded.

Melissa stepped in then. "A bunch of the kids are getting together at the Graysons' house. J.D.'s our local psychiatrist, and his wife's a social worker, and they've got six kids of their own. They live a few miles farther out of town, on the northeast side of the highway. That's where I'm taking these kiddos, and we thought Micahlyn might like to come along."

Nolie chewed the inside of her lower lip. On the one hand, she didn't know these people from Adam. She couldn't just let her daughter go off with them. On the other hand, she did know Melissa's husband, and Micahlyn had been so bored the past week, with nothing to do but sit while Nolie worked. Back in Arkansas, she'd been a very social child. This was the first time she'd even spoken to another child since they'd come here, and there was a gleam of anticipation in her owlish eyes.

Micahlyn tugged at Nolie's hand. "Can I go, Mama?"

"We'll be having a picnic lunch," Melissa said, "and the kids will be very well supervised. J.D. and Kelsey will be there, and me—oh, and J.D.'s father and Miss Agatha will be there, too."

"There they are now," the tall blonde said.

Nolie turned to look as a car pulled off the highway. As soon as the vehicle came to a stop, the three Dalton kids made a rush for it, calling, "Grandpa Bud, Miss Agatha!" Nolie couldn't miss the wistful look in Micahlyn's eyes as she watched them, too.

Miss Agatha joined them. "Good morning, Nolie, Melissa. And good morning to you, too, Miss Micahlyn."

"I been invited to a picnic," Micahlyn announced, "but Mama hasn't said yes yet. Please, Mama, can I go?"

Nolie hesitated only a moment longer. Miss Agatha wasn't a stranger—she and her sister were among Bethlehem's leading citizens, and Chase had known her most of his life. That was enough for her. "Okay, sweetie. But you be sure and mind."

Micahlyn rolled her eyes and started off toward the other kids before returning for a kiss. Then she raced off again.

Melissa offered a business card. "Here's the Graysons' address and phone number and my cell-phone number. I'll bring her back here in three or four hours, and if you're already gone, then I'll take her to the cabin. Okay?"

Nodding, Nolie pocketed the card. "You guys have fun."

It was Miss Agatha who answered, with a slyly innocent smile. "Oh, we always do—both the kids and the kids-at-heart."

Amid a chorus of good-byes, everyone loaded up in the two vehicles, then left Nolie alone in the parking lot with nothing but the steel shelves. She was glad for the company for Micahlyn—and for the opportunity to throw herself into her work without having to worry about her daughter. Now if she just had a little music to work by . . .

She was spraying away and singing softly to herself when the fine hairs on the back of her neck prickled. Breaking off in midchorus, she turned in a slow circle, her gaze scanning. She didn't have far to look for the source of her discomfort. Leaning one shoulder against the cinderblock wall at the opposite side of the building was Chase.

Her first response was a smile. For a man who claimed to want to be left alone, he seemed to be doing his best in the past few days to avoid just that.

Her second response was a grimace. She knew too well how scruffy she'd looked when she left the house that morning, and that was before she'd gotten hot and flecked with paint. Not that it really mattered. She would bet next week's grocery money that he hadn't even noticed she was a woman. Well, except for that day when she'd fallen off the roof and he'd caught her. After all, she wasn't the kind of woman handsome men preferred—thin, pretty, sexy, childless.

She tugged self-consciously at her shirt again and wished her jeans didn't have a large rip just above one knee, then gave herself a mental shake. She was doing messy work, for heaven's sake, and had dressed for it. What did it matter how she looked, or what anyone thought of how she looked?

"You just missed Miss Agatha," she said as a greeting.

"I saw her."

And stayed hidden until she was gone. Naturally. "Melissa Thomas was here, too. Do you know her?"

He shook his head.

"She's married to Alex Thomas. Do you know him?"

Again he shook his head, but without the same certainty, it seemed. Did that mean he did know one but not the other? Was he lying, being evasive, or giving God's truth?

He moved a few yards closer before taking up the same position. "I thought it was the law that all store shelves had to be beige or gray."

She looked at the shelving that stood around her like so many metal skeletons. "I like blue."

"How did you get these out here? You and the kid couldn't have carried them."

"I could have managed somehow if I'd had to," she replied, then relented. "Two of the men who hang out at the hardware store came up this morning and carried them out for me."

"How are you going to get them back inside?"

Her smile was sly. "Well, since you're here . . ." Turning away from him, she gave the paint can a shake, then began working again. "I thought your plan was to vegetate up there on the hill and never go anywhere."

"I go places."

"In Bethlehem?" Without looking, Nolie was pretty sure he'd given another of those shrugs that he passed off as responses. "I didn't think so."

"I prefer to drive to Howland. It's bigger."

She moved to the opposite side of the shelves and crouched to get the lower half. "Howland . . . I drove through there on my way here. As I recall, it offers the same services Bethlehem does, just more choices." Of course, Chase's decision to drive forty-five miles for groceries and a haircut had nothing to do with the greater variety of choices in Howland and everything to do with not wanting to see anyone he knew in Bethlehem. She wished she knew why. "Besides, bigger isn't always better."

"And you know that coming from Whiskey Creek, population—what? Twenty-seven, counting both two- and four-legged critters?"

"If that." Her hometown was so small it had gone unmarked on a couple of official state road maps. Her high school was made up of students from three towns and the surrounding areas, and still hadn't graduated a class of more than thirty. "So if bigger is better, why aren't you in Boston?"

"Because I'm here. Back where I started." His voice was flat, resigned.

Before she could respond to that, he picked up another can of paint and began shaking it, making the ball inside rattle loudly in the still morning. After a time, he pried off the lid, then moved to the next set of shelving.

Nolie stole frequent glances at him as he worked. He really was surprisingly handsome, considering that a mere week and a half ago, his appearance had scared both her and Micahlyn half out of their wits. Cleaned up, he had a rather formal air about him, as if he should be wearing an expensive suit or, at the very least, khakis and an overpriced polo shirt, instead of faded jeans and a white T-shirt. He should be meeting a pretty woman for lunch in a pricey restaurant instead of painting fifty-year-old shelves for a rundown old feed store.

But he looked damn good in faded jeans and a white T-shirt.

"Why didn't you rent a sprayer?" he asked when she paused to shake out the stiffness in her wrist.

"I tried. The rental place won't have any back until Monday, and the hardware store sold their last one yesterday, and I was too impatient to wait. My timing sucks."

Stifling a sigh, she turned to the next set. It was a perfect day for painting outside. The sky was calm, the sun not so warm that the paint dried too quickly, and there hadn't been so much as a rustle of a breeze. She wouldn't mind an occasional rustle—working in even not-so-warm sunshine could make a body hot—but at least she didn't have to worry about dust from the gravel lot blowing onto the wet paint.

She didn't know how much time had passed—five minutes, maybe ten—when Chase spoke out of the blue. "I just went for a walk."

The statement, seemingly in response to nothing, puzzled her. She was about to ask for clarification when he gestured around him with the paint can. "That's how I wound up here."

"Oh." So he wanted her to know he hadn't intended to come here. He'd gone for a walk in the woods and found himself behind the store quite by accident. He hadn't sought out her company on purpose.

Except . . . there was only one trail leading into the woods behind her cabin, and only one place it went—a fact he'd admitted he knew the night before.

But just because *she* stuck to trails didn't mean everyone else did. Some people blazed their own, and it was easier to believe Chase belonged in that category than that he'd come looking for her.

Nolie smiled dryly. All her life it had been easier to believe any number of theories when it came to males than that any man at any given time might be interested in her. Except Jeff. He'd been her best friend since kindergarten, then her boyfriend, then her husband. He'd never minded that she could put on weight as easily as most people put on clothes, or that she was lacking a bit in confidence, and he'd thought she was pretty.

He and her dad were likely the only men who'd ever thought that.

"You know, you're going to have to hire someone to help out here." He stepped back, flexed his index finger, then studied the shelving to make certain no gray showed through on the section he'd finished. After shaking the can again, he bent to finish the bottom half.

"I hope so, eventually. I don't want to work six days a week for the rest of my life."

"You'll need someone when you open. To help with the heavy stuff."

"I can lift the heavy stuff."

"Uh-huh." Chase was fairly certain Fiona had never lifted anything heavier than five pounds in her life. When she traveled, someone else carried her luggage. When she shopped, someone else carried her bags. She wouldn't have dreamed of setting foot in a feed store, and the suggestion that she might heft a fifty-pound bag of feed would earn one of her infamous derisive looks. The thought was almost enough to make him grin.

But Nolie wasn't Fiona. If she believed she could handle this place by herself, hell, she probably could.

Gradually he became aware that she was watching him, hands on her hips. He turned to face her, to wait for whatever she had to say.

"You sound skeptical."

"Me? Skeptical?" he asked dryly.

"I'm stronger than I look."

"Uh-huh."

"I've lived most of my life on a farm, where on occasion I helped haul hay and feed supplement to the stock and drove a tractor and wrestled a calf or two when I had to."

The key phrase there was "on occasion." That could mean anything from once in a while to once every few years.

"To say nothing of the fact that I carried Micahlyn around much of the first two years of her life. You try doing that and see if you don't build some muscles. Of course"—her challenging look faded into sheepishness tinged with self-mockery—"I keep them well hidden underneath all this lusciousness."

Her cracks about her weight seemed designed to forestall any comments he might make. After all, teasing someone wasn't any fun when she made fun of herself first. Maybe she would stop if she knew he wasn't about to say anything disparaging. So what if she was a little plump? Her weight and her satisfaction, or dissatisfaction, with it were her business.

Though Fiona certainly would have offered a few subtly snide comments. Beautiful Fiona, who existed on sugar-free this and nonfat that, who visited the gym as religiously as her old Irish grandmother attended mass, had little tolerance for slackers who let their weight creep one pound over their ideal.

And, for all her physical perfection, look at the kind of person she'd turned out to be.

When the sun was directly overhead, Nolie set down her spray can, stretched her arms over her head, then bent at the waist to ease the kinks out of her spine. "It's time for a break. Want to go to Harry's and get some lunch? My treat."

"I have money."

"Congratulations. And you've spent the last ninety minutes working for free. I think that deserves a free lunch."

"You go ahead."

"Okay, I'll bring it back. What would you like?"

He hadn't set foot in Harry's in sixteen years, but he hadn't forgotten his favorite meal in all that time. "A club sandwich on wheat with potato salad."

She disappeared inside, then returned a few minutes later with her face, arms, and hands freshly scrubbed, her cap gone, and her hair freed from its ponytail. There wasn't much she could do about her clothing, but all in all, she looked fine. Her skin, where it wasn't dotted with freckles, was smooth, pale ivory, her blue eyes were bright, and her mouth . . . His gaze fixed on it, free of lipstick, nicely shaped, with a prominent cupid's bow, and definitely kissable—

The direction his thoughts had wandered made him swallow convulsively and look away as she dug her keys from the pocket of her jeans. "I'll be back in a few minutes."

His only response was a grunt and a nod as he went back to work, keeping his gaze averted as she climbed into the car, then backed out. Once the sound of the engine faded away, he released the breath he'd instinctively held and swore.

He needed a woman. If he had any sense, he would go to one of Howland's numerous bars, have a few drinks, pick one out of the crowd, and spend the rest of the night making up for the past three years. It wouldn't have to be anyone special—just female, breathing, and willing—and he would forget any stupid ideas his extended abstinence might put in his head about Nolie.

Yeah, sure, that was what he would do. Not that he'd

engaged in one-night stands in a long time. But before
Fiona, he'd been pretty good at them, and he was fairly
certain that, like riding a bicycle, it was something you
never really forgot. Besides, he didn't have much choice.
When he had even the faintest sexual thought about a
woman like Nolie, he had to do *something*—and not with
her. For his sake. For hers.

She was gone close to half an hour. When she returned
and got out of the car with a brown paper bag and a card-
board drink carrier, he set the paint can aside and went inside to wash up. By the time he finished, she'd spread a
quilt from somewhere over the concrete stoop and laid out
their lunch.

"Was Harry's busy?" He sat at the near corner of the
quilt, where cinder blocks provided support for him to
lean against. She was doing the same at the other end.

"Very. It's a great place. It reminds me of the café back
home. That was its name—The Café—and it was *the* place
to go if you wanted all the latest news and gossip." Then
she grinned. "It was also the *only* place to go."

He unwrapped his sandwich and took a bite before asking, "How big is Whiskey Creek, really?"

"Let's see . . . with Micahlyn and me leaving, it got de-
moted from 'wide spot in the road' to . . . hmm, I'm not
sure there's a name for places that small. We had one café,
one gas station, a tiny post office, and four churches."

"And you stayed there so long because? . . ."

"It was home. That's where my parents lived when I
was born. That's where Jeff lived . . . and died."

"How?" It took Chase a moment to realize that the
question had come from him. As a rule, he didn't ask such
personal questions just to make conversation. But this
wasn't just small talk. He wanted to know.

She took a bite of her own sandwich—grilled chicken

on thick slices of fresh-baked white bread—and gazed at the traffic passing by on the highway for a moment. "He had an accident at the farm. The tractor rolled over, and he . . ."

The images that immediately popped into Chase's mind were gruesome, and far more than he wanted to know. He murmured, "Sorry," and she gave him a smile colored with sadness. "Me, too."

"Does it bother you to talk about him?"

"Oh, no. I talk to Micahlyn a lot. Even though she was too young to remember him, I want her to know him— what kind of man he was, how much he loved her."

Lucky kid. He didn't know what it was like to have a father's love—and his was still living. Not that he'd given Earl much reason to care. After the less than pleasant eighteen years he'd lived with them, he'd pretty much shut his family out of his life for good, and he didn't miss them at all.

Except occasionally in the loneliest part of the night.

Not wanting to consider that, he asked, "Do your parents still live in Whiskey Creek?"

"No. They died in a car wreck when I was a senior in high school. Jeff's parents took me in, and as soon as I graduated, we got married."

"Sorry," he muttered again.

"Don't be. People we love die. It's a part of life. I'd rather have Jeff, Mom, and Dad alive and well, but . . . at least I got to be a part of their lives while they were here."

"You're much better adjusted than I am."

"Oh, there's a surprise."

He gave her a sharp look. It had been a long time since anyone had felt comfortable enough to tease him. He wasn't sure how he felt that she did.

As he finished his potato salad, she slid another small

foam container across the quilt. "You can have my potato salad, too. I'm saving the calories for dessert."

"And what's for dessert?"

Reaching into the bag, she pulled out a clear plastic box holding three pieces of pastry. "Baklava." She said each syllable distinctly, turning the name into a drawn-out "ahhh" of satisfaction.

"Baklava?"

"It's a Greek pastry."

"I know what it is. When did Harry start selling baklava?"

"Sebastian Knight's new wife is Greek-American, and the recipe is her mother's. Harry made it for her originally— she was having cravings when she was pregnant—but everyone loved it, so he keeps making it."

"And you know this because? . . ."

"Because I spent nearly thirty minutes waiting for our lunch. By the way, she had a girl. In March. Named her Hildred Alyssa. Calls her Alyssa for obvious reasons." She gave him a thoughtful look. "I should have asked Maeve, the waitress, if she knows anyone from Bethlehem named Chase."

He swallowed hard. If she ever did such a thing, she would find herself minus one tenant. It wouldn't take long for someone to remember him—most likely Maeve or Harry themselves—and within minutes, his parents would know he was back. He would have to get out and go . . . hell, wherever. Where did a man go when there was no place left for him?

After polishing off the second container of potato salad, he reached for a triangle of baklava, then carelessly said, "She would have told you no. Not everybody in Bethlehem knows everybody else."

"You must be confusing it with Boston."

The absurdity of her calmly spoken statement brought a long-forgotten sound from him—a chuckle. He cut it off before it finished. "Oh, sure. People make that mistake all the time." It was an easy distinction for him. He'd been happy in Boston. He hadn't been in Bethlehem.

She ate one piece of baklava, then delicately licked the honey syrup from her fingers before she stood up. She gave an exaggerated groan. "I'm not built for hard physical labor."

"I thought you helped haul hay and wrestle calves."

"On occasion," she reminded him, then admitted with a grin, "which was only when I couldn't hide from Jeff's dad when he came looking for help. I wasn't meant to be a farmer's daughter."

"You look like one."

Her gaze narrowed as it settled on him. No doubt she was trying to determine whether he'd insulted or complimented her, and he figured that look meant she was leaning toward an insult. "How does a farmer's daughter look? Corn-fed? Fattened up for market?"

"No." He got to his feet, too, so he didn't have to look up at her. Words came to mind—innocent, fresh, sweet— but he didn't offer them. "Wholesome. Healthy. Robust."

She sniffed disdainfully. "Robust? You like to live dangerously, don't you? Don't forget that I outweigh you, slim. I could hurt you."

He didn't know what devil goaded him to move, to step across the quilt and not stop until he was right in front of her—too close, his defenses warned. So close she had to tilt back her head to look at him. "I don't think so. I'm not as harmless as I look."

She tried to snort with derision, but it came out no more than a soft exhalation of honey-scented breath. This close he could see the subtle shadings of blue in her eyes, could hear the whisper of her breathing and see the pulse beating faintly at the base of her throat. This close she could tempt him to cup his hands to her face, to lower his mouth to hers, to take just a taste, to kiss her just once, briefly, innocently.

And then what? Walk away?

That was the problem.

He didn't know if he could.

Chapter Five

ONE OF THE BEST WAYS TO FIT INTO A SMALL town was to join in the local church services. Cole Jackson had learned that lesson long ago, and had often put it to good use. This Sunday morning he'd gotten up, showered, and shaved, and dressed in pale gray trousers and a white shirt. He'd tossed a darker gray jacket and a tie across the bed, eaten a breakfast of cold pizza left from last night's dinner, and tried to convince himself to finish dressing and leave.

The last of the church bells had stopped tolling fifteen minutes ago, and he was still at home.

He'd had a lot of homes over the years, so many that the word had stopped meaning anything by the time he was ten. A few had been even nicer than this old mansion, but most hadn't existed in the same league. He'd spent more than his share of time in places without heat or electricity, where the rats lived more comfortably than he. Hell, he'd slept plenty of nights in the back of a beat-up old car.

But not anymore. And by God, never again.

Accepting that he wasn't feeling any too pious this morning, he removed the diamond cuff links and rolled his sleeves up. Logic said he should change into jeans and a

T-shirt, walk the two blocks to the office he'd rented, and finish cleaning away a year's grime so he would be ready for the furniture delivery in the morning. But when he moved away from the kitchen sink, where he'd eaten his pizza, he didn't take the back stairs to his bedroom. Instead, he headed down the hall, grabbed his keys, and left, locking the door behind him.

The Miller mansion—*his* mansion—was located catty-corner from the courthouse, which was home to both the sheriff's office and the police department. Beyond that was the town square and downtown Bethlehem. The town was smaller than he liked, but size aside, there was one hell of a lot of money there and in his business, that was all that mattered.

He crossed the small yard that fronted the house and went through the gate. He didn't need to be told that an elderly woman had last lived in the house. One look at the elaborate picket fence and fussy flower beds made that clear, to say nothing of all the crocheted doilies and ruffled fabrics inside the house. The seller, the old woman's son, had offered to remove the furnishings before Cole moved in, but Cole had suggested renting it instead. After all, he needed furniture, and the house was filled to overflowing with it.

The morning was ten degrees cooler than the past few days. Shoving his hands in his pockets, he crossed the street in front of his nearest neighbor, Small Wonders, then crossed the side street and turned toward the square. He'd seen the woman who ran Small Wonders more than a few times since he'd moved into the mansion. She was pretty, dark-haired, and slender. Her business appeared profitable— there was no shortage of customers, and she drove an expensive little SUV that, even now, was parked around the corner from the shop's entrance.

Of course, most businesses in Bethlehem appeared profitable. Wasn't that why he'd come here in the first place? The town had a history of doing all right for itself, helped along by its rather isolated location. When McKinney Industries had moved their headquarters here a few years earlier, *all right* had transformed into *outstanding*. It was rumored the head of MI, Ross McKinney, was worth billions—yep, with a B—and his top people were million-aires twenty or forty times over. That kind of money could make a big difference in a small town.

The square was like something from a hundred years ago—lush grass edged by flower beds, benches, tall trees offering shade, a bandstand in the middle. It didn't require much imagination at all to picture the 4th of July there, with red, white, and blue bunting, flags flapping in the breeze, brightly colored quilts spread across the grass where fami-lies picnicked, and a band offering rousing patriotic tunes. Or an Easter-egg hunt or Christmas carolers in the snow.

At the moment, though, it was pretty much deserted, except for one small boy, driving a dump truck through the grass, and his mother, reading a newspaper on the bench nearby. His neighbor from Small Wonders.

As he debated striking up a conversation with her, the breeze snatched the paper from her hands and sent it sail-ing along just above the ground. With a laugh, the boy went running for one page, and she started after the others. Cole caught them first, folded them neatly, and offered them to her with a practiced smile. "I guess it's true that news really gets around fast in Bethlehem."

She responded with a smile of her own. "You bet it is."

"I'm Cole Jackson."

"I know. You've come here from California, you've bought the Miller house, and you've rented office space on Main Street, across the hall from Alex Thomas." That smile came again. "News travels *very* fast."

"How did you miss the part about my being an investment counselor, thirty years old, and single?"

"Well, I haven't been out much lately." Tucking the newspaper under one arm, she offered her right hand. "I'm Leanne Wilson."

"Fellow businessperson and neighbor." He accepted her hand, finding her grip surprisingly strong and her skin enticingly soft. He'd always had a fondness for soft things, seeing as how they had been lacking for most of his life. After holding her hand a good while longer than was necessary, he released it and gestured toward the boy approaching them, flying the newspaper page like a kite behind him. "Is that your son?"

A tender expression crossed her face as she watched the boy. "Yes, it is."

"Here's your paper, Mom." Folding the double-wide page was beyond the boy's ability, so he handed it to her as was, then turned a dark-eyed gaze on Cole. "Hi."

Leanne lifted the kid into her arms. "This is Danny. Sweetheart, this is Mr. Jackson."

"Hello," Danny said again, extending his hand with grave formality.

Feigning the same formality, Cole shook hands with him. "I'm pleased to meet you, Danny."

Before he could say anything else, though, a shout from across the street—"Hey, Cole!"—interrupted. He turned to watch the twelve-year-old boy running across the street toward them, with surprise, anger, and disbelief building inside. He kept it all off his face, though, and merely stared.

"Who is that?" Leanne asked curiously.

Cole stifled a sigh—or was it a curse?—then stiffly said, "That's Ryan. *My* son."

And why the hell wasn't he in Philadelphia where he belonged?

. . .

WHEN SHE HEARD FOOTSTEPS ON THE PATH BE-hind her Sunday afternoon, Nolie wasn't the least bit surprised. She glanced over her shoulder as Chase appeared through the trees, and nearly walked into a tree herself before swerving back onto the trail. She'd seen him stretched out on the hammock when she'd left the cabin and waved, but he hadn't waved back. Friendly or distant, wanting to be alone or volunteering to spend time with her—she'd gotten to the point where none of it surprised her.

"Where's the kid?" he asked when he fell into step beside her.

"Her name is Micahlyn."

"I know that."

"She went home with the Winchester sisters after church."

"They still invite everybody over for Sunday dinner?"

"They invited us. I declined. Micahlyn accepted. Apparently, several of her new friends from yesterday live near the sisters." Nolie gave him a sidelong look. "I take it you used to go to their church?"

"Do I look the type who would go to any church?"

"Well, now that you mention it . . ." He didn't. He looked too aloof, too sophisticated, too . . . wicked. Though wasn't that exactly the sort of man who *needed* church?

Shifting her attention to the trail as it sloped down to the stream and its bridge, she went on. "Of course, getting to church on Sunday morning is awfully hard when you keep such late hours on Saturday night." She'd seen him drive by barely an hour after they'd finished work at the store, and his cabin had remained dark all evening and late into the night. She knew he'd come home around three-thirty A.M.—though not because she'd been waiting. It had merely been the unfamiliar sound of his truck passing her house that had caught her attention, nothing more. Honestly.

He made an odd choking sound, and when she glanced at him, she saw a blush had turned his cheeks dark bronze. He looked guilty and more than a little defensive. Why? Though she was curious, it was none of her business where he'd gone last night or what he'd done. Especially the what he'd done—and with whom.

As they crossed the footbridge, he changed the subject completely. "Why doesn't the ki—Micahlyn go to school?"

"She's not old enough yet. She just turned five last month, so she'll start kindergarten next fall," she replied absently. Her attention was still focused on the previous topic. She would have thought a man like him had outgrown blushes sometime around the age of six. Heavens, what *had* he done last night?

Then her own cheeks grew warm. Sometimes she was so naive. Saturday night was party night, prime time for unattached singles to go out to bars and clubs, have a few drinks and do their best to become attached, at least for a night or so. Chase was apparently as unattached as they came . . . but he wasn't dead.

"I would have thought you'd had your fill of painting yesterday," she said as the back of the feed store came into sight. By the time they'd painted every single set of shelving, they'd both been bending their index fingers only when necessary and usually accompanied by grimaces. "I certainly have. Once I finish with the store, if I never have to pick up a paint roller again . . . though of course I will. Before long, I'll have to start on the cabin."

"You could have hired someone to do all that work."

She gave him a chastising look. "Oh, yeah, I forgot.

You're the one who pays people to do things for you. I don't, unless there's a very good reason why I can't do the job myself."

His voice was all stiff. "And that makes you better?"

"Not better. Just different." Abruptly she laughed. "I guess I have too much of Great-Grandpa Hiram in me."

"If I'd said that, you would have been insulted."

"Hey, I'm insulted anyway. I told you, by all accounts, he wasn't a nice man."

They came out of the woods behind the store and walked around to the front. The REOPENING SOON sign made a fluttering sound like birds' wings as she unlocked the door, then stepped inside. The smell of paint was strong in the air, completely masking the stale cigar smoke odor. She took a look around, at bright white walls and blue shelves, and smiled privately, proudly. Professional painters could have done the job in a fraction of the time—and at twenty times the cost—but they couldn't have done it any better. She and Chase did good work.

He volunteered to paint the wood trim, and because tedious detail work wasn't her strong suit, she let him and got started on the long countertop and the cabinets that supported it.

After a time, he broke the silence that seemed too often to settle between them. "What did you do in Whiskey Creek besides hide from your father-in-law when he needed help on the farm?"

"I had a part-time job keeping books for Obie—that's Jeff's dad—and several of our neighbors. I wanted to work full-time, since I didn't have much else to do, but Marlene—Jeff's mom—objected."

"What business was it of hers?"

"It wasn't. But I was trying to be a properly grateful daughter-in-law. I didn't want to cause trouble. They'd done so much for us—too much, really. All they wanted was to take care of us, to do their duty by Jeff's widow and child. It made me feel guilty, because all I wanted was *out*."

"So how'd you get *out*?"

She paused in stroking the rich blue paint over the countertop. If she hadn't been so properly grateful, things wouldn't have ended the way they had. If she'd spoken up from time to time. If she'd done the things important to her without letting their opinions sway her. "Everything just built to a head this spring. I wanted Micahlyn to go to day care a couple days a week just so she could play with other kids, but Marlene vetoed the idea. I wanted to work full-time, but she didn't like that, either. When I accepted an invitation to a movie and dinner with an old friend of Jeff's, she was scandalized that I could even consider going out with another man. Then I found out that they had directed Alex Thomas to put this place up for sale and to dispose of Hiram's belongings without even discussing it with me first. That was the last straw. I blew up and said some things, and . . . here we are. I don't think they'll ever get over it."

"So what? You don't need them."

"They're Micahlyn's grandparents—all the family she's got except for a few distant relatives."

"Doesn't sound like she needs them, either."

"You're not a real family type, are you?"

He didn't slow in his painting. "Family's overrated. Most people get along just fine without their relatives butting into their lives."

"What did your parents do to make you feel that way?"

For a long time he continued to paint, cutting in the blue paint in a clean line alongside the white, moving with long, smooth strokes, and she watched him. Watched the way the soft cotton of his shirt stretched across his shoulders with every stroke. The way the muscles in his back alternately flexed, then relaxed, visible even through the shirt. The way his long dark fingers held the brush easily and the way the muscles in his jaw tightened, twitched, as if he found her question too hard . . . or too hurtful.

"You do have a family, don't you?" she asked softly.

That made him glance at her, with something dangerously close to becoming a smile hovering over his mouth. It didn't form, though, to her great disappointment. Some smiles could be lethal, and she was pretty sure his was one of them. "Hard to imagine me as a kid with a mom and dad, isn't it?"

A mom and dad who had failed him. But how?

"Not at all," she lied. "I can just see you as a little squirt, stealing cookies from your mother's kitchen, going fishing with your dad, playing Little League, and tormenting all the little girls around."

Chase snorted. Stealing cookies, yes. Doing anything with his father, no way. Being in the same room together was almost too much to ask, and spending time together alone *was* too much. "You must be imagining someone else. That wasn't my life."

"Then what was?"

He pulled the ladder over—the same one she'd used to reach the cabin roof—and climbed halfway up to paint the trim across the top of the plate-glass window. He generally didn't discuss his family with anyone. Even Fiona hadn't known much about them or his relationship with them . . . though he couldn't recall if that was because he'd never told her or she'd never asked.

"Don't you ever have any desire to talk about yourself?"

The wistful tone in Nolie's voice made him stop in mid-stroke. Slowly he rested the brush across the top of the paint can, then turned on the ladder to face her. He fished a pack of cigarettes from his pocket, shook one halfway out, saw the delicate twitch of her nose, and let it slide back. After flipping the package onto the top shelf of the nearest display, he slid his fingertips into his hip pockets. "Honestly?"

"Always."

He took a breath to say no, no desire, but he didn't think that was the truth. Sometimes he was lonely. He missed spending time with someone. He missed casual conversations, and serious ones, too. Sometimes he would give just about anything to hear another voice, to not feel so alone.

But most of the time he knew alone was the best way to be. People couldn't be trusted. They betrayed you and let you down when you needed them most. They called you friend, then believed the worst of you.

They weren't worth the heartache.

She was waiting for an honest answer, and he gave her the only one he had. "I'm not the neighborly type, or the church type, or the family type, or the trusting type."

The emotion that flitted across her face was difficult to name. Disappointment, maybe, though instinctively he knew it wasn't in *him*. God knows, he'd seen enough disappointment in his parents' eyes to recognize it at a glance.

"I'm sorry," she murmured. "I'm sorry whatever went wrong for you did go wrong, and I'm sorry your family wasn't there to help."

He shrugged as if it didn't matter—told himself it really *didn't* matter. But it took him a long time to pull his gaze from hers, and if voices hadn't filtered in from outside, he might not have managed even then.

Through the open door he saw two women coming across the parking lot toward the store. He jumped the three feet to the ground and headed for the storeroom, ignoring the question in Nolie's eyes. Once inside the dark room, he pushed the door up until it was almost closed, then took up a position beside it, where he could see and hear.

"Good afternoon, Jolie!" the older woman greeted her in a booming voice as they came through the front door. "My, what a wonderful difference you've made in this place."

Nolie glanced toward the storeroom, then turned back to the visitors. "Thank you. It's nice to see you, Gloria, Sophy."

"We were out taking a walk since it's such a beautiful day," the younger woman, Sophy, said, "and we thought we'd stop in and see how you and Micahlyn are getting along."

"Oh, we're fine. She's in town right now—"

"With the Winchesters, of course," Gloria interrupted.

"Yes. She gets bored spending all her time here with me."

"Too bad she's not old enough to help." Sophy stopped next to the ladder and studied the wet paintbrush and the open can of paint. "Though it looks as if you've got someone helping."

"Uh . . . no, I, uh . . . I tend to get distracted. I started on the trim, but decided the counter would be easier."

How had he gotten to know her so well, Chase wondered, that he knew from no more than the tone of her voice that the lie was making her blush? He didn't *want* to know her that well—didn't want to know *anyone* that well ever again.

"Did you also take up smoking?" Sophy gingerly picked up the cigarettes he'd left on the shelves and made a face before letting them fall again.

"No, those aren't mine." This time Nolie sounded relieved that she could tell the truth. "Someone must have left them."

"How's your neighbor?" Gloria asked. "Chance, isn't it?"

"Chase," Sophy corrected.

"That's what I said." Gloria gave a dismissive wave. "You see a lot of him?"

"Uh . . . no, not a lot. He, uh, likes his privacy."

"Too much privacy isn't good for a man." That came from Gloria, and made Sophy shake her head so her curls bobbed. "Humans deal with things in a million different ways. When he's had enough of being alone, he'll give it up."

"A stubborn man like Jace?" Now Gloria shook her own head. "I don't know."

Chase eased back against the wall, his breathing controlled but shallow. There was a sudden tightness in his gut that extended all the way out to curl his fingers into fists. He wished the two women would leave—wished like hell *he* was gone, that he'd never come here. It had been stupid, weakness on his part, to come back to New York, to think he could settle so close to Bethlehem without anyone knowing he was there. Even so, he'd done all right . . . until *she* had come.

He had Nolie to thank for the fact that someone did know.

The conversation between the three women continued, but he didn't listen to anything beyond the drone of their voices. After what seemed like forever, Gloria and Sophy left. A long moment later—after they were out of sight, he guessed—Nolie pushed the storeroom door open. "They're gone—"

He caught her wrist and backed her against the door. "What did you tell them about me? *Why?*"

Her eyes were startled and twice their size. "I didn't tell them anything! You heard—"

He swore, making her flinch. "They knew you have a neighbor."

"They already knew that the first time I met them, right after we moved in!"

"They knew my name. If you didn't tell them, who the hell did?"

She didn't have such a quick answer for that. Her brows arching, she shook her head. "Maybe Alex Thomas. Maybe Miss Corinna or Miss Agatha. I don't know."

"You told the Winchester sisters my name?"

"No!"

"Then they couldn't have told Gloria. And I doubt the lawyer would have told her." Breathing heavily, he stared at her. She looked stunned and surprised, but not scared, and he wondered why the hell not. Why hadn't she tried to pull away? Why didn't she tell him to get out?

Damn it, why didn't he let her go and leave on his own?

Her pulse slowed under his fingertips and the surprise faded from her expression. "I did tell Alex Thomas right after we moved in that there was a man named Chase living in the other cabin, but he's the only one I've mentioned your name to. I don't know how Gloria and Sophy knew, I swear." She swallowed hard, then hesitantly asked, "Are you . . . wanted by the police?"

His laughter was bitter and faded as soon as it started. "Good God, no." He'd served his time, every single day the state of Massachusetts had seen fit to take from him. He wasn't wanted by anyone anymore.

That convulsive swallow came again. "So it's your past you're hiding from."

His past, his present, his nonexistent future. His fingers slid away from her wrist, and he turned to lean against the wall again, staring across the dimly lit room to avoid looking at her. It didn't work, though. From the corner of his eye, he saw her rub her wrist where he'd held her. "I didn't mean to hurt you," he muttered.

"You didn't." But she continued to rub . . . though, in truth, her fingers' slow, easy movements qualified more as a caress. After a moment, with an awkward smile, she stopped. "If I'm ever going to finish this place, I'd better get back to work."

After a few awkward moments of his own, he followed her back into the main room, climbed the ladder, and started painting again.

He should have stayed home. He'd spent the better part of every day for a month lying in that hammock, and he hadn't minded at all. He should have stayed there today, instead of following her into the woods.

But all those days he'd spent slouched in the hammock, he'd been in an alcohol-induced stupor. He couldn't have followed her into the woods, or endured the paint vapors, or climbed this ladder. Well, he could have, but he probably would have broken his fool neck.

There was something to be said for sobriety.

Then he sneaked a glance at Nolie. There was also something to be said for oblivion.

He painted the trim as far as he could stretch, moved the ladder six feet to the right, and climbed up again. Truth was, there was a *lot* to be said for oblivion. For example, he wouldn't care at all if he couldn't remember a single detail from the night before. The forty-five-mile trip to Howland. The first bar, where he'd had a burger with his beer. The second, where he'd had a little friendly conversation and a beer. The third, where he'd relied on ill-tempered scowls to keep everyone away while he nursed his beer.

He'd had one goal—to find a woman. He'd done just that in each bar, then wound up sending them away, staying on his own, coming home alone.

Hell, he couldn't even get laid without screwing up. The story of his life.

The minutes audibly ticked by, even though he knew it was only in his head. The old clock tossed in a box of trash wasn't working, and neither of them wore a watch, which couldn't possibly sound that loud, anyway. His fingers tightened around the brush handle, and his nerves grew tauter with each passing moment. Feeling as if he just might explode, he blurted out the first thing that came to mind. "Who were those women?"

Nolie didn't look up but continued to paint long smooth strokes across the countertop. "The older one is named Gloria, and the younger is Sophy. I don't know anything else about them, except that they did most of the cleaning in here. Oh, and they knew Hiram." She hesitated. "You don't remember them from when you lived here?"

"No." He'd probably met Gloria at some point—she seemed the right age for his mother's group of friends—but Sophy couldn't have been more than a few years old when he left Bethlehem the first time.

There was a part of him that was seriously looking forward to leaving again, only this time he would *never* come back.

And a part that wondered, just for one brief instant, if leaving for the last time might not be harder than the first time. A foolish thought. There wasn't anything here for him, and for damn sure not any*one*.

As he assured himself of that, Nolie came around the counter, traded her roller for a brush, then knelt where the counter butted against the wall. With her lower lip caught between her teeth, she painstakingly painted a thin strip of blue along the edge of the cabinet, taking twice as long as he would have, but getting just as clean a line. A strand of hair that had worked loose from her ponytail brushed her cheek, and she absently wiped it away, leaving a thin smear of blue behind. The hair fell again, and she blew it, making it flutter before it settled once more against her cheek. It looked soft and silky, and when she was outside and the sunlight hit it, it gleamed a rich coppery hue and tempted him to touch it. To see for himself if it was really that soft. To feel the heat it absorbed from and reflected back to the sun. To smell the erotic, womanly scent it gave off.

Chase gradually became aware that his fingers were cramping, and looked down to see that he was gripping the brush as if it were a lifeline. If he were a different man, or even just a different kind of man, he would move down the ladder, cross to her, tangle his fingers into her hair, and tilt her mouth up to his. And then he would—

But he wasn't a different man. He knew right from wrong, good from bad, harmless from dangerous, and at this point in his life, Nolie Harper was definitely dangerous.

Or was it him?

"Is Chase your first name or last?" she asked, completely unaware of the path his thoughts had taken.

"First." When he realized what he'd done—answered a personal question—he turned the subject back to her. "What kind of name is Nolie?"

"It's *my* name."

"Uh-huh. Your parents actually named you Nolie—on your birth certificate and all? Your driver's license and marriage license say Nolie?"

A tinge of pink spread across her cheeks. "Not exactly."

"So what is Nolie a nickname for?"

She rolled paint on the cabinets in a W pattern, then began filling in. "Did I tell you my father was a farmer, too?"

"No."

"Our house was smack dab in the middle of his land. There was a tiny yard, my mother's garden, and acres and acres of flat land planted in corn, cotton, and soybeans. The only trees were the ones my parents planted around the house—a maple, some crape myrtles, two peach trees, and Mom's pride and joy, a huge, beautiful, old"—she glanced at him over her shoulder, saw he was watching, then rolled her eyes—"magnolia tree."

It took a moment for her meaning to sink in. When it did, Chase laughed out loud for the first time in more years than he could remember. "*Magnolia* Harper? You're named for a magnolia tree?"

Her gaze narrowed threateningly. "Which is just between you and me, right?"

"Jeez. And I grew up hating being named after my grandfather. Beats the hell out of a tree."

She continued to scowl at him, unable or unwilling to share his humor. Of course, it was easy for him, since it wasn't *his* name.

"It could have been worse," he said at last.

"How is that?"

He thought of the other trees she'd listed—maple, crape myrtles, and peach—and innocently pointed out, "They could have named you Myrtle."

NOLIE SPENT THE NEXT FEW DAYS PAINTING, OR-ganizing, accepting deliveries for the store, and, in what little spare time she managed, looking for day care for Micahlyn. Though she enjoyed her daughter's company, she knew too well that the child needed to be around other children. She found exactly what she was looking for—or so she hoped—in Angel Wings Day Care. It was located one street over from Main, on a block that was an old and comfortable mix of storefronts and residences.

Angel Wings occupied an old Victorian that was deco-rated with enough flourishes and frills for five such houses, and painted in soft colors—violet, blue, rust, and mossy green. The wood sign identifying it stood at the edge of the brick walk that led to the porch and was cut out in the shape of an angel, head bowed, wings extended.

That Thursday morning would begin Micahlyn's first full day at the center. She eyed everything—the house, the toys and classrooms inside, the teachers, and the other kids—with suspicion. Clutching Nolie's hand, she followed her mother, who was following one of the teachers, down a broad hallway, past a kitchen where fresh cookies were baking, and out the back door to the fenced-in yard where the children in her age group were playing.

"Hey, kids," the teacher called from the top of the step. "Come and meet our new student. This is Micahlyn Harper, and her mother, Nolie Harper."

Eight or ten children gathered at the foot of the stairs. Nolie watched Micahlyn watch them watch her, and her fingers tightened fractionally around Micahlyn's hand. About three-fourths of the kids murmured "hello," and in response, Micahlyn pushed her glasses back up on her nose, then gave Nolie an accusing look. "If we were home where we belong, I wouldn't *have* to go to day care."

Nolie was on the verge of offering to forget the idea, when a familiar face swept in, bending to hug her daughter.

"Why, you don't *have* to come here, Martha Lyn," Gloria said cheerfully. "You *get* to. There's a difference, you know. Do you like to paint and play with modeling clay and bake cookies for a snack?"

Micahlyn nodded, and her glasses slipped.

"And wouldn't you rather play on this wonderful playground than sit in a stinky feed store with nothing to do?"

What a coincidence, Nolie thought as Micahlyn nodded again, that Gloria just happened to pick up on her child's most insistent complaint.

Gloria leaned close and lowered her voice. "Going to the feed store is *work,* you know. Staying here is play. Wouldn't you rather stay here and play all day with me and the other kids than go to work?"

That coaxed one more nod out of Micahlyn, who finally let go of Nolie's hand and took a few steps toward the yard. The teacher took her hand and introduced her to each of the kids while Gloria looked on, beaming. "You made a good choice."

"I didn't know you worked here," Nolie said, then felt foolish. As she'd told Chase, she knew so little about Gloria and her friend as to qualify as nothing.

"Angel Wings. What better place for someone like me to work? I mean, for someone who loves kids and all." Then Gloria squeezed her hand reassuringly. "You can go on about your business now. Michael Lyn will be fine."

Already Micahlyn was sitting primly at a child-sized picnic table with three other little girls and a selection of dolls. As if she felt her mother's gaze, she looked up and smiled when Nolie blew her a kiss, then waved. Then Nolie glanced at Gloria. "I'm sure she will. I'll be back later."

When she reached the sidewalk in front of the Victorian, Nolie stood there a moment. Leaving without Micahlyn seemed to make everything official. Her child was in day care, and she was off to work. She was an honest-to-goodness real single working mother.

Who didn't have anything demanding her time or attention for at least a few hours. Turning away from her car, she strolled to the end of the block, turned the corner, and would have walked on if an outfit in the shop window hadn't caught her eye. The sundress was child-sized, sunflowers on a dark green background, with a matching sash tied around the crown of a floppy straw hat. It was adorable, and that particular shade of green was most flattering for Micahlyn's pale complexion. After hesitating only a moment, she went inside the store and headed for the rack of matching dresses.

"It's pretty, isn't it?"

Nolie glanced at the woman who'd approached, then did a double take. It was Leanne Wilson, whom she'd met at Alex Thomas's office.

"Fancy meeting me here," Leanne said with a laugh. "I should have told you when we met to come by. I've got great clothes for little girls."

"I see." Nolie gave the outfits another wistful look, then sighed. "But the only way I could get that hat on Micahlyn would be to hog-tie her. She thinks life has already been unfair in giving her red hair, freckles, and glasses."

"Someday she'll appreciate it—the red hair, at least. And she can always get contacts. As for the freckles . . ."

"She'll just have to learn to live with them," Nolie said ruefully. It was a lesson she'd had to learn herself, and she still occasionally wished for a creamily perfect complexion.

"I hope you're getting settled in. I don't think I'm going out too far on a limb to say you'll love it here. I never met anyone who didn't . . . well, except for my brother, and that's a whole other story. Where's Micahlyn?"

"I just dropped her off at Angel Wings. It's her first time ever in day care."

"She'll survive—and so will you. I used to bring my son, Danny, to work with me every day. When he turned four, I put him in day care, and when I picked him up that first day, he had two black eyes. One four-year-old's lesson to my only-child-who-always-got-what-he-wanted on the virtues of sharing."

"You must have felt awful."

Leanne laughed. "Oh, yeah, I was eaten up with guilt— *How could I have let him get so spoiled? Why had I made him go there? Why wasn't I a better mother?* He, on the other hand, thought having two shiners was pretty cool."

"I probably would have thought so, too, when I was a kid."

The shop packed an amazing amount of goods in a relatively small space, and Nolie wandered around, looking at it all. There were racks of clothing ranging from the casual to the very-special-event, cribs and cradles, playpens and infant seats and high chairs, lamps, framed pictures, and miniature sculptures. "You've got some great stuff."

"If you're going to go into a retail business, you might as well sell great stuff."

Nolie wrinkled her nose. "Not me. I get to sell feed and insecticide and tomato cages."

"But you still get to be your own boss. That counts for a lot."

It certainly did. And she owed it to Hiram and that stinky, boring feed store. She would learn to love the place for nothing more than that.

"Would you like a cup of tea? I just brewed a pot of Raspberry-Lemon Delight."

The closest Nolie ever got to drinking hot tea was when the ice in her glass melted. But she accepted because Leanne was friendly enough to offer, and she had no place else to go, and it was nice to talk with a woman her age.

She followed Leanne to the back corner of the shop, where a wicker sofa and love seat shared space with an old-fashioned wicker serving cart. While Leanne poured the tea, Nolie took a seat on the sofa and looked out the window at the house across the street. "What a beautiful place."

"It's got nothing on the guy who lives there." Leanne served them both, then curled up on the love seat. "He just moved here from California. You should see him. He gives new meaning to the word *handsome*."

"Is he single?"

"Yeah, but he's got a twelve-year-old son." Then she laughed. "But as a single mother, I don't think I'm allowed to complain about a single father."

"You're divorced?"

"Never married. When I told Danny's father I was pregnant, he disappeared like that." Leanne snapped her fingers. "To borrow a phrase from Melina Knight, he was a real rat bastard. Which comes as no surprise to everyone who knows me. My taste in men is so lousy as to be legendary." After a moment's silence, she cautiously said, "I heard your husband is dead."

Nolie nodded.

"That's tough. I'm really sorry."

"It's been a while." A blush warmed Nolie's cheeks as she looked out the window again. "Jeez, that sounds awful. It was a horrible thing and I wish to God it had never happened and I still miss him so much, but . . . it's been three years. It's time to—to—"

"Get on with your life?" Leanne supplied, her voice soft with sympathy. "You're still awfully young. You can't mourn forever. No one could expect that."

"My in-laws could—and do. That's part of the reason I'm here in Bethlehem while they're in Arkansas." With a wry smile, Nolie shifted the subject. "Does your family live here?"

"Oh, yeah. As long as there's been a Bethlehem, there have been Wilsons and Montgomerys—my mom's family—living in it." Leanne's gaze drifted past Nolie to the window, and a smile warmed her face. "Look, there's Mr. Tall, Blond, and Handsome."

Nolie looked across the street as a man came down the steps of the old house. He wore navy trousers with a light blue polo shirt, and he was everything Leanne had said—

probably a few inches over six feet, as blond and tanned as any California surfer boy, and handsome. He knew it, too, if his self-assurance was anything to judge by.

"Not bad for a neighbor, huh?" Leanne teased.

"Not bad." But not as appealing to look at as *her* neighbor.

The blond crossed the street and rounded the corner. An instant later, the bell over the door *ding*ed. Nolie caught Leanne smoothing her hand over her hair and smiled slyly. "I think I'll leave you to take care of your customer."

"Maybe we could get together for dinner some evening—you and your daughter, me and my son."

"I'd like that."

As Nolie approached the man, waiting near the cash register, he smiled at her in a way guaranteed to make any woman the least bit susceptible to male charm go weak. Fortunately, she wasn't particularly susceptible, since she'd learned by the time she was twelve that she could never compete with most males' ideas of the perfect woman.

Though a smile like that from Chase . . . that might make her forget every lesson she'd ever learned.

Chapter Six

PRETTY WOMAN," COLE SAID AFTER NOLIE HAD left, "if you don't mind the red hair."

"According to surveys, most men think redheads are sexy." Leanne stepped behind the counter as if she had something to do there but wound up resting her hands on the faux stone surface. "I was a redhead once, and I was pretty darn sexy."

"But that had nothing to do with the color of your hair and everything to do with the woman you are." He came to the counter, too, leaning his elbows on the higher of two shelves. "I was just on my way to the office and thought I'd see if the prettiest woman in town will have lunch with me."

He was a sweet-talker, just like every man who'd ever broken her heart. Leanne realized that, but she was still regretful she had to turn him down. "I don't go out for lunch. My part-time help doesn't come in until school's out, so I eat here."

"Okay. I'll provide the meal, and you'll provide the company. What time?"

She should tell him no. Hadn't she sworn off men just last fall when the latest in a line of disappointments had turned out to be married with children? Hadn't she decided the heartbreak was over, right then and there? No more men, no more charmers, no more picking up the pieces.

But did she follow her own advice? Oh, no. That would be too smart. Never let it be said that Leanne Wilson *ever* did the smart thing when it came to men. "Whatever time is best for you."

His smile was even brighter and more pleased than before, as if he'd feared she would refuse. "Great. Is there anything I should know about your likes and dislikes?"

"No. I'm pretty easy to please."

He held her gaze for a long, heavy moment, then the smile became intimate and his voice turned husky. "Good. Because I aim to please." He touched his hand to hers—a casual brush if ever she'd felt one, but somehow it made her skin warm a few degrees and tingle. "I'll see you at lunchtime."

Without waiting for a response, he strode back down the main aisle to the door. After it closed behind him, she murmured, "Sure." Then her mouth tightened in a grimace. She was *not* looking for romance, or sex, or even male friendship. She'd proven repeatedly that she was a loser at love—hell, she didn't even do too well at the game of lust. She was perfectly happy with Danny, the shop, and her family and friends. She didn't need a man. Especially one as handsome and charming as Cole Jackson.

But it was just lunch. Nothing intimate or disastrous— intimacy *was* disastrous, in her experience—could come of that, could it?

Maybe not for most people. But if anyone could turn one lunch into major trouble, it was Leanne—or, rather, the men she was attracted to.

But that was before she'd decided she didn't need a man.

Lunch with Cole Jackson? Nothing to it. Piece of cake. She would be fine.

And she had about two hours to convince herself of that.

SATURDAY WAS THE BIG DAY—THE REOPENING OF Hiram's Feed Store—and Nolie was forced to admit Thursday afternoon that there was nothing more for her to do until then. All the little details on her to-do list were checked off. The painting was finished, the shelves arranged and filled with inventory. She'd opened a commercial checking account, stenciled the hours on the door, and bought a comfortable desk chair to use behind the counter. She'd even taken out an ad in the Friday edition of the Bethlehem newspaper. Now all she could do was pray that Hiram's old customers were out there waiting for the chance to be customers again.

She was sitting in that antique wood chair, rocking back and forth with drawn-out, haunted-house creaks, when a car pulled into the parking lot and a young man got out. As he pushed open the door, then approached the desk, she realized he was just a boy, sixteen, no more than seventeen years old. He was good-looking, too, with hair more blond than brown, a finely shaped jaw, and the sort of long, lean look teenage boys managed so well.

"Mrs. Harper? I'm Trey Grayson. I'd like to apply for a job."

Nolie was bemused. Chase had pointed out that she needed at least one employee, but she hadn't given it much thought. She'd obeyed other people for so long—all her life, really—that it was difficult to imagine being the boss for once. Giving orders, telling other people what to do, being the authority figure . . . a woman could get giddy just thinking about it.

"How old are you, Trey?"

"Sixteen, ma'am."

Too old to be calling her ma'am. Not even ten years younger than she. "Still in school?"

"Yes, ma'am. I'd be able to work afternoons and Saturdays until summer, then whenever you wanted."

She'd told Chase she intended to hire someone eventually, so she could have a day off now and then, but a sixteen-year-old boy wasn't exactly what she'd had in mind. He was very polite, and he seemed sincere about wanting the job, but he was still a kid. Could she in good conscience leave her livelihood entirely in his hands even just one day a week?

"Have you discussed this with your parents?"

"Yes, ma'am. They think it's a good idea, as long as it doesn't affect my school work. I'm on the honor roll, and they want me to stay there. College is coming up soon, and there are six of us kids, so . . ." He shrugged, then swiped back the strand of hair that fell across his forehead.

"Grayson . . . I believe my daughter was a guest at your house last weekend."

He nodded. "Micahlyn. Red hair and glasses."

The curse of being a redhead. Everyone always found it easier to identify you by your hair. Nolie let the chair give one last, great creak before she stood up. "I've never hired an employee before. I don't even know what to ask you. I never ran a business, either. But . . . we can learn together, right?"

A moment passed before his eyes widened. "I got the job?"

"On one condition. Call me Nolie. Not Mrs. Harper, not ma'am."

"Yes, m—Nolie. When do you want me to start?"

"We open Saturday morning at eight. Can you make it that early?"

"Sure. I'm always up early. Thanks a lot, Mrs. Harper. You won't be sorry. See you Saturday."

Nolie watched him leave, smiling at his energy. Then reality set in. She had an employee. That made it official. She was no longer just a mother. Now she was a businessperson, with all the responsibilities that entailed.

She really had to make a go of this place.

For a moment, as she stood there, she considered hyperventilating, then forced herself to take a few deep breaths. She could do this. For Micahlyn's sake, for her own, she could handle this.

Dragging in one last breath, she got her purse from under the counter and headed for the door. She wasn't due to pick up Micahlyn until 6:15, and even if there was nothing left to do at the store, she had plenty of work at home.

It was a short drive up the mountain to the dirt road that led to the cabin. She pulled in, then got out to check the faded yellow mailbox. There was a letter from Marlene and Obie addressed to Micahlyn, and an envelope addressed Occupant for Nolie. She slit it open and pulled out a single sheet of elegant white stationery. It was a letter announcing the arrival of Jackson Investments in Bethlehem.

She fingered the heavy linen paper before tossing it aside and heading up the hill. Cole Jackson must be quite successful at what he did, to use such high-quality paper on a mass mailing. But then, she could have guessed that from his beautiful old house, or the expensive new car parked beside it, or even just the way he carried himself.

Funny that they'd come to town about the same time and were opening their businesses at the same time. But the similarities definitely stopped there. There was no comparison between their houses, their cars, the cost of their wardrobes, their businesses, or the potential thereof.

Not that she cared. She loved her cabin for being hers, and once it was painted and some of the shabby furniture replaced, she would love it for itself. And she'd much rather sell feed and supplements to people so their livestock would grow than take on the responsibility of making their life savings grow.

When she reached the cabin, she wrestled open all the downstairs windows, left the front and back doors open, and started dinner. While the roast beef cooked on top of the stove and brownies baked in the oven, she straightened the living room and started a load of laundry. She was about to start another sewing project—quilt blocks to turn into pillows to brighten the overwhelming brown of the living room—when the phone rang.

She answered absently, her mind still on cutting and piecing the blocks. When she heard her mother-in-law's voice at the other end, though, she snapped to attention. "Hello, Marlene. How are you?"

"I'm fine. Could I speak to my granddaughter?"

I'm fine, too, thanks for asking, Nolie mouthed before answering for real. "She's not here right now."

Marlene's icy disapproval transmitted itself over the phone lines. "Where is she?"

"At day care."

"Day care. Well, you certainly wasted no time getting her out of your way, did you? And you put her in day care so you could . . . what? Watch soap operas all day? Shop? Run around with your new friends?"

Not even a full minute into the conversation, and already Nolie's jaw ached from clenching it. She forced it to relax enough so she could get an answer out, but there was nothing relaxed about her voice. "So I could work. You know—at a job? Get up, go to work in the morning, come home in the evening? Oh, wait. You've never done that. I forgot."

"You never had to do it, either," Marlene coldly reminded her. "Thanks to Jeff and Obie and me."

"It's not a question of *having* to do it. I want to. I've always wanted to . . . but you wouldn't let me."

"Wouldn't let— Oh, so now we're in Nolie's world, where her version of events is the only one that counts . . . no matter how inaccurate it is."

She was wrong. In Nolie's world, who did what didn't matter, as long as she was independent and capable and treated that way. It was in Marlene's world that things got skewed for her purposes. Insisting that Nolie and Micahlyn move in with her and Obie after Jeff's death hadn't been bossy; it had been concern. Refusing to accept Nolie's help hadn't been controlling; it had been giving her a chance to recover. Laying on the guilt every time she mentioned getting a full-time job, looking for a place of their own, or taking responsibility for herself and her daughter hadn't been manipulative; it had been love. And trying to sell off her inheritance behind her back . . . that had merely been looking out for her the best they knew how.

Of course, she was partly to blame for that. She *had* given Obie the authority to handle things for her when they'd first gotten the news of Hiram's death. Small things, like directing Alex Thomas to have the store cleaned out and shut down, or authorizing the lawyer to close out Hiram's accounts and settle his debts. Although renting the second cabin to Chase hadn't fallen under her idea of "small things," it had been okay. Selling off everything without even discussing it with her, hadn't.

"Listen, Marlene, Micahlyn will be—" A creak outside the front door drew her attention that way. Chase stood on the porch, a box in hand. "It's open. Come on in," she called before continuing. "She'll be home—"

"Who were you speaking to?"

"Our neighbor."

"That—that man? The one Micahlyn's so terrified of?" Dismay made Marlene's voice sharper than usual. "You *let* him come into your house, where my granddaughter lives? What's wrong with you, Nolie? Don't you ever *think*?"

There was no way Nolie was going to defend either Chase or herself, especially when he was standing just inside the door—and no way she would defend herself even if he wasn't there. There was no reason. She controlled her life now, not her in-laws. "As I was saying, Micahlyn will be home in a few hours. If you'd like to call back around seven-thirty our time, you can talk to her then. Good-bye."

She missed the cradle when she tried to hang up, and the receiver fell to the floor with a crash. Fishing it back up by its cord, she successfully hung it up on the second try, then pressed her fingertips to the ache between her eyes.

"Let me guess. Your mother-in-law?"

She nodded.

"You could always change your number and not tell her."

"No, I can't," she said wryly, because the idea held a certain appeal. "They're Micahlyn's grandparents." A fact which meant more to her than it did to him, as previous discussions had shown, as his dismissive shrug now indicated. Gesturing toward the box he held, she asked, "What's that?"

"Maybe more trouble. A delivery guy left it over at the cabin."

She met him halfway, took the box, and scowled. It was for Micahlyn. From Marlene. She would really love to hide it and not mention it to her daughter yet, but instead she set it on the coffee table. It would be the first thing Micahlyn saw when she got home . . . and the first thing Marlene would ask about when she called back.

"You ever read Dear Abby and Ann Landers?" Chase asked.

"Sure. But I can't imagine you reading either one."

"I don't, but my secretary used to. One of them always used to say that no one can take advantage of you without your permission."

She sat down on the sofa, then turned her glare from the package to him as he dropped into the armchair. She couldn't argue the point with him, though. She *had* given her in-laws permission to run her life—oh, not expressly, of course, but never arguing, disagreeing, or standing up to them amounted to the same thing. Rather than admit it, she changed the focus of the conversation.

"So . . . you used to have a secretary."

Annoyance flashed across his expression as he realized what he'd let slip. "No. Not me."

"You just said—"

"No, I didn't."

On a good day, she would be up to an argument with him, particularly if it meant finding out something new about his background. The tidbits of his life in Boston were slowly building. They didn't yet amount to much, but hopefully he would continue adding little pieces here and there until she could put them all together.

For right now, though, she let it slide. "The store opens Saturday. I hired someone today."

"A man?" he asked, as if she didn't have the good sense to hire someone competent.

"He's sixteen."

"So he's in school. What are you going to do during the day when you need help?"

She laid on a thick Southern accent. "I'll just flutter my lashes and act like the mindless female you apparently think I am."

His mouth quirked at one corner. "You aren't the lash-fluttering type."

Great. He thought she was mindless—just not particularly feminine. Well, she *was* feminine. Okay, so she'd rather wear jeans and a T-shirt over frilly dresses anytime, and she didn't bother most of the time with makeup, and she was far too strong—and proud—to even think about pretending to be a fragile flower. But she was still feminine. More or less.

She gave him a cross look that matched her cross ego. "You want a job?"

"Hell, no."

"Then mind your own business. Trey and I will do just fine at the store without any input from you."

"You didn't mind my input last weekend."

"I didn't ask for your help. You volunteered."

"Trey who?"

"Grayson. His father's a doctor, and his mother's a social worker. Do you know them?" When he shook his head, Nolie narrowed her gaze. "I find it amazing how you lived here all those years but don't seem to know anyone besides Miss Corinna and Miss Agatha. Could it be you're lying?"

Chase slumped lower in the chair, rested one ankle on the other knee, and fixed his gaze on her. It was no surprise that she thought he was a liar—after all, he *had* lied to her before, the last time mere minutes ago. Still, it was uncomfortable. Irritating.

"What reason could I have for lying?" he asked. "Other than the fact that I've made it clear I don't want to discuss all the things you keep bringing up."

"Talking about ourselves is as natural as breathing."

"Not for everyone." He'd met plenty of people in the years he'd practiced law—to say nothing of the time he'd spent in prison—who were even more closemouthed than he, people who didn't let small details slip. For all his desire to keep his past in the past, sometimes she made him careless.

She made him. Blame didn't really matter, but somehow it was her fault that he said things he shouldn't. In the months between his arrest and conviction, he hadn't confided a damned thing in anyone. He could say the same about his time as a guest of the Massachusetts penal system. He had come out of prison just as much a stranger to the men who shared his cellblock as he'd gone in.

But things were different with Nolie. Maybe he'd reached his limits on how much time he could endure totally alone. More likely, it was something about *her*.

He didn't want to examine the question of *what* too closely, though. He might not like the answers.

"So you prefer to remain a mystery to the people— excuse me—the *person* in your life," she said dryly.

He wanted to take exception to that description. She wasn't *in* his life. That implied friendship. Involvement. A relationship. They were neighbors, nothing more . . . though he couldn't recall the last time he'd gotten a hard-on for one of his neighbors, or gone out looking for a neighbor because she was late getting home, or been tempted to kiss one of them on a sunny Saturday afternoon. He was pretty damned sure that wanting a neighbor had never sent him running to the nearest bar to pick up the first available stranger . . . and that no neighbor had ever been responsible for his turning down the women who'd offered.

Much as he hated to admit it, *this* neighbor had done just that.

"I prefer to keep my business to myself," he said at last.

"That's hardly fair." Judging by the faintly pouting expression she wore, Nolie was fortunately unaware of where his thoughts had drifted. "You know stuff about Micahlyn and me and Jeff and my in-laws, but you refuse to tell anything about yourself."

"You're in the group that likes to talk. I'm not."

She studied him for a long time, not moving even when a timer started beeping in the kitchen. Finally she scooted to the edge of the couch, stood up, then smoothed her shirt over her hips. "I'm sociable. You're not. Is that it?"

"Exactly."

"Bull."

He followed her into the kitchen, where she bent over to remove a pan of brownies from the oven. The faded denim of her jeans clung tightly to her hips and her bottom, then loosened as it stretched the length of her long legs to her bare feet. Something faint stirred deep in his belly, and he told himself it was nothing but hunger, stimulated by the rich aroma of the brownies and a long day without eating.

Hey, they'd already acknowledged he was a liar.

She set the pan on a rack to cool, then lifted the lid from a large pot, releasing more amazing smells into the air. He half-hoped she would invite him to dinner, even though the wise thing to do if she did was refuse. She was way too easy to spend time with, even with her shrill-voiced kid glaring at him the whole time.

"What do you mean, 'bull'?" he asked once she'd finished fussing with the dinner.

"It's a simple concept. If you can't figure it out, maybe your secretary can explain it to you."

"I don't have a secretary."

"Now."

He didn't respond to that.

"What I mean is that you're perfectly sociable by nature. You're just a coward."

This time he was beyond annoyed and irritated, and verging on insulted. He circled the counter that separated the dining room from the kitchen, and him from her, and slowly approached her. "A *coward*? If you knew what I'd been through . . ."

She eyed the distance closing between them and took a step back, then another. "But I don't. I don't know anything about you, and I bet no one else does, because you've chosen to hide away in the woods like some kind of hermit, unwilling to go anywhere or see anybody for fear—"

It was fitting that at the very moment she said the word, the emotion flickered through her eyes. It was the same moment she backed into the corner where two counter-tops met at a right angle, the same moment she realized he had her trapped. But it wasn't fear exactly. More uneasiness. Uncertainty. Maybe even a little anticipation.

She swallowed hard, and braced her hands against the front edge of the counters. She would have been safer—hell, *he* would have been safer—if she'd folded her arms across her chest or, better yet, shoved him out of the way and moved into the open. But she hadn't chosen either option, and the one she had chosen put her in a position that would make it so easy for him to slide his arms between her arms and her body. To move intimately close. To hold her captive. To kiss her.

Instead—for the moment, at least—he rested his hands on the counter's edge, too, outside hers, near but not touching.

He had to give her credit. She didn't tremble or quake. On the other hand, it didn't appear she could take a deep breath to save her life. Still, she bluffed it out, raised her head, straightened her shoulders—and leaned back an inch or two away from him. "What *are* you afraid of?"

You. Me. Doing this. Not doing this. He drew a breath that smelled of faint perfume, sunshine, and shampoo, and wished he hadn't. Who needed air? "You're the one who insists I'm afraid. You tell me."

"I think—" She gulped in a breath. "I think this conversation should have ended a few comments ago. I think it's time for me to pick up Micahlyn at day care. And I think—"

He silenced her with one finger across her mouth, centered over her cupid's bow. Her lips were soft, full, free of lipstick, dotted by that single freckle. "You think too much."

That was his cue to kiss her. God knew, he wanted to. If he thought about it, he could count back to the last time, more than three years ago, he'd kissed a woman—Fiona. Later that same day, Massachusetts State Police officers had taken him from his office in handcuffs, and he'd very slowly begun to realize how deeply someone had betrayed him.

It hadn't been one of his better days . . . though there had been worse.

But that was in the past. He and Nolie were right here. All he had to do was lean forward six, no more than eight, inches. Replace his finger with his mouth. Maybe coax her just a little, but not much, he was sure. Just do it.

The last woman he'd kissed had been his wife. Was he ready to make Nolie the next one?

The answer came as, slowly, he let his finger slide away from her lips and willed himself to back off. Just as slowly his body obeyed the command, taking two steps back before turning away.

Not before he saw the regret flash in her eyes.

Not before he felt it way down deep in his gut.

As he returned to safety on the opposite side of the counter, she tucked a strand of hair behind her ear, tugged at her shirt, then turned her back to him to open the cabinet door. "Do you want to stay for dinner?" Her voice was unsteady, and so were her hands as she began taking dishes from the cabinet.

Did he want to stay? He was hungry, sure, but he had food at his house—not just frozen dinners, but real food that he could add to boxed mixes to make an honest-to-God meal. Or he could drive to Howland for a greasy burger and fries or a steak with all the trimmings. Hell, he could even order a pizza from the delivery place in town. Pizza delivery drivers tended to be kids, and since he'd been gone from Bethlehem sixteen years, odds that he would know any of them were slim.

But whether he wanted to stay had everything to do with hunger of one kind or another and nothing at all to do with food. For that reason alone, he should politely turn her down.

He didn't.

"Okay." He heard the uncertainty in that single word, and wondered if she did. It was hard to tell, with her back still to him.

"Good. By the time I pick up Micahlyn at day care, the pot roast should be done." She set a stack of dishes on the counter, placing three dinner plates near him and sliding a serving platter closer to the stove. "Would you mind staying here while I run into town, to make sure it doesn't burn?"

He looked from her to the pot, steam escaping in a thin column from the loose-fitting lid. "What does that involve?"

"Just check it every so often to make sure it doesn't boil dry."

He nodded. He could do that.

"Also . . ." She set a container of chocolate frosting and a packet of chopped walnuts in front of him. "Could you frost the brownies when they're cool and sprinkle these nuts over them? All you do is stir the frosting, then spread it smoothly across the top with this."

He accepted the utensil she offered—what looked like a wide, flat knife with a rounded edge instead of a point. "I'm not totally useless. I used to watch my mother frost cakes so I could have first choice between the bowl and this spatula thing."

"So you're not an only child."

Chase kept his expression blank. "What makes you think that?"

"If you got first choice, then you needed someone to get second. Like a brother or a sister."

"Or a cousin or a friend or a mother with a sweet tooth."

Her mouth thinning, she gave a shake of her head as she started for the living room. "I'll be back soon."

He walked as far as the doorway between living room and dining room and watched her go, not the least bit hesitant about leaving him alone in her house. He wouldn't feel so comfortable if the situation were reversed. Of course, there were things in his cabin he didn't want anyone to see, bad reminders that he should have thrown away long ago, but kept to remind him of the lessons he'd learned. Don't get involved, don't trust anyone, and never, ever forget.

But Nolie wasn't the sort of woman for secrets. The fact that her name was Magnolia was probably her most closely guarded secret. She had nothing to hide.

Too restless to sit, he walked through the first floor of the cabin—pantry, laundry room, and bathroom off the kitchen, dining room, living room, and, through a door at the foot of the stairs, her great-grandfather's office. The room was small, dark, and stank of cigars and old papers.

As he set one foot on the first step, he hesitated. Likely all that was upstairs was bedrooms and another bathroom. He didn't care where Micahlyn slept, and he didn't need to see where Nolie slept. Better he should just get comfortable on the couch with a book or watch television while he waited.

But instead of turning away, he climbed to the next step, then the next, all the way to the top. The kid's bedroom was to the left, with a twin-sized bed made up in pink-and-white, pink curtains at the windows, and enough toys to stock a small Toys Я Us. The first door to the right led into a bathroom, overly large and boxy, with fittings—clawfoot tub and shower, pedestal sink with porcelain knobs, metal medicine chest with hazy mirror— that appeared original to the house.

Nolie's room was at the end of the hall. Feeling guilty, he didn't set foot inside, but he didn't have to. He could see everything he needed—or didn't need—to see from the open doorway. The furniture, he assumed, was old Hiram's, acquired at a time when he wasn't so miserly. The double bed, dresser, and tall chest were all made of oak, sturdy pieces that would last forever. There was a night table on one side of the bed—presumably the side Nolie slept on— a round table topped with a ruffled skirt that matched the curtains. It held a small beaded and fringed lamp not much better for illumination than a night-light, a telephone, and a book. On the other side of the bed, a wooden rocker that had seen better days was backed into a corner.

It was a far cry from fancy. The walls, a dirty, vaguely

white shade, needed painting, and the wood floor, once painted brown, needed stripping. There was a water stain in one corner of the ceiling, and the closet door, too tall for the opening, had gouged a semi-arc across the floor.

But it looked comfortable. The pastel curtains and tablecloth were fresh and starched, and the pale green sheets helped lighten the room. A half-dozen pillows in pastels and white lace were piled against the oak headboard, and a quilt, in similar colors, was folded across the foot of the bed. It seemed a good place to retreat to at the end of the day.

A good place to spend the better part of the day . . . with the right companion.

Because he was tempted to step inside, he forced himself to go back down the hall and downstairs. He checked on dinner, then frosted the brownies and put them in the refrigerator, then sat down on the sofa to wait with one of Nolie's books.

It was open in his lap when he heard her car approaching, though he couldn't remember a word he'd read. Forgetting it, he watched out the window as she parked. When she got out of the car, she stood there a moment, sunlight gleaming on her hair, her skin as pale and fine as any he'd ever seen, her smile as warm. Then she started toward the house, moving out of sight, and he realized he'd forgotten to breathe.

The kid burst through the door first, full of energy, and skidded to a stop the instant she saw him. He steeled himself for one of her piercing screams, but instead she slowly backed away, never taking her gaze off him, even though she directed her words outside to her mother. "Mama," she said in a loud whisper. "That man is here. In our house. I think he breaked in."

Nolie came through the door, purse in one hand and a

bakery bag in the other. "Why would he break in, babe? All the windows and doors are open."

"So why's he here?"

"He's having dinner with us, and he stayed to make sure it didn't burn while I was gone to get you." Nolie shifted her attention to him. "It didn't, did it?"

"No. I told you, I'm not completely useless."

She tossed her purse on a chair, then went into the kitchen, the smell of fresh-baked bread following. It was enough to make Chase's mouth water. At least, he was pretty sure it was the bread.

He remained where he was, and so did Micahlyn. After a long moment, her gaze finally shifted from him to the package on the coffee table. "Mama, what's that box?"

"I don't know," Nolie called. "It's for you from your grandparents."

A gleam of excitement lit Micahlyn's eyes, tempered by caution. Like any kid, she obviously liked presents. She just wasn't sure she liked them enough to get that close to him, Chase realized.

The adult thing to do would be to move—go into the kitchen, give her plenty of room to open her gift. He didn't. If they were going to spend time in the same room, she had to quit acting as if he was some sort of . . . well, bogeyman.

Twisting her fingers restlessly in the hair of the doll she carried, she shuffled a few steps sideways, then stopped to look from him to the box, then back again. A few more steps, another measuring look, again and again until the package was almost within her reach. Darting forward, she grabbed it, clutched it to her chest, then raced for the kitchen.

The sound of tape ripping was followed by the crinkle

of paper, then a shriek. "Look, Mama! Look what Grandma and Grandpa got me! Isn't she beautiful?"

Chase looked over his shoulder as Nolie crossed to the table, where Micahlyn was holding up a boxed doll. A muscle in Nolie's jaw tightened, and her tone was less than approving as she replied, "Yes, honey, she's beautiful. You know, though, she's not the kind of doll you play with."

"Of course you do, Mama. Jus' carefully. Grandma said. I'm gonna take her upstairs and show her to the others."

As Micahlyn ran off, Nolie grimly shook her head. Chase took the kid's absence as an opportunity to go into the kitchen. "What's the problem with the doll?"

"It's a porcelain collectible that costs about two hundred dollars," she said heatedly as she dumped the contents of the bakery bag—warm buns—into a napkin-lined basket. "It's not an appropriate gift for a five-year-old—not for her birthday or Christmas, and certainly not for no reason at all."

Besides buying her affection, Chase thought. Or getting under her mother's skin.

She slid the basket to the edge of the counter, where a dish of butter and a bottle of ketchup sat. He moved all three to the middle of the table, then removed the packaging from the doll's box. As he picked up the tissue paper, a piece of paper with a photograph attached fell out. "She missed something," he said, laying it on the counter.

Nolie's jaw tightened even more as she read the handwritten note, then looked at the picture. "Damn it," she whispered. "Just when she's finally settling in here, they do this."

Without asking permission, Chase picked up the note again. The photograph was taken in, presumably, the Harpers' backyard. Off in the distance was a barn and several outbuildings, with acres of something green stretching

off in all directions. The focus, though, was on an elaborate playground setup—swing, jungle gym, slide, teeter-
totter, and fort, all connected by tunnels, bridges, or stairs.

Hey, Mikey, the note read. *Look what Grandpa built for
you. The sooner your mother brings you home, where you belong,
the sooner you can play on it. Isn't it great? Love, Grandma.*

Marlene Harper's brand of love was the kind that turned
otherwise normal families dysfunctional. What kind of
grandparent would manipulate her only grandchild that
way?

"Why don't you talk to her?" he asked as he picked up
the silverware and napkins that had appeared on the
counter while he was preoccupied with the note.

Nolie snorted. "Lately I try to avoid talking to Marlene
as much as I can."

He didn't blame her. He hadn't spoken to his mother in
six years, or to his father in sixteen. But he wasn't trying to
maintain some sort of relationship between either of them
and their grandchild. If he and Fiona had had children—
something she'd always said she wanted as much as he did,
but somehow the time had never been right—they would
have to have been satisfied with the Kelly relatives for their
only family. He wouldn't even have been inclined to let
them meet his sister, not after she'd sided against him with
their parents.

But Nolie was different. She thought family was important. More than that, he suspected she felt she owed it to
Jeff to get along the best she could with his parents or,
failing that, to see that Micahlyn had a good relationship
with them.

"When Marlene called this afternoon, our conversation
lasted less than six, seven minutes. In that time, she accused
me of putting Micahlyn in day care so I could watch soap
operas all day; she reminded me that she, Obie, and Jeff

have supported me since my parents died; she called me a liar; and she criticized me for letting you come over." She stepped into the doorway and shouted, "Micahlyn, dinner's ready!"

"She was always smothering and overly critical," she went on, "but ever since I told her we were moving here, we can't carry on a conversation anymore. In her eyes, I've turned into this selfish, ungrateful, disloyal creature who's stolen all that's left of Jeff from her. She's not interested in anything I have to say if it doesn't include 'We're moving back to Whiskey Creek.' "

"Then have a lawyer talk to her."

She stopped in the act of setting the serving platter on the table and stared at him.

"Grandparents have some rights." He sounded impatient, and made an effort to neutralize it. "But the bottom line is, *you're* Micahlyn's mother and legal guardian. You're responsible for raising her, for all the decisions affecting her, and they're interfering with that. Ask Alex Thomas to write them a letter stating that there are stipulations to their continued access to their granddaughter. Trust me, Thomas will be so reasonable and pleasant that they'll think it was their own idea."

Nolie snorted again. "You don't know Marlene though it sounds as if you do know Alex Thomas."

"I already told you I don't." Had already lied to her. Shrugging as if that fact didn't bother him, he pulled out the chair where he'd sat last Friday, waited for her to sit on his left, then sat down. "Take my advice or don't. It doesn't matter to me. You're the one who has to deal with them."

He was out of the family-dealing business, and the problem-solving business.

Forever.

Chapter Seven

WHEN SATURDAY ROLLED AROUND, NOLIE was prepared for a slow start to business. Even with the ad in the local paper, she figured it would take a week, maybe even longer, for Hiram's customers to come back. But when she got to the store at 7:45 that morning, not only was Trey Grayson waiting for her, so were a half-dozen customers.

That was just the start of a steady stream. She met more people than she could remember, both serious customers and the friendly sort who stopped in to support a new business and meet a new neighbor. By the time she turned over the Closed sign at six P.M., her face was aching from so much smiling, almost as much as her feet did from long hours on hard concrete. When she finished balancing the cash register, she tucked the day's deposit into a bank bag, then watched as Trey finished sweeping up.

"We didn't discuss salary." She named an amount. "Does that seem fair?"

His first response was a grin. "You bet. Want me to come in Monday after school?"

"That would be great."

After he'd returned the broom to the back room, Nolie

switched off most of the lights, then walked to the door with him. "You have plans for this evening?"

"Some of us are going to Howland to dinner, a movie, maybe play a little pool. What about you?"

"I'm putting my feet up on something soft and letting Micahlyn wait on me. I'm not as young as I used to be."

"Huh. You're not *that* much older than me." After she locked the door, he gestured overhead. "Who changed the sign, and when? It didn't say that when I got here this morning."

She looked up, too, and her gaze fixed on the banner. The red-and-gold color scheme was the same, but now, instead of REOPENING SOON, it read OPEN FOR BUSINESS. "I don't— There must—" She sighed. "I don't even know where those signs came from. I thought Gloria and Sophy had someone put the first one up as sort of a welcome gift, but . . ."

"Who are Gloria and Sophy?"

"The two women who cleaned the store so I could get it painted. They've lived here a long time. They even knew Hiram. Gloria works at Angel Wings Day Care, and Sophy . . . heavens, she can't be more than a few years older than you. You must know them."

He shook his head. "Never heard of either one."

That wasn't so strange, Nolie told herself. He was a teenage boy, and usually a teenage boy's biggest interests were sports and teenage girls. "Well, have a good time this evening, and be careful."

"Yeah, you, too."

Trey was gone and Nolie was backing out of her parking space when the beeping of a horn caught her attention. She stopped, and the red SUV pulled up beside her, with Leanne Wilson behind the wheel. "Hey, sorry I didn't make it for the grand reopening, but I got tied up at the shop. How did it go?"

"Great. I was surprised by how many people showed up."

"How about a celebration? My friend Maggie McKinney has offered to baby-sit for us tonight if you'd like to go out and kick up your heels."

Nolie had never been the heel-kicking type, but the idea of an evening out with a new friend sounded like the perfect end to an almost perfect day. "We wouldn't have to go all the way to Howland to do that, would we?"

"Oh, no. We would go to the Starlite Lounge, right here in town. That's where most of the single folks in town will be. We can have dinner there, if you happen to be craving a hamburger and fries, or we could eat at Harry's or McCauley's Steakhouse or, if you want to dress up, we could go to McBride Inn for heavenly food and sinful desserts."

Sinful desserts were Nolie's weakness, but she was afraid the kind of dressing up required for dinner at McBride Inn would deplete what little energy she had. "A hamburger and fries sound fine, but let me check with Micahlyn first. She's not used to spending so much time away from me."

"Okay. I've got to pick up Danny at my folks' house. Why don't you call me at home when you decide? My number's in the book."

Nolie nodded, then returned Leanne's wave as the other woman drove off. As she drove in the same direction, she wondered what kind of place the Starlite Lounge was. It sounded like one of the shabby little bars that dotted backcountry roads across the South, and not the sort of place a responsible single mother and respectable businesswoman would hang out. But wasn't Leanne a responsible single mother and respectable businesswoman, too? Besides, what did she know about bars? She'd never once set foot in one.

And she'd never once imagined she would ever be a single mother, or would leave the only home she'd ever known for another halfway across the country, or be attracted to a man with no apparent means of support and more secrets than any character on Marlene's favorite soap operas. It appeared the old saying was true—there *was* a first time for everything.

When she reached Angel Wings, Micahlyn was one of only a half-dozen kids playing in the yard under Gloria's supervision. She called that she would be ready in just a minute, and while Nolie waited, Gloria greeted her warmly.

"I was just talking about you a few minutes ago with Trey Grayson," Nolie commented.

"Oh, Troy. Isn't he a wonderful young man? His parents have a lot to be proud of with him."

"I can see that. He didn't seem to know who you were. Of course, I couldn't give him your last name because I never remembered to ask it."

"You know how kids are. Us old folks all sort of run together in their minds." Gloria grinned slyly. "I understand you're celebrating your opening day success with an evening out on the town."

"How did you know—?"

"Small town. News travels fast. Let's see . . . it will be you and Louanne—"

"Leanne."

Gloria gestured dismissively. "—dining and dancing at the Starlite Lounge."

"Well, dining and talking. I don't dance."

"You should learn."

Nolie shook her head. How often did a woman alone

get the chance to dance? Especially one so abundantly lush. Except for that one friend of Jeff's who'd asked her out and, of course, Jeff himself, most of the guys she'd known preferred their women in a size six, not a sixteen.

Though her weight didn't seem to put Chase off. She would have sworn he was going to kiss her the other day in her kitchen—but he hadn't. She'd been disappointed, then annoyed for the disappointment. If Chase considered her anything other than a pesky neighbor who refused to be brushed off, it was a friend, or a friendly acquaintance. Not a prospective date, girlfriend, or lover. And she was okay with that. Really, she was.

"Have you ever been to the Starlite?" she asked, to get her thoughts back on track.

"Me? Oh, no. But I have been to the Four Pines Tavern before. Or is it the Five Pines? Hmm. Whatever, now *that's* a place you don't want to go. It's a tough joint."

The last words struck Nolie as amusing, coming from grandmotherly, plump-cheeked Gloria. "Is the Starlite a place I'd want to go?"

"It's about as respectable as a bar can get. After all, this *is* Bethlehem." Gloria patted her arm. "Go. Have a good time. Michael Ann will have a wonderful time with the McKenzies. She won't miss you at all."

Nolie didn't bother to correct either her daughter's name or the McKinneys, as Micahlyn was approaching. "I'm ready, Mama. Bye, Gloria. See ya tomorrow."

"Not tomorrow, dear, unless it's in church. Sunday's the Lord's day. But I'll see you bright and bushy-tailed Monday morning, all right?"

With a giggle, Micahlyn bobbed her head, then skipped ahead to the car. All the way home, she chattered about her day, in such a good mood that when Nolie cautiously broached the idea of leaving her with a babysitter that evening, she agreed cheerfully. She liked Miss Maggie, whom she'd met at day care, and her little girl, Rachel, and their big dog, Buddy, and, oh, by the way, could *they* have a dog, too? Nolie was so pleased by her easy acceptance, she almost said sure, why not. Thank goodness, she caught herself in time.

And so it was that Nolie found herself sitting at a table across from Leanne at the Starlite Lounge. All the booths around the outer walls were occupied, as were most of the tables and the stools along the bar. The bandstand at one end of the building stood empty, though a sign nearby announced that the live music would start at nine P.M. instead of the usual seven.

So this was a bar. What would Marlene think if she knew Nolie had abandoned Micahlyn to a stranger's care so she could spend the evening in a low-down honky-tonk—Marlene's words for such places, not Nolie's. But it wasn't up to Marlene to do Nolie's thinking for her anymore. She was free from that at last. Now if she could just stop caring what her mother-in-law thought of her.

"See anyone who interests you?" Leanne asked. "I'd be happy to perform introductions."

It took Nolie a moment to understand what she was offering, then she shook her head. No, no, she wasn't up to a fix-up of even the most subtle type. Introductions to customers, neighbors, prospective friends—that was fine. Introductions in a man/woman looking-to-get-together-temporarily way, no way.

"Come on, I know everyone here, and for the most part, they're nice guys. There's one or two you ought to stay away from. Like Mickey over there." She gestured, and Nolie turned to look. "He's not bad when he's sober. Trouble is, he's hardly ever sober. Give him one beer, and he totally forgets the meaning of the word no. And Jerry back in the corner." Another gesture, another look. "He's not a bad guy, either—just going through a bad divorce and pining for his ex. Gil, in the red shirt, has been divorced so many times he's got it down to an art. His ex-wives don't even hate him."

"Why aren't you married? Are you pining for Danny's father?" Immediately Nolie blushed. "I'm sorry. That's none of my business."

Leanne didn't seem to mind as she shrugged. "It's no secret. I told you, I have lousy taste in men. Greg ran out on me when I got pregnant. Steve knew all about Danny when we started dating and swore it was no problem, then broke up with me once I'd gotten serious, because he didn't want a ready-made family. After that came Richard. He was a sales rep who passed through here every month or two. It took a while for him to convince me he was the marrying type, the father type, and the make-a-commitment-and-stick-to-it type. I was starting to fantasize about the perfect wedding, and then I found out he'd made a commitment, all right—to his wife and kids back home in Rochester."

"Ouch."

Leanne's smile was thin. "Funny. That's exactly what he said after I punched him in the nose." Tilting her head to one side, she studied Nolie, her gaze measuring. "What about you? Are you looking to get married again?"

"If I meet somebody I can't imagine living the rest of my life without, sure. But just for the sake of being married?" She shook her head.

"Sometimes I think marriage for its own sake has a lot going for it. Someone to share the responsibilities and financial obligations. A father figure for Danny. Sex." Leanne's voice turned wistful. "I know Greg, Steve, and Richard were rats, but . . . I certainly do miss regular sex."

Nolie nodded, agreeing but also wistful. It had taken a

long time after Jeff's death for her hormones to come back to life. She could even pinpoint the day it had happened. She had gone to the grocery store with Micahlyn and Marlene, where they'd run into Jeff's old friend, the store manager, in the produce section. While the others went on, Nolie chatted with him a bit. He'd asked her out, and like a bolt of lightning from above, she'd realized instantly that he was handsome, had a nice smile and a nice body, and was rumored to show his girlfriends a very nice time. It had been so long since she'd had a very nice time, and she'd been tempted.

Just not enough to stand up to Marlene.

Across the table, Leanne waved her fingers in front of Nolie's face. "I take it by that dazed, distant look you're wearing that you miss regular sex, too. Look around. Take your pick, and you can end the dry spell tonight."

"It's not that easy."

"Of course it is."

"Sure, with your hair, your face, and your body. Besides . . . I've never been with anyone but Jeff. I'm a tad inexperienced." Truth was, the thought of being with anyone but Jeff—of being that intimate, that vulnerable—was almost enough to make a life of celibacy seem . . . well, doable.

"Oh, please. There's nothing wrong with your hair, your face, or your body. Guys love red hair, women covet skin like yours, and men like curves." Resting her elbow on the table, Leanne tapped one fingertip to her lips. "But, for the inexperienced part, we need to find someone special. Hmm . . ."

At the mention of someone special, an image of Chase popped into Nolie's head as he'd looked Thursday afternoon when he'd cornered her in the kitchen and moved so close and looked at her as if . . . as if he *really* wanted what he saw. Of course, he'd turned away without taking it, even though she would have gladly offered if she'd had the faintest confidence he wouldn't have rejected her.

Eager to turn the subject away from her, Nolie gestured toward the door. "Speaking of someone special . . . Tall, Blond, and Handsome just walked in, and he's all alone."

Leanne swiveled to look, then laid her napkin on the table. "Ooh, Cole Jackson. I knew there was a reason the Starlite was calling out to me today. Do me a favor, would you? Trip any female who appears to be heading his way."

Nolie smiled as Leanne made a beeline for the man, then the smile slowly faded. She was new at this sitting-alone-in-a-bar business—for that fact, sitting-alone-anywhere—and she couldn't help but notice that everyone else was in couples or groups. Of course, Leanne hadn't exactly abandoned her. She would be back sooner or later, alone or with TB&H in tow. Still, Nolie felt obviously uncomfortable.

With a sigh, she stacked their dishes together for a waitress to eventually claim. She'd polished off every bite of her hamburger and fries, while Leanne had eaten little more than half of hers, which was one of the reasons Leanne was thin and she wasn't. But what could she say? She liked food. She found comfort in it, especially in sweets. A meal without dessert was no fun.

Granted, neither was weighing a hundred and—well, what she weighed. Maybe she would start a diet Monday, and maybe, with most of the Marlene-and-Obie stress removed from her life, she would stick to it this time. After all, she was getting a lot more exercise these days than when she'd lived in Arkansas. She'd noticed just the evening before that she wasn't as winded as usual after climbing the hill from the store to the cabin.

And what if she was successful this time? Maybe the

men in the bar would look at her the way they looked at Leanne and a number of the other women there—was that what she wanted? Not particularly, though of course it would be nice.

Maybe Chase would corner her in the kitchen again, only this time he would kiss her? Oh, yeah. That would be way better than nice.

Turning in her chair, she located Leanne and Cole on the dance floor, swaying to a tune on the jukebox. Four other couples shared the space with them, but there was something special about them. It might have been merely that they looked good together—two very attractive people, one fair, the other dark, each apparently lost in the other. Whatever it was, it stirred a yearning deep inside Nolie that made her restless and anxious to get away.

She waited through a second song, then a third, before picking up Leanne's purse and her own shoulder bag and seeking them out on the dance floor. "Sorry to interrupt," she said, and Leanne blinked as if she'd completely forgotten her. "I'm going to head on home. It's been a long day."

Leanne did another slow blink. "Oh. Okay. Uh, let me take you back to your car—"

"That's okay. I'd enjoy the walk."

"Are you sure it's safe?" Cole asked. "We can give you a ride."

"Safe?" Leanne echoed. "This is Bethlehem, the safest place on earth. I doubt a serious criminal has set foot inside the city limits in fifty years. But, Nolie, it *has* been a long day, and I know you're tired. At least let me give you my keys—"

"I'm not that tired. I just want to pick up Micahlyn and get home. Here's your bag. You guys have fun. I'll see you."

. . . .

CHASE LAY IN THE HAMMOCK, HIS ANKLES CROSSED, a pillow under his head, and stared in the direction of Nolie's cabin. It was 9:15, the parking space out front was still empty, and the only lights burning were the ones she left on every day when she went to the store. She was probably out celebrating the reopening of the store with some of her new friends. It didn't take a person long to make friends in Bethlehem. Its residents tended to be some of the nicest people in the whole damn world.

But so what if she was out with other people? It was none of his business. He'd chosen to live alone. She hadn't. She was younger, practically, than he could remember being, and she deserved some fun.

"I can't believe you're freakin' jealous," he said aloud, scowling hard into the darkness.

But he was. He'd gotten used to her being around. Once she made other friends, especially friends who weren't in hiding, she wouldn't have much time left for him. Not that he considered her a friend.

He wondered how things had gone at the store, whether her teenage helper was worth the salary she was paying, how many people she'd met that he would know. Who was she celebrating with—just Micahlyn or maybe the Winchesters or the Thomases?—and how damn long did it take?

Leaning over to the floor, he picked up a pack of cigarettes, shook one out, and lit it. He was down to a quarter of a pack a day, and he hadn't had a single beer all day. He was cleaning up his act . . . but why? For whom? Himself? Or Nolie? Either way, it wasn't as if he had much of a future.

The sound of a car engine broke the night, laboring up

the steepest part of the hill. He watched and waited for the headlights to break through the trees, shifting here, there, as she drove around the last curve. Finally the car appeared, angling into the parking space.

The interior light came on, then went off again, as Nolie got out. She circled the car to the passenger side, lifted Micahlyn out, and settled her on one hip. She was moving slowly, as if she was tired. After ten hours at the store, then partying, she probably was.

As far as he could tell, she didn't even glance in his direction, though once she'd climbed the stairs, the shadows were too deep to see. A click in the still night indicated she'd gone inside and closed the door behind her. This late she would put Micahlyn to bed without a bath, and then she would probably go to bed herself, lying on pale green sheets, her hair a deep copper contrast against the lace-embellished pillowcase. He wondered if she slept in a T-shirt, nightgown, or nothing at all, and his body immediately responded to the possibilities.

Better not think about that.

Closing his eyes, he shifted one foot to the floor and set the hammock swaying. If he gave himself half a chance, he could probably fall asleep right there. The night air was comfortable enough, the woods quiet enough. He'd never been particularly fond of camping as a kid, though he'd done it often enough with the Scouts and, in high school, with buddies who preferred to do their underage drinking away from home and parents. But this wasn't camping. It was just relaxing.

"You fall asleep with a cigarette and burn yourself up and my cabin down, I'm going to be very unhappy."

His impulse was to jerk his eyes open—and demand to know where she'd been, with whom, doing what—but he forced himself to do it slowly instead. She stood on his left, at the end of the porch and wore a loose, T-shirt-looking dress that fell all the way to her ankles and looked as comfortable as he now felt. Then he noticed that her feet were bare, and a little of his comfort turned to not-unpleasant tension.

Still rocking the hammock, he lazily said, "I'm not going to fall asleep."

"Huh. You should see yourself from my point of view." She seated herself at the front edge of the porch, leaning against the post, knees drawn up and hands clasped around them.

"Want the hammock?"

"No, thanks. I imagine there's a weight limit on it."

"I meant, I'd get up and let you have it."

"That's what I meant, too."

His jaw tightened and he scowled at her. "Why do you talk as if you're so heavy?"

Her smile was flippant. "I'm what's called a plus-size woman. An abundant woman. I don't believe I've been smaller than a size ten since I *was* ten. I'm excessively lush."

"Men like curves," he said, and realized he was developing an appreciation for them himself. Every woman he'd ever been involved with had been tiny, petite, and delicate, but damned if he could remember at that very moment what it was about them that had attracted him.

"Funny. You're the second person tonight to tell me that."

The jealousy he'd forgotten returned with a vengeance, gnawing at his gut and making his voice stiff. "Who was the other?"

"Just someone I was talking to."

"Where?"

"At the Starlite Lounge. Their menu has only four items—hamburgers, cheeseburgers, fries, and onion rings—

but the food's good, the beer is cold, and all the pretty women in town go there. There's pool and dancing and live music on weekends. You should drop in sometime."

Why, unless she was planning to start spending every Saturday evening there?

He was debating how to question her further without sounding like the lawyer he was, grilling a hostile witness, but she didn't wait. "Why did you bother lighting that cigarette if you're not going to smoke it?"

He glanced down at the glowing tip radiating heat onto his fingers, then leaned over and dropped it in a gallon coffee can half-filled with dirt. "Satisfied?"

She made a noncommittal sound.

"How was opening day?"

"Excellent. I never expected so many people."

"How did the kid work out?"

"He was excellent, too." She smiled smugly. "I made a good choice."

"Hiring someone who could be there during the day would have been a better choice. How are you going to make deliveries when you're there alone until Junior gets out of school?"

"I'll send Jun—Trey with them when he gets there."

"How are you going to load two hundred pounds of feed for a customer?"

"I'll manage."

"Oh, yeah, I forgot. You'll flutter your lashes," he said sourly.

"Oh, yeah, you forgot. I'm not the lash-fluttering type. I'm just mindless," she said just as sourly.

"I didn't say you were mindless."

She made a *hmph* sound, but didn't speak.

A whiff of fragrances—perfume, shampoo, Nolie—

drifted to him on the still night air, and he half-wished he still had the burning cigarette to block it out.

He also half-wished he could pull her into the hammock with him, close enough that he couldn't smell anything else. But if he did that—if she came along willingly—then he would want to kiss her, and then he would get turned on, and then . . .

He'd better not go there, or he would get hard without even touching her, and she would probably run away home and lock her windows and doors.

"Bethlehem's a nice town," she remarked.

"You think so."

"I do. You can't tell me it wasn't a good place to grow up."

He could, if he wanted to lie to her again, which he didn't. Not this time, at least. "It wasn't bad. It was clean, safe, lots of stuff to do. Real family-oriented." And that was his problem. He hadn't been running away from Bethlehem when he'd left. He'd been escaping his family.

"So you liked the schools, the activities, the people. Then your trouble must have been with your family."

He glared at her. Damn it, she might as well have read his mind. "I thought we'd established the fact that I don't have a family." So much for not lying again . . . though it wasn't completely a lie. Yes, he had blood relatives, but they weren't a family to him in the real sense of the word.

"Actually, we haven't established many facts about you at all. I keep trying, but you're very good at evasion."

"So quit trying."

"Then what would we talk about? You already know everything about me. I don't know anything about you. I still don't even know your last name."

Then don't talk. Go home. Leave me alone. But he didn't want to be left alone. And he didn't know everything about her. He didn't know how she tasted, or if her skin was as impossibly soft as it looked, or how she looked naked, or how she would feel underneath him in bed. He didn't know if an attempt to kiss her would frighten her, or if she would kiss him back, or if she wanted him half as much as he was starting to want her.

He didn't know any of the important things.

He exhaled heavily, swung his left foot to the floor next to her feet, then sat up and faced her. "As far as I know, my mother, father, and sister live in Bethlehem. To say we aren't close would be a gross understatement. Growing up, I couldn't wait to get out and they couldn't wait for me to get out. When I graduated from l"—he broke off, then made a substitution for law school—"college, I invited them to come, though I hadn't seen them in years. Only my sister showed up. When I got married, I invited them to the wedding. That time, not even my sister came. Every time I tried to arrange a visit to bring Fiona here to meet them, I was told it wasn't a good time, until I gave up trying. I haven't been in touch with any of them since then."

"I'm sorry."

"Of course you are." He didn't mean it as harshly as it sounded. She was the one who valued family. He didn't doubt that she really was sorry about his. Of course, being sorry didn't mean she was willing to let the subject drop.

"Feeling the way you do, why did you come back here?"

He rolled out of the hammock and settled on the floor, facing her. "I didn't have a lot of choices."

"You had a whole world full of them. Remember, I know how much your rent is. You could spend that same amount of money virtually anywhere else in the country, with the added advantage that you wouldn't have to hide out to avoid seeing anyone you knew. So why Bethlehem?"

Because he'd already offered the only answer he had, he shrugged. "You tell me."

For a long time, she sat still and thoughtful, studying him as if she could find answers to all her questions if she just looked long enough. Finally she rested her chin on her knees. "Maybe you came back because you have unfinished business here."

"I finished with this town and everyone in it sixteen years ago."

"Maybe you need to resolve things with your family. To convince yourself that the break wasn't your fault, that you've done all a reasonable adult could be expected to do."

"You're wrong."

"Then why didn't you settle in California, Louisiana, or Missouri? Why didn't you head west to Montana or south to Florida? Why settle for this kind of existence?"

"This kind of existence? You make it sound as if I'm living under a bridge and eating out of garbage cans. I *wanted* to be left alone. I didn't want to bother with people or neighbors or questions. Bethlehem was convenient. That's all." He shrugged to ease the tension knotting the muscles in his shoulders. "You know, you can go home now."

He half-expected her to ignore him. Instead, she stood up, smoothed her dress, then pushed her hands into her pockets. Without so much as a *screw you,* she walked a dozen feet, then turned back. "I think you're kidding yourself, Chase. I don't believe for a minute that you came back here because it was *convenient.* But if you want to pretend to believe that, go ahead."

Then she strolled back to her cabin, a pale figure in the moonlight. A lush figure, yes, but womanly. Desirable.

But she was still wrong. He hadn't had any ulterior motives when he'd moved here. He didn't have the slightest need to resolve anything with his family. He just hadn't had the energy to find someplace new. An unexpected and nasty divorce, a criminal trial, a wrongful conviction, and twenty-two months in prison could sap the initiative right out of a guy. He'd been lucky he'd made it here. He *could* have just walked in front of a bus in Boston.

No matter how much she wanted to believe differently, she was *wrong*.

He was convinced of it.

So, when he stood up long after she'd disappeared inside, why did he head for his truck instead of his bed? And when he reached the end of the dirt road, why did he turn right, toward Bethlehem, instead of the other way?

About the time he passed the feed store, he took his foot off the gas pedal, and the SUV began slowing. This was stupid. He had nothing to prove by going into town and no one to prove it to. He didn't care how the town had changed in the past sixteen years. None of the old places that had meant anything to him back then mattered now.

Still, he passed up a half-dozen chances to turn around.

This late on Saturday night, there wasn't a lot of traffic—but, hell, at five P.M. on a Friday afternoon before a weekend holiday, there wasn't a lot of traffic. He drove Main Street from one end of town to the other, then turned onto a side street. An awful lot hadn't changed at all. The old houses still looked the same—some of them grand, some not, all of them well cared for. Even the majority of businesses downtown had been around a long time—Harry's, the bank, the bakery, the clothing stores, the movie theater. What had once been Herbert Thomas's law office was now occupied by his nephew, Alex Thomas, and the sign outside Dr. Hawkins's dental clinic now read Hawkins and Hawkins.

Chase would recognize these streets in his sleep.

He drove past the schools he'd attended from kindergarten on, past the stadium where he'd played football—until he'd gotten kicked off the team for disciplinary problems—and, next door, the field where he'd played baseball not very well for a season or two. He went by the church they'd attended, still every bit as solid and permanent as he remembered. And why shouldn't it be? It had stood in the same spot for more than two hundred years.

He also looked up the Starlite Lounge, stopping alongside the curb fifty feet away. It might be late for most of the town, but the bar wouldn't close for three or four hours more. The parking lot was filled with cars, and loud music drifted out each time the doors opened. He'd been too young to go there before he'd moved away. He was certainly old enough now, but couldn't find the appeal in it. The kind of woman he was likely to develop an interest in wasn't likely to hang out in a place like this . . . though it was exactly where Nolie had spent her evening.

With whom? Had she danced? Had a drink? Turned down any invitations?

He was relatively sure she hadn't been drinking. Not having had a beer in more than twenty-four hours—a long time for him lately—he would have smelled it on her. The rest he didn't know about. He wished he did.

Headlights flashed in his rearview mirror. He watched as a police car passed, then pulled into the street, intending to head home. He'd seen enough.

But on the way home was City Park, now home to a swimming pool in addition to the playground equipment and the ice rink he remembered. And across the street from City Park was an old brick house. . . .

Refusing to consider his actions, he pulled into one of the park's parking lots, shut off the engine, and walked to the swing set that faced the house. He'd spent a lot of time on these swings when he was a kid. He'd learned to skate at the ice rink, had picnics under the trees, and jumped his bike off a mound of dirt that had later been turned into a ball field, breaking his arm in the process. If it had been his sister, she probably would have gotten her favorite dinner and ice cream, plus a toy to cheer her up. He'd gotten grounded for two weeks.

Sitting on a swing seat, he stared at the house. It was two stories, square, built of dark brick and roofed with green tile. Around back, a detached garage with a long-unused apartment above was just visible at the edge of the property. Up front, the two upstairs windows on the right had been his room, the two on the left his sister's.

He wondered how long it had taken them, once he'd moved out, to erase any sign of his existence from his room. Probably no more than a few days.

"Isn't it a lovely evening?"

Startled, he jerked his gaze around to see Nolie's friend Sophy standing at the other end of the swing set. Smiling politely, she straddled the seat and faced him, chain at her back. "First time you've seen the house?" she asked.

He glanced from her to the house, then back again. "What are you talking about?"

"Your old family home. Is this the first time you've seen it since you came back?"

"How did you know—?"

The look she gave him was chiding. "Some people think they know everything. They annoy those of us who really do." Unexpectedly, she extended her hand. "Sophy Jones."

He offered neither his hand nor his name.

"It takes more than unfriendliness to offend me." Pivoting around, she planted her feet in the dirt, gave a great push, then stretched her legs straight out and reached into the sky. Dressed in baggy shorts and a too-large shirt, with her blond curls and big eyes, she looked about twelve. Well, okay, twenty-two, but not a day older. Too young for him to have known from before.

"They still live there, you know," she said as she pumped the swing higher. "Your parents, I mean. Your sister has a place of her own, of course."

"Do you think I care where they live?"

"Isn't that why you're here?"

"No."

He was about to stand up, but before his brain had even formed the command, she said, "Oh, sit down, Chase. Don't get all hostile. It's perfectly natural to wonder about your parents when you haven't seen them in half a lifetime."

"I don't wonder about them at all."

She looked sideways at him in a way that reminded him of Nolie's long, searching gaze. "Then why are you here?"

"You translate visiting a place where I used to play into curiosity about people who aren't a part of my life and haven't been—by their own choice—for years?" He shook his head disgustedly. "You're jumping to some pretty big conclusions there."

"You're sitting on a swing staring at the house where you grew up, where your parents still live, and you expect me to believe it's got nothing to do with them?"

"I don't give a damn what you be—"

When her swing came forward and reached its highest point, she jumped from the seat—a good way to sprain an ankle, he'd learned when he was seven. But Sophy landed with much more grace than he'd managed. Like some damn gymnast or something, she landed on her feet and stuck. Grinning, she shoved her hands into her back pockets. "What I believe doesn't matter. What you *think* you believe really doesn't matter, either. You had a reason for returning to Bethlehem, and it had nothing to do with no other options or convenience or energy or initiative. You came here"—she gestured wide to indicate the town—"for a purpose, just as you came *here*"—this time she pointed at the swings—"for a purpose. The sooner you admit it, the sooner you can fulfill it."

Chase's jaw tightened till his teeth ached, as her words echoed in his head . . . *it had nothing to do with no other options or convenience or energy or initiative*. Damn Nolie. What had she done? Oh, so casually sauntered home, then rushed inside to call Sophy and repeat everything to her? Why the hell would she do that, and who the hell was Sophy to care?

"Nolie didn't tell me anything," she said, making his head whip around so fast his neck ached. "In fact, I haven't seen her since that day at the feed store. If you think back, you'll remember that the only excuses you gave her this evening were no-other-options and convenience. The energy and initiative bit came after she was gone."

He stared angrily at her, about to unleash his temper, when the porch light coming on across the street momentarily distracted him. The front door opened, and a small yippy dog, the kind his mother had always preferred, ran into the yard, did his business, then dashed back to the house. The door closed again without his catching a glimpse of even the hand that closed it. He turned back to Sophy. "Who the hell are y—"

She was gone. The swing swayed slightly, as if touched by a breeze, but there was no sign of her. Not in the park, not on the street, not as far as he could see. She was damn quick on her feet, he told himself, and quiet, too. But she was as wrong as Nolie had been. About everything . . . except one thing.

He *hadn't* said anything to Nolie about energy and initiative—hadn't said it at all. They'd just been thoughts in his mind.

So how in sweet hell had Sophy Jones known about them?

Chapter Eight

"MAMA?"

Nolie didn't look up from the sink, where she was peeling potatoes. "Yes, babe?"

"Is that man coming over for dinner again?"

"That man?"

"You know. Him." Taking a moment from her coloring, Micahlyn waved in the direction of the other cabin with a hot-pink crayon.

"No, hon, he's not." Nolie hadn't seen Chase since he'd told her to go home Saturday night. It seemed like forever, but in reality had been only three and a half days . . . not that she was counting. She didn't care. Her friendly nature only went so far. If he wanted to live over there like a hermit, drink, smoke, and not bathe, fine. He was welcome to his privacy—to his loneliness.

"He's not really the bogeyman, is he?" Micahlyn asked.

Nolie's smile was strained. "No, babe, he isn't."

"I didn't think so. Deontae, at day care, says the real bogeyman is green and slimy and lives in a cave way up the mountains. He's seen him before, so he knows."

"Sweetheart, there's no such thing as a real bogeyman."

"Uh-huh. Deontae says."

Nolie rinsed the last potato, sliced it into a pan of water, and set it on the stove to boil. Her favorite way to eat potatoes was baked and slathered in butter and sour cream—not exactly allowed on this diet she'd started Monday. Her second favorite was to boil them until soft, drain, and add milk and Velveeta cheese. Also not diet food. In fact, in only three days, she'd figured out that very few of her favorite dishes could find a place on any weight-reduction diet. Tonight she planned to mash Micahlyn's potatoes with milk and butter, and have hers simply boiled. Yum. Or did she mean yuck?

She was pouring frozen peas into a bowl to microwave when the phone rang. For just one instant, she wondered if it might be Chase—but how could it be? Presumably, he didn't have a phone, and if he wanted to talk to her, he would simply walk over and knock at the door.

"I'll get it," Micahlyn sang out and hopped across to the wall phone. "H'lo? Hi, Grandma."

Nolie rolled her eyes. Either Marlene or Obie, or both, had called Micahlyn every night this week. They didn't talk long, and they never asked to speak to Nolie, but still it bothered her. Of course, she couldn't forbid them to call—what harm was in it? And no matter what Chase thought, she couldn't tell them to back off or sic her lawyer on them, regardless of how nice Alex was. She just wished they would let her and Micahlyn have their own lives.

The thought made her feel guilty, because she knew how much the Harpers had loved Jeff and how much they loved his only child. And feeling guilty made her hungry for something much more comforting than a boneless, skinless grilled chicken breast, plain boiled potatoes, and green peas. Something like the cherry pecan vanilla ice cream she'd polished off Saturday night after the unsatisfying end to her last conversation with Chase. Or the refrigerated cinnamon rolls she'd eaten for breakfast Sunday morning, the French silk pie she'd had with lunch at Harry's, or the super-duper nachos she'd fixed for dinner that night, all in preparation for her diet on Monday.

Man, she'd really love to have some nachos right now, heavy on the cheese and sour cream, with a baklava chaser.

Micahlyn stretched the phone cord through the doorway and across the living room to the couch. Five years old, and she liked to take her phone calls in private. Nolie couldn't help but wonder what she was going to be like at fifteen.

By the time Micahlyn hung up, Nolie had dinner on the table. She waited until they'd each had a chance to eat a bit before asking, "What did Grandma have to say?"

"Oh, not much," Micahlyn replied airily. "We talked about Maria Diane." That was her new, too-expensive doll. "Grandma's making some clothes for her. And we talked about the play toys Grandpa built for me."

"Did she say anything to you about coming to visit?"

"Just that then I could play on the new toys. And be sure to bring Maria Diane." Micahlyn speared a piece of chicken and ate it, then sighed. "I sure do like fried chicken better 'n this."

Who didn't? "We can have fried chicken once in a while. Just not every week."

"Grandma says you're tryin' to get skinny so you can get a boyfriend."

Nolie's face flushed. Hadn't the thought of being more attractive to males entered her mind—even helped cement her decision to diet again? Even so, she had no compunction about lying. "Your grandma's wrong. I want to lose weight so I can be healthier."

"You can walk all the way up the hill without goin' like

this." Micahlyn panted heavily. "Are you hopin' if you get skinny, he'll kiss you?"

"Who?"

"Him." This time she jerked her head toward Chase's cabin. "Grandma says you're gonna replace my daddy with him."

Nolie's temper flared, and her hunger disappeared at the same time her craving for something sweet and comforting kicked into high gear. She laid her fork down. "Listen to me, Micahlyn. Your grandmother had no right to say that. I loved your daddy, and no one can ever take his place. But . . . he's gone. He's been gone a long time. Someday I might get married again, but not right now."

"Huh. Grandma says—"

"Let's not talk about Grandma anymore tonight, okay?" Though Nolie had every intention of talking *to* Grandma the very instant Micahlyn got into her bath.

Though her appetite was gone, Nolie ate the rest of her dinner—or she would regret it later—and even enjoyed the fresh berries with Cool Whip Lite they dished up for dessert. As soon as she could possibly justify it, she hustled Micahlyn upstairs and into the tub, then returned to the kitchen phone to call Whiskey Creek.

After five rings with no answer, she disconnected, then immediately dialed back. This time she gave it ten rings before hanging up. Seething, she stalked across the living room, outside, and onto the first porch step, where she clenched her fists, tilted her head back, and gave a satisfying shriek.

"Primal therapy?" asked a low, dry voice behind her, and she shrieked again, whirling around to find Chase standing in the shadows next to the door.

"What are you doing skulking around on my porch?"

"I'm not skulking. I don't even know how. I was about

to knock, and I saw you were on the phone, so I waited, and then you stomped out and screamed."

She let her expression settle into a pout. "I didn't stomp. I walked heavily."

"Well, forgive me for not being up on the subtle nuances between stomping and walking heavily." After a moment, he asked, "Bad news?"

"No. The miracles of modern technology." With a deep sigh, she moved to lean against the porch railing, her arms folded over her chest. "I was trying to call my mother-in-law, to tell her she was way out of line in her most recent conversation with my child. Of course, Marlene and Obie have Caller ID, so they knew it was me calling. They wouldn't answer, and they even turned off the answering machine so the damn phone just rang and rang."

Chase simply stood there next to the door, where little of the light spilling out reached him. She couldn't make out his expression, but she could actually feel the quietness radiating from him. "What? No advice?"

"When you're in the advice-giving business, you learn to save your breath with people who don't want to follow it."

"Gee, you're a great help." She stomped—er, walked heavily—to the first rocker and plopped into it. More calmly, she said, "It's not that I don't want to follow it. It's just that . . ."

"You were raised the way most girls are—to be the peacemaker, to get along, to respect your elders and not make waves."

"Exactly."

"But that doesn't mean you can't stand up for yourself when the situation warrants it."

"Yes, it does. I'm a big weenie when it comes to confrontation."

That rare, stiff laughter she'd heard once before came from the shadows. "You don't have any trouble confronting me. You've bullied me since you moved in here."

"I have not—! Well . . . maybe . . . a little bit. But you have to admit, you needed bullying."

"I don't have to admit anything."

He moved past her and sat in the second rocker, where light spilling through the window allowed her to see the right side of his face. His jaw was heavily stubbled with beard, as if he hadn't bothered to shave that morning, which gave him a wickedly disreputable look. If it wasn't too much to state the obvious, he looked exactly like the sort of man mothers warned their daughters about—or, in her case, mothers-in-law.

"What did your mother-in-law say to your daughter that was so out of line?" he asked.

Nolie set her chair rocking. There was no way she could tell him that Marlene thought she was on a manhunt and he was the intended victim. Instead, she shrugged. "Just more of her plan to keep things stirred up. She's manipulating my child, and trying to manipulate me, and I don't like it."

"Trying?" he repeated dryly, but that was all he said.

After making a face at him, she returned to his earlier comment. "So you were in the advice-giving business back in Boston. Certainly not as an advice columnist like Dear Abby. Let's see . . . were you a minister?"

"I haven't set foot in church in sixteen years, and I'm none too eager to do so again, lest God strike me down for my sins."

"Okay. A psychologist?"

"I don't care about the workings of anyone's mind but my own."

"Counselor?"

"Don't care to mess with whiny people who can't handle their own problems."

"Hmm. Doctor?"

"The sight of blood makes me queasy."

"Cop?"

He snorted derisively.

"Matchmaker?"

Another snort. "Only if my life had become hell on earth."

Who else made a practice of giving advice? Overbearing parents, nosy friends, bartenders, accountants, consultants, lawyers— "Were you a lawyer?" She wasn't sure why she'd chosen that one out of the last three. He just didn't seem nerdy enough to be an accountant, but too edgy to be a consultant.

He sat motionless, one half of his face illuminated, the other half in shadow. His expression gave away nothing, but the tension that held him so still said a lot. She waited a moment, barely breathing, then softly asked again, "Are you a lawyer?"

For a time he looked as if he'd turned to stone. Gradually, though, as though he'd reached a decision, the stiffness drained from him, and he leaned back in the rocker and propped his booted feet on the porch railing. "I used to be."

The enormity of his admission wasn't lost on Nolie. With nothing more than that small detail and his first name, she could learn an awful lot about him. Chase wasn't unheard of as a first name, but it wasn't common, either. How many lawyers named Chase could the state of Massachusetts have? From that, she could get his last name, and with that, she could find out about his marriage and divorce, why he'd left Boston, why he said he *used* to be a lawyer, and why he wasn't anymore.

More important, she could find out who his parents were.

All it would take was a little time on the Internet, maybe a phone call or two, and she could uncover most, if not all, of his secrets.

And he would never trust her with anything ever again.

"I bet you were a very good lawyer," she said at last.

"I was. I could reason, argue, lie, and manipulate with the best of them. I went into court with clients who'd confessed to every last detail of their crimes and got them acquitted in spite of themselves. I was damn good . . . but not good enough."

Nolie was about to ask what had happened when she remembered his comment that she bullied him. Instead, she reworded the question. "Do you want to talk about it?"

The look he gave her was disbelieving. "*No.* Why would I?"

"Hey, you're the one who volunteered one of his secrets. I didn't want to appear rude by not following up on it." That earned her a flicker of a smile that made her smile, too. "Have you eaten?"

"I'm not destitute. You don't have to feed me."

"I know that. So . . . have you eaten?"

"Yeah."

"Really?"

"Really. I had Hamburger Helper. I used to live on that stuff in la—" He hesitated, then must have remembered he'd already spilled the beans. "In law school."

Clomping steps sounded inside the house, then Micahlyn called out, "Mama, where are you?"

"Out here, babe."

The screen door banged, then Micahlyn joined her, clomping because she was wearing a pair of Nolie's sandals along with one of Nolie's T-shirts to double as a nightgown. "I took my bath and I'm all ready for bed except—" Seeing Chase, she abruptly broke off, sidled closer to Nolie, then climbed into her lap and offered a brush. "Comb my hair, please."

Her long red hair was dripping water. Nolie dried it on the excess shirt fabric, then began gently tugging the brush through her hair. Ignoring the jerks and yanks Nolie was doing her best to avoid, Micahlyn fixed her gaze on Chase. "You're *not* the bogeyman." Her tone was accusing, as if he'd laid claim to the title himself instead of having it bestowed upon him by none other than her.

"No, I'm not," Chase agreed.

"You don't even look anything like him." She sighed. "You're just a man."

Not *just* a man, Nolie thought. A wickedly handsome man. A competent, capable, wounded man. A man who had almost kissed her, whom she couldn't help but fantasize about his really kissing her.

"Sorry to disappoint you," Chase said. "If it would make you feel any better, I can snarl at you from time to time."

Micahlyn's response was prim, with her mouth held in that prissy way she'd learned from Marlene. "That's okay. You're not green and slimy, and you don't live in a cave and eat little kids for dinner. It wouldn't be the same." That quickly she changed the subject. "Mama, can I cut my hair?"

"No, you may not."

"But why not? Gracie's got short hair. And Chrissy. And Brandi and Caitlyn."

"But your hair is so pretty. You don't really want—"

Chase cleared his throat rather loudly, and Nolie broke off to glance at him. His expression, what she could see of it, was totally innocent. But that was okay, because in that brief silence, she'd heard the sentence finished in her head in a dozen different ways, all in the same voice. *You don't really want to stay all alone in this trailer with the baby, Nolie. You don't really want to bother yourself with housework or cooking. You don't really want to spend all day at a job you don't need and away from Micahlyn. You don't really want the burden of that old feed store in New York.*

Lord knew, she didn't really want to sound like Marlene. And who was she to decide how long Micahlyn's hair should be? She kept hers barely to her shoulders, because anything longer than that was a hassle. It was hot and sticky in the summer, blew wildly in the wind, and tangled at the drop of a pin. And if it was a hassle for her, it was probably just as much a hassle for her daughter.

"If you really want it cut, I'll find someone to do it, okay?"

"Okay. Tomorrow, please." Micahlyn slid to the floor. "I'm goin' to bed now. Come tuck me."

She clomped back inside, the screen door slamming behind her, and up the stairs. Nolie looked at Chase. "Thanks."

"I didn't say anything."

"You didn't have to." With a sigh, she pushed herself to her feet. "I must go tuck the child and read her a story. Will you be here when I finish?"

"No." He stood up, too. "I should go home."

They walked together, Nolie stopping at the door, Chase on the top step. She opened the screen door, then let it close again. "For the record ... I won't do any snooping with the information you gave me tonight."

He approached her, his steps slow and measured. When he came close, she leaned back against the door frame just because it was there, not because she needed its support. He didn't stop until nothing more than a whisper of caution separated them. Even so, she could feel the heat and strength of his body, and it made her hot and weak.

He leaned so near that his features blurred and every breath she took smelled of him, clean and sexy and dangerous and male. Her eyes automatically closed, and in self-defense she resorted to soft, shallow breaths. His mouth brushed hers—just a touch, not a kiss—as it moved lightly to her ear. "For the record," he murmured, his voice tickling, his lips grazing her earlobe, "I know."

Then he walked away.

B ACK IN THE DAYS BEFORE CHASE'S DIVORCE, Friday night had been dinner-out night. Of course, he and Fiona had eaten dinner out almost every other night as well, but Friday nights were reserved for her favorite restaurants—the fanciest, the most expensive.

In the Harper house, Friday night was hot-dog night. He couldn't imagine two more different ways to spend an evening. Dinner out had meant a suit for him and dressing to kill for Fiona, multiple courses, a long evening, and dropping a few hundred bucks or more. Neither Nolie nor Micahlyn cared what he wore for hot dogs, there was nothing else on the menu but chips and salsa and fresh berries for dessert, and the damage, which he didn't even have to pay, couldn't have been more than ten dollars.

And there was no question which one he preferred.

This time he'd learned how to light the grill, then set everything on the table while Nolie cooked the hot dogs. He was standing between two chairs at the table, a hand on the back of each, and waiting for her to join them when Micahlyn, her hair newly cut, pointed to the chair across from her with a tortilla chip. "That's your place, and this one's Mama's."

His place. How long had it been since he'd had a place at anyone's table? In anyone's home? He wouldn't be welcome in his own parents' house, or his sister's, or any one of Fiona's, but he had a place of his own in Nolie's house. That felt better than he had any right to expect.

Nolie set a platter of plump, grilled wieners on the table, then slid into her seat. Chase sat, too, and Micahlyn mumbled a quick blessing with a mouthful of chips.

"How was day care?" Nolie asked as she passed around the wieners, then buns.

"Fine. I made a scul—a scup—a statue today. I get to bring it home tomorrow. It's really good."

"I bet it is, sweetie." Nolie glanced at him. "And how was your day?"

He blinked at the unexpected inclusion. "I got tired of lying on the couch watching TV so I went out and laid in the hammock and watched the clouds."

"You need a job."

"I like being a bum."

"Your mind is going to molder away until you don't do anything, don't know anything, and don't remember anything."

He smiled smugly. "Sweet oblivion."

"Uh-huh. I take it you're not interested in prac"—she glanced at Micahlyn—"in returning to your previous profession."

It would be a little difficult when he'd been disbarred, which he couldn't tell her without telling her why. Would she believe him when he said he wasn't guilty? Jeez, it was such a cliche. Every man in prison pleaded innocence at one time or another, and in general, the ones who weren't lying were untruthful.

But would he return to practicing law if he could? Two years ago, probably even two months ago, his answer would have been an automatic yes. He liked the challenges. It was the only thing he did well, the only thing he'd ever wanted to do. But now . . .

"I'm not interested in any profession at the moment." Deliberately he changed the subject. "You lose your appetite?" The other time he'd shared hot dogs with them, she'd loaded hers with so many extras—sauerkraut, chili, onions, and cheese—that she'd had to eat it with a fork. Tonight the wiener looked lonely in its bun with nothing but mustard and a few onions.

Before she could speak, Micahlyn did, her full bottom lip curling into a pout. "Mama's on a diet. We haven't had any ice cream or cookies or fried chicken or anything good all week."

A blush turned Nolie's fair skin pink all over, even extending down her throat and disappearing beneath the V neck of her dress. "Thank you, Micahlyn. I appreciate you announcing that to everyone."

"You're welcome, Mama." Micahlyn smiled prettily, then sprawled in her chair, one knee drawn up, and ate her own hot dog without regard for her plate.

"They don't learn the finer points of what to tell and what to keep quiet until they're older," Chase said, his tone mild. Then he let his gaze slide down what he could see of Nolie—pink throat, bare arms, full breasts, curvy hips. "You don't need to go on a diet."

"Oh, no," she agreed. "I could just keep eating and eating until I pop."

"Oh, yeah, like that's gonna happen. You look fine."

"Sure, I do. What size was Fiona?"

Chase's jaw tightened. He'd bought her a new wardrobe twice every year they were married, along with various incidental purchases throughout the year. It was fair to say that the cost of clothing her for three years exceeded the cost of his three years in law school. But he'd usually just written the checks and admired her in the clothes. He'd rarely made any purchases himself.

"Well?"

"I didn't buy her clothes . . . except . . ." He glanced at Nolie and found her waiting impatiently. After drawing a breath, he exhaled loudly and blurted it out. "Once I bought a sweater she'd picked out. It was a petite extra small."

As he expected, Nolie's eyes arched toward her bangs. "Extra small? I didn't even know women's clothes *came* in extra small. You're sure she was a woman and not a little porcelain doll?"

"She was a little of both, I suppose." With a good measure of duplicity tossed in to keep her from being too precious. He'd never suspected she was having an affair, never expected she would divorce him and marry her lover . . . but then, *she'd* never imagined he would wind up in prison. She'd signed on for better and for worse, but not for prison and living on a budget.

Nolie shook her head, her hair capturing the light shining down from above and gleaming richer, deeper, with it. "If I shriveled away to nothing but skin and bones, I'd still be bigger than an extra small."

"But, Mama, you feel just like a mama's s'posed to," Micahlyn chimed in. "Tiffany's mama back home, when she used to hug me at church, everything poked 'cause she's so skinny. But you're soft and cuddly, like a mama should be."

Chase hid a smile. Soft and cuddly—just how every single twenty-something woman wanted to be described. But he could share Micahlyn's sentiment. He'd slept a lot of nights with skinny, and soft and cuddly looked damn fine at the moment.

"Thank you, sweetie. But no more talk about diets and my weight tonight, okay?"

"Okay." Micahlyn shoved the last bite of her hot dog into her mouth, then hung one arm over the back of the chair. "Can I be excused?"

"May I," Nolie corrected.

Michalyn responded with a grin, "Yes, you may. Can I, too?"

"Yes. Take your dishes to the sink."

As she obeyed, then raced upstairs, Chase polished off his third hot dog and a handful of chips, then leaned back comfortably in his own chair. "Did you ever talk to your mother-in-law?"

"No. When they finally turned the answering machine back on, I left a couple of messages, but she hasn't called."

"Look on the bright side—as long as she's avoiding you, she won't be calling to talk to Micahlyn, and you get to bask in your weenie-ness and not have to confront her."

She started clearing the table and he got up to help her, though it seemed that every time he moved, he was bumping into her or she was sidestepping to avoid him. He wouldn't have thought anything of it if she didn't seem so jumpy about it. Still embarrassed over the discussion about her weight?

Or did it have something to do with the other night, when he'd sort of almost kissed her?

He hadn't known at the time what made him do it, and hadn't figured it out yet. Yes, he was attracted to her, and would like to do a hell of a lot more than just sort of kiss her. But she wasn't the kind of woman a man used, then walked away from. She was sweet, innocent, insecure. She would be easy to hurt.

Hell, it would be damn easy for *him* to get hurt.

With everything else done, he leaned against the

counter and watched as she finished loading the dish-washer. When she straightened, she washed and dried her hands, then brushed her hair back. "Would you like dessert now or later?"

"Later." Corny as it sounded, he liked the idea of a "later."

She squirted lotion onto her hands, then went into the living room as she rubbed it in. He followed, and continued to do so when she circled behind the sofa and went outside onto the porch. She didn't sit in one of the rockers, but took a seat on the top step. He sat beside her, a foot or so separating them. Twelve inches too much, twelve miles too little.

"Isn't the sky pretty?" she murmured.

He murmured in agreement, though it wasn't the sky he was looking at.

"When I was a kid, most of the boys at school wanted to be farmers, like their dads, and most of the girls wanted to be nurses or teachers or mommies, like their mothers. But I wanted to an archaeologist or an astronomer. I loved studying the stars, and I went on so many digs in our back-yard and in the fields that Daddy finally had to hide the shovels from me. I believe that was the year they found out my precious buried artifacts were actually the potatoes and carrots Mom had planted in her garden."

"Did you ever seriously consider doing it? Going to college? Making a career of it?"

She shook her head. "Even if they'd lived, my folks couldn't have afforded college. When you're a small farmer, everything pretty much goes back into the land. Besides, I had Jeff. He was perfectly content to spend the rest of his life farming with his dad in Whiskey Creek, and I was perfectly content to be a farmer's wife."

"So you got to be content for a couple years."

"Four years. We married right after we graduated from high school. We were eighteen. He died four years and two months later."

"That's more than a lot of people get."

"More than you got with Fiona."

He nodded, though she wasn't looking. Instead, she was gazing at her left hand, where the thin gold band glinted in the dim light. After seeing it for the first time that day he'd caught her falling off the roof—the day he'd gotten turned on like a sex-starved teenager by nothing more than brief contact—he'd pretty much forgotten it, though he guessed she wore it every day. Was it sentimentality? Habit? Did she still love Jeff? Or was it a reminder that she wasn't yet ready to take another man into her life or her bed?

He couldn't speak to sentimentality himself. The day he'd found out about Fiona's affair, he'd removed the gold-and-diamond band she'd given him and thrown it into the Charles River. She had asked for it back in the divorce settlement, and he'd politely told her to get it herself and where to find it.

"What was she like?"

"Fiona?"

"No, the girl you took to your senior prom. Of course, Fiona."

He scowled at her, but he was just going through the motions, and she knew it. "She was . . . expensive."

"People shouldn't be expensive."

No, he agreed. But some of them were. In one way or another, damn near everyone in his life had cost him more than he could afford.

What would be the price for this time with Nolie?

"Is that all you can say about her? She was expensive?"

He stood up, descended the steps, paced to her car, then leaned against the hood and faced her. She was backlit by the light coming through the windows and door. He was in shadow.

"She's five feet four, slender, delicate. She has black hair, eyes almost as blue as yours, and skin almost as fair as yours. She's beautiful, elegant, and graceful in any situation."

That last wasn't exactly true. Fiona was as much at ease in a four-star hotel or visiting some friend's Cape Cod hideaway as she was in her own home. She could talk to governors, presidents, and royalty as easily as the current Hollywood heartthrob. But for all her poise and grace, she wouldn't be able to carry on a conversation with a normal, everyday-average person. The only real people she ever had contact with were there to serve her in some capacity—housekeeping staff, waiters, shop clerks. She could give them orders, but she couldn't chat with them.

She functioned beautifully in Boston, New York, or Paris, but set her down in Bethlehem, and she wouldn't know what to do.

"She has this ability to make a person think he's the most important thing in her life, when the truth of it is, she can't even remember his name. She was—and I'm sure, still is—ambitious as hell. She'll tell you exactly what you want to hear and make you believe it, as long as she gets what she wants in return. She's charming, beautiful, intelligent, and one hell of an accomplished liar."

He waited, hands resting on cool metal, for Nolie's response. It came after a moment, her voice soft, her tone thoughtful. "And yet you loved her."

He wished he could deny it, but Nolie was intelligent, too. She wouldn't believe him. "Everyone's entitled to at least one mistake."

"And Fiona was yours."

He shrugged. How his ex-wife would hate hearing herself referred to as a mistake. He would bet she didn't view their marriage the same way. No, for her their marriage had been the first step on the way to a better marriage, a better life.

Nolie rose gracefully, dusted her bottom, then strolled down the steps. "I guess I've been very fortunate, because I haven't made my mistake yet."

"Come over here and I'll help you with it."

The instant the words were out of his mouth, he regretted them—regretted that he'd said them out loud, that they'd made the air between them practically hum with tension, and regretted most of all that she wouldn't take him up on the offer . . . would she?

A shiver flitted through Nolie as she gazed at him. The darkness hid his expression, but that didn't stop her from searching anyway for some guidance.

Come over here and I'll help you with it. Was that a joke, just one friend teasing another, or a serious offer? His voice hadn't given a clue. He'd sounded . . . normal. Not teasing, not particularly serious. Even now, he offered no hint. He didn't repeat his words, didn't move toward her or away, didn't laugh it off.

If she knew he was serious, she would force her feet to unroot from the earth below and carry her the short distance to him. Even without knowing how he was defining *it.*

Come over here . . . But who was she kidding? Men like Chase didn't say things like that to women like her and mean them, just as men like him didn't kiss women like her. His type of woman was everything she wasn't—slender, delicate, beautiful, elegant. Her type was nice, average guys, the ones who couldn't get any farther with beautiful women than she could with handsome, sexy men. And if by some faint ghost of a chance he *was* serious, he would have to come to her, because she was frozen in place.

And he didn't look as if he had any intention of going anywhere.

Because one of them had to break the heavy silence between them and he showed no intention of doing that, either, she found her voice and schooled it into something resembling casual. "So that was life with Fiona. What about—"

"Coward."

Lifting her chin, she gazed at him. "Excuse me?"

"You don't even have the courage to walk ten feet."

"To do what? Make a mistake?" She managed to smile in spite of the butterflies in her stomach. "Whether it's cowardice or intelligence depends on your definition of *mistake*. Besides, I think you're changing the subject back because *you're* a coward—because you don't want to talk about yourself any longer."

"Maybe. But you'll never know because you don't have the courage to come over here and find out."

Nolie's insides were quivering like Jell-O—with anticipation, fear, insecurity, temptation. The desire to prove him wrong was great. Just not as great as her need to spare herself any unnecessary embarrassment, presuming he'd made the offer only because he'd been positive she wouldn't take him up on it.

Instead, she folded her arms across her middle. "Why would it, whatever it is, be a mistake?"

"In case you haven't noticed, personal relationships aren't my forte."

"And what does that mean? Anything you start is doomed to fail? If I come over there, you'll break my heart?"

"Or you'll break mine."

Though deep inside she found herself wistful at the idea she could break *anyone's* heart, she couldn't contain the laugh that burst free. "That's about as likely as me hitching a ride on the tail of the next comet that comes through here and traveling to the outer reaches of the universe." Finally able to move, she took a few steps toward him. "I hate to break this to you, Chase, but telling me you're not good with people is kind of like telling a hog farmer his pigs stink."

"Do they?"

"Oh, yeah, I forgot—you turned yourself into a bona fide city boy. Yes, hogs stink. The only thing worse than being downwind of a hog farm is being downwind of a chicken farm . . . maybe."

"I can imagine—" He broke off, and she could feel the tension that streaked through him even from five feet away. She looked around but saw nothing, listened and heard the faint rumble of a car's engine. They couldn't hear highway traffic from there, which meant the car must be coming up their road. Unannounced company late on a Friday evening? Not likely. Kids looking for an isolated place to park, or someone who'd taken a wrong turn.

The headlights appeared first, all but blinding her. The engine had that low-throated growl Jeff had equated with power and she'd always thought signified the need for a tune up. The growl didn't fade when the car rolled to a slow stop in front of her cabin.

She glanced at Chase, who'd edged a few feet farther to her left, deeper into the shadows of the nearby tree. At least he didn't disappear completely, leaving her to face her visitor—or intruder—alone.

The car was a Camaro Z-28, a convertible, Jeff's most favorite vehicle in the world after his Ford pickup truck and his International Harvester tractor. With its powerful engine and dark-tinted windows, there was a vaguely sinister air to the vehicle, at least until the front window glided down silently and the woman behind the wheel flashed a friendly smile.

Nolie had an instant to take stock before the woman spoke. She was beautiful, dark-haired and dark-skinned, and looked as if she could double on the runway for any supermodel out there. Her voice was her saving grace. She didn't sound cultured, elegant, or sophisticated, but as normal as Nolie herself.

"Hi. I'm looking for a cabin rented to Lorraine Giar—"

"Raine?" Chase emerged from the shadows, bypassing Nolie without a glance and striding toward the car. "What are you—"

She was out of the car in a flash, throwing her arms around him. Nolie was more than a little jealous that he hugged her back.

Lorraine Giardello—Raine. So this was the woman Obie had rented Nolie's other cabin to. Definitely beautiful, shorter than she'd looked seated, probably five foot four, no more than five foot five without those ridiculous heels. Her red dress clung like a second skin and ended so high on the thigh that it would have been considered indecent in some places, and her black hair was cut in a sleek, sexy, breathtakingly short style. A Fiona clone? Nolie wondered uncharitably.

The woman was definitely happy to see Chase.

And vice versa.

Feeling invisible, Nolie took a step back, followed by another and another until she tumbled over the first of the porch steps and sat down hard on her butt on the third step. The sound of her falling and the grunt it knocked from her were enough to make them finally step apart and glance her way. She hoped the night was dark enough that they couldn't see the blush heating her face.

"Lorraine Giardello, this is Nolie Harper," Chase said. "She owns my cabin."

So it was Lorraine now, Nolie thought darkly. Was Raine a pet nickname only he was allowed to use? And that was the best description he could think of for her? *She owns my cabin?*

Lorraine didn't even teeter in the high heels and the soft dirt as she approached. "It's a pleasure to meet you, Nolie." Her handshake was firm, her skin extraordinarily soft. "That's an unusual name. Short for Magnolia?"

If her mother hadn't raised her better, she would have sent a killing look in Chase's direction . . . not that he would have noticed. His attention was all Lorraine's. Instead she forced a smile and said, "Nice to meet you," through gritted teeth and ignored the question about her name.

She was saved from spending another minute with them by the creak of an upstairs window. "Mama!" Micahlyn called out. "Me and Maria Diane are gonna take a bath, okay?"

Nolie scrambled to her feet. "I, uh, need to go," she said with a smile that kept slipping. Hurrying inside, she closed the door behind her, then leaned against it, listening for voices, car doors, the sound of the car driving away. The door actually vibrated against her back when the engine revved . . . or maybe that was just her heart thudding too hard in her chest.

She peeked out the curtain over the front window and saw taillights in front of Chase's cabin. They disappeared, and a moment later lights came on inside the cabin.

"Mama?" Micahlyn stood at the top of the stairs, naked except for pink-hearts underpants, holding the porcelain doll in her arms.

"I'm coming, babe," she said, and started up the stairs.

"Maria Diane does not need a bath—not now or ever, understand?"

"She does, too. See?"

When she reached the second floor, Nolie took the doll and held her to the light. Her porcelain face was garishly colored, courtesy of the play makeup kit Marlene had given Micahlyn, with the spillover splattered onto her once-exquisite white lace dress. Swallowing a curse, Nolie said, "You get into the tub. I'll take care of the doll." The doll who, incidentally, looked better with or without makeup than she did. Who had a nicer body than she'd ever had. Who had black hair and delicate features and was amazingly beautiful. Who made Nolie feel woefully inadequate.

Geez, *another* Fiona clone?

As Micahlyn climbed into the filling tub, Nolie went into her bedroom and laid the doll on the bed. She didn't turn the lights on, but walked to the window, looking toward the other cabin. Moonlight glinted on the Camaro, and more subdued light spilled out from the cabin's windows, but with the door closed and the drapes drawn, that was all she could see.

It was more than she wanted to see.

Chapter Nine

TELL ME ABOUT NOLIE."

Chase was in the kitchen, emptying ice cubes into a glass for Raine's soft drink, when she issued the request from the doorway. He'd left her a moment ago looking around the living room, though God knew, there was little enough to look at. A couch, a coffee table, one chair, a television. No pictures on the walls, no newspapers or books, nothing personal at all. Even the most observant person couldn't spend more than a few minutes observing in there.

"What about her?"

Raine came closer, walking with that easy, graceful stride men everywhere admired. She was the sort of woman who commanded attention wherever she went—like Fiona. Unlike Fiona, Raine didn't accept it as nothing more than her due. "Well, for starters, do you have a thing for her?"

"Define 'a thing.' "

"Hmm, evading questions. Interesting."

"Not evading. Clarifying."

"Right. Don't forget, Chase, I've watched you work. I know evasion when I see it, so knock it off." She smiled teasingly. "The court orders you to answer the question."

"I'm not under oath, so I can't be held to anything I say."

"So you'd want to lie to me about her. Ooh, interesting."

He handed her the drink, refilled the ice tray, and returned it to the freezer, then took a beer from the refrigerator. In the past week or so, his alcohol consumption had dropped to practically nil, and he hadn't had a craving for a cigarette all day. What did it mean that he wanted both now?

Truthfully, he didn't want to know.

"Nolie is—" He caught the beginnings of Raine's grin itching to form and scowled at her. "Don't laugh. She's a very nice woman."

"If you think I'd laugh at that, you must have mistaken me for Fiona. I happen to like very nice women. Hey, I happen to *be* a very nice woman."

"You'll get no arguments from me." He gestured toward the living room with his beer bottle, and she lazily strolled that way. With the same ease, she sat down in the chair and modestly crossed her legs—an amazing feat, considering how short her dress was. He slumped down on the sofa.

"So she's a nice woman who has a child? . . ."

"Micahlyn. She's five."

"Pretty, like her mother?"

When they'd first moved in, Chase remembered, he'd thought the kindest word to describe Micahlyn was homely. Long, frizz-prone red hair, ghostly white skin, and Coke-bottle glasses hadn't exactly matched his idea of pretty. But impressions changed. She'd stopped shrieking, scowling, or whining every time she'd seen him and started acting like the pampered but fairly well-behaved child she was, and somewhere along the line, he'd begun thinking of her as cute, with the potential for beauty someday. When had that happened?

"Yeah," he said at last. "Like her mother."

"Is there a husband and father in the picture?"

He shook his head. "He's dead."

"Jeez, too bad." After a moment, Raine's grin returned. "Well? What else? Tell me the good stuff."

"What do you consider good stuff?"

"Oh, I don't know. Like . . . have you gone out with her? Kissed her? Done the deed with her?"

Chase felt his face growing hot, and did his best to disguise from her what he was feeling. Hell, he didn't even know exactly what he was feeling. Embarrassment because she'd brought up the subject of sex? Uneasiness because he *wanted* to have sex with Nolie? Chagrin that she had read him so easily? "What makes you think we aren't just neighbors?"

"Call it woman's intuition—plus the fact that you two were obviously up to *something* out there in the dark when I arrived."

"We were talking."

"Uh-huh. I'll believe it if you want me to."

His need to change the subject was so strong that he didn't bother with finesse. "What brings you down here? Not that I'm not glad to see you, but it's a long drive for a chat."

"I had some vacation time and my plans fell through and I'd been wondering about you. I was afraid you'd hole up out here and forget to eat and withdraw from the human race. So . . . here I am."

He didn't tell her just how right she'd been—and would still be if not for Nolie. Raine would probably respond by becoming her newest best friend.

"What were your vacation plans?" he asked.

She gazed down at her glass, jiggling it just enough to make the ice cubes clink together. When she finally looked up again, there were shadows in her eyes. "Oh, nothing special. No great disappointment. Tell me, is there any place to stay in this town of yours besides the motel on the highway with the NO VACANCY sign?"

"I don't know. You can find out tomorrow if you want, and spend the night here."

"Uh-huh. And how will that look to Nolie?"

"It's not as if we have a . . . thing," he said, resorting to her word for lack of a better one.

"Oh, yes, you do. You just haven't found the nerve to do anything about it. Yet." She hid a yawn behind one hand. "But in any case, if you're offering me your couch, I'd be more than happy to accept."

"Then put on a smile." He slid to his feet and went to the hall closet to get clean linens, then grabbed the extra pillow off his bed. What was wrong with this picture? he thought grimly on his way back. He hadn't had sex in more than three years—so long he could hardly remember how good it had been. Finally a beautiful, sexy, sensual woman was spending the night with him, and he couldn't stir up even the slightest enthusiasm for a seduction attempt. Raine was exactly his type, and he thought he might have a better-than-even chance of succeeding if he did try to seduce her.

He just didn't want to.

Because she wasn't Nolie.

The screen door was just closing behind Raine when he got back to the living room. She tossed her car keys on the coffee table, then set a small suitcase on the floor next to it.

He gave her the bedding to use how she wanted, then retreated to the hallway. "If you need anything, just yell."

"Oh, if I need anything, I bet I can take care of it myself." She shook out one sheet over the sofa cushions and tucked it under, then spread out another sheet for cover.

"It's good to see you, Raine."

"I wasn't sure you would think so," she said, flashing him a smile. "I had visions of finding a wild-eyed crazy man and having to drag you back to Boston in chains."

If he looked up bogeyman in the dictionary, would *wild-eyed crazy man* come after *green, slimy, and lives in a mountain cave* or before?

"I'm only wild-eyed and crazy on Tuesdays." He should turn around now and go to his room. It was late. Raine was tired. Any other conversation could wait until the next day. But his brain refused to give the command, and he doubted his feet would have obeyed it just yet. There was one question he needed to ask first. "Do you . . . Have you heard anything about Fiona?"

Raine straightened, holding the pillow to her chest, and an expression uncomfortably close to pity clouded her eyes. "It's kind of hard to avoid hearing about her and Darren. For a wedding present, her father set him up as head of his own firm. With you out of the way, he gets the high-profile cases you always got, but he doesn't win as many of them. They still live in your—in the house you bought, and . . . she's pregnant. I'm sorry, Chase."

He knew those two words covered a lot. *I'm sorry the wife you loved two-timed you, sorry she broke your heart and divorced you, sorry you were wrongly convicted, and sorry she's carrying the baby you wanted but she would never agree to.* He was sorry about all those things, too, but he chose to interpret her words differently.

"Yeah, me, too. No kid should have to grow up with Fiona and Darren for parents." He smiled faintly. "Goodnight."

•   •   •

LORRAINE GIARDELLO SPENT THE NIGHT WITH Chase.

Nolie learned that first thing after a restless night by peeking out the window facing the other cabin, hoping against hope that the Camaro would be gone. Not only was it not gone, but Lorraine, hair tousled, barefooted, and wearing only an overly large T-shirt, was relaxing in the hammock with what appeared to be a cup of coffee. Even rumpled, she looked beautiful and sleek and satisfied.

And that T-shirt . . . Granted, Nolie wore one to sleep in, but Lorraine didn't strike her as the T-shirt type . . . unless it was the only thing handy to put on.

Chase, however, was the T-shirt type, and it was big enough to be his.

Nolie's scowl didn't fade the whole time she showered, dressed, rousted Micahlyn from bed, and fixed breakfast. She caught herself snapping at Micahlyn for dawdling over her cereal and had to apologize, then did it again when she sent her daughter upstairs to dress and Micahlyn returned in a church dress instead of play clothes.

"You're awful grumpy today," Micahlyn announced with a scowl of her own when she came back in shorts and a top. "Grandma never talks mean to me."

That was true. Marlene saved her mean talk for Nolie. Which was beside the point. "I'm sorry, babe. I didn't sleep well last night, and I *am* kind of grumpy." Grumpy. Not jealous, not hurt, not feeling rejected. Just cross due to lack of sleep. "Come on, let's get going or I'll be late for work."

"Wait a minute. I want to finish my toast in the car."

Nolie flushed guiltily. She'd rinsed their breakfast dishes while Micahlyn was changing clothes, and she'd seen no reason to waste an untouched piece of toast slathered with butter and homemade peach jam, so she'd . . . um, eaten it. After a week on her diet, it had tasted so good that she'd been tempted to sit down with the jam and a spoon and pig out.

"Mama!" Micahlyn wailed from the dining room. "You throwed my toast away!"

"Not exactly," Nolie murmured, then forced a smile. "Sorry, kiddo. But you know I clean up while you get dressed, so you should have told me to save it. Come on now. We've really got to go." She slung her purse over one shoulder, opened the door, and shooed her daughter outside, then hastily locked up.

She was determined not to look in the direction of the other cabin. She followed Micahlyn down the steps, her gaze on the ground, and unlocked the car door. Slide in, back out with only the barest of glances, then drive away, and she'd be safe.

She was too optimistic by half. She was about to get in the car when the banging of the screen door at the other cabin caught her attention. She didn't mean to look, honestly, but it was reflex, and once she'd looked, she couldn't turn away to save her life.

Chase stood on the porch, wearing jeans and no shirt, looking like he'd just rolled out of bed, and Raine was in his arms. He wasn't kissing her—that might have been easier to bear. No, his head was tilted back and he was laughing—*laughing* out loud. Nolie had coaxed a laugh from him *once,* and it had been at her own expense, when she'd told him she'd been named for a tree. The rest of the time she was lucky to catch him with a smile.

Apparently, Lorraine gave him more to laugh and smile about.

Her face burning, Nolie got in the car, cranked the

engine, and backed up without even a glance. But as she drove away, she couldn't resist looking in the rearview mirror.

They looked good together.

And she felt like a fool.

Micahlyn chattered nonstop as Nolie drove on auto-pilot to Angel Wings. She signed Micahlyn in, then kissed her good-bye before returning to the car. When she should have turned back toward the store, though, instead she made a detour past the bakery and bought her most favorite treat in the world—doughnut holes. Three dozen of them, still warm. She ate one dozen before she reached the store, giving herself twelve more reasons to feel rotten.

As the morning passed, she shared the remaining dough-nut holes with Trey, waited on customers, and brooded. Somehow she'd gotten the idea that Chase had been pretty much alone since his divorce. Not that she could blame it on anything he'd said. She'd just assumed the divorce had been difficult and he'd more or less mourned his loss until recently.

Obviously, that wasn't the case.

The surprise was that she was surprised. Hadn't she thought before, when they'd talked about Lorraine, that the woman must have been important to him? He hadn't said much—*Lorraine is very real*—but it was the way he'd said it. As if she was special. As last night had proven.

And here Nolie had been indulging in fantasies about being someone special to Chase herself. She was such an idiot.

Dimly she became aware of a steady gaze fixed on her. She gave herself a mental shake, then looked up to find Trey standing on the opposite side of the shelves from her. He grinned. "Have a nice trip?"

Puzzled, she raised her brows in silent question.

"You were obviously miles away. You've been straightening that same shelf for ten minutes." Coming around the corner, he took her by the shoulders and steered her toward the counter. "There aren't any customers at the moment, and I've done all the sweeping, dusting, and restocking that can be done. Sit down. Read a book. Listen to music. Or, hey, tell me what you want for lunch, and I'll go get it."

"I had two do—too many doughnut holes this morning." To say nothing of her own low-fat breakfast and her daughter's toast. "I think I should probably skip lunch. But you go ahead."

"Are you sure you don't want a burger and fries? Maybe a chocolate malt?"

Oh, she hadn't had a chocolate malt in longer than she could recall, and just the mention of it was enough to make her mouth water. But then she caught a glimpse of her reflection in the plate-glass window and regretfully sighed. "You're a kid. You'll burn off all those calories before dinnertime. But they'll spend eternity on my hips and thighs."

"Aw, you look fine. If you change your mind, you have my cell-phone number. Just let me know."

Watching him leave, she gave an affectionate shake of her head. Yeah, he could say she looked fine, because she was way too old for him. But it was probably a sure thing that when he looked at girls his own age, wondering who to ask to the next school dance, he didn't linger long on the overweight girls but went straight to the beautiful, thin, cheerleader types.

Just as Chase had completely forgotten lush Nolie last night, once beautiful, thin, sexy Lorraine arrived.

And speaking of Lorraine . . . It seemed the bell over the door announced her *after* she was already inside and halfway to the counter, robbing Nolie of the opportunity to duck into the back room. Instead, she was stuck, standing at the counter with no place to hide and nothing to do but watch as Lorraine moved far too gracefully toward her, arms full. "I come bearing food."

Nolie looked from her to the pizza boxes, then back again. Pizza was one of her many weaknesses, and these pies were steaming hot and fragrant enough to make a hungry woman weep. Under normal circumstances, she would have no desire to spend even one minute in the woman's company, but when she came offering pizza . . . that was a hard thing to turn down.

Setting the boxes on the counter, Lorraine lifted both lids, and the aromas actually made Nolie's mouth water. Weakness was definitely the right word to describe it. She couldn't possibly be hungry. She'd eaten—and eaten— only . . .

It was a few minutes after one, she saw with a glance at the clock. Six hours since breakfast and past lunchtime, and she *was* hungry, especially for something that smelled so incredible.

As if sensing she was wavering, Lorraine fanned the air above the pizzas with the napkins she'd brought. "I know good pizza when I see it—trust me, I'm Italian—and these look damn good. Surely you can eat a slice or two."

Or three or five.

"This one has everything but anchovies," Lorraine said, picking up a slice from one box, "and this one is vegetarian—Chase's favorite. But you probably know that."

Watching her bite into the pizza pushed Nolie way past wavering. Grudgingly, she gestured toward the stool at the end of the counter, then pulled up her own and reached for a slice of everything. It tasted as wonderful as it smelled.

"I tried to get Chase to come with me," Lorraine said,

"but you know how he is. He's so . . . determined not to risk running into his family."

"I would have said scared."

"I almost did," Lorraine said with a grin. "Do you see them often? I can't imagine a town this small has *that* many people with his last name."

"I don't really know." The urge to ask what his last name was, was almost too strong for Nolie to resist. With the help of a generous mouthful of pepperoni, Canadian bacon, onions, peppers, and cheese, she managed. Well, that, plus the fact that she wasn't about to admit to this total stranger just how little she knew about Chase.

"He doesn't talk about them much, does he? I swear, he knows just about everything about *my* family and I know zilch about his, aside from the fact that he has nothing to do with them."

At least she knew his last name. That still put Lorraine a big step ahead of her.

Oh, yeah, and she'd slept with him. That put her in, like, another realm or something.

Suddenly the pizza didn't taste so good, but Nolie finished the piece anyway and took a bite from another. It was what she did, all right? Comfort herself with food. It was stupid and unhealthy and had helped her right into a size sixteen, but the middle of a crisis of insecurity wasn't the best time to change.

"So . . . how well do you know him?" Lorraine was looking at her in a speculative way that made Nolie feel extremely exposed . . . and heavy . . . and scruffy.

"Not as well as *you* do." She hoped her expression was bland, but feared she was scowling again.

Lorraine's expression, on the other hand, was perfectly bland. "That sounded rather . . . hostile. Any particular reason?"

"I'm not hostile," Nolie muttered with a mouthful of pizza.

"Okay. Rather than hostile, how about jealous?"

"I'm *not* jealous."

"Because if you are, you have no reason to be. Chase and I are friends. We used to be more—he was my boss—but that ended over three years ago. I like him, respect him, and care about him a great deal, but not romantically. We're just friends."

Nolie gazed at the pizza, her need for food finally following her appetite's lead and disappearing. She wanted to believe Lorraine, but should she? Could she? Besides, *just friends* could mean different things to different people. Some friends slept together. Some got married. And not being romantically involved didn't automatically rule out being sexually involved.

"I slept on Chase's couch last night," Lorraine patiently went on, "only because the motel didn't have any vacancies. We've never had sex, never gone out on a date, never kissed, and never wanted to." She shrugged. "Just friends."

Maybe she was being honest, though Nolie couldn't imagine being as close to Chase as Lorraine apparently was and wanting nothing from him but friendship. She couldn't pinpoint exactly when she'd started wanting more, but it seemed like forever.

She wiped her hands on a napkin, walked to the trash can in the corner to throw it away, then slowly turned back and aimed for evasion. "I don't know why you think any of this matters to me."

Lorraine snorted. "So you wouldn't mind at all if I'd spent last night in Chase's bed instead of on his sofa?"

"What business would it be of mine?"

Again Lorraine subjected her to an intense study, then

abruptly gave a careless shrug. "Sure. Whatever you say. I guess I just read both of you wrong."

She wouldn't ask, she wouldn't ask, she wouldn't— Oh, hell. "What do you mean?"

Lorraine's smile was triumphant, but somehow it didn't seem as smug as it should. "Obviously he likes you."

The hopes she hadn't even been aware of rising dashed down again. "He's lonely and bored."

"Maybe. Probably. But if he didn't like you, he would rather be lonely and bored than spend time with you."

With a shrug, Nolie slid back onto her stool and rested her elbows on the counter.

"Besides, he said you were, and this is a direct quote, 'a very nice woman.' "

Oh, that was great. First he introduced her not as a friend or neighbor but as the woman who owned his cabin, and then he called her *a very nice woman*? He had a lot of nerve. That had probably been his way of letting Lorraine know he had zero interest in Nolie. He was just passing time with her until he left or the people in town discovered he was back or something forced him out of his solitude.

"You don't look pleased."

"You ever hear the phrase, 'damn with faint praise'?" Nolie asked dryly. "Jeez, isn't it every woman's dream to be told she's 'very nice'?"

"Oh, no, it's a compliment, really. I'm a very nice woman, too, so I know. You see, Chase's ex-wife was a whiny bitch who betrayed, manipulated, and two-timed him. She wounded his pride, cleaned him out financially, and broke his heart. What he needs now more than anything is a nice woman, one exactly the opposite of Fiona." She smiled brightly. "One like you."

"Why not one like you?"

"Because I'm pretty sure that kissing Chase would be like kissing my brother, if I had one." Lorraine made a dismissive gesture, as if the thought of getting romantically involved with him had truly never crossed her mind. She seemed so sincere, in fact, that Nolie was on the verge of believing her, whether it seemed reasonable or not.

But she wasn't on the verge of believing that the same thought hadn't crossed Chase's mind.

"Look, Lorraine—"

"Please call me Raine. Only my mother calls me Lorraine, and only when I'm in trouble."

Knowing that it wasn't Chase's pet name for her relieved Nolie more than she wanted to admit. "Okay, Raine, whatever I feel, whatever you think he feels, the bottom line is, I'm not his type."

The noise coming from the other woman was crude and unrefined, but got her point across perfectly. "I don't believe in types. You're nothing like Fiona, but he's attracted to you. I bet he's nothing like your husband, but you're still attracted to him."

That was true. Chase had graduated from college and law school while Jeff had barely squeaked through high school. The only future he'd ever wanted was on the farm, and the lessons he needed there weren't taught in the classroom. Chase had been an outstanding lawyer, with an outstanding income to match, while Jeff had worked long, hard hours for very little reward. Chase was handsome, wicked, with a hint of danger about him, while Jeff had been average in looks and as harmless, straightforward, and uncomplicated as a man could be. And yet she'd loved Jeff with all her heart and, with very little encouragement, she suspected she could care as much about Chase.

She half-wished Raine would stop offering encouragement.

In an effort to turn the subject away from herself, she asked, "If you have such an appetite for matchmaking, why haven't you made your own match?"

Raine's smile faded, and a look of such sorrow came across her face. Nolie wanted to call back the words, to apologize, or to hurriedly change the subject again, but in the end she quietly said, "Feel free to tell me it's none of my business. I won't take offense."

Before Raine had decided what to say, a customer came in to buy two fifty-pound bags of feed for his horses. Nolie rang up the sale and accepted his check, then offered to carry one of the bags to his truck. Like all her other male customers, he refused her help and went the added step of practically bristling at the suggestion he should let a woman do his heavy work for him.

"Chauvinism is alive and well," Raine commented once he'd hefted the second bag over his shoulder, then left with a wave.

"I grew up with men who considered it their responsibility to look out for the women in their lives, who were taught to open doors, hold chairs, and do the heavy lifting. I kind of like it." Then Nolie grinned. "At the same time, I lived my whole life on a farm, so I know I can do whatever's necessary myself if I have to."

Sliding from the stool, Raine roamed to one end of the counter. She paused a moment to study the quilt project Nolie kept there for slow times, read the copy on a stand-up display of irrigation nozzles, then gazed out the window at the woods and the highway that wound through them like a silver ribbon on its way out of the valley. When she finally spoke, her voice was soft, emotionless. "I told Chase I decided to come here when my vacation plans fell through. No place else to go, nothing else to do."

Quietly Nolie slid the remaining pizza into the box

with Chase's vegetarian pie, then threw the crusts, crumbs, and greasy napkins away. That done, she circled the counter, but stopped a half-dozen feet from Raine.

"Truth is, more than my vacation fell through. My fiancé has been working in Raleigh for the past three months. He's a computer whiz with a big consulting firm— a good Italian boy whom my family loves almost as much as they love me. When he first got to North Carolina, he invited me down this month for a couple of weeks, to visit and finalize the wedding plans, but . . ."

There should be some law against stories with a "but," Nolie thought. So very little that was good ever followed a "but."

Raine turned back, wearing an unsteady smile. "When I got there, he realized he'd forgotten to tell me he had met someone else and that planning *our* wedding would be a bit of a problem, because, well, gee, he'd already planned his wedding with *her*. It happens in two weeks."

"I'm sorry."

"You know, I hadn't heard much from him since he went down there, but he's lousy at writing letters and too cheap for long-distance calls. His E-mails seemed a little abrupt and less affectionate, but some people don't communicate as well via E-mail as they do in person." She shrugged again. "Anyway, I flew back to Boston, but I couldn't face my family just yet, so I picked up my car and came here. So, you see, I definitely don't have anything going with Chase besides friendship, because I'm never getting involved with another man as long as I live . . . or until I get really desperate."

"I really am sorry."

Raine nodded, then gazed around, looking at last at the pizza box. "Oh, God, I can't believe I ate all that pizza. The night the jerk dumped me, I checked into a motel, then went shopping at the strip center across the street. I had ice cream, M&Ms, Oreos, and enough takeout from the Chinese restaurant there to feed three ravenous football players. All I could think was that I'd outgrow the wedding dress hanging in my closet or die trying. Looks like I'm still trying."

On the one hand, Nolie was comforted to know that Raine found the same solace in food that she did. On the other, the fact that Raine controlled her eating so much more successfully than Nolie reminded her of the diet she'd blown that morning and made her feel like a failure all over again.

After a few deep breaths, Raine came to the counter and reached for the pizza box. All the hurt and sadness were gone from her expression, leaving her looking warm, friendly, and without a care in the world. "Can we have dinner tonight? You, me, your daughter, and Chase? As you know, he won't go to a restaurant in town, so it would have to be a home-cooked meal, and as you also know, he doesn't have much in the way of furniture, so it would probably have to be at your house. Don't you like that?" she asked with a laugh. "A near stranger inviting herself and a friend to dinner at your home? But I'll provide the food, help with the cooking, and do the cleanup."

"Sure. I'll take care of the food, but I'll gladly let you clean up. How about seven?" Nolie agreed, not because she wanted to have dinner with Chase. Not because she'd missed him or anything like that. Because she was a neighborly person and cooking for four wasn't much more work than cooking for two. And because—a sly voice whispered in her mind—she wanted to see Chase and Raine together, to see for herself whether there was anything between them. She was *this* close to believing Raine had no interest in him, but she couldn't feel entirely comfortable until she knew *he* had no interest in *her.* Before she risked any more of herself than she already had, she wanted promises. Guarantees.

A sure thing.

That wasn't so much to ask, was it?

THOUGH HE WAS ACCUSTOMED TO WORKING ALL kinds of hours, Cole Jackson felt an unusual sense of relief when he walked into the house late Saturday afternoon. He left his briefcase on the hall table, loosened his tie, then shrugged out of his jacket on the way to the kitchen, where he got a beer and a slice of pizza left over from last night's dinner.

"How'd it go?"

Looking over his shoulder, he saw Ryan leaning against the door frame. The kid wore jeans that were two inches too short and a T-shirt that was stretched to the max, and his brown hair looked as if he'd combed it with a mixer. "Didn't I just buy those clothes two months ago?"

Ryan shrugged. "I'm growing."

"Yeah, well, stop it. Keeping you in clothes that fit is gonna break me."

"So . . . how did it go? The meeting with the doctors?"

Cole grinned. "We have four new investors."

"Which brings the total to? . . ."

"About $180,000."

Ryan gave a whoop, then came closer, pulling the beer from Cole's hand. He had the bottle lifted to his mouth when Cole swiped it back. "Sorry. You miss the minimum drinking age by nine years."

"So what? I've had beer before."

"Not in Bethlehem. You drink here, and they'll throw me in jail."

"It's not as if you haven't been there before," the boy scoffed.

"Youthful indiscretions," Cole said, then sternly added, "and I don't plan to go there again. What are you doing home? I thought you were going to play baseball at the park with those kids you met the other day."

"We played. I've been back since two o'clock."

"Any problems?"

"Why do you always assume I'm causin' problems?" Ryan shoved his hand through his hair, making it stand on end. "We played ball for a couple hours, then they was all goin' to a party for some girl they know. I wasn't invited 'cause, hey, I never *met* her, so I came home. No big deal." He grabbed a piece of pizza from the box, crammed half of it in his mouth, and stalked out of the room.

No big deal. Cole knew better. His old man had kept them on the move a lot, and he'd always been the new kid in town, the one who didn't have any friends or get invited to any parties. If he made the mistake of actually finding a friend, before long his dad always moved them on, and he had to start all over again. He'd learned by the time he was Ryan's age that it was better to always be the outsider than to keep leaving people he cared for behind.

Ryan had learned that lesson pretty well, too. But, damn it, what could Cole do? His line of work required him to relocate frequently. He couldn't turn Ryan over to his mother, since no one knew where the hell she'd gone after abandoning him at a St. Louis bus station. This time he'd tried leaving him with his dad in Philadelphia, so the kid could finish the school year, but that had lasted only six days—five, if you didn't count the day he'd spent on the bus to Bethlehem.

Of course, he could look for a new line of work. Too bad this was the only thing he knew how to do.

Wearily, Cole climbed the back stairs to the second floor, then went down the broad hall to his room, situated at the front of the house. He changed into pleated and pressed khaki shorts and a knit shirt, wishing for a moment he could dig out his favorite pair of faded, ripped cutoffs, then went to the window to look out.

He ignored the back view of the courthouse and the wedge of the square and instead looked straight across the street. On eye level was Leanne Wilson's bedroom. If he lowered his gaze to ground level, he could see inside her shop, to the sofa and love seat where she often sat when the shop wasn't busy. As luck would have it, where she was sitting right now.

Impulse sent him to the nightstand, where an old-fashioned rotary phone sat atop a Bethlehem phone book. It took longer to dial the shop's number than it did to look it up in the slim volume. He stretched the phone cord back to the window and watched as Leanne picked up the cordless phone from the cushion beside her on the first ring.

"Small Wonders. This is Leanne."

"I can see that."

She straightened, looked around, then peered in his direction. Rising from the sofa, she walked to the plate-glass window and raised one hand in a wave. "I thought you worked all the time."

"Sometimes it seems that way. You're not one to talk, though. You're in the store six days a week yourself."

"But I have a child to support."

"So do I." He thought of Ryan sulking downstairs and felt a twinge of guilt that he wasn't doing a better job at taking care of him. "You have plans tonight?"

"Yeah. An easy dinner—probably frozen—followed by a whole evening of doing nothing. No cleaning, no dealing with customers, no paperwork."

"I know an easier dinner, and it'll taste better, too. Why don't you and your son come over and eat with Ryan and me? I'll do all the cooking—steaks, baked potatoes, whatever. All you'll have to do is sit and watch and eat."

A smile curved her lips. "You know how to cook?"

"I've been doing it since I was ten."

"What about your mother?"

"Didn't have one." At least, not much of one. Her name was Eloise, and she'd been in and out—mostly out—of their lives for as long as he could remember. She and his father were like oil and water, or gasoline and fire. They couldn't get along together but couldn't stay apart. In their times together they'd had six sons, who'd pretty much raised one another in their times apart. "Why don't you and Danny come over around six-thirty?"

"Sounds great. We'll see you then." She disconnected, waved, then turned away from the window.

Whistling softly, Cole ran down the elaborately carved main staircase and, on his way to the kitchen, stopped at the living room, where Ryan was sprawled on the couch, watching a ninja movie. "Hey, kid, I need you to go to the grocery store."

With a sigh, Ryan followed Cole into the kitchen where he was making a shopping list. "For what?"

"We're having company for dinner. I need you to pick up some stuff."

"Who?"

"Leanne and her son."

Ryan leaned against the island. "You looking to get her into your investments or your bed?"

"Everyone's a prospective client."

"And every pretty woman is a prospective one-night stand, too."

Cole gave him a wounded look. "Not every pretty

woman, and rarely just for one night. Besides, haven't we had this conversation before? The one where I remind you that my sex life is none of your business?"

"Yeah, yeah, yeah. I suppose it'll be my job to entertain her kid."

"I suppose so." Cole handed him the shopping list, then pulled two fifties from his wallet. "Pay for everything this time, would you? And bring me some change."

"Jeez, I shoplifted *one* thing, and you never let me forget it."

"*One thing?* You stole enough books—though, granted, one at a time—to create your own library." Though he'd never admitted it, Cole had been relieved it was just books Ryan had taken from the variety store near their apartment in Cleveland. It would have been just as easy for him to walk out with knives or even a gun from the sporting goods section, or with drugs from the pharmacy or cash from an unwatched register.

Rolling his eyes, Ryan stuffed the list and the money in his pocket. "I'll be back soon—with a receipt *and* your change."

Cole felt another twinge of guilt as he watched the kid leave. Maybe he wasn't helping any by treating Ryan more like a grown-up than a kid, though a grown-up he could still boss around. The trouble was, the kid had never been much of a kid. His mother had never been much of a mother—that seemed to be a common complaint—and she'd left him pretty much on his own since he was little. By the time he'd come to live with Cole, he'd already skipped childhood. He'd been a thirty-year-old in a nine-year-old body, and he hadn't gotten any more childlike as he got older.

Maybe that was something Leanne could help him with.

Then he thought of her, of the time they'd spent dancing a week before, of the way he'd kissed her goodnight in the Starlite parking lot and how she'd kissed him back, and he grinned.

Ryan was only one of many things Leanne could help him with.

And he sure intended to ask.

Chapter Ten

WHEN CHASE AND RAINE ARRIVED AT Nolie's a few minutes after seven, Micahlyn greeted them at the door. "Mama's out back," she announced through the screen door. "She says we can eat outside 'cause it's a pretty night, and 'sides, her quilt stuff's all over the dining table."

"Do we get to come in, or do you want us to walk around the house?" he asked.

The kid somberly looked from him to Raine before shifting her dolls to her other arm, then unlatching the screen door. "Who are you?" The question was directed to Raine, and Chase left her to answer it and headed for the kitchen.

He wasn't too eager to see Nolie, was he?

"I thought *he* was the bogeyman," Micahlyn was saying as he turned the corner into the kitchen. "He was scary and mean-looking, and—"

Nolie was just coming in the back door. Her hair was up on her head in that style that shouldn't possibly be sexy but was, and her dress was soft, summery, and reached almost all the way to her bare feet. She stopped short when she saw him, tucked a loose tendril of hair behind her ear, then moved to the sink. "Hi."

It took a couple of tries to get out a simple response. "Hi." Then he cleared the huskiness from his voice. "Micahlyn says we're eating outside so you won't have to clean off the dining table."

"Why, that—" She gave him a warning look. "She did not."

"No, she didn't. But she gave that impression." He stopped beside the counter, where six quilt blocks were laid out. It took him a moment to figure out the pattern, but once he did, he recognized it as the same pattern of the quilt on her bed. Where that one was done in pastels, the colors of this one were richer—burgundy, hunter green, navy-blue, rich purple. "Pretty. Who is it for?"

Finally she dared come closer, gathering up the squares and moving them to the table to join other pieces and yardages of the same fabric. "It's not necessarily for anyone. I just like to quilt." But there was a flush in her cheeks, making him wonder if just maybe she'd started the quilt with him in mind.

"Where is Raine?"

He looked over his shoulder into the living room, but it was empty. "I guess she and Micahlyn went upstairs."

"She probably made the mistake of pretending an interest in Micahlyn's dolls, so now she'll get to meet the whole family—and there's a lot of them. Mostly blond, buxom, and beautiful."

When she would have walked past him to the kitchen, he caught her wrist. "Some people don't care for blond and buxom."

The color in her cheeks deepened. "True. Some prefer dark and petite."

Like Fiona. Like Raine. "And some like red hair and curves."

The comment surprised him almost as much as her. He hadn't known where he was going with the conversation, and didn't know why he'd chosen that path. But he wouldn't take the words back even if he could. Why would he, when they were true?

Now her face was crimson, the color extending underneath the rounded neckline of her dress. Her pulse beat against his fingertips, and her breathing grew shallow and uneven.

After a moment, she regained her composure and gently freed her wrist. "I need to check on . . ." Without finishing, she grabbed a stack of plates and silverware and disappeared outside again.

Chase went to the sink to watch her through the window. The patio table was covered with a green gingham cloth that went well with the green-striped cushions on the chairs, and Nolie was setting four places around the table. He'd bet money she would put Raine and Micahlyn between them if she could. But that was all right. It would leave him directly across from her, and he liked looking at her.

The aroma of warm, fresh bread drew his attention to the stove. The towel-covered basket held rolls, kept warm by the heat of the mushroom gravy simmering on the front burner and the red potatoes on the back. Steaks were marinating in a dish nearby, a corn-onions-and-peppers dish sat next to them, and some sort of flaky pastry was cooling on a wire rack next to the oven.

Raine hadn't suggested dinner until early that afternoon, and Nolie had worked until six, picked up Micahlyn, gone to the grocery store, and gotten all this done. He was impressed. The only thing Fiona could make for dinner in an hour or less was reservations.

Nolie came back inside. That strand of hair had fallen again, and he thought about brushing it back—hell, about kissing it back. But if he kissed her once, he wouldn't stop until he'd done it again and again and dinner would be ruined and he . . . he would be lost.

Or found.

"I don't suppose you've ever grilled steaks before," she remarked, her tone making it clear she knew the answer.

"Nope. But you can teach me."

"Grab the meat and those tongs." She gestured with a bottle of ketchup, then picked up two bottles of steak sauce, plus salt and pepper shakers.

It was a warm evening, the sun low on the horizon, the air still and fragrant with the scent of pines and, the instant she placed the steaks on the grill, the hunger-inducing aroma of beef cooking.

"Do you know how Raine likes hers?"

"Medium."

"And yours?"

"Rare."

She went to the table to arrange the bottles in the center, then turned back, hands on her hips. "I don't imagine many men remember how their former secretaries like their steaks."

"Raine was as much a friend as a secretary. Probably the only real friend I had in Boston."

She hesitated, bit her lip, then quietly asked, "Just a friend?"

He watched the flames leap and sizzle from the meat drippings before glancing at her. "Maybe it takes someone who doesn't have many friends to understand how important they are. No, not *just* a friend. But not a girlfriend, not a lover. A very good friend who stood by me when things went wrong, when no one else did."

She came a few steps closer. "What things?"

It was an excellent opening to tell her the last of his secrets. How someone he worked with, someone he'd probably considered a friend of sorts, had embezzled more than a million dollars from the firm. How whoever it was had planted evidence to make *him* look guilty. How he'd been trapped so thoroughly, the second-best defense lawyer in Boston—he'd been the best, of course—hadn't had a chance in hell of winning an acquittal. How he'd spent six hundred and ninety-three days in prison.

In his first months in prison, he'd lived for the day he could get out and somehow prove his innocence. He'd wanted revenge against whoever had set him up, wanted to make them, and everyone who hadn't believed in him, pay dearly. Six months inside, though, and he'd forgotten about clearing his name and seeking revenge. What good would it do? It wouldn't win Fiona back. It wouldn't make him forget all the people who'd thought he was guilty. It wouldn't give him back the six hundred and ninety-three days he'd been locked up, or his career, or his good name.

Vengeance wouldn't give him back Nolie once she found out the whole truth.

When he answered, he offered only a partial truth. What things had gone wrong? she wanted to know. "Fiona. The divorce."

And that bit of truth satisfied her, because she thought he was being honest. She trusted him. That made him feel lower than dirt.

But it didn't make him pour out the rest. "How was business today?"

"Steady."

"How's the kid working out?"

"Trey's great."

He walked to the table and poured lemonade from the

pitcher into one of three matching glasses filled with ice. There was a plastic cup with a lid for Micahlyn, pink-and-white with Barbie dolls smiling from its sides. Stopping in front of Nolie, he took a long drink, then remarked, "We can't have a conversation if all your answers are going to be two syllables or less. You want to try again?"

The smile she gave him was meant to be mocking but was tempered by too much sweetness. "Business was fine—not too busy, not too slow. Time to get things done, but not enough time to sit and pray for six o'clock to crawl around. And Trey's working out great. He's sweet, funny, reliable, responsible, and a good worker. Even though *someone* thought I should have hired some guy full-time, I couldn't ask for a better employee than Trey."

"Smart ass."

Surprise flashed across her face, then she smiled. "You asked for it."

"Is that your policy—ask and you shall receive?" He gave her a long look from head to toe, then smiled. "I'll have to keep that in mind."

She turned pink from head to toe. "I, uh . . . the steaks need to be turned. I'll, uh . . ." She gestured toward the house, then bolted.

Chase flipped the steaks, rested the tongs in the dish, and gazed off to the west. For the first time in longer than he wanted to remember, he felt utterly, totally, completely contented. It was a simple thing—spending the evening with Nolie, Raine, and Micahlyn, grilling steaks, watching dusk descend—but he couldn't think of anyplace else he would rather be, or anyone else he'd rather be with. The only thing he would change would be the inevitable end to the evening. He would much rather spend tonight—and a few thousand more—with Nolie than alone.

When the back door creaked open, it wasn't just Nolie,

but a parade of females bearing dishes. Micahlyn came first, clutching the corn dish in both hands. Behind her was Raine, carrying serving spoons plus the potatoes. Nolie brought up the rear with the bread basket, a tub of butter, and the mushroom gravy. As soon as she set her load down at the table, she came to the grill and moved two of the four steaks to the edge.

"Reinforcements?" he murmured.

She replied in an equally soft voice. "I didn't ask them to come out. I simply told them dinner's ready."

"You lied."

"That's such an ugly word. I, ah, overestimated how quickly you could finish their steaks."

"Oh, sure, blame it on me."

"What are you two whispering about over there?" Raine asked.

Chase and Nolie both turned to look at her. While they'd talked, Raine had none too subtly rearranged the settings at the square table. Instead of seating one person per side, now it was set up for two on one side, two opposite, and she and Micahlyn had claimed the two seats opposite.

He grinned. Nolie looked more than a little wary.

"We're not whispering," he replied. "We're talking softly. And if we wanted you to hear, we would have raised our voices."

"Ooh, personal, private, *intimate* conversation," Raine teased. "Maybe Micahlyn and I should have stayed inside a while longer."

He chided her. "Don't embarrass your hostess."

"I'm not embarrassed," Nolie denied. Then, apparently feeling the blush the others could see so clearly, she shrugged. "It's just the heat from the grill."

"Uh-huh. Of course." Raine was grinning broadly, like

a proud Italian mama who'd been proven right for the thousandth time.

Saved by the steak. That was the first thought in Chase's mind when Nolie gratefully declared the last two pieces done, transferred them to a serving dish, then took them to the table. "Raine, you should probably let me sit next to Micahlyn," she suggested as she dished the steaks onto their plates. "I'll have to cut her meat, and she sometimes spills stuff."

"Oh, I'm used to eating with kids," Raine replied. "I've got four nieces and three nephews, and I still get stuck at the kids' table at family dinners. Can I cut your meat for you, Micahlyn?"

"Yes, please," the kid answered, earning an eye roll from her mother.

"Nice try," Chase murmured as Nolie sat down next to him. He earned a scowl from her.

The food was outstanding, and so was the company. By the time they finished, darkness had fallen, leaving only the light above the door to illuminate the patio. For a few minutes, they sat in silence, until finally Raine groaned. "Oh, Nolie, you are an excellent cook, and Chase, you're a good helper."

"And Raine 'n' me are gonna be good cleaners, ain't we?" Micahlyn added.

"Yes, ma'am. As soon as I can move."

Micahlyn sprawled back in her chair, trying to mimic Raine's relaxed position. "Mama, does this mean you're off your diet and we can eat real food again?"

Nolie gave her own groan. "Don't mention the word diet. After two weeks of doing so well, I totally blew it today."

"Woo-hoo! No more diet!" Micahlyn practically swooned. "We can have fried chicken again!"

Raine straightened. "Do you fry your own chicken, Nolie? Hell, Chase, marry this woman so I can eat someone's fried chicken besides the Colonel's."

From the corner of his eye, he saw Nolie lower her gaze abruptly as if the mention of marriage made her uncomfortable. And why not? It made *him* damn uncomfortable. After the divorce, he'd sworn he would never marry again, and he'd meant it. Fiona had provided him with enough misery to last a lifetime. He would never go looking for more.

And even if he did, he wouldn't go looking with Nolie. She wasn't his type. He wasn't hers. She was staying in Bethlehem. He wasn't. She needed another husband like Jeff, and Micahlyn needed another father like Jeff, while he needed . . . he needed . . .

Not to get involved in a relationship that had no future. Not to get himself hurt again. Not to hurt Nolie.

But not getting involved, not getting hurt or doing the hurting, would require strength he wasn't sure he had. He didn't think he could stay away from her. All he knew for sure he could do was regret what happened after the fact.

"I have a suggestion." Raine leaned her arms on the tabletop, and beside her Micahlyn did the same. "It's such a pretty evening. Why don't you two take the Camaro, put the top down, and go for a leisurely drive while Micahlyn and I put away and clean up and play with her dolls?"

"You don't have to do that," Nolie said at the same time Chase said, "All right." She gave him a warning look, then went on with her protest. "I can help with the cleanup, and heaven knows, you don't have to play dolls—"

"But, Mama, she likes dolls," Micahlyn broke in. "D'you know she has an old, old, old Barbie doll from when she was a little girl?"

"Honey, I'm not *that* old," Raine gently corrected her. "But I do play with dolls. I told you, Nolie, I have seven nieces and nephews. I play dolls, war games, video games—you name it. They think I'm the coolest aunt in the world. You guys, go on, have fun. Micahlyn and I will take care of everything, won't we?"

Micahlyn's enthusiastic yes was the push Nolie needed. She rose from her chair and picked up a handful of dishes. "All right. But we won't be gone long."

"Oh, honey, you're both adults. You can stay out all night if you want," Raine said with a wink.

Chase would vote for that.

Even if it might be the worst mistake he'd ever made.

A NYWHERE IN PARTICULAR YOU WANT TO GO?"
Nolie glanced across the small car at Chase. They were sitting at the end of the driveway, the highway in front of them stretching off in either direction. They could turn left and climb out of the valley, could drive for miles passing occasional houses but not find another town until they reached Howland. Or they could turn right and be in Bethlehem in a matter of minutes. "You decide."

She expected him to go left. When he didn't, she directed a surprised look his way but didn't say anything. She just settled back in the plush leather seat and relaxed.

The engine sounded like a powerful, undomesticated cat—loud and rumbly. The car was one of the last Camaros made, Raine had told her, and she intended to keep it forever, or until Chevrolet came to their senses and started production again, whichever came first. Though Nolie had never developed that kind of attachment to any vehicle, she could understand it. The car was sleek, flashy, and drew more than its share of attention—rather like Raine herself.

Amazingly, Chase drove right through the heart of

Bethlehem—but not so surprisingly, when they reached the far edge of town, he didn't turn around but kept on going. The road climbed and twisted its way up the mountain. Where it went, she had no idea, since she'd never gone as far as the town limits on this side, but the traffic was sparse, as were the road signs.

After six, maybe eight, miles, he slowed, then turned onto a narrower road. It was paved but, judging from its condition, saw little use and less maintenance. He had to drive slow enough to dodge potholes, a few of which looked capable of swallowing the Camaro whole. She didn't mind the lack of speed, though, because the night was so comfortably cool and the stars were twinkling overhead and the absence of the rushing wind made conversation possible. "Where are we going?"

"There's a lake up here. It's one of the few places around here I remember . . ."

"Fondly?" she suggested.

His only response was a shrug.

"Did you come here often when you were growing up?"

"Some."

"With your family? Your friends? Your girlfriends?"

"My family never did much of anything together, besides go to church, which was pretty much a joke. We fought constantly—at least, my father and I did—but we were in church every Sunday morning and, by God, we pretended to be happy."

"In avoidance mode, are we?" Nolie injected a teasing note into her voice but deliberately kept it gentle.

"I'm not avoiding anything. I'm answering in the order you asked. That covers family, so . . . yeah, I came here with friends a lot. We'd camp out, drink, go skinny-dipping." The dashboard lights combined with the moon-

and starlight to illuminate his grin. "Want to give that a try when the water's warmer?"

Now there was a thought to make a woman hot. She'd never been skinny-dipping in her life—she was too modest by far—but the idea of a hot summer's night, of stripping off her clothes and slipping into the cool water, of watching him do the same . . . She could use a cold shower just thinking about it. With her luck, she would be thinking about it in bed tonight . . . and tomorrow night . . . and the next . . . and all the while, she would be alone.

Who needed a cold shower when she could face cold reality instead?

"You'd better watch it," she warned quietly. "One of these days you're going to say something like that and I'm going to take you up on it, and then what are you going to do?"

He brought the car to a stop so slowly she hardly realized it, then turned to meet her gaze head-on. "Probably get down on my knees and thank God, and then make sure you don't regret it."

She couldn't breathe—couldn't swallow, couldn't move. He looked so damned serious and sounded it, too, and she felt . . . exhilarated. Touched. Wary. Unsure. Cautious. Bewildered. "Don't-don't say things like that unless you-you mean them."

"I never do," he replied, still deadly sincere. After a long moment, he broke the contact and gestured ahead. "We're here."

While she was trying to get a grip on her emotions and shake off the daze that had settled over her, he got out, circled the car, and opened her door. Feeling suddenly clumsy at the prospect of getting out of the small, low-to-the-ground vehicle, she swallowed hard, took the hand he offered, and let him help her out, and without stumbling, struggling, or stepping on his foot even once.

The road ended in a clearing with the lake spread out before them and a grassy area in between. There were three concrete picnic tables and benches evenly spaced around the grass, and what looked like a beach straight ahead. Up close it wasn't the most inspiring sight she'd ever seen, but the lake beyond, with the night-dark woods snugged close to its shores, with a few rugged bluffs across the way and the moon and stars reflected in its smooth surface, was really very lovely.

She started toward the center table and Chase, still holding her hand, came along. Once they were seated on the cement, still warm from the day's sun, she sneaked a glance at him. "You never finished answering my question."

"Questions," he pointed out. "I answered two."

"Did you bring your girlfriends here?"

"Yeah. A few times. Where did you and Jeff go when you wanted to be alone?"

"The back forty. The hayloft. The usual places you'd expect two farm kids to hide out." She said it with a grin, only half-teasing. "Truth was, we didn't need a lot of privacy. We didn't . . . ah, do anything until our wedding night."

"And you've never been with anyone else."

He wasn't asking but stating, so sure of himself. She didn't know whether to feel insulted or complimented. Did he think she would have a tough time attracting very many men, or only that she wasn't the type to engage in indiscriminate sex? Deciding to believe the latter, she shook her head.

"I haven't been with anyone since Fiona. I went to Howland one night, fully intending to pick up the first woman I saw, just to—to take the edge off, but I wound up going home alone. Do you want to know why?"

Oh, she did, almost as much as she was afraid to. She wasn't like other women, confident women, who flirted and expected nothing less than the attention they got from men. She wasn't accustomed to discussing sex with men, and she certainly wasn't accustomed to tantalizing statements—*get down on my knees and thank God, and then make sure you don't regret it*—from men like him.

He shifted on the table to face her. "Because they were the wrong women. They weren't you."

Nolie didn't have a clue how to react—whether to look at him or speak, whether to laugh as if he surely must be teasing or to brush him off. She wound up nervously combing her hair back, then pressing both hands between her knees. Her fingers all but disappeared in the soft folds of fabric, then knotted tightly. "I . . . I don't know . . ." She drew a deep breath that straightened her shoulders, then faced him. "I don't know what to say to that."

A ghost of a smile crossed his mouth. "Well, you didn't shriek in dismay and run away. That's a good start."

There was humor in his voice, but she didn't share it. Heat warmed her cheeks and butterflies tumbled in her stomach. She was, by turns, aroused, excited, and unsure. For the next few moments she wanted to be someone different—bold, daring, confident. She wanted to take what she wanted, to offer what she thought he wanted.

But she didn't know how to be anyone but Nolie McVie Harper. Never bold or daring and rarely confident.

Bless him, he changed the subject and eased the tension holding her stiff . . . as well as fueled the disappointment that pumped through her veins. "What's that constellation?"

She followed the line of his pointing finger up into the

sky. It was impossible to know exactly which stars he was pointing at, but she dryly made the obvious guess. "You mean the Big Dipper?"

That quick smile came and went again. "It's the only constellation that actually looks like what it's supposed to be, to me."

"Me, too," she admitted. "I figure the others were named by wildly creative people. Their minds must have been frightening places."

"Do you wish on stars?"

"Every night," she murmured. "When I was growing up, my parents each had their own bedtime routine with me. Mom would read to me and listen to my prayers, and Dad would wish on stars with me. We'd choose the biggest, brightest star and say the rhyme *Star light, star bright, . . .* and when we got to the wish part, we closed our eyes and said our wishes silently." She gave him a side-long look. "Otherwise, you know, they don't come true."

"What kind of things did little Magnolia wish for?"

"That no one would ever find out my real name. That someday Daddy would change his mind and let me have a horse. That I wouldn't have to wear my braces as long as the orthodontist said and my hair would magically turn brown and my skin would tan. Silly things."

She sneaked another look at him and wondered if he was sitting closer than he'd been before and, if he was, which of them had moved. She didn't remember either of them shifting position while she'd stared at the sky, but now he was close enough to touch. To sway a little to the right and bump. To hear the steady in-and-out of his breathing.

He was close enough that no effort would be required to lean across and kiss him. Just the slightest of movements, and gravity would do the rest.

Or was that chemistry?

"Tell me about your family." She didn't realize she'd even thought the words until she heard them in her own voice. Breath caught, she waited, half-expecting him to pull away, to grow stiff and distant and dismiss her request out of hand.

He did pull away, but not far—just got to his feet, then held out his hand to her. She accepted it, stepped to the ground, then followed him across the grass to the water's edge. The beach wasn't much of a beach—a strip of sand about ten by fifty feet. Just past the distant end, the remains of an old dock glistened in the shallow water.

They stood on the sand, softly lit by the moon, and watched the water's surface ripple as it lapped against the shore. Occasionally a fish plopped, and somewhere distant a boat putt-putted along. It was a perfect moment, a perfect night, a perfect place.

And Chase made it even more so when he tugged her down on the sand beside him, then finally broke his silence. "There's not much to tell. My father sells insurance, my mother is a housewife, and my sister is two years younger than me."

"What was she like?" While waiting for him to choose the answer he would share, she slipped off her shoes and wriggled her toes into the cool sand. This would be a lovely place to spread a quilt on a hot summer's evening, to share with a handsome man, a cooler of icy drinks, and, hanging in the nearby trees, a melodic set of chimes. Or to come on a chilly winter night, to build a fire and roast wieners and marshmallows and enjoy the heavy fragrance of woodsmoke. Either instance would, of course, call for snuggling and cuddling, for kissing and petting and making love under the stars.

The longing the images stirred inside made her sigh aloud.

Lying back, Chase pillowed his head on his hands and gazed at the sky. "She was Daddy's little princess. Pretty, smart, reasonably adept at wrapping both parents around her little finger. She was everything they wanted her to be . . . and I was nothing they wanted me to be."

Nolie's only goal for Micahlyn was for her to be happy. Whether she went to college or not, whether she had a career or a minimum-wage job or stayed home and took care of her family . . . all that mattered was that she be satisfied with her choices. That was all any parent should want for their children. Why had it been too much to ask of Chase's parents?

"The more my father tried to mold me into his image, the more I resisted being molded. The madder he got, the more rebellious I got and the more upset my mother became, because he was one tough bastard to live with in a good mood. In a bad mood, he was damn near unbearable." He gave a shake of his head. "When I left home, I didn't have a clue how I was gonna make it. I was eighteen, and the only money I had was what I'd made at a summer job after graduation, and my father had made it clear he wasn't wasting anymore of his hard-earned cash on me. Even so . . . the sense of relief that I was finally free was incredible."

Nolie shivered with a chill that came from the inside out. She'd loved her parents dearly, and they'd doted on her. She couldn't begin to imagine the person she would be if not for their love and influence. She couldn't believe the man Chase had become without that sort of love and support.

His fingers curled around her wrist. "If you're cool, come down here and I'll keep you warm."

She gazed down at him, smiling, and shook her head. If she let him warm her, they would probably spontaneously combust, and who would take care of Micahlyn then?

"Are you afraid?" One fingertip pressed against her pulse, measuring her heartbeat, before he rubbed his fingers sensuously over her skin.

"Heavens, yes. I'm an intelligent woman. How could I not be?"

"Of what? Me? Or yourself?" His hand closed in a tight but gentle grip around her arm, and he began pulling her to the ground. If she really struggled, she could free herself . . . but she couldn't find the energy, or the desire, to struggle. Instead, she let him draw her closer.

"Neither," she lied. "I just think . . ."

He settled her against his side, her head on his shoulder, his arm around her. He didn't try to pull her on top of him, didn't try to touch her intimately or do anything inappropriate at all. He simply held her.

That was one of the things she'd missed most since Jeff died.

"You just think what?"

She wet her lip with her tongue. "I think you're bored. And I'm not your type. And we want different things. And you could break my heart. And we don't even play the same games."

For a moment, he stiffened. She could feel it everywhere they touched. Then, with a deep breath, he deliberately relaxed again. "I'm not bored."

Was that the only one of her comments he could dispute, or was he taking the remarks one at a time, as he'd done earlier? She didn't wait to find out. "Of course you are. You're smart, capable, and accustomed to working long hours at a demanding job and living a totally different life. How could you not be bored?"

"I needed a break."

"And you've had it. Now it's time to get back to living life instead of vegetating in the hammock all day."

He didn't admit to or deny that. Instead, he shifted until he could tangle his fingers in her hair. "Why do you think you're not my type?"

She snorted. "That one's not even open to debate."

"I'll give you some free advice—never debate with a damn good lawyer. You'll lose every time." Again he shifted, rolling onto his side, gazing down at her. "What do we want that's so different?"

"You want to be alone. I want to have a family. You want to leave Bethlehem. I intend to stay here forever." Any man she fell in love with was going to have roots planted as deep in Bethlehem soil as the giant tree that shaded her house.

She wished he would disagree with her, and really mean it, but all he did was nod slowly, because what she'd said was true. Before she could give in fully to the regret growing inside her for even bringing up the subject, though, he kissed her.

It was sweet, full of temptation and hunger and need, and it warmed her all the way through with that private little thrill that came with each new first kiss. It made her want more, made her think that risking her heart for more seemed a perfectly logical move.

Easing closer, he turned it into a teasing, tasting, exploring sort of kiss, as if he had all the time in the world to get to know her mouth and intended to take it. As her breathing grew short and ragged, so did her patience, but if she'd ever known how to subtly ask for more, she'd forgotten. When her nails bit into her palms, she realized that unclenching her fists might be a good thing, and touching him might be even better.

Blindly she raised one hand, brushed his shoulder, then slid her fingers into his dark hair. Lifting her other hand, she found, once again, his shoulder, then his throat, then his jaw. His skin was warm and prickly with beard stubble, and enticed her to touch more of him—much more, like the arousal pressed against her thigh—but she'd never been one to ask for a lot out of life. For the moment, this was enough.

It ended too soon to satisfy her, too late to save her. Chase freed her mouth, nuzzled her ear, then lifted a handful of the hair that had worked free of its clasps. "I'm glad your hair didn't magically turn brown and your skin didn't tan." His voice was husky, his tone as velvety-dark as the sky above them. "Dark-haired women are a dime a dozen, and not one of them can compare to you for sheer loveliness."

She couldn't stop the choked sound. It worked free entirely on its own. "Loveliness? Is that what they call washed-out redheads these days? The same way I refer to my extra forty pounds as lushness?"

He didn't argue, didn't try to convince her of his sincerity. For a long time he did nothing but gaze at her, the expression in his eyes impossible to read but intense enough to send a few anticipatory shivers through her.

"If I thought you were fishing for more compliments, I'd be pissed," he said at last. "You are the blindest woman I've ever known when it comes to yourself. It never occurred to Fiona that the entire world didn't find her as beautiful as she found herself, but I'd swear it's never occurred to you that anyone could find you beautiful."

"That's because I know I'm not." She managed a fairly steady smile in spite of the fact that she would dearly like to believe he thought she was pretty. "It's one of my better qualities. I see things as they are and don't kid myself otherwise."

He murmured an obscenity. "*I* see things as they are. You, on the other hand, suffer from skewed vision."

"Skewed vision? When the rest of the world agrees with me, then *your* vision is the one that's skewed. I try not to use the F-word very often—"

A frown narrowed his gaze as he apparently considered, then discarded, the obvious choice. "Which word is that?"

"Fat. It's what I am. Not plump or chubby or generously proportioned. Not lush or plus-sized or ample. Just plain f—"

He kissed her again, cutting off her words effectively even though his mouth was nowhere near hers. No, he was kissing the delicate skin in the hollow where the swell of her breasts started—a simple, hot, open-mouthed kiss that turned her breath to vapor, and sent a shock of tingly heat all the way to her extremities.

When he lifted his head, his eyes seemed darker than ever. "Womanly. That's what you are." Idly he undid the first in the row of buttons that stretched from her neckline to hem, then nudged the second one open. His fingers explored the newly exposed skin, followed by his mouth.

Womanly. Whenever she'd bemoaned her weight, Jeff had always told her she looked fine. Her mother had sympathized with dismissive comments about unlucky genes, and her friends had shared their own laments. Even sixteen-year-old Trey Grayson had told her she looked fine.

No one but Chase had ever told her she looked womanly. Even if it wasn't anything more than semantics, it made her feel prettier. More desirable.

"Never debate a lawyer, huh?" she repeated, her voice breathless from the kisses he was trailing along the upper edges of her bra.

"You'll lose every time."

And sometimes losing was even better than winning.

Chapter Eleven

I T WAS AFTER MIDNIGHT WHEN THEY RETURNED home. Chase's cabin was dark, while only the living room lights showed in Nolie's. He parked next to her station wagon, then followed her halfway up the steps before realizing that Raine was sitting in one of the rockers. Micahlyn was asleep in her arms, snoring softly.

"I told you guys you could stay out all night," Raine said, a note of chastisement soft in her voice. "Though I guess it's just as well you ignored me. Micahlyn fell asleep while we were talking, and I kept putting off taking her inside and now I think both my legs have gone numb."

"I'll take her," Nolie said, but Chase tugged her back. "Have a seat. I'll carry her upstairs."

"But—"

Stepping past her, he scooped up the kid from Raine's lap, opened the screen door, and carried her inside. She looked unsubstantial as hell, but she was a solid weight in his arms—a weight smelling of sweet soap and baby shampoo, looking innocent and owlish with her eyes closed and her thick glasses still perched on her nose.

He didn't bother with a light as he turned into her bedroom. Two night-lights, one a mermaid and the other a dancing hippo, provided enough illumination to lay her on the twin bed. He removed her glasses and set them on the night table, then watched as she immediately huddled into the pillow, her mouth pursed, and settled once again into deep sleep.

He'd always wanted children—at first because it had seemed the thing to do, later because he'd . . . well, he'd *wanted* them. Wanted someone to love, teach, and influence. Someone to pass on the best parts of himself to. Someone with his name and his values, who would live long after he was gone.

Someone to prove that he was a better man than his family believed?

Bending, he brushed Micahlyn's hair from her face, then eased the sheet over her. She sighed and squinted up at him. "G'night, Mr. Bogeyman."

His smile was unsteady. "Goodnight, Mica." Turning away, he made it only a few feet before soft voices filtered through the open windows from below.

"Looks like you had fun." That was Raine, her born-and-bred-in-Boston voice a far cry from Nolie's lazy, softer Arkansas equivalent.

"Wh-why do you say that?" Nolie's response made him smile. She was the kind of witness lawyers loved—or hated, depending on the testimony offered—to get on the stand. She couldn't lie, or even avoid the truth, worth a damn, and everyone knew it.

"Well, your hair was so neatly done up when you left."

"Oh, uh, the top was down, and . . . the wind . . . you know . . ."

Raine sounded greatly amused. "Did the wind also undo the buttons on your dress?"

"I-I-I—" Nolie gave up, and in the silence that followed, Chase presumed she was refastening the buttons.

"Besides, you have that look, and so does Chase."

"What look is that?" Nolie asked guardedly.

"*That* look. You know, the gee-that-felt-good-when-can-we-do-it-again look."

"Oh, no. No, no, no—"

Grinning, Chase turned away from the window and headed downstairs. When he reached the porch, Nolie was still stammering out her denial. He sat down on the bench near her chair and noticed that she had, indeed, buttoned her dress. Feeling a strong twinge of regret at that, he politely interrupted. "She's teasing you, Nolie. Don't give her the satisfaction."

"Much as it pains me to say this, he's right, Nolie. I'm just having fun." With a laugh, Raine stretched her arms above her head. "I'm afraid I've got to head to bed, so you'll have to share the dirty details with me tomorrow. Thanks so much for letting me invite myself to dinner. I can't remember when I had such a nice evening. Chase, you want to give me the keys, I'll take the Z home and you can wander along when you're ready."

He handed her the keys, added his goodnight to Nolie's, then waited until Raine was pulling away to speak. "I'd probably better go, too."

"Then you should have gone with her."

"And miss the opportunity to kiss you goodnight?"

The pale light spilling through the window showed her faint blush and roused a long-forgotten tenderness inside him. Though the women he involved himself with inspired a great many emotions, tenderness generally wasn't one of them. But how many times had he reminded himself that Nolie wasn't the others?

A fact he was appreciating more every day.

"You kissed me goodnight at the lake," she primly pointed out.

"That was just a peck. This time I think I'll kiss your socks off."

She extended both legs to show her bare feet. "I'm not wearing socks."

No, but she *was* wearing a few other garments he would like to rid her of, starting with that plain white bra that had kept his explorations at the lake far less intimate than he would have liked. But he'd been afraid to push her too far too fast, and . . . well, hell, there was something to be said about anticipation.

When he stood up, so did she, and for every step he took forward, she retreated one. Finally the screen door was behind her, and there was no place left to go but inside. He blocked that easily enough by resting his palm against the door frame above her head and leaning his weight on it. She was trapped between him and the cabin wall, but she didn't look trapped. In fact, if the satisfied smile curving her mouth was anything to judge by, she was exactly where she wanted to be.

He smoothed away the smile with one fingertip. "Don't tempt me. Did I mention that I haven't been with a woman for more than three years? I'm a strong man, but I have my limits."

She bit gently at his finger before brushing it away. "Nolie the temptress. Improbable, but I like it."

"Improbable?" Nudging her feet apart, he slid his hands to her bottom and lifted her against his erection. "Does that feel improbable?"

Her only response was a whimper, which aroused him almost as much as her hips, soft and heated, cradling his. More than anything, he wanted to be inside her, wanted to see her naked, to kiss her all over, to fill her over and over until neither of them could bear anymore. More than anything he wanted . . .

. . . to do this right. To please her, satisfy her, love her, in ways no one else ever had. To protect her. To protect himself.

Slowly, with a groan, he let her feet slide to the floor. Eyes closed, jaw clenched tightly, he buried his face in her hair and took long sweet breaths of perfume, shampoo, Nolie, woman. Finally, from somewhere, he found the strength to raise his head, to look down at her, to touch his mouth to hers.

"Goodnight," he whispered. "Sleep tight. And don't forget to wish. . . ."

He walked away quickly, not looking back until he reached his own porch. There he looked, but it was too dark to tell whether she still stood in the shadows. It wasn't too dark, though, to find a thousand twinkling stars overhead. He settled on the brightest of them all and silently recited the rhyme. *I wish I may, I wish I might, have the wish I wish tonight. I wish . . .*

It was so childish, believing in wishes—far too innocent and optimistic a thing for a man like him. But that didn't stop him from finishing.

I wish for Nolie.

For now? For always? Forever?

For now, he repeated again. For all the reasons she'd pointed out at the lake, all the reasons he'd brought up himself earlier, there was no future for them. *For now* would have to be enough, because his only choices were that or nothing.

Just for an instant, he would have sworn that the wishing star, the brightest of them all, twinkled even brighter in response. But it was only his imagination.

Funny. Most people back in Boston never would have believed he even had an imagination.

•   •   •

"D ON'T YOU LOVE WHEN THINGS WORK OUT THE way they're supposed to?" Gloria said in her pleased-with-the-world voice. "And twinkling the star—that was a nice effect. Sort of like adding an exclamation point."

Sophy nodded modestly. She liked effects—shooting stars to carry prayers to heaven, a hint of a soft voice carried on a freshening breeze, though, truthfully, Gloria used that more often than Sophy.

"There's still much to be done, though. Chase is no closer to dealing with his family than when he came here, stubborn man." Gloria planted her feet on the shingles that roofed Chase's cabin, then rested her arms on her knees and her chin on her arms. "This is gonna be a tough one."

"You always say that."

Gloria gave her a long, steady look. "And I'm always right."

That was true, too, Sophy admitted, though she didn't say so out loud. She didn't need to. Gloria's preening made that clear.

"I'm not preening!" the other guardian denied.

Sophy didn't bother arguing the point with her. "These two are safe for the night. Come on. We've got places to go and other people to watch over."

Gloria disappeared first, her voice murmuring after her, "A guardian's work is never done." With a grin, Sophy followed, leaving behind nothing but a sprinkling of angel dust where, seconds ago, she'd sat. Just a whisper of glittery gleaming that sparkled in the air before fading away to nothing.

Did she mention that she liked special effects?

•   •   •

THE RELENTLESS *BEEP-BEEP-BEEP* OF AN ALARM slowly penetrated Cole's sleep and forced him to fling out one arm to fumble for the clock so he could throw it across the room. The night table was in the wrong place, though, so he encountered wood where there should have been air, bruising a knuckle, and for his effort, all the table held was a lamp.

The beeping, coming from the other side of the bed, abruptly stopped, then a warm body rolled close against him. Just the feel of all that soft, bare skin brought back a flood of memories, including how he'd wound up sleeping on the wrong side of the bed. Dinner Saturday night, followed by incredible and endless sex with Leanne. Except for work Monday, they'd hardly come up for air since Saturday's dessert. No wonder he felt so good—and so tired.

"Tell me it's not really time to get up," she mumbled.

"You set the alarm, darlin', not me." He turned to face her, wrapping his arms around her, drawing her near. "It's barely dawn. Stay another half hour."

"It's nearly seven o'clock. In another half hour, there are going to be a lot of people out and about."

People she would rather not have seeing her leave his house and, so obviously, his bed. It was a logical precaution, one he usually took whenever he spent the night at a woman's house. There were times when talk was good, and times when it wasn't. When it involved sex, he'd learned, the less said, the better.

So why did it bother him that she was being cautious?

"Are you ashamed to let people know you've been staying over here?"

That opened her eyes wide. "Of course not. I'm thirty-two years old. I've had enough serious relationships that it won't surprise anyone I have a sex life. It's just . . ." She flashed a wicked grin as she slid out of bed. "I don't want to share you yet."

"You don't have to worry about that." Cole leaned against the headboard, pulled the sheet to his waist, and watched her. She worked quickly—maneuvering into her panties and bra, then her dress; smoothing out the wrinkles; combing back her hair; scooping up her earrings from the nightstand; stepping into her shoes. Even just awakened after too little sleep, she looked incredible.

He would miss her when he was gone.

The thought disturbed him—not because he was already thinking about when he would leave. He always left; it was what he did. And he always missed the various women who had brightened his life and shared his bed. He just didn't make a habit of missing them in advance. That was all that bothered him. He wasn't getting attached to her. Hell, he didn't even have the emotional capacity to do that.

Decent enough for the stroll across the street to her apartment, she came to sit on the bed beside him. "I had a good time," she said, all prim and proper.

He grinned, though he didn't really feel like it. "Your mother raised you right, huh?"

"No, but I turned out well anyway." She brushed a kiss to his jaw. "I'll grab Danny and be on my way."

"We can bring him over when he wakes up, hopefully at a decent hour."

"You don't mind?"

When he shook his head, she started toward the door, then came back and planted a kiss on him. "Thank you," she whispered, her eyes dark with emotion. "See you later." Without waiting for a response, she left.

He listened until he heard the front door close, then with a groan, he slid down in the bed. He'd seen that look in her eyes before—not in hers, specifically, but the same look. In other women's eyes. The getting-serious look. The damn-near-adoring look.

The she's-gonna-be-trouble look.

All he wanted from a woman was good sex and companionship. Talking could be interesting. Having someone to eat dinner with was a nice change. Not going to sleep in an empty bed every night was worth a lot. But that was all he wanted, and only on a short-term basis. He had no intention of settling down. Who needed the complications?

If he had half a brain, the next kiss he gave Leanne would be good-bye. He wouldn't even have to tell her it was over. He was an expert at breaking things off without saying anything at all. Become unavailable, put some emotional distance between them, let her see him with other women . . . She was a smart woman. She would get the hint.

All he had to do was give it.

After a while, he eased out of bed, feeling every one of his thirty years, showered, dressed, then checked on the boys. Ryan's room was at the other end of the hall from Cole's. Had all that distance been his choice or Ryan's? Cole couldn't remember.

Fifty years ago it had been the Miller boys' room. The walls were still papered with a faded baseball theme, and the twin beds were still covered with decades-old spreads in Yankee colors. Ryan had griped that it was a kid's room, then moved in without further complaint.

He was asleep now, the bedside lamp scooted closest to his bed, its light too dim to compete with the morning sun filtering through the sheer curtains. For as long as Cole had known him, he'd insisted on sleeping with a light on. He wasn't afraid of the dark, he'd sworn in his blustery, grown-up way. He just liked to see where he was the instant he woke up. One night, though, probably two years ago, the bulb had burned out and Cole had been shocked out of a sound sleep by a spine-chilling scream. It had taken two hours to get Ryan settled down, and for months after that, Cole had left two lights burning. He'd never known what caused the nightmare—no doubt, something the boy's worthless mother had done. Truth was, he hadn't wanted to know. It was easier for him.

And he did have a tendency to do what was easiest for *him,* he thought sardonically.

In the other bed, Danny was lying on his back, his eyes open, his mouth turned up in a friendly grin. He wiggled his fingers, then said in a loud whisper, "Ryan's still asleep."

"You want some breakfast?" When Danny nodded, Cole lifted him up in one arm and carried him into the hall. When he would have lowered the kid to the floor, though, Danny held on, so, because it was no big deal, Cole gave him a ride downstairs to the kitchen.

After settling Danny at the table, Cole nuked a half-dozen frozen sausage links and toasted the same number of frozen waffles. He turned his into sandwiches, which he ate standing up. Danny turned his into boats, floating on an ocean of syrup dotted with islands of melted butter.

"I have to go to day care," Danny announced, syrup dripping from his chin.

"Yeah?" Cole handed him a napkin, then watched him swab his whole face and still miss the syrup.

"Does Ryan go to day care?"

"Nope." That was one thing Cole had never had to mess with. The kid had been taking care of himself since he was out of diapers, and was better at it than Cole would ever be.

" 'Cause he's a big boy." Danny nodded knowingly,

then said in a solemnly disappointed voice, "And I'm just a kid."

"The older you get, the tougher life gets. Stay a kid as long as you can, son." *Son?* Jeez, where the hell had that come from? He'd never even called Ryan that . . . though it was true his own father had rarely called Cole or his brothers anything else. It was easier than keeping six boys and their names straight.

Once Danny finished eating, Cole wiped his face and hands—and pajamas—with a washcloth, then settled him in the living room with cartoons on TV while he went upstairs to dress in a pale gray suit, white shirt, and burgundy tie. He added cuff links and a diamond-studded tie clip, slid his Italian leather wallet into his pocket and his Italian leather loafers onto his feet, then checked the mirror. His taste in clothes was conservative at best, downright boring at worst. Truth was, he didn't trust himself to experiment. Besides, conservative wasn't a bad thing for an investment broker.

Switching his briefcase to his other hand, he knocked loudly at Ryan's open door. "Hey, lazy bones, you plannin' to show your smiling face in school today?"

"Go away," the kid groaned from under his pillow.

"Come on, or you're gonna be late."

"It's a holiday."

"Uh-huh. Right."

"It's a teacher workday." Ryan slid the pillow aside, leaving his hair standing on end. "I'm sick. The school burned down. The principal gave me summer vacation early because I'm so smart. I'm under house arrest. If I leave the house, aliens will beam me up."

"Are those the best excuses you can come up with?" Cole grinned. "Come on, get your butt in gear. I'm gonna run Danny across the street. Soon as I get back, we've gotta get going."

Scowling, Ryan got out of bed. "Just for the record"—he paused in front of Cole on the way to the bathroom—"enrolling me in school was a really dumb idea."

"Hey, you're the one who showed up here and left me without a choice. Besides, it keeps you out of trouble."

Ryan snorted. "You 'n' me both know better 'n that."

"Ten minutes," Cole called an instant before the bathroom door slammed. He took the stairs three at a time, dropped the briefcase, and picked up Danny, then headed for Leanne's. This would be a good time to start putting some distance between them, he reminded himself as he rang the bell next to her apartment door. Easily said, easier done.

Then she opened the door, smiling brightly enough to light the staircase at her back, and distance was the farthest thing from his mind. That quick, he wanted her again, as if they hadn't had incredible sex five or six times in the past two and a half days.

"Hey, sweetie," she greeted Danny. "You want to run upstairs and get some breakfast?"

"I already eated. See?" He tugged at his pajama top, sniffing the stain there. "Sausage." He sniffed, then licked, a second stain. "An' pancakes wif butter 'n' syrp."

"Don't lick your clothes. Go on and get dressed." Leanne gave him a playful swat as he pushed past her and thundered up the stairs. "Thanks for feeding and delivering him."

"Anytime." Cole forced himself to take a step back, then pivot back toward his own house.

"Hey . . . how about dinner tonight? I'll cook."

Okay, this was it. There were a thousand simple answers: *I've got a late appointment. Ryan's got something at*

school. I promised the kid this would be father/son time. I'm un-
der house arrest. The kitchen burned down. The kitchen might
burn down if you and I get in there together. . . .

Or even simpler: *No, thanks.* And walk away.

But she looked so damn . . . sweet standing there, and
there would always be plenty of time to break it off with
her in the future. It wasn't as if he was in danger of falling
for her or anything.

"Sure. I'll give you a call later."

THE WEATHER FORECAST CALLED FOR RAIN ON
Wednesday, and was dead-on. Nolie awakened to a
room that was still night-dark at seven A.M. and the sound
of a deluge beating on the cabin roof. Wishing she could
stay curled up in bed—or, better yet, curled up in Chase's
bed—she delivered Micahlyn to day care in the rain, then
dashed through it from the car to the store, soaking her
feet in the process. It thundered on the store's tin roof,
kept traffic on the highway to a minimum, and made customers practically nonexistent.

By one, she'd waited on two people, quilted until her
fingers ached, and contemplated bringing in a cot for
dreary lazy days. She'd read until her eyes crossed, polished
off two candy bars bought in prediet, and turned down an
invitation from Leanne Wilson for a take-out lunch from
Harry's. She'd regretted it, too, because she hadn't seen
Leanne since the night they'd gone to the Starlite, and
Raine had gone home the day before, and Nolie was discovering all over again how much she missed having girlfriends.

But mostly what she did that long, gray day was think,
and mostly what she thought about was Chase. Thought

about? Change that to mooned over. Fantasized about. Dreamed of.

And kissed. Sunday, Monday, *and* Tuesday nights, he'd kissed her goodnight—sweet, lazy, hungry, intoxicating kisses. The kind that could make a woman forget her relative inexperience. The kind that could make even a size sixteen feel slender and desirable and worth getting naked for. The kind of kisses that could rob a woman of her last bit of good sense and make her say yes to just about anything.

The problem was, he didn't ask for anything.

He wanted her—she'd been achingly aware of his arousal on more than one occasion—so what was he waiting for? For her to make the first move? For the planets to align? For someone better to come along?

Maybe.

It hurt her to think that, and scared her to not think it. She was just so damn insecure, and he was so . . .

Oh, yeah. *So* . . .

When the bell over the door rang, she eagerly jumped to her feet. She didn't care who it was, or if they bought anything. She was just happy for the distraction.

The figure came up the center aisle, bundled in an electric-blue slicker a size too big, its hood shadowing the wearer's face. Rather dowdy polyester pants—the forgiving kind that Nolie's mother had favored—were tucked into lemon-yellow rain boots, and the handle of a hot-pink umbrella disappeared up one oversized sleeve. Whoever it was certainly didn't want to be overlooked in the limited visibility.

"Can I help you?"

One pale hand slipped out to push the hood back, then Gloria beamed at her. "Isn't it a lovely day?"

"Only if you quack when you talk and waddle when you walk."

"Oh, a little rain is good for us. It can wash away a multitude of woes." Gloria propped the umbrella against the nearest shelves, shrugged out of her slicker, and hung it on the upended handles of a display of shovels.

"I'm surprised they gave you time off from the day-care center," Nolie remarked. "The kids all adore you."

"Of course they do, and I adore them, too. They know I'm an angel, you know."

"I didn't realize that." Nolie bit back her smile. The woman had made the statement so sincerely, as if it were God's honest truth. And who would argue with her? Anyone who could happily, wholeheartedly care for a few dozen children, most under the age of six, all day, day after day, certainly qualified as an angel in Nolie's book.

"Oh, yes. Of course, children are much more astute about those things than adults." Gloria gave herself a shake to dislodge stray raindrops, then turned on the megawatt smile. "And how are you settling in Bethlehem, Jolie?"

"Just fine." She thought of Chase and smiled. "I'm glad I came here. It's a great town."

"Oh, yes, it certainly is. Not that there's anything wrong with Whiskey Creek, besides that name. And the fact that Case isn't there. Where is he now? Hidden away at that dusty old cabin?"

"Probably lying in the hammock and enjoying the rain."

Stillness swept over Gloria for an instant, then abruptly she bobbed her head. "You're right—he is. You know, that boy needs a job. It's not good for a man with a mind like his to sit around idle all day."

Nolie was surprised by the protectiveness Gloria felt,

especially since Nolie'd said the same thing not long ago. "He'll get one when he's ready."

"Yep. But more than a job, he needs you and Martha Lyn."

Nolie's gaze jerked to the older woman even as a blush began creeping up her neck. "You think so?" The plaintive, hopeful note in her voice was pathetic, but she couldn't do anything about it.

Gloria was wearing that earnestly sincere look again. "Oh, no, Nola, I know. It's a sure thing."

Maybe in your world, Nolie scoffed silently. In *her* world, nothing was sure besides death and taxes and her boundless love for Micahlyn. Though she would very much like to believe Chase was, too.

Gloria reached across the counter to pat Nolie's hand. "Our worlds are one and the same, dear."

A chill snaked down Nolie's spine. "Wh— How—" Then she smiled uneasily. "I didn't mean to say that out loud."

"Good. Because you didn't." Gloria beamed at her, then looked around the room. "This place brings back memories. Did I tell you I'd worked in this old store before?"

"No, you didn't. For my great-grandfather?"

"I did my best, but he was a difficult man to help. Always wanted things his own way, hardheaded, wouldn't compromise to save his life. A little compromise *might* have saved his life."

"What do you mean? He died an old man."

"His life was over long before he died." Gloria's voice was soft, distant, and underlaid with pity. "He drove that girl of his away and was too proud to go after her and make things right. He never got to see her grow into a woman or become a wife and a mother. He denied himself the chance to meet his only granddaughter and her only daughter. He lived all those years bitter and alone because he was more hardheaded than anyone I've known." Her gaze cut to Nolie. "Do you take after him?"

"Oh, no. No way."

"I hope not. But you've got a streak of hardheadedness . . ."

Nolie's mouth dropped open. *Her? Hardheaded?* Oh, no way, nohow, not in the least! She was the one who hated confrontation, who was such a weenie about standing up for herself, who went along to get along. She didn't have a stubborn bone in her body.

"When you get your mind fixed on something and refuse to change it, no matter what, that's stubborn," Gloria said pointedly.

"I agree, but that's not me."

"Oh, no. Man tells you you're beautiful, and you laugh in his face . . . that's not being hardheaded at all, now, is it?"

"I didn't— It's not—" Nolie drew a heavy breath, then, for reasons she didn't even understand, she solemnly confided, "I have a mirror back there in the bathroom, several in my car, and even more in my house. I look at myself every day, and I see—"

"What you expect to see. Fair skin, freckles, a few extra pounds. You know what Jase sees? Shiny, coppery red hair that's fine as silk and soft as satin, pale porcelain skin, eyes the color of a summer sky before a storm, a cupid's-bow mouth with one freckle right in the center of one arch. He sees strength and curves and sweet, pure womanliness." Gloria raised both hands in a shrug. "He sees beauty."

Her insides quavering, Nolie breathed deeply again, then sank into her chair. "He told you that?" she asked, expecting a negative answer.

"He didn't have to tell me. He told *you*."

Without giving her a chance to respond, Gloria went on. "I have a suggestion, Nolie—it *is* Nolie, isn't it? Why don't you turn the store over to me for an hour or two and take Louanne up on that lunch invitation? You'll only have three more customers today, and I can wait on them as easily as you."

Nolie wanted to go back to the subject of Chase, to demand answers to a dozen questions, while at the same time she wanted to declare him off-limits in conversation. And if it was questions she had, well, how did Gloria know about Louan—Leanne's invitation? And how in the world could she possibly know there would be only three more customers?

"It's my job to know," Gloria said in a reassuring voice. She stepped through the back-room door to retrieve the rain jacket Nolie had hung there, then reached without hesitation into the drawer—out of nine!—where Nolie kept her purse and presented both to her with a pleased smile. "I may have a problem with names, but I keep track of everything else."

"But—"

"Go on, dear, and don't worry for a minute. I know exactly where to go for help if I need it." She rolled her gaze heavenward, then gave a big wink and a laugh.

It wasn't the best idea in the world. Some part of Nolie recognized that, but she couldn't come up with a single reason to say why. She had no doubt the woman was trustworthy, or the good folks of Bethlehem would never let her work with their children. She did need to get out, just for a while, and she really did want to see Leanne, and . . . Suddenly it seemed a perfectly wonderful idea. She shrugged into the jacket, dug her keys from her purse, and stepped outside into the rain.

"By the way, Noreen." Gloria stuck her head out the door and grinned. "If there's a God's honest truth, is there also a God's *dis*honest truth?" With another wink and a grin, she disappeared back inside.

Nolie walked to her car in a daze. Okay, so the woman was psychic or something. She could read minds like the people Nolie had seen on late-night infomercials, only she was for real. That was the only way to explain it.

Well, either that, or . . .

She really was an angel.

FOR THE MOST PART, THE HAMMOCK WAS PRO-tected from the rain, though an occasional gust of wind blew a sprinkling of drops across Chase's legs, turning the denim indigo. It had been coming down for hours, slacking once in a while to give the saturated ground a chance to recover, then returning with a vengeance. It made everything smell rain-shower clean—hey, wasn't that the scent of the soap in his bathroom?—and turned the greens and browns of the hillside into deeper, richer shades.

It was also creating a nice, shallow lake between his cabin and Nolie's, and gouging the ruts on the last uphill section of the road a little deeper. It was a lousy day for being out and about, but just about ideal for being lazy at home. In fact, if he closed his eyes and slowed his breathing for just five minutes, he could probably go right to sleep and stay there until Nolie came home from work.

He was trying it when raindrops splattered across his face. Not even the strongest wind had brought them higher than his knees, and he hadn't felt even the slightest of breezes just now. Irritably curious, he opened his eyes and saw a familiar face watching him. Familiar—not necessarily welcome. "Sophy, isn't it?"

Smiling, she sat down on the porch floor, back against the wall. "At your service. Is this how you spend all your days?"

"Can you think of anything better to do?"

"Oh . . . how about helping people? That's the business I'm in. That *used* to be the business you were in. Don't you miss your law practice?"

He lifted his head to scowl at her. "How do you know—?"

"Don't go blaming Nolie again. Remember, I told you—I know everything."

"You're arrogant enough to be a lawyer yourself."

Modestly she shook her head. "My talents are better used elsewhere. Did you know your church is having a picnic Saturday afternoon at City Park? Lots of people will be there . . . including your folks. You should go."

He didn't bother to point out that *he* didn't have a church, not anymore, or that the last people he wanted to see were his parents . . . or maybe Fiona and her current husband. He considered it a moment, then shook his head. No, it was his parents. If he never saw them again, he could die a happy man.

"Nolie and Micahlyn will be there, too, at least for a little while."

"Good. They'll have fun."

"Your sister will also be there."

The last time he'd seen his sister popped into his mind as clearly as if it had been yesterday. She'd been twenty-four years old, so much more grown-up than the eighteen-year-old he'd left when he went away to college. Defying their parents to attend his law school graduation hadn't been easy for her—defiance wasn't one of her strong suits—but she'd done it rather than leave him to mark such a momentous occasion by himself, and he'd been more grateful than he could say.

And more hurt than he could say when she hadn't been willing to do it again to attend his wedding.

"Then I assume she'll have fun, too."

"And her son. Your nephew. You didn't know you were an uncle, did you?"

Her casual question sent an old pain stabbing through him. No, he hadn't known. But he wasn't surprised. Leanne had been raised with the notion that she could have anything she wanted, and what she'd wanted most, at least as a teenage girl, was a husband, home, and children of her own. He should have met his brother-in-law, though, and he certainly should have met his nephew. He should have known. *She* should have told him.

Like he'd told her about Fiona? An invitation to the wedding, sent in care of their parents, was the only information he'd offered.

Like he'd told her about the divorce? His arrest? His subsequent twenty-two months in prison?

Like he'd told her he was back?

"Who did she marry?" he asked stiffly.

"Who? Your sister? Oh, no one. After she got pregnant, the father decided he wasn't ready to *be* a father, so he took off. She's raising Danny alone. He's a cute kid. Looks like his mother, and a little like you. He's got that Wilson coloring."

"How did you—" He broke off, and his jaw tightened. "I forgot. You know everything. Well, do you know what I'm thinking right now?"

Sophy gave him a poor-sap look, then shook her finger in admonishment. "It's not nice to think such things. The grandfather whose name you bear would wash your mouth out with soap if he were here."

Lucky guess. Of course, how lucky did a person have to be to match the thoughts she couldn't see with the hostility she could? Still, a twinge of discomfort spread through him as he slowly sat up. He didn't know this woman from Eve, but she seemed to know an awful lot about him. On top of that, she was one hell of a busybody. Could she be trusted to keep her mouth shut, or would she amuse herself by telling precisely the people he didn't want to know that he was back?

"Where did you come from?" His tone was a sharp indication that his patience was stretched thin. She must have heard it, but it didn't seem to concern her.

"A long time ago in a place far, far away . . ." Once more she smiled, looking about fifteen with her blond curls frizzing around her face. "Oh, you meant just now, didn't you? I hiked through the woods."

"Why?"

"Because I don't drive."

"Where were you going?"

"Here."

"Why?"

She gave him a look that made him feel like a very slow child. "What have we been doing the last few minutes? Talking."

"So you hiked through the woods in the rain to talk to me."

"Bingo."

"Even though I have no desire to talk to you."

"Sometimes people don't want to talk to me. Sometimes I have to sort of force the issue." She shrugged carelessly. "That's what I do."

"You annoy people. *That's* what you do."

That earned him another charming grin. "Aw, I'm not annoying you, Chase. You just say that because I make you think about things you've spent the last half of your life ignoring."

He eased to his feet and walked past her to the door. There he turned back. "If I'm so good at ignoring things, then maybe I can learn to ignore you."

"Don't count on it." She scrambled to her feet and dusted her damp clothes. "I'm impossible to ignore—but easy to forget."

"I doubt that," he said dryly, letting the screen door slam behind him to punctuate the words. He didn't make it more than five feet, though, before he went back and pushed the door open again. "Hey—"

All he'd wanted to do was tell her—warn her—to keep what she knew to herself. But he slowly closed the screen door without saying a word.

Because she was gone. Disappeared. Vanished.

And damned if he could figure out how.

Chapter Twelve

THE NEAREST AVAILABLE PARKING SPACE TO Small Wonders Nolie could find was half a block away and across the street. By the time she stepped into rather than over the minitorrent rushing along the curb to the drain, then hustled down the block, her shoes were soaked again. Fortunately, she'd managed to spare the hem of her dress by lifting it practically to her knees. Leanne's warm greeting when she walked through the shop door made up for the chilly discomfort, though.

"I thought you couldn't make it."

"So did I, but . . ." Nolie shrugged out of her jacket and hung it on the bright red coat tree just inside the door, then sloshed her way to the back. "Have you eaten? Since I'm already wet, I can wade over to Harry's."

"No need. I ordered a sandwich from the sub place down the block, and it's big enough for three. Come on back."

Nolie slipped out of her shoes while Leanne served the sandwich on paper plates with chips—baked, but hey, not everything could be fattening. They curled up on the wicker sofa and love seat, ate, and discussed the sort of things Nolie used to talk about with her girlfriends back in Arkansas. Nothing of major importance—kids, clothing, weather, TV shows—but comforting all the same. While Chase was way beyond nice, he didn't have quite the same interest in hairstyles or diet woes that Leanne did. It was a lovely way to spend a rainy afternoon . . . at least, until an older woman walked through the door.

Leanne rose from the couch, a smile ready on her lips before it started slipping. "Oh. Mom. Look, Nolie, it's my mother." She grabbed Nolie's hand and pulled her to her feet and toward the woman who stopped near the cash register, almost as if she intended to use her as a shield. "Mom, Nolie Harper. Nolie, my mom, Phyllis Wilson."

"I think she got the idea, Leanne." The woman's cool gaze swept Nolie up and down, and her mouth tightened, as if to keep in the admonishments fighting to get out. Nolie could all too easily imagine them: *Barefoot in a place of business? Eating when you certainly can afford to skip a meal or two or twenty? If that hair color's natural, something can be done about it, you know, and if it's not natural . . .* Followed by a disapproving shake of the head.

"Nice to meet you, Mrs. Wilson."

"Yes, of course." Phyllis turned her attention to her daughter. "I called you Saturday evening. I wanted Danny to spend the night with us."

"We were out."

"So I understand. Georgia Blakely over at the grocery store told me she saw you and Danny coming out of the Miller house on her way to work Sunday morning. At nearly seven A.M. Not going *in*. Coming *out*. As if you might have—oh, dear, is this jumping to conclusions?— spent the night there."

Appalled, Nolie edged back to stand next to a rack of tiny frilly dresses. Her mother *never* would have taken that tone with her. Heavens, she would swear her mother couldn't have scrounged up that much sarcasm to save her life.

Apparently, it wasn't an unusual thing for Phyllis, because Leanne didn't seem the least bit surprised. "What I was doing Sunday morning is none of Georgia Blakely's business, Mom."

And it's none of your business, either. Nolie silently urged her to say the words, but Leanne was a better person, or at least in better control of her impulses.

"No denial. So it must be true. This-this Jackson person moves into town one week and you're in his bed the next." Phyllis rolled her gaze heavenward. "It must be your father's influence."

"Leave Daddy out of this, Mom."

"God knows, I did the best I could. I sacrificed for you and your brother. I made a home for you. I took care of you. And this is the thanks I get. My daughter can't find a single man to meet her high, high standards for marriage, but has no problem finding plenty of them to sleep with, and my son—"

"Leave him out of this, too." Any hint of politeness, patience, or resignation was gone from Leanne's voice, making the words hard and icy, to match the pale, frigid look she wore.

Phyllis opened her mouth, then closed it again. Wise choice, Nolie thought, retreating farther by trading the frilly dresses for the cover of a display of summer shorts and tops.

"Did you come by for any reason other than to find out if I'm sleeping with Cole Jackson?" Leanne asked.

A miffed expression pinched Phyllis's face. "Actually, I want Danny to come over this evening."

"Sorry. We have plans."

"I can guess what plans you and Cole Jackson have," Phyllis responded with a sneer.

Leanne's only response was a shrug.

"Well, when do you think I might be allowed to see my only grandchild?"

"How about at the church picnic Saturday afternoon?"

"You know, Leanne—". Apparently Phyllis thought better of whatever she'd been about to say. She nodded once, stiffly, and said, "Very well." Then, head high, mouth pursed sourly, she turned on her heel and stalked out of the store.

For a long time the shop was quiet. Finally, Leanne exhaled loudly. "I'm sorry about that."

"Don't apologize." Nolie had been part of a few ugly scenes before, notably her last few conversations in person with Marlene and Obie. Thankfully, though, she'd been spared any witnesses to hers.

They returned to the sitting area and the cookies they'd moved on to after the sandwich and chips were gone. Leanne nibbled at hers before regretfully laying it down. "My plans tonight aren't with Cole. He's got a couple of late appointments, so I'm taking Danny and Ryan to dinner and a movie."

"Why, Leanne!" Nolie said in a scandalized voice. "You *lied* to your mother?"

Leanne laughed. "I didn't exactly lie. She assumed, and I let her, though I'm sure that's still lying in her book."

"So . . . tell me about Tall, Blond, and Handsome."

Leanne's gaze drifted across the street to the Jackson house, and a tender look came across her face. She was smitten, Nolie's grandmother would have said, and Nolie would agree 100 percent.

"He's very sweet, very charming . . . and incredibly *hot*." Her wicked grin came and went, replaced by a faintly troubled frown. "I like him a whole lot—more than I should. Maybe more than is safe for me."

"Why is that?" Nolie asked the question, though she knew the answer perfectly well. Broken hearts were slow to mend and tough to live with in the meantime.

Leanne shook her head regretfully. "I wasn't looking for a relationship. After the last loser, I swore I wouldn't get involved with another man again. Then I met Cole, and I thought it couldn't hurt to have lunch with him, or to dance with him at the Starlite, or to have dinner with him last weekend. But I was wrong. It could hurt, because here I am, already sleeping with him and half in love with him, and truth is, I've only known him a few weeks."

"Sometimes it doesn't take very long," Nolie gently pointed out.

"No kidding," Leanne agreed with great feeling, then turned pensive again. "When I'm with him, I think . . . he just might be that elusive Mr. Right we're all supposed to be searching for. He's interesting, he's good with his son, he talks, he cooks. Danny likes him and worships his son. Ryan's the big brother Danny's always wanted."

"But when you're not with him? . . ."

"I keep wondering when the Jekyll/Hyde transformation is going to start. You know, they're *all* charming and sweet in the beginning, but eventually their true colors show through. Greg took off because I got pregnant. Steve dumped me because of Danny. Richard was already married. What's it going to be with Cole? He's gay?"

Nolie snorted. "Not if he spent Saturday night with you."

"And Sunday night. And Monday." Leanne colored a bit even as she languidly fanned herself. "Oh, my, my . . . So maybe he's on the FBI's Most Wanted list, or he's an alien from outer space seeking to colonize earth."

"Well, they do say men are from Mars." Nolie took one more cookie from the bag, swearing it would be her last. "Here's a novel idea: Maybe he's exactly what he seems—a sweet, charming guy who's a good father, a prospect for a good husband . . . and incredibly *hot*."

"Mr. Right. Wouldn't that be something after all the Mr. Wrongs I've had?"

"Hey, hope for the best. You deserve it."

As did *she*.

Was it any surprise that Chase sprang immediately to mind?

I WISH YOU'D CHANGE YOUR MIND AND GO WITH US." It wasn't the first time Saturday Nolie had made the remark, but it *was* the first time it had sounded so plaintive to Chase. She was referring to the church picnic, of course. She'd closed the store at noon, then come home to change clothes and try one more time to change his mind. Once he convinced her that wasn't possible, she would pick up Micahlyn, then head for City Park.

Half the town would be there regardless of whether they attended the church, and there would be more food than any three such gatherings could consume. The women would gather in groups and talk, the men would gather and gossip, and the kids would play as if there were no tomorrow. Everyone would make Nolie and Micahlyn feel as if they'd lived there forever, and they would have a great time and make new friends.

Friends who didn't mind going out to dinner or a movie or a picnic, who didn't have reason to hide from everyone. People with whom spending time might appeal to Nolie more than hanging out at home with him night after night.

Still, he shook his head. "Sorry."

A frown wrinkling her forehead, she stared at him a moment, then accused, "No, you're not. You're perfectly happy being the hermit up here."

He didn't bother to tell her she was wrong. Lately he'd noticed an increasing restlessness, a desire to do *something*. He just didn't know what. Pack up and take off? Get a job—any job that would occupy his time? Look into the possibility of getting his law license reinstated? Oh, yeah, right, now there was a goal for him. It would be a cold day in hell before he'd go back to practicing law. Nearly two years in prison had cost him his interest in and his respect for the judicial system.

Maybe he could just spend time with people. Lead a normal life. *Make* a normal life for himself.

But to have a normal life, he would have to have people to share it with, and the only people he wanted to share with were the two he had no future with.

Deliberately he shifted the subject. "Are you opening the store again after the picnic?"

"Probably not. It depends on what time we leave—and whether any of our customers *aren't* at the park." She gave him one of those pursed-mouth looks, then sighed. "I guess I'd better go, then."

"Have fun."

Her snort made his mouth twitch with a grin. Primly she said, "You don't know the meaning of the word."

"Oh, I know. But if I show you, you'll never make it to the park, and Micahlyn will be disappointed." Placing his hands on her shoulders, he turned her toward the car parked in front of his house and walked her down the steps. "Go. Have fun. Make new friends." But not too much fun, he silently clarified, or too many friends, and certainly none that was male.

Reluctantly she got into her car, waved, then drove away.

Long after her car disappeared from sight and the sound of its engine faded into the distance, he still stood there. Just stood. He had no place to go and nothing to do. No one to visit, no one to miss him, no one to give a damn whether he stood there in the pine needles and dirt the entire rest of the day and into the night. He felt empty. Forgotten.

Or maybe he was just feeling sorry for himself because everyone in his immediate world got to go where they wanted and do what they wanted, while he was stuck out here— What was it Nolie had said? *Being the hermit*. Being. Not playing.

So where did he want to go? Somewhere. And what did he want to do? Something.

"You're a great help," he muttered aloud as he stalked back to the porch. "You don't even know what the hell you want."

Besides Nolie.

He went inside the house and fixed a frozen dinner for lunch, ate a couple of bites, then threw it away. Stretched out on the sofa, he surfed the channels, looking for something that could hold his interest on TV, but found nothing. There wasn't any cleaning to do, or any need pressing enough to justify the ninety-mile round-rip to Howland. He was edgy and restless and bored, and couldn't find a damn thing that helped.

Swearing, he grabbed his keys and went to his truck. Driving was good, even without a destination. He could get out of the valley, clear his head, and pass the few hours— five at the most—until Nolie was home again.

Unless she met someone she liked at the picnic.

Someone with more to offer than nothing.

When he reached the end of the dirt road, his natural inclination was to turn left. He tried his damnedest to follow it this time, but for some perverse reason he turned right instead. He made another right at the first street he came to, then continued a zigzag route to a little-used lot on the back side of City Park.

The streets around the park had been reduced to one lane of traffic, thanks to the vehicles parked on either side. The food was spread out on tables under the trees, and people were everywhere, with folding chairs, quilts, or boulders for seats. The kids seemed to run wild, though he knew from past experience that there were always a few adults watching over them, usually Miss Agatha—yeah, there she was, with Miss Corinna, sitting on a blanket at the top of a small rise.

He couldn't pick Nolie out of the crowd, or his sister or, thankfully, his parents. He did see some familiar faces, as well as plenty that weren't. But what could he expect after sixteen years away?

If he had any guts at all, he would get out of the truck and go in search of Nolie, Leanne, and the nephew he'd never known. He challenged himself to do just that, and even went so far as to grip the door handle when the crowd seemed to part, and standing there, not a hundred feet in front of him, were his parents. His mother was wearing the vague smile he hated, the only one she'd ever smiled after a few years of living with his father, Earl was doing his friendly have-I-got-a-deal-for-you salesman shtick, and each was ignoring the other.

Other than a few more lines on their faces, more gray in Earl's hair, and an extra twenty pounds around his middle, they looked the same as Chase remembered. One strong, hypercritical man and one weak, uncaring woman who never should have married, much less produced children.

Thirty-six years they'd been married and, judging from the way they were avoiding each other now, thirty-six years they'd been miserable.

Damned if he would give them the chance to make him miserable again.

Not even for Nolie.

Still gripping the door handle, he started the engine and left.

THE PARK WAS BUSTLING WITH ACTIVITY, EXACTLY the way a park should, Sophy thought with satisfaction. Tables stretched end to end under the ancient shade trees, their pale pink cloths fluttering in the light breeze, their weight capacity put to the test under the vast display of food. There were salads of every type and ethnicity, serving dishes filled with fried chicken, chicken salad, chicken and dumplings, sweet-and-sour meatballs, Italian meatballs, and barbecue meatballs, ribs and sliced ham, deep-fried turkey and egg foo yung, side dishes and desserts . . . ah, desserts to make a woman—er, angel—sigh.

She did just that from her place on a sturdy branch of the tallest of the trees, directly above the first of a half-dozen dessert tables, and swung her legs in the air. There were so many familiar faces—Nathan and Emilie Bishop and their brood; Kelsey and J.D. Grayson and their half-dozen; Police Chief Mitch Walker and his family; Tom and Holly Flynn and her half sister, Bree. Little Rachel McKinney rode on her father's shoulders, wide-eyed at the sights and sounds but keeping her mother, Maggie, in sight, and Alex and Melissa Thomas strolled arm in arm in the warm sunshine, chatting with Gabe and Noelle Rawlins.

As if she'd heard her name whispered in Sophy's

thoughts, Noelle, a former guardian herself, looked high up into the tree, smiled, and gave a little wave. Sophy wiggled her fingers back at the only soul around at the moment who could see her, then continued to survey the scene.

Below, Ben Foster and Sebastian Knight were making selections from the dessert tables for their wives. Both Lynda and Melina loved sweets and were fortunate enough to burn off the extra calories with no trouble at all. Nolie Harper, choosing between salads a few yards away, wasn't blessed with as efficient a metabolism, but that didn't seem to matter one bit to Chase Wilson . . . though the stubborn man wasn't here today to show it.

Abruptly the branch dipped and leaves rustled as Gloria settled next to Sophy. She was smiling brightly—when wasn't she?—and balancing a plate of Miss Corinna's no-bake cookies and Miss Agatha's favorite peanut butter cookies. Gloria's favorite, too, judging by how many of them she'd piled on the plate.

"Where have you been?" Sophy asked. "Besides raiding the food table."

"I took some cookies," Gloria admitted, "but I was also putting a dish out."

"Since when did you bring food to any of Bethlehem's potlucks?"

"Why, isn't that the way these things work? Everyone shares in the cooking, and everyone shares in the bounty." Gloria's attempt at innocence wasn't a rousing success, and after a moment of enduring Sophy's sternest look, she sighed heavily. "Oh, all right, so I never have before, but we have a job to do, you know. Sometimes it just requires little nudges, like the one that persuaded Selena Knight—"

"Melina."

"—to make Julia—"

"Julie."

"—a part of her family." Airily, Gloria waved at the quilt beneath a maple, where the private investigator and the formerly homeless teenager were surrounded by family and friends. "But sometimes we have to shov—er, nudge a little harder."

Sophy frowned at the woman. It probably wasn't appropriate to be so suspicious of another guardian, but she couldn't shake the feeling. "Where is this dish you brought?"

"Oh, it's gone now. It was green pea salad, with chunks of ham and cheddar and sweet onion, and with just a bit of sour cream mixed in the mayonnaise dressing—just the way Nolie's mama used to make it." With an appreciative smile, Gloria smacked her lips as if she could taste it even then.

Leaning forward, Sophy looked at the spot on the table where the salads sat. The bowl from which Nolie had served herself was gone—and, when she spotted Nolie sharing a quilt some distance away, she could see the generous portion Nolie had served herself was gone, too.

Straightening again, she turned a reproachful and suspicious gaze on the other guardian. "Heavenly stars, Gloria, *what* have you done?"

SIX O'CLOCK CAME AND WENT WITH NO SIGN OF Nolie and Micahlyn. So did seven. And eight. Chase told himself it was no big deal. She'd probably gone back to the store after the picnic, then gone out with someone. She'd done it before, on the day of the store's reopening. Hadn't gotten home until nine-thirty, and never had told him who she'd been with.

But things had changed between them since then. If

she'd had plans, she would have told him . . . but if she'd made the plans at the picnic, the only way to do that was to drive out and tell him in person. Maybe keeping him informed so he wouldn't worry wasn't that important to her. Not that he was worried. He was just . . . just . . .

Hell, yes, he was worried. For the second time in a day—a record for his months in Bethlehem—he got in his truck and headed into town. On the way, he pulled into the feed store parking lot. Her station wagon was parked there, but the CLOSED sign was on the door and only a couple of low-wattage lights burned inside. Though he knew it was pointless, he drove past City Park, thinking just maybe she and her new friends had decided to make a full day of it.

The park was empty.

The uneasy feeling in his gut began growing, tightening. He drove back up the hill, parking in front of her cabin. Maybe she'd had car trouble and she and Micahlyn had come home by way of the trail through the woods.

Though the usual lights were on, the house was locked up. Besides, even if she'd walked home, he would have known. She would have come over, if for no other reason than to invite him over.

In less than five minutes, he was back in the feed store lot, banging on the door, shouting her name, then Micahlyn's. He wasn't going to panic, he counseled himself. She wasn't hurt or dying somewhere. She was just being inconsiderate—having a good time, celebrating with new friends, forgetting about him. If anything, he should be pissed, not anxious. He should put her out of his mind and go home, and she would come wandering in when she was ready. Just like the day the store opened.

The counseling session didn't work. As he turned away

from the store, apprehension knotted his stomach. Something *was* wrong. He was sure of it. He just didn't know—

Leaning against the front fender of his truck, Sophy offered a tight smile. "Looking for Nolie?"

"Where is she?"

She chewed her lower lip, then said, "I can't tell you."

"I thought you knew everything."

"I do, but I can't tell everything. You'll have to find out for yourself."

Scowling, he jerked the SUV door open. "And how the hell am I supposed to do that?"

"Who are the go-to people in Bethlehem for information?"

In the city it would be the police, politicians, or the media. What they didn't know, they could find out. In Bethlehem it was simpler—the Winchester sisters.

As he climbed into the truck, Sophy stepped away and onto the sidewalk in front of the store. "When you see her, tell her Gloria's really sorry," she called.

With a nod, he slammed the door and backed up with a spray of gravel. As he waited to pull onto the highway, he glanced in the mirror at the storefront behind him. There was no sign of Sophy. This time he wasn't even surprised.

The first pay phone he came to was outside a gas station on the edge of town. He found Corinna Winchester Humphries in the phone book, dropped in some coins, and punched the numbers.

She answered on the third ring, her calm cool voice immediately transporting him back to sixth grade, when it had taken no more than that voice to keep a class of girly girls and rowdy boys in line.

"Miss Corinna, this is— I'm Nolie Harper's neighbor. She—" What if he was overreacting and about to make a fool of himself?

And what if he wasn't?

"Nolie's really late getting home, and I was wondering—"

For the first time in his memory, Miss Corinna interrupted. "Oh, dear, you must not have heard. They had to rush her to the hospital after the picnic today. I don't know exactly what was wrong—"

He didn't wait to hear the rest, dropping the receiver. He got into his truck and drove on autopilot into town, turning onto one quiet street after another until he reached the hospital. Feeling oddly calm—tense as hell, but calm—he parked in the first empty space he came to and climbed out. He didn't hesitate at opening the door, didn't give more than a brief thought to running away and hiding. Though it was the hardest thing he'd done since coming back, he crossed the parking lot and went in through the emergency room's walk-in entrance and straight to the desk.

The woman behind the desk looked vaguely familiar, but he made no effort to place her face with a name. "I'm looking for Nolie Harper. I understand—"

"Chase?"

The voice came from the waiting room behind him and was soft, feminine, and heavily shaded with emotion—surprise, maybe, or disbelief. It was familiar, too, but it wasn't Nolie, who was the only person he was interested in in this entire building.

Still, he turned around and noticed for the first time that the waiting room was filled with people, and right in their middle was the one who'd spoken. The one who'd recognized him.

His sister, Leanne.

. . .

WHEN MICAHLYN BEGAN STRUGGLING, LEANNE slowly let her slide to the floor, then watched as the child raced across the lobby to Chase. She launched herself toward him, and he crouched to scoop her up, then stood again, holding her possessively, as if he had every right to.

Leanne took a few halting steps toward them. She'd thought she would see icicles in July before she would see her brother again, and in Bethlehem, no less. He'd left swearing he would never return, and he'd made good on that vow for sixteen years. And now there he was, standing a dozen feet in front of her, looking older and handsome and so dear . . . and trapped. He hadn't wanted to run into her, hadn't wanted her to know he was back, and that cut more deeply than she could say.

She forced back the impulse to throw her arms around him and welcome him home, unsure *he* would welcome her embrace. Instead, she folded her arms tightly across her middle. "My God, Chase. I can't believe . . ." Couldn't believe he'd come back. Couldn't believe he'd been back a while, apparently, else how would he know Nolie and Micahlyn?

Micahlyn cupped her small hands to his cheeks, demanding his attention. "My mama got sick at the picnic and Leanne had to bring her to the hop–hospital, and the doctor said the food poisoned her and *she* says she's never gonna eat again. I was *scared*. Mama's never sick, but she just about turned *green*."

"She'll be all right," he said automatically, patting her back. Then he looked at Leanne. "Won't she?"

He was asking for reassurance for himself as well as Micahlyn, Leanne realized—a fact that puzzled her all the more. "She'll be fine. She apparently ate something at the picnic that didn't agree with her." Brusquely she changed the subject. "My God, what are you doing here? How long have you been back, and why didn't you let me know?"

He delayed by setting Micahlyn on the floor. "Mica, can you go over there for a minute?"

She looked up, her eyes magnified to twice their size by her glasses, her full bottom lip showing the faintest quiver. "You won't forget me, will you?"

"No, of course not."

Now there was an image Leanne couldn't have dreamed up—Nolie Harper's fatherless little girl looking at Chase Wilson as if he was the only security in her suddenly shaken world.

They both watched as Micahlyn skipped off to join Danny on the floor with his crayons and coloring books. After a moment, Leanne turned back to Chase. "You want to take the questions one at a time? When did you get back?"

"A few months ago."

"A few—" The hurt that answer sent spearing through her was enough to make her breath catch. She wanted to cry. To turn around and walk away from him and never look back. Hell, she wanted to smack him. Hard.

She settled for doing it verbally. "You've been in Bethlehem a few *months* and you never let anyone know?"

"Who was I supposed to let know? Mom and Dad? As if they would have cared?"

"*I* would have cared! My God, Chase, do you have any idea how many times I've tried to call you? How many letters I've written? Do you know how much I've missed you?"

His mouth thinned, and his eyes turned a few degrees colder. "Yeah. So much that you couldn't even be bothered to show up at my wedding."

That was a low blow. He was her only brother, her

protector, and, yes, on occasion, her tormentor. But she'd always loved him dearly and had always believed he felt the same about her. But how could he get married without her? "Your wed— You're married?"

"Not anymore."

"Why didn't you tell me?"

"What'd you want? An engraved invitation?" He smacked his forehead with the heel of his palm. "No, wait, we *sent* you one."

"I never got it."

"Oh, come on, Leanne. I addressed them myself. One to you, one to our parents."

She didn't want to think what she was thinking—hated it almost as much as she hated that she'd missed her only brother's wedding . . . and divorce. She didn't want to believe that either of her parents could be so heartless or so deceptive, but she had to know. "Both to the same address?"

After all these years, she was still able to read the suspicion forming in his mind. He stared at her a moment, his eyes dark with pain, then they suddenly went blank and his jaw tightened. "Yeah. The last I'd heard, you still lived at home. Even if you didn't, I figured Mom would make sure you got it."

"She didn't. Or Dad made sure she didn't. Who knows?" Her brother's relationship with their parents, particularly their father, had never been an easy one. Earl had pushed, and Chase had pushed back. Earl had set limits, and Chase had exceeded them. Earl had been overly critical, so Chase had given him plenty to be critical of. By the time he was sixteen, he'd been unable to spend five minutes in the same room with Earl without tempers flaring and exchanging ugly words.

Her sigh was heavy with years of regret. "I'm sorry,

Chase. I wouldn't have missed your wedding for anything."

Then, surprising herself almost as much as him, she smacked his arm hard. "You've got a hell of a nerve. Why didn't you call me? How could you just assume that I'd chosen them over you? You knew me better than that!"

"I thought I did. That was why . . ."

Trailing off, he shrugged and avoided her gaze. That was okay. She knew him well enough to know what he'd chosen not to finish. *Why it had hurt so bad.* The biggest day in his life—at least, to that time—had arrived, and the only family he'd always been able to count on, hadn't. She was so sorry for his disappointment and wanted to sweep him into her arms and make it all better, the way she did with Danny. But Chase wasn't four years old, and his hurts didn't heal as easily as Danny's.

He shrugged again. "You lived with them. They supported you. You were the favored child. And you'd been so worried about them finding out you'd gone to my graduation from law school. I just thought . . ."

"You just thought wrong. Don't think I'm over being pissed, because I'm not," she warned, "but . . . can I hug you?"

When he shrugged a third time, she wrapped her arms around him tightly. After a moment, he hesitantly slid his arms around her. It felt . . . amazing.

When she finally drew back, her eyes were damp and she sniffled a time or two. "I've got so much to tell you— and apparently, you've got even more to tell me, starting with your wedding and ending with Nolie. But first, come over here. There's someone I want you to meet. Danny."

Clutching a red crayon in his left hand, Danny joined them. Leanne lifted him to her hip, then turned him toward Chase. "This is Daniel David Wilson, my son.

Danny, this is your Uncle Chase. Remember, I've shown you pictures of him and told you he lived in Boston?"

Danny nodded vigorously. "He's the one that made you lose your front teeth when you were little, ain't he?"

Chase scowled at Leanne. "You couldn't tell him about the time I beat up the new kid for picking on you, or the time I carried you home when you hurt your foot, or all the years I tutored you in math, could you? No, you pick the time I accidentally made you fall."

"You *tripped* me."

"I was a growing boy. I didn't realize my feet had gotten so big. One of them just sort of got in your way."

Danny tilted his head to one side and studied Chase with eyes very much like his own. "How come you're my uncle?"

"Because your mom's my sister."

"How come you don't have the same mama and daddy?"

"We do, hon," Leanne answered.

"Huh-uh. I asked Grandpa once, and he said he didn't have a son. Just a princess." Danny giggled. "That's what he calls Mama. Did Grandpa lie?"

Leanne would have given an awful lot to say no. Or to have introduced her son to his only uncle right after his birth. Or to have seen Chase more than twice in the past sixteen years. Or to have a normal family where everyone loved one another and usually even liked one another. But not the Wilson family. Oh, no, words like *normal* and *love* and *like* didn't even belong in the same sentence with them. She might as well be wishing for the moon.

"Yes, hon, he lied, and I will have a talk with him about it tomorrow."

"Boy, is he gonna be in trouble. Can I go color with Micahlyn some more?"

"Sure." She swung him to the floor, then watched him go. After a moment, her gaze shifted a few yards past him, where Cole was reading a magazine between looks at them. When she caught his gaze, she smiled just a little. He didn't smile back, but she felt the warmth of his gaze clear across the room.

"What happened with Nolie?"

Chase's question made her swivel back to face him. "She went back to work after the picnic, then called and said she was sick. She just wanted a ride home, but she looked so awful, we brought her here instead." She studied him a long moment, then said, "I assume she didn't call you because . . . you don't have a phone?"

He shook his head.

"And I assume you know her because you're living in that other cabin out there."

This time he nodded.

A nurse came to the waiting room to call a patient back just as a new patient came in the door. Taking Chase's arm, Leanne drew him off to a relatively quiet spot against one wall. "Why did you come back if you didn't intend to let anyone know you were here?"

"Nolie says I had unfinished business here."

"Damn right you do." She started to punch him again, thought she probably should have outgrown that behavior by now, then did it anyway. "And what do you say?"

"I thought it was the only option left to me." He dragged his hand through his hair. "I don't know. Maybe she was right."

Before she could pursue that line of thought, Nola Matthews came through the doorway separating the treatment area from the waiting room, glanced around, then headed toward them. "Leanne. You brought Nolie Harper in, didn't you?"

"Yes, I did." Leanne barely got the words out before Chase demanded—er, asked, "How is she?"

When the doctor turned a speculative gaze on him, Leanne said, "Dr. Nola Matthews, my brother, Chase Wilson. He and Nolie are . . ." Lacking the insight to complete the sentence, she shrugged.

"She's had a rough night," Nola said briskly. "The vomiting, chills, nausea, etcetera, are pretty much gone, and we've pumped a couple liters of fluids into her to keep her from getting dehydrated. We've been watching her back there for the last couple hours, and she seems to be over the worst of it. Too bad—her first big event in Bethlehem, and she gets food poisoning from it."

"Has anyone else been sick?" Leanne asked.

"No one I've heard of. Weird, isn't it? Half the town ate all the same foods—well, almost all. She mentioned a green pea salad that I didn't see there—luckily, because I would have pigged out on it if I had, and then I could have shared an emesis basin with her."

"Can she go home tonight?" Chase asked.

"Yeah, we're not going to admit her. She's getting dressed now. Poor kid's exhausted, so hopefully, with all the meds in her system, she'll sleep well tonight and life will be worth living again tomorrow." Nola stuck out her hand. "Nice to meet you, Chase. Leanne, see you around."

After Nola disappeared through the double doors again, Leanne leaned against the cool tile wall. "I thought you might want to finish that sentence for me, about what's between you and Nolie."

He leaned back, too, where he could scan the faces in the waiting room. "She's not from here, is she? The doctor, I mean."

"I know their names are similar, but I think it was pretty

clear I said *Nolie,* not *Nola.*" Then Leanne relented. "No, she moved here a few years ago."

Moment after moment slipped past while he said nothing and refused to even look at her. Probably afraid she would see too much. Well, she was pretty good at waiting games herself.

As long as no one interrupted. This time it was Nolie. Her hair had come out of its braid and hung limp, and somehow she managed to look even paler than usual. There were shadows under her eyes and her smile and whole demeanor was shaky, but at least she was no longer green, groaning, or throwing up.

"Quick, get me out of here before they change their minds and start sticking me with needles again," she said, her voice hoarse and unsteady.

Chase spun around, and Nolie's eyes doubled in size. "Oh my God . . . you came into town. I can't believe . . ."

"What? You thought I wouldn't worry?" he asked, a scowl narrowing his features.

"No, of course not, but . . . you came into *town.* Around *people.*"

Leanne watched them as they looked at each other, and had her answer. Chase and Nolie were *involved.* Big time. Whether they knew it themselves or not.

Pushing away from the wall, she hugged Nolie. "I'm glad you're feeling better. If you need anything, give me a call." Then she faced Chase. "I have about a million questions for you, but they've kept for years. They'll wait a little longer. Take her home and put her to bed. And get a phone. Someone might be trying to reach you." She started to pinch the fleshy part of his arm, another habit from childhood, but gave it a quick, affectionate squeeze instead.

As she walked away, she heard Nolie ask, "How do you know Leanne?"

Her steps slowed and her breath caught in her chest as she waited for his response. It came quietly and—yes, she thought with overwhelming relief—affectionately. "She's my kid sister."

Chapter Thirteen

NOLIE AWOKE THE NEXT MORNING FEELING like a new woman—albeit, one who'd done some struggling to come into being. She felt a little punchy from the medications the doctor had given her, her mouth was dry, and her abdomen was still tender from the severe cramps she'd thought might kill her, but other than that, she felt pretty darn good. In a moment, she would get out of bed, get Micahlyn up, then start breakfast—

Her stomach clenched at the thought of food, and she grimaced. Maybe she would just lie here and recuperate a while longer.

All in all, Saturday had been quite a day. She'd had a ball at the picnic, had met more people and gotten better acquainted with many who'd come to the store's grand reopening. Micahlyn had made a dozen new friends, and the food . . . well, never mind that. The only downside—not counting the food poisoning—had been walking up on Leanne arguing with her parents because Danny hadn't wanted to spend the night with them and she wouldn't make him. Actually, Phyllis Wilson had done most of the arguing, while Earl Wilson alternately rolled his eyes or made snide comments designed to make his wife even angrier.

Phyllis and Earl Wilson. The parents Chase harbored such resentment toward. It was hard to imagine—at least, with Earl. Once Phyllis had stomped off in a fit of frustration, he'd been friendly and welcoming with Nolie. Clearly he loved his daughter and adored his grandson, and everyone who'd spoken to him, with the exception of his wife, had been affectionate or respectful. He'd reminded Nolie of her own father and, in better days, of Obie.

Phyllis, on the other hand, was bitter, angry at the world, unhappy, and blaming everyone but herself. She was a sharp-tongued, hot-tempered shrew, and Nolie completely understood why Chase had had nothing to do with her for sixteen years.

Slowly, she sat up, testing for any sign of the weakness that had plagued her last night, then eased to her feet. She was still wearing most of her clothes from the day before— when Chase had brought her upstairs shortly before midnight, he'd removed her shoes and helped her with her jeans before she'd collapsed into bed. He'd opened the windows, then tucked the sheet around her and—she thought—sat beside her for a while. She'd wanted to ask him a million questions, like Leanne, but it was a testament to how rotten she'd felt that she had fallen right to sleep instead. Judging by the stiffness in her joints, she hadn't moved once the rest of the night.

She took a quick shower, wrapped a robe around her, then started downstairs. Nearly at the bottom, she came to an abrupt stop. Chase was stretched out in the recliner across the room, sound asleep, and curled in the crook of his arm was Micahlyn, also asleep. Her favorite storybook was open on his lap, and Maria Diane had tumbled down between his side and the chair arm.

The bogeyman had been tamed, Nolie thought, one hand pressed to her heart to ease the ache that seized it. They looked so comfortable together—so trusting of each other, and neither of them, she knew well, gave that trust easily.

Maybe Gloria had been right. Maybe Chase really did need them.

In the same scary, exciting, uncertain way *she* needed *him*.

As she moved on down the stairs, the next to the last step creaked loudly and Chase stirred, breathing deeply, then reached up to rub his jaw as he opened his eyes. He saw her right away and looked at her as if . . . oh, Lord, as if he really did need her.

He eased out of the chair, carefully laid Micahlyn down again, then followed Nolie into the kitchen. While he leaned against the counter, one ankle crossed over the other, she started a pot of coffee, then poured herself a glass of water. If her stomach could handle that, then she'd think about something else to take the edge off its emptiness.

Finally, she combed her fingers through her wet hair as if it needed it, though it was slicked straight back from her face—not the most flattering style for a plump face like hers. Too late to do anything about that. Besides, he'd seen her last night looking almost her worst—worst had been when Leanne and Cole Jackson arrived at the store to find her doubled over in pain, sweating, moaning, and heaving up the contents of her stomach for the hundredth time—and he hadn't run away.

She leaned against the counter opposite him and laced her fingers around the glass. "There's so much to talk about that I don't even know where to start."

"How about we start right here?" He pushed away from the counter, reached her in two long strides, slid his fingers into her hair, and kissed her hungrily. His tongue coaxed her teeth apart, not that she needed coaxing, then stabbed into her mouth. It was a quick, hard kiss, over too soon, then his dark gaze searched her face. "How do you feel?"

"Well . . . my blood's pumping now." She raised one hand to curl her fingers around his wrist. "I'm going to survive."

"Damn straight you are."

"Chase Wilson." She whispered his name, had whispered it to herself over and over on the way home last night. She finally had a name for her neighbor, friend, the object of her erotic fantasies . . . for the man she was *this* close to falling in love with. Under ordinary circumstances, she would have learned his full name the first time they'd met. But there'd been nothing ordinary about *their* circumstances.

Hearing the final drips of the coffeemaker, she took two mugs from the cabinet, then crossed to the counter where the machine sat. She filled the mugs, offered one to him, then moved the sugar and powdered creamer to a spot between them. At last, she said, "I met your parents."

He didn't scowl or make some obscene sound, as she expected. He acknowledged her comment with a slight nod, then said, "I met my nephew."

"Danny's a doll, isn't he?"

"He gets that from his mother."

"She must get it from her brother." Still somewhat bemused by the fact that he was the brother Leanne had mentioned on occasion, she gave a shake of her head. "How did you know where to find us?"

"I checked here, the store, and the park. Sophy suggested I call the Winchesters, so I did, and Miss Corinna

said you'd been taken to the hospital. By the way, Sophy
said to tell you Gloria was really sorry. About what?"

"I don't know, unless she made the pea salad." The
mention of it brought a sour taste to her mouth, which she
washed away with the stronger, bitter taste of undoctored
coffee. "And just like that, you came." The wonder of it
amazed her. For weeks he'd stayed close to home, making
serious efforts to avoid the town and all its residents. But
he'd broken his self-imposed exile, and he'd done it for *her*.

Now he scowled at her. "All Miss Corinna said was that
you'd been rushed to the hospital. For all I knew, you
could have been dying. If I'd known it was just a little
stomachache . . ."

"Hah! Stronger people than you have been laid low by
less," she retorted. "Micahlyn thought I was dying, and
there were a few moments there where I was convinced
dying couldn't possibly hurt worse." She added one packet
of sweetener to her coffee and stirred it, then dropped the
spoon in the sink. "Leanne must have been thrilled to
see you."

"I don't know. She punched me twice."

"Oh, she did not."

"She did, too. I've probably got the bruises to show for
it. You want to see?"

It was an innocent question. She was 95 percent sure of
it. But damned if the response flooding through her, all hot
and tingly, was as far from innocent as could be. If her coffee wasn't already hot, she could make it steam by doing
nothing more than holding the mug. "Sure," she said, or
tried to, but her voice was husky. She cleared her throat.
"Roll up your sleeve and show me."

His eyes gleamed with mischief, wickedness, humor—
she didn't know what—as he shook his head. "I didn't say
she punched me on the arm. I'd have to take my shirt off."

Her hands started to tremble, and she swore her terry robe had suddenly developed the warming capacity of a half-dozen mink coats. Afraid she might get burned, she set the coffee down. Afraid she might get burned worse, and not caring, she hoarsely replied, "So take it off."

Whatever had gleamed in his gaze, fled, leaving him serious and solemn and intense. "How late does Micahlyn sleep?"

She glanced at the clock. "As late as she was up last night and with all the excitement, she should be out for another few hours."

"That's all, huh?"

"How long does it take to show me some nonexistent bruises?"

"A couple hours, at least. Probably five or six to do it right. But"—his smile was tentative and disappeared practically before it formed—"we can make the best of what we've got . . . if you want."

He moved to stand a few feet in front of her and offered his hand. She stared at it, fascinated by the strength in his long, tanned fingers, stunned by the intensity with which she wanted to take it, but unable to do so . . . yet. Tugging at her robe's belt, she raised her gaze to his. "I–I'm not very good at playing games, Chase. I don't know if you're flirting or teasing or deadly serious."

"Yes," he said simply, to all three, then apparently took pity on her. "Just so there's no misunderstanding, if you go upstairs with me, I'm going to do my damnedest to seduce you. I want to see you naked. I want to kiss every inch of your body. I want—" He swallowed hard, and an exquisitely fierce look came over him, making his voice raw and sharp. "I want to make love to you, Nolie."

She wanted to say yes and drag him upstairs . . . to say

I'm sorry and run away. She was aroused and frightened, flattered and intrigued and unsure.

He waited patiently, his gaze never wavering, his need never slipping.

"I–I've never been with anyone but Jeff," she said at last.

"I know."

"I'm not exactly experienced."

The faintest smile quirked one corner of his mouth. "Trust me. I know what to do."

She smiled a bit, too, then tugged tighter at her belt. "I'm not on–on the pill or–or anything."

Gently he pulled the belt from her hands. "Stop that, or we'll have to cut you out of that robe." Then . . . "I have a box of condoms in the truck."

Of course he did. Be prepared—the motto of the Boy Scouts and single men everywhere. Not that he'd used them yet, even though he'd had every chance.

Finally he took her hands. "Nolie, it's all right if you want to say no. Just tell me it's too soon or you're not ready or you don't"—his voice steeled—"don't want me. I'll be disappointed, but I'll deal with it."

Mouth pursed, she shook her head. "I can't do that, because it wouldn't be true, and I try really hard to always tell the truth." She watched as the understanding that she was going to go upstairs with him dawned. Instead of looking relieved, though, he seemed fiercer, tauter, than ever. Almost as if her simple agreement aroused him even further.

"But you have to promise me one thing. When I take this robe off . . . don't compare me to any of the other women in your life, okay?" Her voice had started out strong and confident, but by the *okay*, it had deteriorated into a plea that heated her face with embarrassment.

"There are no other women in my life. Just you," he

said as he pulled her closer. Once her body was snug against his—against his arousal—he brushed a kiss to her temple, another to her cheek, and a third, long, deep, intimate kiss to her mouth, then said, "And just for the record . . . when you take that robe off, honey, I'm gonna get down on my knees and thank God, and then I'm gonna make damn sure you don't regret it."

So she was *this* close to falling in love, huh? She might still be on her feet, but no doubt about it . . .

She'd just finished falling.

WHEN HE WAS SIXTEEN, CHASE HAD LOST HIS VIRginity with his high school girlfriend, a pretty little dark-haired thing. Until that night, he'd thought she was a virgin, too, but she'd had a few surprises in store for him. Logically, the fact that she knew what she was doing should have relaxed him, but it had made him more nervous instead.

He felt the same way now, as if he were taking a monumental step and he'd damn well better not screw up.

Though, of course, he would. Making love with her when he still had no intentions of sticking around forever, when she still didn't know the truth . . . no matter how he looked at it, it was wrong.

And no matter how wrong it was, he was going to do it anyway. He needed it.

He needed *her*.

Carrying the box of condoms in one hand, he quietly closed the door behind him, then checked on Micahlyn, snoring softly in the recliner. Nolie was upstairs, wearing nothing but that robe, probably waiting beside the bed with its summer-light sheets and quilt. The idea turned him on and made his palms sweaty and his mouth dry.

Skipping the step that creaked, he climbed to the top, walked to the open bedroom door, and stopped. Nolie was, indeed, waiting next to the bed. She'd closed the blinds, turning the room shadowy. With Fiona, it would have been vanity—she believed every woman benefitted from soft lighting. With Nolie, he'd bet it was a combination of modesty and insecurity. He planned to do his best to banish both feelings from her wide range of emotions.

She smiled nervously as he stepped inside and closed the door, then tossed the box on the bed. "Do you always carry condoms in your truck?"

"Never before. But I told you—I went to Howland one night intending to end my three-years-plus of abstinence. I bought them then."

Her fingers nervously worked at her belt, this time undoing the knot instead of tightening it. He wondered if she knew her actions had caused the robe to loosen so that the vee that earlier had ended modestly above her breasts now dipped almost to her waist, revealing the curves and shadows of her full breasts. He wanted to walk across the room, brush her hands away, and slide his own inside the robe so bad he damn near hurt with it.

He did circle the bed to her, but when he touched her, it was her face, cupping one palm to her cheek. "I'd ask if you have any idea how beautiful you are, but I already know the answer. You see red hair. I see rich, coppery hair that's silky and soft. You see pale skin, freckles, and blue eyes, and I see skin as fine as porcelain, creamy and smooth and soft, and eyes the blue of a summer sky. You see yourself as generously proportioned, and I see incredible curves. I see a beautiful woman."

Her breathing had turned shallow as he spoke, then she stopped breathing completely, or so it seemed, when he kissed her. He slid his arms around her—outside the robe, damn it—and drew her tightly against him, and lazily, hungrily, but with all the time in the world, kissed her. His erection strained against his jeans, against her stomach, reminding him how long it had been, but he couldn't hurry. Not this first time. Maybe not the first fifty times.

She raised her hands to his chest, then slid down, searching for and finally finding the bottom of his shirt. Undressing him seemed a bold move for someone so shy, but he realized that wasn't her intent, not yet, at least, the instant her palms flattened against his bare skin. Her touch was tentative, relatively innocent, no more than gentle caresses across his middle, but she left a sharp, aching heat everywhere she went. When one hand eased higher and one fingertip brushed across his nipple, he sucked in his breath and lifted his mouth from hers. His gaze locked on hers, wide and watchful but unafraid, as he put a few inches between them, then deliberately slid his hand inside her robe, brushing across her nipple in the same way.

Her lips parted, but she didn't make a sound, and when he cupped her breast in his palm, a sweet heavy weight, her eyes fluttered shut. Pushing the robe back from that side only, he stroked her breast, toyed with her nipple, making it swell and harden. Impatiently, he pushed the other side of the robe away, guiding the fabric off her shoulder, then maneuvering so he could sit on the bed. She moved willingly between his thighs, giving a soft gasp when he took her nipple into his mouth. He felt her pulse pounding, the rate damn near doubling when he suckled harder at her breast, and heard her shallow, rapid breaths.

The knot in the belt came free and the robe fell away, but he didn't take time to admire her. Sliding his hands to her hips, he lifted her with him as he rolled back onto the bed. The condom box crushed beneath his weight, but he didn't mind that, either, as he continued to suck, nip, kiss, and caress her.

"Chase . . ." She managed little more than a whisper, quavery and raw with need.

Lifting his head, he saw her expression, dazed, but purely, painfully, pleasured. "What, babe?"

"Take off your clothes. I want . . ."

To see him naked? To feel him inside her? To not be the only one vulnerable and exposed? He didn't care which was the right answer. Rolling off the bed, he jerked his T-shirt over his head and kicked off his jeans and briefs, all under her steady gaze. Naked, he stretched out beside her, leaning his head on one hand so he could watch her, using the other to stroke lightly across her breasts, her stomach, her hips. When he reached the curls between her thighs, she caught her breath. When he slid one fingertip over that hypersensitive spot beneath the curls, her thighs tightened as if to stop him at the same time her hips arched, inviting him to continue.

He stroked inside her, then all the way back out, making her whimper as she clenched his wrist. "If you don't stop, you're going to make me . . ." In spite of her plea, though, she wasn't pulling his hand away, but pressing it harder against her flesh.

He chuckled. "We're gonna have to do something about your shyness, darlin'. And making you . . . is kind of the point, isn't it? Again and again . . ."

Wearing a smile that was wicked and womanly and not the least bit shy, she turned onto her side, trapping his hand where he couldn't tease her, then wrapping her fingers around *his* flesh, stroking every stone-hard, aching inch of it. Sensation flooding through him, he gave himself the feeble order to pull her hand away, but—déjà vu—instead molded his hand to hers and thrust desperately, once, twice, three times, against the incredible friction she created.

Even though his eyes were squeezed shut, he swore they'd crossed, and his chest was so tight he couldn't manage more than the slightest of breaths. "Ah, damn . . . sweet damnation, Nolie. . . ."

"That's kind of the point, isn't it?" she whispered. "Make love to me, Chase. Please."

He moved to his knees between her thighs, then unrolled a condom into place, clenching his jaw at the tremors rocketing through him. "This isn't going to last long," he warned. "It's been a long time."

"I know. For me, too." She reached for him, and he slid inside her, breaking out in a cold sweat at the need to hold out and the stronger need to make good on his warning. She took the choice from him, shifting her hips, drawing a shuddering groan from him, and smiled that wicked smile again. "That's why we get to do it again and again."

MICAHLYN WAS STANDING ON THE CHAIR SHE'D dragged to the kitchen counter, carefully pouring milk on her cereal, when the ring of the telephone made her jump and milk spilled onto the counter. She looked from the spill to the phone, not sure which to take care of first. When the phone rang again, she set the milk down, jumped to the floor, and skipped across the room.

"Tough choice," Gloria murmured from her seat on the opposite counter.

Sophy snorted. "You would have gone for the phone, too."

"Probably. Talking is so much more enjoyable than cleaning, even though the cleaning's gotta be done."

"Usually by someone else," Sophy retorted. "That's one thing you and Micahlyn have in common."

Gloria looked hurt—for about a second. Then she stuck her tongue out at Sophy.

Stretching onto her toes, Micahlyn picked up the receiver in midring. "H'llo."

"Hi, Mikey, it's Grandma. What are you doing?"

"Pourin' some milk on my cereal so's I can have breakfast, but I spilled some, so I have to clean it up."

"Why isn't your mother pouring the milk?"

Micahlyn stretched the cord to the counter, pulled her cereal bowl over, and shoveled a big bite into her mouth, crunching before she answered. "She's asleep. We all slept late 'cause it was late when we got home last night. Guess what? Mama got food poisoning from green pea salad—"

Sophy turned a chastising look on Gloria, who squirmed guiltily.

"—and she had to go to the hospital, but she's all right now. I'm sure glad I don't eat peas, 'cause they're icky, and I bet now she won't never try to make me eat 'em again."

"Oh, no, peas aren't icky. They're *good* for you," Gloria said. Of course, Micahlyn didn't hear.

"You said you all sleeped—slept late," Grandma said. "You mean, both you and your mother?"

"And Chase. He slept with *me* last night, and him and Mama are in bed now. I changed clothes all by myself, and brushed my teeth, and now I'm fixin' my own breakfast, and I'm bein' real quiet so's I won't wake them. And you know what, Grandma? We went to a picnic yesterday, and I met a whole lot of kids, and they're lots nicer than stinky ol' Laura back there. And let's see . . . what else did I want to tell you? Oh, yeah, did you know . . ."

He slept with me *last night, and him and Mama are in bed now.* Sophy winced. Too bad Chase had unplugged the upstairs phone last night. All he'd wanted was to let Nolie sleep without any disturbances, but compared to the trouble Micahlyn's conversation was going to stir, one little phone call wouldn't have disturbed a soul.

"Oh, dear," Gloria murmured, then sighed philosophically. "Well, every relationship needs a little trial by fire, doesn't it?"

And Marlene Harper would be Nolie and Chase's. Sophy hoped they survived.

T HE DISTANT RING OF THE TELEPHONE DIMLY PENEtrated Nolie's brain, making her open one eye and look at the phone on the night table. When it remained silent, she snuggled deeper into the pillow. The ringing phone must have been on TV, since this one rang loud enough to wake the dead.

She was about to drift off to sleep again when a warm, hard body moved snugly against her, with emphasis on *hard*. Chase's hand slipped around to cup her breast, gently squeezing her tender nipple, and his arousal was hot and solid against her bottom. She couldn't believe he was ready again, when they'd made love twice in the past few hours. Granted, the first time had practically been over before it started for both of them, though was no less satisfying for that, but the second time . . . She'd never known it could last like that. By the time it had finally ended, they'd both been trembling, slick with sweat, and she'd thought she just might burst into a million pieces if he'd kept her from reaching orgasm one instant longer.

He hadn't . . . but she'd burst into a million pieces anyway.

"I think I heard stirring downstairs," Chase murmured

into her ear. "If we're quiet and quick, can we do it one more time?"

Quick was no problem, they'd already proven, but quiet? She wasn't a screamer, but neither of them would win any awards for quietness. Heavy breathing—theirs. Whimpers—hers. Groans—his. Erotic little sounds. Erotic little turn-ons. She liked knowing she could make him groan in that guttural, sexy, helpless way, liked that she could double his heart rate and his respirations with nothing more than a well-placed caress.

She liked knowing he could do the same to her.

He coaxed her to lift her leg, then his arousal probed between her thighs before sliding home. With an already-satisfied sigh, she twisted her head for his kiss and arched her back to press her breast harder against his palm. When he slid his hand between her legs, she gave a soft cry. When he rubbed that spot and brought her to orgasm, she would have cried out much louder, but his mouth muffled the sound, just as she muffled his groan.

Withdrawing from her body, he moved back enough that she could turn over to face him. He brushed her hair from her flushed face, then placed a kiss on her nose. "You are beautiful."

For the first time, she didn't argue with him, in her own mind or out loud, because for the first time, she *felt* beautiful. No, make that the second. The first time was when he'd compared her to silk, porcelain, and a summer sky. . . .

A frown brought her brows together. The words sounded oddly familiar, but she was positive no one had ever spoken them to her before. Those were the kind of compliments a woman never forgot, especially a woman who'd never received many such compliments. Especially when they came from a man like Chase.

He traced his fingertip over the lines in her forehead. "What's wrong?"

"Nothing." She stretched lazily, raising her arms above her head, then brought one hand down on his arm. "So . . . where are those bruises you were going to show me?"

"Hmm. Don't guess she hit me that hard, after all. Though I may have gained a few scratches and teeth marks since we came up here." He grinned so lasciviously that Nolie blushed from the top of her head all the way down her body.

Before she could apologize—or demand to see the proof—Micahlyn's voice bellowed up the stairs. "Ma-maaa! We got company! Can I let 'em in?"

Nolie retrieved her robe from the floor and was about to put it on when Chase tugged it away, apparently thinking he'd left her with no choice but to go to the door naked while he watched openly—and with interest. Making a face at him, she sashayed to the closet door, where she grabbed her other robe and shrugged it on. The green satin provided far less camouflage than the heavy terry cloth, but it beat being naked.

"Ma-maaa!" Micahlyn shouted from the top of the stairs just as Nolie opened the door a few inches.

"Who's here, babe?"

"Danny and his mom. Can I let them in?"

"Okay. Tell Leanne I'll be down in just a minute." Closing the door, she began gathering underwear from the dresser, along with a summer dress from the closet. "I believe this company is for you. I'll entertain her until you're ready to face her."

Arms full, she went into the bathroom, where she dressed and pulled her hair back into a ponytail. A few unruly strands fell over her forehead, making it painfully clear that she'd made little effort with her appearance that morning. Oh, well, Leanne liked her for her personality, not her dazzling beauty, and Chase, poor fool, thought she was beautiful anyway.

By the time she made it downstairs, Micahlyn had let the Wilsons in and was telling them how she'd dressed herself and fixed her own breakfast. The dressing part wouldn't have been a difficult guess, since she wore a green-and-white-striped T-shirt with yellow-and-pink polka-dotted shorts.

"How are you feeling, Nolie?" Leanne asked when Micahlyn finished her recitation.

"I'm fine." Better than fine. She felt tingly and satiated and wicked and besotted and about a hundred other things. "Thanks for helping me out last night."

"Anytime." Leanne's grin turned sly and knowing. "Hope I didn't interrupt anything."

That blasted blush flared again as Nolie took a seat on the couch. "Oh, no, not at all. I've already been up and had a shower and some coffee and—and—"

"Uh-huh. My brother wouldn't happen to be here, would he? There was no answer at his house, and I figured that truck out front must be his." She made a point of looking at the man-sized running shoes on the floor next to the recliner where she sat, then grinned even bigger.

"I— He—uh—"

"Yes, I'm here." Chase came down the stairs, moving gracefully into the room. He was dressed, and he'd combed his hair, and though his feet were bare, otherwise he looked perfectly and innocently presentable, or so Nolie told herself. No one would notice that lazy, satisfied, just-had-great-sex look in his eyes, or catch the warmth in his gaze when it brushed over her, or even think twice about the careless way he touched her shoulder on his way to the other end of the sofa.

But Leanne wasn't no one. Despite their long separation, she probably knew him better than anyone around. Judging from her own satisfied look, she noticed everything.

"Why aren't you in church?" Chase asked after he sat down with his shoes and began putting them on. "You raising my nephew to be a heathen?"

"Like uncle, like nephew." Leanne made a face at him. "We go to church most of the time . . . well, unless we have a good reason not to, don't we, Danny?"

He looked up from the storybook Chase had read to Micahlyn the night before. "Uh-huh. But sometimes we go have breakfast at Harry's, an' then play in the square instead."

"That's your definition of a good reason?" Chase asked his sister dryly.

She shrugged. "This morning we definitely had a good reason to skip. It's not every day that a woman's brother comes back after disappearing for all those years. I told you last night, my questions would wait a while, but I'm all out of patience. I want to know *everything,* starting with when you're going over to see Mom and Dad."

He glanced at Nolie, as if making sure she was still there, then replied, "I don't know that I am."

"Oh, Chase—"

"Oh, Leanne—" He copied her tone, sounding as pesty as anyone Nolie had heard. Last night it had been kind of hard to imagine him as anyone's brother. His mimicry and resulting grin made it easier this morning.

"They're your parents."

"No, they're *your* parents. For me they're just the people who provided a place to live until I could support myself. They didn't help with a dime of my college expenses, they refused to come to my graduation from college or law school, they refused to attend my wedding or to even meet my wife. Dad lived for the day I would be out of his house and his life, and Mom never cared either way."

Nolie wished desperately that Leanne would disagree—that she could point out times when their parents had treated Chase the way they'd treated her. But Leanne didn't dispute his recall, and it wouldn't have mattered if she did. He'd felt unwanted and unloved, and *that* was all that mattered.

"Mama, can I show Danny my room?" Micahlyn asked.

"Sure, babe."

Chattering about all her toys, Micahlyn led the way upstairs. Once they were gone, Leanne sighed. "Okay. I really can't blame you. I try to avoid Mom as much as I can these days, and the two of them together . . ." Grimly, she shook her head.

"I'm surprised they still are together," Chase remarked dryly. "I can't remember them ever being happy."

"Me, either. Speaking of still being together . . ." Leanne's gaze flickered from Chase to Nolie, then back again. "What happened with you and your marriage?"

"The marriage was fine. The divorce was hell."

"What happened?"

Nolie stood up, intending to slip off into the kitchen. She wanted to know the details of his divorce, but not like this, not because she was sitting in on what should be a private reunion with his sister. Besides, she knew both from him and Raine that Fiona wasn't a nice person, but he'd loved her anyway. His mistake, he'd called it. She couldn't help but wonder, though. . . . How bad did a not-nice woman have to get, to lose her husband's love?

"I—I'll fix us something to drink," she said as she moved behind the couch.

Chase caught her hand, though, and refused to let go.

"You've had more questions than anyone I know, and now all you can think about is playing the perfect hostess?"

Blushing, she lowered her gaze. "You and Leanne should be alone. This conversation—your parents, your marriage—is personal."

His thumb rubbed lazily over the pulse in her wrist, sending a languid heat through her veins. "Honey, it doesn't get anymore personal than you and me. If you're uncomfortable, you can go hide in the kitchen, but . . . I wish you'd stay."

Oh, sheesh, all but telling his sister they were lovers, touching her like that, looking at her like that—it would take a stronger woman than Nolie to walk away now. She returned to the couch and was about to sit at the end when he gestured for her to move closer. She sat beside him, and he laced his fingers through hers.

"My ex's name is Fiona," he said. "I invited you guys to the wedding. No one came. I called Mom a half-dozen times afterward, trying to arrange a trip to Bethlehem to introduce her to all of you, but according to Mom, there never was a good time. We were married six years ago, and she divorced me three years ago when the man she was having an affair with—one of the lawyers I worked with, by the way—agreed to marry her. Next question?"

His tone was even, pretty much emotionless, as if this were ancient history that meant nothing to him, but Nolie knew better. Fiona had broken his heart, but a person could never guess it listening to him now.

Unless . . . the broken heart had healed and the devastation really was ancient history. Unless someone had replaced Fiona in his heart. Someone like . . . oh, gee, maybe *her*?

The arrogance of her assumption made Nolie suppress a

smile. Not long ago she'd wished to be bold, daring, and confident. Maybe some wishes did come true.

"Why aren't you practicing law?" Leanne asked.

"Don't want to."

"Why not?"

"Maybe I decided to live down to the old man's expectations and amount to nothing."

Leanne scoffed. "You were a hotshot lawyer making tons of money. You're way past amounting to nothing." Abruptly she went on to her next question. "Why didn't you ever call me?"

His fingers tightened fractionally around Nolie's. "If our parents wouldn't pass on your invitation to the wedding, what makes you think they would have let me talk to you on the phone?"

"I'm in the phone book. I have been for years."

Again his fingers tightened, then relaxed when he blew out an impatient breath. "When you didn't come to the wedding, I was pissed. As far as I was concerned, from then on I didn't have a family." He tensed at her flinch, then turned the question back on her. "Why didn't you call me? I was in the phone book, too, at least, for a while."

"For a long time I was swamped with trying to get the shop up and running, and then I got pregnant and Danny's dad ran out on me, and things were getting worse with Mom. . . . There's nothing like having a baby to make you realize how important family is, and I was pretty much estranged from two-thirds of mine. Nothing I did could fix things with Mom, but you were always so much more reasonable." She smiled dimly. "I called the last number I had for you, but it belonged to some fifteen-year-old kid. I called the firm where you'd worked and all they would tell me was that you were no longer with them. I sent letters to the firm asking them to forward them, and every one of them came back unopened. I called the state bar in Massachusetts to find out where you were practicing, and they didn't have a clue."

For a moment silence settled over the room, heavy and stiff. Then Leanne's stomach growled loudly, easing the tension. "Let's go into town and get some lunch," she suggested. "If we hurry, we can get to Harry's or McCauley's Steakhouse before all the church people show up."

Nolie was torn between hoping he would agree and wanting to stay home. Though she would love to go out in public with him, they were sure to run into people he knew who would want to say hello. Besides, there was something awfully nice about a quiet, private family meal.

When Chase looked at her, one brow raised, she shrugged, leaving the decision to him. He studied her a moment, then turned back to his sister. "Why go to McCauley's when Nolie's teaching me how to grill steaks? You two go to the store, I'll watch the kids, and when you get back, I'll show you what I've learned."

Grinning, Leanne stood up. "Sounds great. Get some shoes on, Nolie, quick, before the kids realize we're sneaking out."

Nolie was almost at the top of the stairs when Leanne spoke again. "One more question, Chase. You and Nolie . . . is it serious? Because, you know, I've always wanted a sister."

Nolie couldn't help it. She stopped at the top of the stairs, not moving, not breathing, and listened for his response. If it was verbal, though, she couldn't hear it.

It was just as well. If he was serious or if he wasn't . . . a woman should learn information like that firsthand, not pick it up eavesdropping.

Though darned if she wouldn't take it any way she could get it.

Chapter Fourteen

SINCE HIS ARRIVAL IN BETHLEHEM, COLE HAD made a practice of having lunch most weekdays at Harry's, the place to see and be seen. He'd learned more about the town and its residents in that thirty or forty minutes each day than he could have picked up in a week elsewhere. He was a regular now, had his usual table, and was greeted by all the other regulars when he walked in the door.

But Monday, Tuesday, and again on Wednesday, he'd called the sub shop around the corner and asked them to send up a sandwich. He didn't feel like being a regular today—didn't want to smile and joke and be friendly as hell.

He wanted out of Bethlehem.

The town was getting too comfortable. Sometimes he caught himself thinking about it as a permanent relocation, as if he would be there weeks or months down the line. As if his future was there.

And the people . . . Since Leanne had understandably spent Sunday getting reacquainted with her long-absent brother, he'd gone to church that morning and dragged Ryan along. The elderly sisters who lived a few blocks away had invited them to dinner, and everyone had made them feel as if—as if they belonged. The kids had welcomed Ryan into their midst without reservation, and the adults had done the same to Cole. They'd liked him, trusted him, been open and honest and friendly.

While he'd done nothing but lie since he set foot in this town.

If he had a conscience, he would think the town had gotten to him, but he'd been raised conscience-free. By the time he was ten, his father had taught him everything a boy needed to know about picking pockets and picking locks, choosing a mark and relieving him—or her—of whatever it was you wanted, creating a diversion and feigning innocence, sacrificing your partners and saving your own hide. Any gaps left in his education by his father had been filled in by his mother. His parents had been the best con artists the great state of Texas ever produced.

And he was better than both.

For the first time in too many years—maybe ever—he didn't find any pride in that.

He slumped lower in his leather chair and scowled at the diamond cuff links on the desk blotter. Funny that a boy from the wrong side of the tracks in Dallas could be living in the Miller mansion, driving a sixty-thousand-dollar Lexus, and wearing diamond cuff links. None of it was his, of course. The Lexus was a rental. By the time the deal fell through on the house, he would be long gone, and the cuff links he'd stolen from a rich divorcée in Palm Beach.

There wasn't much in life that was his. Even the things he'd bought, like this Armani suit, had been paid for with money he'd taken from others.

No wonder Ryan had thought nothing of stealing all those books for his personal library. Cole had thought if he kept the kid out of the business—his only unbreakable rule—Ryan would grow up decent and law-abiding, but how could he expect the kid to show respect for the law when he saw Cole and the rest of the family breaking it all the time?

The kid deserved a better family.

He damn well deserved a better father.

A soft knock at the open door interrupted his brooding. Expecting the tall, gangly kid from the sandwich shop, he looked up to find Nolie Harper instead. "Hi. I guess your secretary's out, so . . ."

He glanced past her to the empty desk in the waiting room. "I don't have one." A secretary was a luxury he couldn't afford, not when the investment opportunities he was selling didn't exist, certainly not when the clients' money he was taking in had already been funneled to a different bank account under a different name, just waiting for him to leave Bethlehem and reclaim it.

"The kid at the sub shop was too busy to deliver this, so I volunteered." She came farther into the room to hand over a paper bag. "He said to tell you he'll put it on your tab."

Another trusting soul he'd be stiffing. His jaw tightened. "Thanks. How are you feeling?"

Her face turned a becoming pink. "I'm fine."

"Tired of people asking you that?"

"A little." She glanced around the office, appraising it. Everything was top quality. One of Cole's earliest lessons had been that a man had to spend money to make money. The chairs were leather, the bookcase solid oak. The file cabinets—mostly empty—were oak, too, and antiques, as was the desk. The fountain pen resting on an open file was a Mont Blanc and cost about the same as a good used car. It was stolen, too, from the same widow who'd provided his cuff links.

The office was impressive, an efficient tool in gaining his marks'—his clients'—trust. And their money.

"Can I ask you something?"

He raised both hands palm up. "Ask away."

"You've been awfully busy since you came here, building your client base, visiting all the business owners in town. But you've never approached me. Why not?"

Good question. Granted, Hiram's Feed Store didn't appear to be the most prosperous business in town, but he knew better than anyone that appearances could be deceiving. Maybe he'd given her a break because she was so young and widowed and raising her little girl alone, or he'd decided not to part her from her money because they came from the same part of the country.

Or maybe it was because she was a friend of Leanne's.

Sentimental crap.

He smiled his used-car salesman's smile. "You're on my list. Are you looking to invest?"

She shrugged, then slid into the chair across from him. "My husband died three years ago, and I'm saving his life insurance for Micahlyn's college. It's been in CDs, but the last time they matured, I stuck them in a savings account until I could decide what else to do. If you have something better to suggest . . ."

Yeah. Keep yourself and your money far, far away from me. That money would be better served spending the next twelve years in a low-interest savings account than in providing him flash money for another scam in another town.

Still, he didn't turn her away. That wasn't the Jackson way. "Let me put something together for you, and I'll bring it by the store."

She smiled, as open and honest and trusting as all the other damn fools in this town, and stood up. "Okay. Thanks."

He walked with her to the reception door, watched her leave, then closed that door and returned to his desk. "Oh, yeah, babe. Thank me for screwing your daughter out of an education."

He unwrapped the sandwich, stared at it a moment or so, then tossed it in the trash.

It seemed he'd lost his appetite.

As Nolie carried lunch into the feed store, she noticed the bell over the door remained silent. She gazed up at it a moment, wondering exactly who to call to fix it. She was pretty sure there wasn't a listing in the Yellow Pages for "Annoying bells over doors in stores." Maybe she would just let it stay broken. After all, it *was* annoying, and it wasn't as if the store was so big that she wouldn't notice a customer.

Chase was kicked back in her chair, his feet propped on the desk, when she walked behind the counter. He laid down the magazine he'd been reading and let his gaze slide over her in that way that made her knees weak and her heart pitter-patter. "You're back."

Oh, yeah, and about to dissolve into a puddle at his feet. She managed to open the drawer where her purse went on the third try, then set the sandwiches on the counter. Though they were wrapped in identical wrappers, they were easy to tell apart. His was the monster with everything on it, including two kinds of melted cheese and a rich creamy dressing, while hers was the roasted chicken with no cheese, no dressing, no anything but a handful of pickles and onions. Yes, she was back on her diet, and doing pretty well. Stripping down naked every night with a gorgeous man provided an incentive she'd never had before.

"Any customers?" she asked as she handed his sandwich and a bag of chips to him, then slid onto the stool with her own sandwich and baked chips.

"No one I couldn't handle."

"I should hope there's no one in this county a hotshot Boston lawyer couldn't handle."

His only response to that was a vague nod. In the past few days, he'd come clean about a lot of stuff—Leanne had left him little choice—but he was still evasive or downright nonresponsive when his law career came up. He'd told Leanne he didn't want to practice law any longer, but being a lawyer was all he'd ever wanted to be, she'd reminded him the night before. It was what he'd excelled at—what he'd loved.

Not that his reasons really mattered to Nolie. Hey, she'd gone and fallen in love with the guy without even knowing his last name. She wasn't going to quibble about a minor matter like a career change.

"I stopped by Cole Jackson's office on my way back," she announced.

"Why?"

"I offered to deliver his lunch to him because the sub shop was so busy, plus I wanted to talk to him about investing Micahlyn's college money."

Chase scowled. "What do you know about this guy?"

"I like him. About half the town's got their money invested with him. And your sister's pretty much in love with him."

"Well, there's a good reason not to trust him. Leanne admits herself that her taste in men sucks."

It was hard to argue the facts, so she just shrugged. "I think Cole's different."

"Or maybe you're just dazzled by his blond hair and blue eyes."

"Good-looking blonds are a dime a dozen. I happen to prefer dark hair and brown eyes."

"But you think he's good-looking."

"Heavens, yes." Then she smiled primly. "But I think you're gorgeous."

The compliment pleased him, but at the same time it turned his eyes dark and wary. He opened his mouth as if to speak, then closed it again and grimaced.

The moment sent a wary shiver down her spine. He still had secrets, and sometimes she couldn't help but wonder if one of them was that he was merely amusing himself with her. Most of the time, she didn't believe it—he was so sweet and so sincere—but she still had her weenie moments when it was easier to believe he was using her than that he was falling in love with her.

He drew a breath as if he needed it badly, then returned to the subject. "Before you give this guy any money, let me check him out, okay? Just to be sure."

"Okay." It seemed a reasonable suggestion, though she was certain others in Bethlehem had already done so.

A quick rush of customers arrived as soon as they'd finished lunch. Once the store was quiet again, Chase turned on the radio, then slid his arms around Nolie from behind and lowered his mouth to her ear. "If it stays quiet this afternoon, I have a suggestion to liven things up."

"I bet you do," she replied with a smile and a lazy sigh. "You always have something in mind."

"And you enjoy every minute of it."

"Absolutely." She turned, then slid onto the counter. He immediately stepped between her legs, wrapped his arms around her, and pressed his just-awakening erection against her.

"We could make love right here, right now," he teased. "We wouldn't even have to undress, since you so conveniently wore a dress today. All I'd have to do is lift your skirt"—he did so, bunching the fabric around her waist—"and undo my jeans and slide inside you right here." He scraped one fingertip over the crotch of her panties, pulling the cotton taut and making her whimper.

"Wh-what about the-the windows?" she murmured breathlessly. "Someone c-could see."

"That's part of the fun. Besides, all they could really see is that we're doing something and it *might* be indecent, but—"

"Excuse me."

The voice came from behind Nolie, and startled them both. He jerked away a few inches as she yanked down her skirt, scrambled off the counter, and—her face burning—whirled around to see who had interrupted.

She stared.

And stared.

"Oh, God," she whispered. "Oh, my God."

Chase was standing close behind her—probably to hide the fact that he was turned on, she thought blankly. As if she didn't have much bigger problems to worry about.

"Nolie?" He laid one hand on her shoulder, but she couldn't tear her gaze from the couple standing in front of them.

"Oh, my God," she repeated. "Marlene. Obie. What are you doing here?"

THERE WAS NOTHING PARTICULARLY REMARKABLE about Nolie's in-laws. Obie Harper stood just under six feet, was a large, muscular man with a belly protruding over his belt, and had steel-gray hair and the weathered look of a man who'd spent most of his life outside. Marlene Harper had probably been pretty at one time in her life, but now she mostly looked tired. She was a half-foot shorter than her husband, sturdily trim in the way women of a certain age managed, and her hair was brown streaked with blond, probably to hide her gray hair. Her mouth was pursed in an angry, bitter line that reminded Chase of Saturday's glimpse of his mother.

Life had let Marlene Harper down, and she wasn't going to take it anymore.

Nolie pressed one hand to her chest. Her heart was probably pounding like his. Getting caught making out was bad enough, but getting caught by her in-laws, who weren't even supposed to be on this side of the Mississippi . . .

"Wh-what are you doing here?" she asked again.

Obie started to speak, but Marlene stilled him with one hand on his arm. "Where are your manners, Nolie? I know your mama raised you better than that. Introduce us."

"M-Marlene, Obie, this is Chase Wilson. Chase, my-my in-laws." She glanced nervously over her shoulder, her gaze worried. Chase reassured her the only way he could, touching his hand lightly to her spine, out of sight of the older couple.

At least she didn't refer to him as *the man who rents my cabin,* he thought humorlessly as he moved to stand beside her and extended his hand. "Mrs. Harper, Mr. Harper."

The older couple eyed his hand suspiciously, neither of them deigning to shake it. So where were *their* manners? Didn't their mamas raise them better than that? he wondered cynically.

"I'm-I'm surprised to see you," Nolie said, then baldly asked again, "What are you doing here?"

Again, it was Marlene who responded. "We're looking out for our granddaughter's best interests. *Someone* has to."

Uh-oh. Chase shifted a few inches away from Nolie. This wasn't good. Grandparents showing up out of the blue, hostile as hell, spouting about the best interests of *their* grandchild . . . not good at all. And finding their daughter-in-law necking on the counter in the middle of the day with the boyfriend who wasn't their son . . . Damn.

Marlene's sanctimonious pronouncement had one good effect—it shook the embarrassment and nervousness right out of Nolie. She quit smoothing her hands over her skirt as if she could erase the fact that it'd been up to her waist when they walked in, and rested her palms flat against the counter. "Yes," she agreed, her voice even and cool. "Someone does have to look out for Micahlyn—her mother. That's me. So . . . let me ask you for the last time. Why are you here?"

Finally Obie found his backbone and ignored his wife's gesture to let her do the talking. "We miss you and Mikey. We just wanted to make sure everything's all right and to have a look-see at this new home"—when Marlene elbowed him in the ribs, he colored and corrected himself—"this new town of yours."

"Where is Mikey?" Marlene asked.

"In day care."

"Tell us where and we'll go get her."

A few days ago, in a poetic and painfully aroused state, Chase had compared the color of Nolie's eyes to a summer sky. More like a *stormy* summer sky at the moment. "You can't. Chase is the only one besides me who can pick her up."

That didn't set well with Marlene. Her face took on a mottled look, and she was preparing to voice her displeasure when Nolie went on. "Have you guys had lunch, or can I get you some coffee or pop?"

"A cup of coffee would be . . ." Obie trailed off after a shrewish look from his wife.

Smiling tightly, Nolie went to the end of the counter, where a coffeemaker shared space with foam cups, creamer, and sugar. Neither of them were big coffee drinkers, but she'd learned a fair number of customers appreciated a cup while they gabbed—er, shopped. She stirred in one cream and two sugars, then handed the cup across the counter. Obie softened his taut smile with a wink his wife didn't see.

"What about you, Marlene? Can I get you something?"

"Yes. My granddaughter."

"Why don't you get settled in—"

"We've done that. We've got a room at the motel up the road."

That bit of news did nothing to ease the sense of foreboding settled in Chase's stomach. These four people had lived together for three years, and yet on their very first visit, the Harpers not only showed up without warning, but checked into a motel without even considering the possibility of staying with Nolie?

"Go on," Marlene commanded. "I'm sure . . . *he*"—said with a disdainful glance in Chase's direction—"can take care of things while you're gone."

Clearly, Nolie didn't want to obey, but just as clearly, she couldn't think of a reason not to. Marlene and Obie *were* Micahlyn's grandparents, after all, and she'd missed them a lot. Of course she would want to spend as much time with them as possible.

"All right," Nolie said at last. "But before I go . . . it took a long time for Micahlyn to adjust to Bethlehem as her new home."

Marlene sniffed.

"But she has adjusted. She has friends here. She likes it here. Don't talk to her about going back to Whiskey Creek to live, because it's not going to happen. *This* is her home now. Okay?" She waited until her father-in-law nodded and her mother-in-law shrugged, then took her purse from the drawer. "I'll be back in a few minutes," she said, more to Chase than the others. The look she gave him was apologetic.

All he could do in response was smile.

The instant the door closed behind her, the store seemed a smaller, unfriendlier place. He'd spent plenty of time in smaller rooms with unfriendlier people—thieves, drug dealers, murderers—and never found himself at a loss for words, but damned if he couldn't think of a single thing to say to these people.

It was Obie who finally broke the silence. Looking around the room, he nodded and said, "Nice store."

Marlene snorted. "For God's sake, Obie, it's a *feed store*."

"And it's a nice one."

Chase kept his attention partly on Marlene, but directed his answer to Obie. "Nolie's done a lot of work on it."

"How's business?"

"Pretty good. The next nearest feed store is forty-five miles away, so she's got no competition."

"She have help besides you?"

"A teenage boy comes in after school and on Saturdays. I don't work here. I'm just kind of helping her out."

"Helping her out of what? Her clothes?" Marlene snorted again. "We saw an example of your kind of *help*."

Heat rushed into Chase's face again. "We were just—"

Turning her back, she cut him off and tapped one foot impatiently. "What's taking so long? We drove through that dreary little town. She could have gone all the way to the other end and back by now."

For the first time in his life, Chase felt compelled to defend his hometown. "Bethlehem must not compare to the cosmopolitan charm of Whiskey Creek, home to . . . let's see, a café, a gas station, a post office, and four churches."

Her shoulders straightened and the toe-tapping stopped, but that was the extent of her response.

Fortunately a customer came in in the ensuing silence. Unfortunately, the man was one of his father's old fishing buddies. He carried a couple gallons of spray for his fruit trees to the counter, set them down, and pulled his wallet out before doing a double take. "Chase Wilson. I was just in your dad's office, asking him if it was true that you were back. He said he didn't know and—" He looked at the Harpers, then left the sentence dangling.

Didn't know and didn't care, Chase silently finished for him. "You should have asked Leanne instead."

"She sure turned out pretty, didn't she? Your dad's just prouder 'n a peacock of her."

Because she was pretty? Hey, he had it on good authority that he was passably good-looking himself, but it had never made a difference in the way Earl treated him. "That's $19.46."

The old man handed over a twenty, then slid his change in his pocket. "You oughta drop in and see your folks sometime. Parents oughta know when one of their kids moves back home, doncha think?"

He thought there came a time when the bond between some parents and their kids—and kids-in-law—should be severed forever. For him that time had come sixteen years ago. He was afraid it had just arrived for Nolie.

Of course, he didn't say any of that. He just thanked the man for his business and watched him leave.

"So . . ." Obie picked up a pair of pruning shears, tested the blade with one callused thumb, then returned them to the shelf. "You've been away a while."

Chase nodded.

"Ever regret leaving?"

"No." Though he did regret not making a more intensive effort to stay connected with Leanne. An awful lot about the past few years would have been easier if he'd had her support.

Marlene smiled snidely. "Then maybe you shouldn't have come back."

He smiled, too, but kept his emotions out of it. "I don't have any regrets about that, either. In fact, it was probably the best decision I ever made."

That expended their store of small talk. No one said another word until the door swung open and Nolie guided Micahlyn into the store, one hand over the kid's eyes. "Can I see the surprise now?" she asked excitedly. "Is it a dog? Did you get me a dog?"

Nolie removed her hand. Micahlyn's eyes opened wide and she squealed. "Grandma! Grandpa!"

Marlene opened her arms wide. "Mikey! Come here and— Oh, my God, what happened to your hair?"

"I got it cut," Micahlyn replied at the same time her grandfather said, "And it looks good, *doesn't it,* Marlene?"

"Touching," Chase murmured when Nolie circled the group hug and joined him. He really didn't mean to sound cynical. There was a lot of love between those three, no doubt about it.

And no doubt at all that the only best interests Marlene had at heart were her own.

IT WAS AFTER MIDNIGHT WHEN NOLIE SCRUBBED her face, brushed her teeth, and pulled on her satin robe, then went into the bedroom. Chase insisted he liked the way she looked in that particular garment, and heaven knew, she liked the way she felt when he looked at her in it—sexy. Beautiful. Special.

Wearing nothing but jeans, he was standing at the window, looking out. Though she would have sworn her bare feet had made no noise, when she got close, he extended his arm without looking, then drew her snugly against him.

"You okay?"

I am now. There was something amazingly reassuring about being in his arms. Bad things could happen—Obie and Marlene walking into the store today was proof of that—but as long as he was there to hold her at the end of the day, everything would be all right.

Naturally, she didn't dump all that on him. Instead, she rested her head against his shoulder and murmured, "I'm fine."

"A long day, huh?"

"Very." Against her better judgment, she'd let the Harpers take Micahlyn for the afternoon. After work, they'd all met for dinner at McCauley's, where the steak had been easier to cut than the tension, then walked the few blocks to the ice cream shop on the square for dessert. Nolie had been about to order a sugar-free frozen yogurt when Marlene, her timing impeccable, asked if she'd put on a few pounds since coming to Bethlehem. In response, she'd ordered strawberry ripple instead, licked the cone clean, then eaten it for good measure . . . exactly what Marlene had wanted her to do. She'd felt like such a spineless puppet . . . also what Marlene had wanted.

Afterward, they passed an excruciating two hours at home before Obie had finally been able to draw Marlene away. She'd wanted Micahlyn to spend the night with them at the motel, but he'd reminded her they had only the one bed until a room with two came available.

Nolie had been grateful, because, truth was, somewhere

way down inside, she wasn't comfortable with the idea of Micahlyn spending too much time with them. They'd helped raised her, changed her diapers, supported her, entertained her, and loved her, and that hadn't changed, but one thing had—their feelings for Nolie. And *that* made her uncomfortable with giving them unlimited time with her daughter.

"Do you think they really just missed Micahlyn and wanted to see Bethlehem?" The wistfulness in her voice was impossible to ignore. She desperately wanted Chase to tell her yes, that was all, there was no reason to worry, and if he did, she would pretend to believe him.

But he didn't, and no matter how hard she'd pretended, she never would have convinced herself.

"No." Chase's voice was soft, his breath stirring her hair. "I don't know why they're here, but I don't think it's anything so innocent." He tensed, then shifted against her as if to hide it. "Do you think . . ."

Waiting for him to continue, she watched a shooting star streak across the sky—her first since coming to New York. She'd been about ten and terribly disappointed when she found out that shooting stars weren't stars at all. Just tiny objects flying through space at such speeds that they became incandescent when they entered the atmosphere. She'd eventually gotten over her disappointment, though, and considered shooting stars the best stars of all to wish on.

I wish I may, I wish I might . . .

After a moment, Chase cautiously continued. "Do you think your in-laws would do something rash?"

"You mean, like . . . kidnaping Micahlyn?" she asked, surprised he could even suggest it.

"Like trying to get custody of her."

"Oh, no. No, no, no, they would never do either of

those things. They're not real happy with me right now, but they love her dearly, and they know I do, too. I would do *anything* for her."

"Except move back to Whiskey Creek and under Marlene's control."

She smiled without humor. It hadn't taken him long to size up the relationship with Jeff's parents. When it came to farm matters, Obie ruled. On everything else, they were the epitome of that bad old joke—*When I want your opinion, I'll give it to you.*

"I know they were very disappointed by my decision to come here. They would have stopped me if they'd been able to. Heavens, Obie tried to sell everything without my knowing it."

"A move orchestrated by his wife, no doubt."

She nodded. "But I don't believe they would ever try to take Micahlyn. It's just hard for them, not having that last little bit of Jeff around."

"Then . . . *you* believe their only reason for coming here is to see Micahlyn."

The silence drew out, long and heavy, before she finally managed to whisper her answer. "No."

That truth worried her more than she could say.

"Well, babe, it's one problem we can't do anything about right now. But I've got another problem that I think might take your mind off of it . . . if you're up to it."

When he slid her hand to the bulge in his jeans, she laughed. "You certainly are. By all means, darlin', take me away."

AFTER THEY'D MADE LOVE AND HE'D FALLEN ASLEEP holding her close, Nolie gazed drowsily into the night sky. What wish had she made on the falling star? Oh, yeah, for *this*—Chase in her bed, her daughter safe down the hall, utter satisfaction, love, and pure, sweet pleasure.

For the last few nights, that wish had been reality, and for at least one more night, it would stay true.

And Marlene and Obie couldn't change it. She wouldn't let them.

FRIDAY'S HOT-DOG NIGHT WASN'T QUITE THE EASY, relaxed event Nolie had gotten used to over the past six weeks. For one thing, there were more people—the three of them, Marlene and Obie, Leanne, Danny, and Ryan Jackson. Cole hadn't been able to come, Leanne had said, but he'd sent the investment prospectus he'd promised. It sat on the end table, its white folder elegantly embossed with Jackson Investments in gold foil.

For another, Nolie had caught Marlene telling Micahlyn about the wonderful backyard gym awaiting her in Arkansas, describing it in such wondrous terms that even Danny appeared ready to kiss his mother good-bye and head west. When she'd seen Nolie's frown, she'd returned it with such coldness that Nolie had been shaken all the way to her core.

And, the icing on the cake, Leanne was so low her chin practically bumped the floor when she walked. She was doing her best to hide it, especially from Chase, but Nolie saw through her phony smiles and chatter.

"Just a little bit longer, kids, and dinner will be ready," Nolie announced before she headed for the kitchen. The chili and sauerkraut were heating on the stove, and Leanne was chopping onions. Chase and Obie were on the patio, sharing the grilling chores but not much else, judging from their body language when she looked out the window.

All that was left was to grate the cheese, pour drinks,

figure out seating, find out what was wrong with Leanne, and endure another painfully uncomfortable evening with her in-laws. Then she could crawl into bed with Chase and hide until the sun came up the next morning.

"What's the wicked witch doing?" Leanne whispered when Nolie started work on the cheese.

"Nice description," Nolie whispered back. "She's trying her best to incite a mutiny. To hear her tell it, Bethlehem is the armpit of the world and Whiskey Creek is heaven on earth. You'd better make sure Danny doesn't stow away with them when they leave."

"When will that be?"

"Darned if I know. I feel funny about asking them outright, but they seem not to catch my hints."

"Your hints are probably so polite, *no one* could catch them. It's your life, Nolie. Walk in there, look her in the eye, and say, 'The Wizard called. They need you back in Oz ASAP.'" With the back of the knife, Leanne scraped the chopped onions into a bowl. "You know, it took me a long time to see the bright side of Greg taking off before Danny was born. Just think—if he'd stuck around, we could have gotten married and I could have had a mother-in-law like that." She shuddered as if horrified by the possibility.

"She wasn't always this bad. In fact, before Jeff died, she was a nice woman."

Leanne looked skeptical. "Was she really nice? Or just pretending to be because you all let her have her way?"

Watching shreds of sharp New York cheddar fall into the bowl as she grated, Nolie considered the question. All the major decisions in her and Jeff's lives—when they would get married, in what kind of wedding, where they would live, even where they would eat their evening meals—had been orchestrated by Marlene. She'd chosen Nolie's wedding gown, had planned their anniversary dinners, and had replaced Nolie's choice of christening outfits for Micahlyn with her own. And it had never occurred to Nolie to argue with her. She'd been a good little girl, had gone along and gotten along.

"I don't know," she said at last. "I don't know whether she changed after Jeff died . . . or I did."

"God, it must have been tough, outliving their only child. If I lost Danny . . ."

"I know." As one, they turned to look at the kids. Ryan was sprawled sideways in the recliner, watching TV. Danny was curled up on his lap, and Micahlyn sat on the sofa looking at a storybook with Marlene.

When she turned back, Nolie asked, "Is Cole working tonight?"

"*So he said.* I hear my lazy brother's working at the store with you. If you get tired of him, send him my way. I'm getting new shipments every day, and I could use a little help."

"Me? Get tired of him? I don't think so."

Leanne studied her with an intensity that matched Chase's, then nodded once. "I don't think so, either."

Nolie wanted to change the subject and pursue that *So he said* response, but before she could, the back door opened and Chase came in, carrying a tray of nicely grilled wieners. There were lines at the corners of his mouth, emphasizing its taut set. These past couple of days had been hard for all of them. Every conversation with Marlene— and there'd been too many to count—had been stiff and awkward, if not outright hostile. All Nolie wanted was for the Harpers to go home, and that made her feel guilty— because they were Jeff's parents and they'd been so good to her and Micahlyn—and selfish, because she just wanted to get on with her life.

There was incredible tension in the air, and it wore on her nerves. It was like waiting for an explosion, helpless to do anything but hope everyone survived the fallout. It was awful spending all her free time that way, and even worse for Chase, since he didn't *have* to be a part of it. He was doing it for her, and she loved him for it.

Someday she was going to tell him.

Leanne took the tray from him and dumped the wieners in a warm dish, then set it on the dining table. "How do you want to do this, Nolie? Half of us eat outside and half here?"

"Only if we get the half that doesn't include Marlene," Chase murmured.

"Why don't we all eat in the living room? The kids can use the coffee table, and I've got some folding trays stored in Hiram's office."

"Is that the door by the stairs?" Obie asked as he closed the door behind him. "I'll get 'em and set 'em up."

"Thanks."

The next voice she heard from the living room was Marlene's. "We're eating in here?"

How many times had Nolie heard comments like that from her? Couched as questions so she could always fall back on a defense of *I wasn't criticizing—just asking* if anyone took exception, and usually asked in a tone that was sweet, friendly, concerned, or curious. Implied criticism had suited her better then. Now she didn't rely on implications. Her tone made it clear exactly what she thought.

A response came from the least likely person in the house—Ryan. "What's wrong with that?"

"What if one of you children spills something on the floor?"

"So what if they do? It's wood. Hot dogs aren't going to ruin a wood floor."

"Attaboy, Ryan." Chase scooped up four glasses of lemonade, then grinned at Nolie. "You ready?"

"*No*. But I'll go in if you will." Though he walked off, she dawdled over picking up two glasses. She'd just turned from the counter when Leanne's voice, strong and friendly, came through the doorway.

"So, Mrs. Harper, are you going home sometime soon?"

Nolie smiled. She didn't know what Earl and Phyllis Wilson's problems were, and she didn't much care. But she had to give them credit for one thing. By luck, accident, or—more likely—noninvolvement, they'd created two great kids.

And she loved them both.

Chapter Fifteen

EANNE FOOLISHLY THOUGHT SHE WOULD ES-
cape the Harper shindig without facing any questions more difficult than Chase's *You okay?* After
helping with the cleanup, she'd started gathering the
kids—funny that leaving with two kids who'd brought
nothing with them required "gathering," but it was true—
and was about to say her good-byes and escape, when
Nolie hooked her arm through hers.

"We haven't had dessert yet. Ryan, would you help
Chase serve, please? Leanne and I need to step outside for
a moment."

"Hey, if we're talking sweets, I'd rather stay—" But she
couldn't wriggle free of Nolie's grip, so she let herself be
dragged out onto the front porch. Released—and cornered—she leaned against the railing and folded her arms
over her chest. "Is this your way of telling me I need to
watch my weight?"

"You want a piece of cake, honey, I'll send the whole
darn thing home with you. What's up?"

"The stock market? TV ratings? My blood pressure?"

Nolie didn't smile at her rotten attempt at humor, but
that was okay, because neither did Leanne. She was all out

of phony smiles and fake cheer and pretending everything was fine when it wasn't. She just wasn't sure she was ready to share yet.

"When I asked if Cole had to work late, you replied, 'So he said.' Does that mean he lied to you or brushed you off or what?"

"It means he said he had to work tonight."

Nolie looked at her in the dim illumination from the porch light, and for the longest time she just looked back. Then she sighed and her whole body seemed to collapse, her shoulders rounding, her chin dropping. "I told him— I told him I loved him," she mumbled.

"You what?"

"I woke up this morning, and he was lying there asleep and looking adorable and sweet and so damned sexy, and I-I just—I said it. 'I love you, Cole' " She raised one limp hand to cover her eyes, as if she could block out the memory by blocking her vision, but it didn't work. "The idiot wasn't asleep. He just had his eyes closed. At least until I opened my mouth. He got this panicked look, like . . ."

"A deer caught in headlights?"

Leanne's smile was shaky. "Trust you small-town Arkansas girls to know just the right words. Not that I've ever seen a deer caught in headlights, but, yeah, it would probably look exactly like Cole. Once he got over the initial shock, he couldn't get away from me fast enough. He claimed he was running late for an early appointment and rushed me out the door so quickly I didn't even have time to dress Danny."

"Maybe he really did have an appointment."

"Maybe. But he canceled lunch. No, wait, *he* didn't cancel it. He asked the mayor's secretary to cancel it for him. He was having lunch with him instead."

"He's a businessman, Leanne. I would imagine being

friendly with the mayor can't hurt, especially when you deal in money and dreams and trust."

"You sound like Chase, so cool and rational. But you didn't see that look in his eyes this morning. He's gonna be like everyone else. He's gonna break my heart."

"Maybe not. Maybe he was just . . . surprised. A lot of men don't deal with emotions. Maybe he just needs time. Don't go looking for trouble, Leanne, or you might create it where there isn't any."

Leanne scowled. "It's easy for you to give advice. You've got my brother following you around like a big ol' lovesick puppy. I've got a guy who uses me for great sex and baby-sitting services and very well may not want anything more."

"How great is the sex?"

The easy laughter bubbling up inside surprised Leanne, but she was happy to give in to it. Anything to make herself feel better, even if for only a moment.

Nolie came to lean against the railing beside her. "Do you really think . . ."

That seemed as far as she was willing to go, so Leanne replied anyway. "I think Chase has fallen head over heels for you, and I couldn't be happier. I've got my brother back, and I've always wanted a sister. I'll warn you, though, Wilsons come with responsibilities, like feeding me cake when I get dumped—again. And putting up with our parents on occasion. Though if you can handle the wicked witch, you'll do fine with our folks."

Nolie was quiet a long time—absorbing what Leanne had said about Chase falling. Finally she swayed to the side, gently bumping Leanne's shoulder. "I don't know about parents, but I'll be happy to provide cake. Did I mention that the one they're eating inside won a blue ribbon at the state fair a few years ago?"

"Mm-mm-mm. Welcome to the family, Nolie. Please may I have a piece before I take my guys home?"

Nolie pushed away from the railing and started toward the door. "I told you, I'll give you the whole thing."

And she did—every luscious leftover bite, packing it in a covered pan that she pressed into Leanne's hands as she followed the boys on their way out. For a moment Leanne actually considered refusing it, then thought better of it. There weren't many places she could go for a sweets fix in the middle of the night if it became necessary. Better to be safe than sorry.

The Miller mansion was dark, the driveway empty, when she parked across the street. Mumbling his thanks, Ryan started in that direction, but she grabbed him by the collar and stopped him short. "Where do you think you're going, slick?"

"Home. I've got a key."

"You're too young to stay home alone at night."

The look he gave her should have withered her to nothing. "I'm *twelve*."

"See? Too young. C'mon." Trading his shirt for a grip on his shoulder, she guided him ahead of her to her apartment door, with Danny skipping in front.

"This is stupid," Ryan grumbled. "I've been takin' care of myself ever since I was little. Jeez, it's not even nine-thirty yet."

"Humor me, child." She unlocked the door and Danny ran up the stairs.

Shuffling his feet and still complaining, Ryan clomped up behind him. "Cole won't know where I am."

"He knows you were spending the evening with us. He'll figure it out." And when he did, would he call and say, "Send my kid home"? Or would he find the nerve to come over and face her?

She was betting on a phone call.

She got Danny ready for bed, who then nagged Ryan into reading him a half-dozen stories. When she went to check on them, she found them both asleep in the small bed. For a moment she watched them, thinking how Danny was designed from his genes out to be a little brother, not an only child, and how Ryan seemed designed to be a big brother, not a lonely only also. They could be a family—these two boys, Chase, and her.

Oh, yeah, right, and they could live happily ever after, too, couldn't they? And the sun would always shine, bad times would be banished, and life would be perfect.

Sighing—whether at her wistfulness or cynicism, she didn't know—she shut off the lamp, pulled the door shut, and was on her way back to the living room when the doorbell rang. She detoured for a look out her bedroom window and saw the Lexus parked in the Miller driveway. So he'd opted for the face-to-face. She hadn't expected it.

Running her fingers through her hair, she hurried down the stairs and opened the door. Cole stood on the sidewalk, wearing gray trousers and a white shirt. The sleeves were rolled up, the tie around his neck loosened, and he looked as if he'd combed his hair with his fingers a time or three. He looked . . . troubled? Or just tired? If he'd really had an early appointment that morning, it had been a hell of a long workday for him.

She *really* wanted to believe he'd had that appointment.

"I believe you have my son."

She leaned one shoulder against the jamb. "He fell asleep reading to Danny. He can spend the night if you'd rather not wake him." *You can spend the night, too, if you'd give the slightest hint you want to.*

He copied her pose on the other side of the door. "How was dinner?"

"Tolerable. Nolie's mother-in-law is a bona-fide witch."

"With warts on her nose and a pointy black hat?"

She gave him a chiding look. "That's so stereotypical. Witches can pass for real human beings. Trust me on this. My mother's one, too." She considered inviting him in, and her heart rate increased a fair amount, so she went ahead. After that cake, she could use a cardiac workout. "Nolie baked a blue-ribbon-winning cake for dessert and sent the leftovers home with me. Would you like a slice?"

"No, thanks." His cool blue gaze remained steady on her face. "But I'd like to make love to you."

It was difficult to say which was stronger—the instantaneous arousal that streaked through her or the relief that threatened to buckle her knees. He wasn't running away after her unfortunate wake-up this morning. It wasn't as good as a declaration of love, but it meant something, right? He cared for her—he must, or he would have opted out of spending the night, wouldn't he?

"Ooh, that's better than cake anytime," she murmured, taking his hand, then strolling up the stairs.

THE SCREAM RIPPED THROUGH THE QUIET NIGHT, jerking Cole out of a sound sleep. In the moment it took him to remember where he was and why, Leanne had already pulled out of his arms, grabbed a robe, and was on her way to the door. He pulled on his boxers as the second shriek split the air, then hustled across the short hall into Danny's room. The bedside lamp was on, and Leanne was sitting on the edge of the bed, arms wrapped around Ryan, stroking his hair and murmuring to him. Danny was sitting up, eyes wide and startled, his lower lip trembling, and Ryan was shaking like a leaf, but not crying. No matter how bad things got, the kid never cried.

And those nightmares must be pretty damn bad.

Damn it, he should have noticed there was no light under Danny's door when he'd followed Leanne into her bedroom. How could she have known Ryan was afraid of the dark? He sure as hell wouldn't have told her.

But no, Cole had been too focused on his own needs. The kid really needed a better parent—something he'd often thought, but now was beginning to believe.

Squeezing into a space on the bed, Cole ruffled Danny's hair and gave him a reassuring wink, then laid his hand on Ryan's back. "You okay, son?" he asked gruffly.

The boy's shudders were steadily lessening. Leanne's arms were a comfortable place to be, and must seem doubly so for a kid who'd had so little mothering in his life. His breathing slowed, and those frantic little panicked sounds stopped completely. In another minute, embarrassment would set in, and he would shrug away their concern as if he hadn't just scared them half to death.

Sure enough, in thirty seconds or so, he pulled out of Leanne's embrace, his face burning red, stared at the floor, and muttered, "I wanna go home."

"Okay. Let me get dressed." It was as good an excuse as any to walk away from Leanne and spend the rest of the night alone. Might as well start getting used to that again, because it wouldn't be long before Bethlehem was just a memory.

He dressed quickly, then returned to Danny's room. Leanne was standing beside the bed now, her hair mussed, her eyes dark with concern. "Cole—"

He brushed a kiss to her forehead, then gestured for Ryan to lead the way. "I'll talk to you later."

"But—"

Pretending he hadn't heard her, he hurried Ryan down the hall and the stairs and out the door. Even then, though, he didn't feel safe. He suspected he wouldn't until he'd put a few thousand miles between himself and Bethlehem . . . and Leanne.

CHASE DIDN'T GO IN TO THE STORE ON SATURDAY, not when Trey Grayson would be there to help out. Instead, he kissed Nolie good-bye, then walked to his house. In the past week, he'd spent little time there, mostly just showering and changing clothes, but he didn't want to hang out at Nolie's house when she wasn't home.

After a shower, he changed into clean jeans, microwaved a frozen breakfast, then went out onto the porch. Upon eating the last bite, he contemplated spending the rest of the day in the hammock—not an appealing idea. He could go into town and let Leanne give him the grand tour of her store, or drive by the golf course on the north side of town where his father had spent every Saturday morning Chase could recall, weather permitting. If the old man's habits held true, Chase could use the time to see his mother. Not that he particularly wanted to. It just seemed that maybe he should.

But it wasn't such a strong feeling that it actually moved him out of the hammock. No, it took a familiar rental car coming up the hill to do that. The Harpers knew the store hours as well as he did, so why were they going to Nolie's house when they knew she wasn't there?

The car didn't park in front of the other cabin, though, but came on down toward his house. And it wasn't both Harpers. It was Marlene. He'd seen enough of her in the past three days to last a lifetime. Hell, she even managed to make the prospect of visiting his mother more appealing. Too bad he'd delayed.

He stood up as she parked out front, then climbed out

of the car. Though the wind was blowing out of the west, her gray-streaked blond hair didn't so much as flutter, no doubt shellacked into place. Or maybe Marlene could intimidate even inanimate objects. She sure as hell intimidated *him*.

Wishing he'd put on a shirt and shoes, he waited at the top of the steps. "Mrs. Harper."

She stopped at the bottom of the steps and gazed up at him. Sheer height should have given him some sort of psychological advantage, but she didn't seem to feel the slightest bit disadvantaged.

"Nolie's not here."

"I wouldn't have come if she was. Some conversations are better had in private." She said the words with a smile that didn't touch her eyes and couldn't camouflage their ominous sound.

"What do you want to talk about?"

"I understand you were a lawyer." She waited for his nod. "Why aren't you practicing law now?"

"I don't want to."

"Don't want to . . . or can't?"

Cold inside, he sat down on the step. He had a really bad feeling in his gut about this and, from the start of his legal career, he'd learned to always trust his gut feelings. He wanted to order her off the property, go inside and lock the door, or tell her to go to hell . . . but he couldn't do any of that. He also couldn't tell a lie that could come back to haunt him—or, worse, Nolie—so he said nothing at all.

"I'm not real knowledgeable about the law, but it's my understanding that once you've been disbarred, you *can't* practice. Isn't that right? So what you *want* has nothing to do with it." Her voice softened. "And you have been disbarred, haven't you? For embezzling $1.1 million in client money. And you went to prison. And Nolie doesn't have a clue."

Sweat trickled down his spine, and his throat grew tight, making his voice hoarse, choked. "How did you learn that?"

"I hired a private detective—one of those that specializes in checking out cheating spouses and lovers. The point is, Nolie doesn't know, does she?"

He didn't bother confirming what she already knew, so instead he lied. "I plan to tell her." Sure, he did. He just hadn't decided when would be the best time—at work, when she was trying to earn a living to support her child, or in the evening, when they sat at the dinner table with Micahlyn, like some sort of little family, or how about in the middle of the night, when they'd just made love and she was feeling lazy and lucky and satisfied?

"Oh, it's too late for that. You should have told her *before* you weaseled your way into her life and her bed, before she became infatuated with you, before Mikey came to care for you." Her features hardened. "You've lied to her from the moment you met. You've betrayed her trust, used her, and made a fool of her. Deep inside she already suspects it. Good-looking lawyers from the city—even ones who are ex-cons—don't fall for plain, plump girls like Nolie. She knows that. We all know it. But having to face it will break her heart."

He wanted to protest that he hadn't lied to Nolie. He just hadn't told her everything. But that wasn't much, if any, better than outright lying. But in the beginning he'd had no reason to tell her, and by the time he had found one, as Marlene said, it had been too late. He'd had something that never should have been his, and damned if he'd been unselfish enough to risk losing it.

Now he would, and Marlene would like nothing better than being the one taking it all away from him.

He studied her—the age lines around her eyes, the stress lines around her mouth. She was probably eight or ten years younger than his mother, but she looked that much older. He agreed that fate hadn't been kind to her, but just because she was unhappy, did that mean everyone in her sphere of influence had to be the same?

"Tell me something, Mrs. Harper. Are you really this selfish?"

Her face flamed red, suggesting that someone else—Obie?—had made the same comment. Embarrassment didn't temper the haughtiness of her voice, though. "Maybe my actions appear selfish to you, but only because they conflict with your own selfish desires. I just want what's best for my granddaughter."

"You don't get to decide what's best for Micahlyn. That's her mother's right."

"It should be. But when Nolie's clearly not considering Mikey's welfare, someone has to step in. Obie and I are the only other family Mikey has. That makes it our responsibility."

"How is Nolie not considering Micahlyn's welfare?"

Folding her arms over her chest, she started tapping one foot. "She never should have uprooted that child from the only home she'd ever known and brought her here. She never should have taken her away from her only family. If Nolie wasn't happy living with us, we could have worked things out. We could have converted the garage into an apartment for her, or moved Jeff's old trailer out back. We could have compromised."

"And how do you define compromise, Mrs. Harper? You get everything you want, and Nolie learns to live with it?"

She made a dismissive gesture. "Oh, I'm sure she's filled your head with stories about how awful it was, living with us. All we did was help her out when she needed it, but to hear her tell it, we treated her like a prisoner. But you tell me—why in the world should she work when we could give her everything she needed? And getting a place of her own—that was just ridiculous. There aren't any houses or apartments for rent in Whiskey Creek, and even if she'd found one, how would she manage? She would have had to work to pay the rent, and bring Mikey out to the house every day and pick her up every night, and do housework and cooking and laundry. . . . Why make life so hard on herself—and on Mikey—when I already did all those things for her?"

The stirring of sympathy inside surprised Chase and wasn't entirely welcome. He didn't want to feel anything but hostility toward the woman who had caused Nolie such headaches, who threatened everything between them. But he couldn't help it. Marlene Harper was hurting. She'd lost her son to death, her daughter-in-law and her granddaughter to the need for lives of their own. The harder she'd tried to hold onto them, the harder Nolie had fought to get away.

"What about the date with Jeff's friend?" he asked quietly.

She frowned until the memory clicked. "Oh, that. She wasn't ready to start dating again. I know she thought differently, but she wasn't seeing things clearly. She was still heartbroken over Jeff. It was too soon."

"It had been three years. When do you think would have been the right time? Five years? Ten? Never?"

Her mouth pursed primly. "I don't expect her to stay single forever. But Jeff was perfect for her. He was the only man she'd ever looked at. They were so much in love, and you just don't get over a love like that. She'll always love him."

"Yes, she will," Chase agreed evenly. He wouldn't expect anything less from her. "And she'll always love me."

He didn't mean to say the last words. They just slipped out before he realized it, unexpected and arrogant . . . but true. He knew she loved him, because he felt the same way about her.

For a long still moment, he thought about that. He'd sworn he would never marry again, or get too involved with Nolie, or set himself up for getting hurt again. He'd been so sure he could handle having her for a neighbor, then being friends with her, then becoming lovers with her, while never losing sight of the fact that there was no future for them. And then he'd gone and fallen in love with her.

He'd been kidding himself.

Was it possible that he'd also been kidding himself about their future, or lack thereof? Could he trust her enough to accept the truth about him? Could he stay in Bethlehem, or persuade her to leave with him?

Could he risk hoping for something good . . . and bear the disappointment if it didn't come?

"She's not in love with you," Marlene scoffed. "She just thinks she is."

And there was even more arrogance. How could she presume to know Nolie's feelings better than Nolie herself? Then he answered his own question. Because that was what Marlene did. She dictated lives, controlled people, and believed she knew best. That was the hell of it—what made it so hard for people like Nolie to stand up to her. She truly believed in her heart that she was doing what was best for them.

"What do you want from me, Mrs. Harper?"

"I want you out of my daughter-in-law's and granddaughter's lives."

"And that'll help your cause how?"

For the first time—at least, when Micahlyn wasn't around—she smiled a smile that was happy, anticipatory, and her voice took on a warmth he hadn't heard before as she leaned forward. "As I said, she's infatuated with you. She thinks there's something more than sex between you. If you break it off with her unexpectedly, without explanation, she'll be hurt, and she'll have no reason to insist on staying in this dreary place."

Arrogant, dictatorial, and manipulative, but not thinking too clearly. "Nolie loves Bethlehem. She likes running her own business, making her own decisions, being in control of her life. She's got friends and customers who need her. She's part of the community. She's not going to give all that up and run back to Arkansas just because I'm no longer part of the picture."

"You overestimate her," she said dismissively. That was what she did, too—simply brush off as without merit any opinion that didn't support hers. There were only two points of view in Marlene's life, hers . . . and the wrong one.

"I don't think it's possible to overestimate Nolie." Rising to his feet, he leaned one shoulder against the post. So Marlene wanted him to break Nolie's heart and spirit so thoroughly that she would have no choice but to return to Whiskey Creek, admit her mistakes to the Harpers, and settle once again into the suffocating existence that was life with them. It was a broken heart that had led her into the situation in the first place, and he seriously doubted another one could send her back to it. She was too strong, too smart.

Besides, Marlene's plan had one major hole—why would he agree to such a thing? To keep Nolie from finding out he'd gone to prison? Maybe, was his first, panicked thought. He would give a lot to keep that information to himself. Hell, he would give everything if it had never happened.

But break her heart just to keep it secret?

"How did you plan to get me to agree to this?" he asked conversationally. "Are you going to blackmail me with my sordid past?"

"That's part of it, though a small part." Marlene climbed the steps until she was standing one below him. For a woman of average height, below-average weight, and past the half-century mark, she was damned formidable. "If you don't cooperate, Obie and I will have no choice but to sue for custody of Micahlyn. Her mother shacked up with a felon, a common thief, allowing him liberties with her child. . . . It's just not a healthy environment for a five-year-old."

"*What* liberties?" Just the word had a dirty feel to it and made his skin crawl. Kiddie perverts were the only dregs of society he'd refused to represent when he was practicing law. To have something like that even hinted at . . .

"Do you deny sharing a bed with Mikey last weekend?"

"Yes, I do!" Last Friday night he'd slept alone in his own bed, and Saturday night had been divided between looking for Nolie and the hospital, then—"Jeez, you're talking about when Nolie was sick? Micahlyn and I were reading and we fell asleep in the chair. We were both fully dressed. There was nothing improper about it."

"So she told me. Trust me, I've questioned her about it repeatedly, and her story doesn't change. But no matter how innocent it was, being a big-city lawyer ex-con, you can see how creepy it would sound in court, can't you? Even child molesters usually start with something innocent."

The sympathy he'd felt earlier was gone, for good this time. Once more he wished for a cigarette, only screw the beer. He needed a few stiff shots of whiskey instead. "Let me see if I have this straight. Either I dump Nolie, or you'll drag her into court, trying to take her little girl from her and branding me some kind of pervert. Is that about it?"

"About. Except that the case would probably be heard by Judge Harrison Clinton, one of Obie's oldest friends."

"No conflict of interest there," he said bitterly.

She smiled with smug satisfaction. "Our county's small. We only have two judges, one who hears criminal cases and one who handles everything else, and everyone knows everyone, of course."

Of course. He knew how incestuous court systems could be. No matter how unfair it was—hell, how *illegal* it was—sometimes the interests of the judge won out over the interests of justice.

"It's a good thing your son is dead."

The color drained from her face and she drew back, mouth open, eyes wide. "You-you— How dare you—"

"If he knew what you were doing to his wife and daughter, it would break *his* heart." He didn't wait for her to recover from her shock. "I may not own this property, but renting it gives me some rights. Get the hell off of it now, and don't come back."

Her jaw tightened as she took a step back. "I'd like your answer."

He wanted to snarl at her not only *no,* but *hell, no.* He didn't, though. How could he when she was threatening Nolie's daughter? "You know, if Nolie ever finds out about this, you will have destroyed your relationship with her."

"As long as Jeff's daughter is safe at home where she belongs, that's all that matters." She waited impatiently. "Well?"

He had to practically pry his jaw apart to force out the words he hated saying. "I'll think about it."

"Don't take too long, or I'll make the choice for you."

Turning on his heel, he went inside, closed the door, and locked it, then swore—once, twice, three times.

What the hell was he going to do?

I T WAS A LONG BUSY DAY AT THE STORE, LEAVING Nolie too tired to feel anything but relief at going home. She put away the groceries she'd picked up on her way—makings for pizzas—then went upstairs and got out of her grubby work clothes and into the shower. Marlene and Obie had said they would bring Micahlyn home around seven, which would give her just enough time to dress and walk over to the other cabin to say hello to Chase.

She'd missed him, she thought as she pulled on a loose green dress and a pair of sandals, then combed her damp hair. It had been only one workday since she'd seen him, less than twelve hours, but it felt like forever.

The evening was quiet and warm, with just a hint of a cooling breeze. Soon summer would be there, the days long and hot, the nights warm and lazy. She loved summer and swimming and picnicking and gardening and walking barefoot and airy clothes and late sunsets and gorgeous sunrises.

She loved autumn, too, with its fresh, crisp, woodsy smells, the changing colors of the trees, the crackle of fallen leaves underfoot, the nippier reminder that winter was on its way, the lovely endings and the promise of new beginnings.

Of course, winter was also pretty special, she thought, laughing aloud at herself as she climbed the steps to Chase's cabin. And who could resist spring?

Raising one hand, she rapped sharply on the screen door, then gazed back toward the road. She'd bought plenty of pizza stuff in case Marlene and Obie wanted to stay for dinner, but she sincerely hoped they would just drop off Micahlyn and leave. She wanted a quiet, peaceful evening, just her, Micahlyn, and Chase, with no tense undercurrents, no sharp voices or patronizing or manipulating. She loved her in-laws, truly, but she really needed a break from them.

Her brow wrinkling, she knocked on the door again, then walked to the far end of the porch. Chase's SUV was gone, a fact which gave her an enormous letdown. He hadn't mentioned plans to go out that morning before she left for work . . . not that he had to clear it with her, of course. Besides, he might have made the decision after she was gone. Maybe he'd gone into town to see Leanne, or some old friend, or even his parents. Or maybe he'd developed a taste for a particular meal and had gone to buy the ingredients, or he'd just needed to get out of the house for a while.

He knew she would expect him for dinner. He would be back soon.

Heaving a sigh, she strolled back to her cabin. She'd just seated herself in one of the rockers when the sound of a car broke the silence. She was hoping for Chase. Instead it was her in-laws.

Obie parked next to her car, got out, and scooped a dozing Micahlyn into his arms from the backseat. He smiled at Nolie as he climbed the steps. "If you'll open the door for me, I'll lay her on the couch."

Nolie hastily obeyed, remaining in the doorway while he gently lowered Micahlyn to the couch, then brushed a kiss to her forehead. When he came back, she returned to the porch with him. "Looks like she had a busy day."

"She's like her daddy—plays hard and sleeps hard."

Nolie winced inwardly. Micahlyn *was* like her father, and she'd never minded the comparisons before. She hated that it somehow made her feel guilty now.

She closed the screen door quietly, then laced her fingers together and summoned a smile. "You and Marlene are welcome to stay for dinner if you'd like. I'm fixing pizza."

He glanced at the car where Marlene sat in the front seat, face turned away, then gave a shake of his head. "I don't think so."

Didn't think they would stay? Or they were welcome? Either way, the result was what she wanted—a quiet, peaceful dinner—and another twinge of guilt.

But how peaceful would dinner be if Chase didn't show up?

"Where's Chase?"

She blinked, as if thinking of him had somehow prompted Obie's question. "He had something to take care of." It wasn't a lie. Whatever he was doing surely qualified as "something," even if it was just getting a change of scenery.

"Well . . . I'd better get going. Don't want Marlene getting impatient." He moved as if to hug her, caught himself, and smiled apologetically instead.

Crossing her arms over her chest, Nolie watched him get into the car, then freed one hand for a wave as he backed out. Then she went back to waiting.

Micahlyn woke up a short while later and told Nolie all about her day. They chopped onions and peppers and fixed their pizza, but Nolie didn't have much appetite. She bathed Micahlyn and wished on stars with her, then put her to bed and read her a story, and still Chase didn't come home.

Maybe he'd gone to Howland or to the Starlite Lounge. Maybe he was tired of her company and had gone looking for someone prettier, more accomplished, skinnier. Or maybe he was making up for sixteen years with his family. The entire Wilson clan could be having a welcome-back reunion even as she brooded.

By midnight, she couldn't keep her eyes open. She got ready for bed, then slept with her windows raised, just in case the rumble of the SUV's engine might wake her from her sleep.

It didn't, and she discovered why when she got up the next morning—apparently, he hadn't come home. His cabin was quiet, locked up, his truck was still absent, and she had a knot the size of a basketball in her chest. She wanted to know where he was, what he was doing, and with whom.

Though she was really afraid she wouldn't like the answer.

She'd never had a jealous moment in her life with Jeff. They'd been together so long—best friends forever, sweethearts all through school, then husband and wife. He'd never looked at another woman, and she'd never thought twice about another man. They'd been so sure of each other.

She felt anything *but* sure with Chase.

When he finally came home, she was sitting on the porch, a magazine open but unread in her lap. The Harpers had picked up Micahlyn for church and would bring her back sometime that afternoon. She'd made a lunch of cold leftover pizza, then thrown it away after two bites. It was hard to eat when her stomach was knotted with apprehension.

Practically faint with relief, she waited for him to pull into the space beside her car, but he drove past to park beside his own cabin. He got out, stood there a moment, then reluctantly walked back, as if he'd rather face anyone but her.

When he reached the steps, he sat on the top one, the post with the carved hearts at his back. There was no smile, no hug, no kiss, for her. Just a grim gaze that he couldn't even bring to hers.

She forced a phony smile. "Have a nice time?"

"Why do you ask?"

"You've been gone a long time. You must have enjoyed whatever it was you were doing."

That earned her a brief glance and a shrug. His hair was tousled, his jaw unshaven, and his eyes were bloodshot. Too little sleep, too much booze, too many hours in a smoke-filled bar? She didn't want to know, almost as much as she did.

"I would have appreciated a note or a call."

"I'm an adult. I'm not accustomed to reporting my movements to anybody."

Anybody. Was that a step down from *the woman who owned his cabin* or a step up? It felt like a downhill slide. "And does being an adult also relieve you of any obligation to consider someone else's feelings?"

His mouth thinned in a taut line and his voice matched, sharp, flat. "I didn't know I was supposed to check in, okay? Sorry. Can we drop it now?"

"Sure." She picked up the magazine, turned from the page she hadn't read to a page she couldn't read, not with panic building inside, robbing her of the ability to focus. Pretending disinterest, she turned another page, then another, then forced a casual tone to her voice. "Have you had lunch?"

"Yeah."

"Because we have leftovers from Micahlyn's the-best-of-everything pizza."

He was silent a moment before grudgingly asking, "Where is she?"

"She went to church with her grandparents this morning. She'll be back soon."

Twenty-four hours ago they would have spent a morning without Micahlyn in bed, playing, laughing, making love. Right this moment she wondered if they would ever make love again. He was acting so strangely, as if he didn't want to be there, didn't want to talk to her or even look at her, and it fed every insecurity and fear she had. If he would just look her in the eye, just drop the attitude and *tell* her what was wrong. . . .

Dropping the magazine, she moved to sit in front of him. He immediately scooted back until his spine was straight against the post, putting as much room between them as possible. She knew he wouldn't welcome her touch, but she reached out anyway, wrapping her fingers around his.

It hurt way down inside when he just as easily unwrapped them, then rested both hands on his thighs.

"What's wrong, Chase?" Her words were soft, her voice quavering. Pride warned she should have more dignity than to let him hear that she was hurt or upset, but she hadn't had much experience at masking her emotions. Jeff had never given her any reason to.

For a long time it appeared he wasn't going to answer, but finally he raised his head and looked at her. His gaze was as hostile and bitter as it had been that first day they'd met when, for one fearful moment, she'd half-believed the bogeyman *had* come to drag them away. She'd never imagined that a few short months later, he would break her heart.

"Look, Nolie . . ." He dragged his fingers through his hair, then breathed deeply. "This thing between us . . . it's not working. It was nice and-and convenient, but . . . like you said at the lake, I've been bored and you're not my type, and now that I'm not stuck out here any longer, never seeing anyone but you, I'm ready to-to find someone more-more suitable."

She couldn't breathe, couldn't think, could only stare at him through eyes filling with tears. Her chest hurt, and her stomach, and there was a knot in the back of her throat, locking her voice inside, along with the sobs rising slowly all the way from her toes.

"Don't get me wrong," he went on, his gaze fixed somewhere around her chin. "You're a nice woman, and you're pretty, but . . . my type is more like Fiona or Raine and you're . . . not." Again he combed through his hair, and again sucked in a deep breath. "There's no way I'm gonna stick around Bethlehem and no way I'm gonna get serious with a woman like you, and sure as hell no way I'm gonna play father to some other guy's kid, so . . . I'm sorry. I didn't mean to give you the wrong idea. I-I'm sorry."

He sat there a moment longer, but when the first tear fell, sliding slowly down her cheek, he muttered an obscenity, sprang to his feet, and walked away.

And she sat there alone and cried.

Chapter Sixteen

H E WAS A BASTARD.

Chase lay in bed, the cabin dark and still, the bottle of whiskey cool where it rested against his skin. He didn't know what time it was—the wee hours of morning—and wished he didn't know what day it was, but he did. It was Tuesday. The start of the third day without Nolie.

The start of his third day of pure hell.

He'd known it would be hard giving her up, though he hadn't known *how* hard. He had thought he could handle it—after all, he'd survived Fiona breaking his heart three years ago. Jesus, he'd been an idiot. Losing Fiona had nothing on losing Nolie.

And losing Nolie would have nothing on being the reason she lost Micahlyn. There wasn't a love in the world strong enough to survive that. Even if there was, certainly *he* wouldn't inspire it.

He'd put six hundred miles on his truck Saturday night and Sunday morning, had driven mile after mile, trying to find a way out of this mess and failing. Only a year into his law career, he'd become cynical as hell about the court system. Justice wasn't blind. As often as not, it went to the highest bidder—the one with the best, most expensive lawyers and the best, most expensive witnesses. Testimony could be bought and sold, jurors manipulated, the law itself manipulated and twisted and perverted. Verdicts had little to do with guilt or innocence, or right or wrong.

Even in the best-case scenario, with a fair and impartial judge, Marlene could use him to make Nolie look bad. For practical purposes, they had been living together, having sex while her five-year-old slept fifteen feet down the hall. Regardless that he'd been wrongly convicted and had served his sentence, he was still a felon. And no matter how innocent his falling asleep with Micahlyn had been, any decent lawyer could make it look like the first step to molestation.

Told to a judge with a vested interest in making his dear old friends happy . . .

He'd had no choice but to do Marlene's bidding. If Nolie knew, she would agree. There was no place in her and Micahlyn's lives for him.

And there was no life for him without them.

He rolled onto his side, bringing his arm up to cover his eyes. The first time they'd met, he'd come back home, intending to pack up and leave that very day. He never would have gotten to know them, never would have fallen in love with them, and never would have hurt them. But, no, he'd taken the easy way out and stuck around.

Now they all had to pay for it.

I T WAS NOTHING LESS THAN AMAZING THAT A PERson could go on about her life, functioning perfectly well, when her heart had broken into a dozen pieces. Never having had a broken heart before, Nolie would have expected it to be more crippling. She would have thought a newly broken heart would cower in bed, crying, asking *Why?* and pleading for another chance.

But not her. Oh, she'd done her share of crying—Sunday afternoon when Chase had walked away, that night after Micahlyn was asleep in bed, and again Monday night. She'd wondered obsessively about the *why* and had wanted desperately to plead.

But she'd gone about her business as usual. Taken care of Micahlyn. Handled things at the store. Waited on customers and dealt with Marlene and Obie and joked with Trey, all as if nothing had happened. If anyone had noticed the hurt in her eyes or the fragility that made her feel she might shatter given the slightest nudge, no one mentioned it. No one seemed to notice anything out of place.

No one but her, and she was trying so very hard to pretend it wasn't so. Life would go on as normal, and so would she.

It was Tuesday, the end of Obie and Marlene's first week in Bethlehem, still without any mention of going home. For the first time since they'd arrived, Nolie didn't care. They could leave today or stay forever. It didn't matter to her either way.

With a deep breath, she turned her attention to the mail on the desk in front of her. There were just a few bills, along with a reminder to deliver a check to Cole Jackson. Chase had wanted to check him out before—

She swallowed hard. Screw Chase. He didn't want her anymore, so he had no say in what she did anymore. Grabbing the checkbook, she scrawled out a check to Jackson Investments for every single penny of Jeff's $30,000 life insurance proceeds, plus three years' interest, tore it out, and laid it aside to deliver later.

She was writing a check for the electric bill when the door opened just as an eighteen-wheeler rumbled by on the highway. Making a mental note to get that blasted bell repaired, she fixed a smile on her face and managed to keep it in place even though the new arrivals were Marlene and Obie—without her daughter.

"Where's Micahlyn?"

Naturally, it was Marlene who answered. "She wanted to stay for storytime at the library. Corinna Humphries offered to watch over her while we take care of some business."

Nolie counseled herself to count to ten, but made it only to three. "You shouldn't be leaving my daughter with someone else without asking me first."

"I told you—" Obie started, but Marlene silenced him with a look. In the next instant, she dismissed Nolie with a wave. "Corinna's a pillar of the community. You know her, and you would have let Mikey stay with her if we'd asked, so we didn't bother."

"That's not the point, Marlene. It's my decision to make, not yours."

Marlene rolled her eyes. "Oh, pardon me. I raised my son and helped raise you, but I'm not good enough to make one small decision about my granddaughter."

"That's not what I—" Nolie broke off, and made it to ten this time. She just couldn't play her mother-in-law's games. She didn't have the emotional fortitude for it.

The silence dragged on until finally Obie cleared his throat. "Where's Chase?"

Nolie's hands curled into fists as she willed the pain to remain manageable and the tears to stay inside where they belonged. "He's home." Maybe. Or in town visiting someone. Or finally waking up after a long, busy night in some other woman's bed—some *suitable* woman's bed.

As opposed to Nolie's *convenient* bed.

Unwilling to follow a line of thought that could only

lead to tears, she smiled brightly, phonily. "What business did you have to take care of?"

Obie looked at Marlene, as if trying to send her a message with nothing more than his gaze, but Marlene turned away from him and focused on Nolie. "It concerns Chase. You're a trusting woman, Nolie—too trusting. You rented a house to this man, you became friends with him and . . . more." Her lips thinned, as if she found the idea of Nolie having a sex life too distasteful an idea to contemplate. And why not? She considered Nolie even being friendly with another man a betrayal of Jeff's memory.

"I didn't rent—"

"You invited him into your home and your life—into your daughter's life—without bothering to find out anything about him, just taking him at his word. For all you know, he could be a criminal, a thief, a liar, or worse."

The last thing Nolie wanted to do was discuss Chase, and the *very* last thing she wanted was to defend him. Still, broken heart aside, she couldn't *not* do it. "Chase—a criminal? He was a highly respected lawyer in Boston, Marlene. It may not be the most honorable career in America these days, but it's a far cry from being a criminal."

"Not in his case."

The words hung in the air, quiet, practically vibrating with certainty. Nolie looked at Obie, who wouldn't meet her gaze, then turned back as Marlene withdrew a red-white-and-blue Express Mail envelope from her purse and laid it on the counter.

"You might be willing to allow strangers into your life, but we were concerned, and it turns out we had good reason to be. We hired a private investigator, and he sent us this."

For a long time, Nolie didn't touch the envelope. It had been sent in care of Angels Lodge, the motel where her in-laws were staying, and it bore a return address in Boston. Obviously, the information inside wasn't good— Marlene didn't like it, and expected the same response from Nolie. Why?

At the moment her brain was too befuddled to think of any possibilities, which left her little choice but to open the envelope. Inside was a sheaf of papers, topped by a letter from the investigator that offered little—*Here's what I've uncovered so far. If you want more detailed information, let me know.* Underneath was a copy of Chase and Fiona's divorce decree, a letter from the state confirming that disciplinary action had resulted in his disbarment, and copies of newspaper articles.

ATTORNEY ARRESTED.

ATTORNEY CONVICTED IN EMBEZZLEMENT CASE.

ATTORNEY SENTENCED TO THREE-YEAR TERM.

Her first reaction was shock, the second disbelief. The Chase she knew wasn't a thief. Sure, he'd used her because she was convenient. He'd let her fall in love with him, then left her with nothing to show for it but heartache. He was going to take forever to get over. But an embezzler? A common thief? No way. He wasn't that kind of person.

Her third reaction was shock again, stronger this time.

She went back to the beginning and started reading. Her hands were trembling, so she laid the pages on the counter, touching them only to turn to the next one.

There was only one photograph accompanying the newspaper articles, and that was the first one. It showed Chase being led out of an office building in handcuffs. He looked far more than three years younger and bewildered, but there was a certain confidence about him, too, that said this was all a horrible mistake and would soon be cleared up. She wondered how different a photo accompanying the last article—*Attorney Sentenced to Three-Year Term*—would have been. Where would that confidence have gone?

"Well?"

The impatient question came from Marlene. Nolie looked up at her, at the cool smile that curved her lips and the triumphant gleam in her eyes. She expected Nolie to be stunned right out of her socks by the news—to be hurt, betrayed, angry, weepy.

Nolie had news for her. She was *already* hurt, betrayed, angry, and weepy. This news hardly registered, compared to the little bombshell Chase had dropped Sunday afternoon.

She was stunned, granted, and hurt that he'd never confided in her, and she was damned angry—at the authorities who'd wrongly arrested and tried Chase, the jurors who'd chosen the easy verdict, and the people who'd set him up in the first place. She was angry that he'd gotten such a raw deal and beyond angry that Marlene thought to twist it to her advantage.

Grateful that her hands were once again steady, Nolie straightened the papers and slid them into the envelope, then held it out.

"Keep it," Marlene said. "We've got copies." For the first time since their arrival in Bethlehem, she touched Nolie, taking her hand, squeezing it tightly. "I know how hard this is for you. You thought you were lucky that such a handsome man was attracted to you. You thought he actually cared about you. But you see now that he's a thief, a liar, and an ex-con. He was just using you."

Pain spasmed through Nolie, making her tremble as she

pulled her hand back. "You really don't think much of me, do you, Marlene?"

Her mother-in-law's forehead wrinkled in a frown. "I don't know what you mean."

"You don't believe I'm pretty enough or smart enough or likable enough to attract a handsome man. You can't believe that Chase could possibly want anything besides sex from me, and you think he wanted that only because . . . what? I was easy? I was handy?" The hell of it—that Marlene was right—brought tears to Nolie's eyes. Hugging herself tightly, she blinked to keep them at bay.

Marlene opened her mouth, closed it, then opened it again, her manner brusque and annoyed. "This isn't about you, Nolie. It's about your so-called boyfriend, the convicted felon. The ex-con. For God's sake, forget your hormones and open your eyes! It's all there, in black and white. Chase Wilson is a thief! He stole more than a million dollars and—"

"Bullshit." The obscenity, sharp and succinct, came from behind the Harpers and from the unlikeliest source to defend Chase in all of New York—Earl Wilson.

I really have to get that bell fixed, Nolie thought.

Marlene rounded on Earl. "This is a private conversation, so kindly mind your own business."

"That's my son you're talking about, which makes it my business," Earl retorted. "I admit, he was a wild kid, in and out of trouble all the time, living to make his mother's and my lives hell. But I can tell you this—that boy's never stolen anything in his life. He wouldn't."

Earl Wilson's creed, Nolie thought, too numb to smile even cynically. *He* could criticize his family all he wanted, but by God, no one without Wilson blood flowing through his veins got the same privilege. Jeff had been that way. He could complain about his mother all he wanted when she'd driven him crazy, but heaven help the poor fool, even Nolie, who chimed in.

Marlene pointed to the envelope. "The state of Massachusetts says otherwise."

"Then the state of Massachusetts is wrong."

"He's a convicted felon."

Earl's only response to her was to repeat the obscenity, with more emphasis this time.

Nolie tried to send a plea for intervention Obie's way, but he was still refusing to look at her. He was ashamed to even be there, she thought, reading his slumped shoulders, downcast gaze, and stiff posture. It was too bad he didn't have more of a backbone, but then he had to live with the woman . . . or thought he did.

Marlene did what she did best—ignored Earl and his opinions—and fixed her gaze on Nolie. "We don't want him around our granddaughter, Nolie. We're God-fearing and law-abiding people, and that sort of influence is something she doesn't need and we don't want."

"He's innocent." Nolie couldn't find a single doubt inside her.

"What? Did he tell you so?" Marlene asked snidely. "I bet he also told you you're beautiful . . . just before you let him in your bed. Men lie, Nolie. Heavens, he's got you thinking he cares for you—maybe even loves you. How could you not know he's lying?"

Nolie bit the inside of her lip until the tears slowly seeped back where they belonged. Before she could come up with a response, no doubt a pathetic one, Earl spoke again.

"If he told her she's beautiful, it just proves he's got good taste."

Marlene shot him a killing look. "I believe I asked you to mind your own business."

"No, you told me. And I told you, Chase *is* my business. Besides"—he gave Nolie a sidelong look and a wink—"as I understand, this girl's gonna be my daughter-in-law someday. Let's see, that gives me two reasons to butt in while you only have one, so maybe you should butt out."

Marlene's mouth dropped open, her face turned cherry-red, and Nolie swore she could see each thud of the woman's heart in the vein throbbing wildly in her neck. It was a fair bet that nobody in the world had ever told her to mind her own business, and she didn't like it one bit.

It took her a moment to regain enough composure to speak again, her control rigid but liable to shatter at any moment. "You think about what you're going to do, Nolie. You think long and hard, because it will determine what we're going to do. Right now, we're going to pick up our granddaughter at the library. We'll be in touch with you to find out—"

"No." Nolie blurted it out before she lost her nerve.

Eyebrows reaching toward her hairline, Marlene stared at her. "No? You think you can turn us away without an answer to this problem?"

"I mean, no, you can't pick up Micahlyn. I'll do it."

Finally Obie found his voice. "But we promised her—"

"Don't push me, Nolie," Marlene said, her voice soft but menacing.

Nolie matched her, note for note. "Don't threaten me. I'll get Micahlyn. Call this evening, and I'll let you know when you can see her again."

Marlene stared at her as the clock on the wall loudly ticked off ten seconds, twenty, thirty. Then she spun and regally swept down the aisle toward the door. Obie took a step toward Nolie, squeezed her hand, and shrugged, then went after Marlene.

Closing her eyes, Nolie sank onto the stool next to her, then covered her face with both hands. Her limbs were heavy, her knees unsteady, and if her heart hadn't been thoroughly broken before her in-laws had walked in the door, it was now.

But not all her problems were gone. Earl came around the counter and laid his hand on her shoulder. "I've got to give you credit. You don't look strong enough to stand up to that old battleax. She's been getting her way longer than you've even been alive."

Drawing a deep breath, she faced him. "Thank you." He'd taken her side when her own father-in-law—her surrogate father!—hadn't. It meant a lot, both in her feelings toward Earl and her feelings for Obie.

He shrugged, then confirmed her earlier thought. "A man can't stand by and let some stranger talk bad about his family. Leanne tells me you're all but part of us."

"Actually, no. Chase broke up with me Sunday."

Earl snorted derisively. "I said he wasn't a thief. I didn't say he showed good sense. Why didn't you tell the old battleax that? It's obviously what she wants."

"Tell her she's right? That a man like Chase couldn't possibly care about a woman like me?" she asked, hating the wistful note to her voice. "No, thanks."

He patted her back in a reassuring manner. "She's not right. Any man with eyes in his head can see that." The friendly tone of his voice not changing one bit, he went on. "Though, if I were you, I'd probably be talking with my lawyer about this."

Chills danced down her spine. *Do you think your in-laws would do something rash?* Chase had asked. *Like trying* to get *custody of Micahlyn*. Oh, no, she'd confidently, foolishly, replied. No, no, no.

Dear God, please don't prove me wrong.

CHASE LAY IN THE HAMMOCK, A BOX OF STALE CEreal in one hand, a can of beer on the floor beside him. He wore the same jeans he'd worn the day before, and the past couple days before that, and his T-shirt was wadded up and stuffed under his head for a pillow.

He needed to get out of Bethlehem, though he didn't know where he could go—someplace west or maybe south. Someplace where he didn't know a soul and could keep it that way. Someplace away from Nolie, and hell and gone from Marlene.

But that wasn't part of Marlene's plan. If he left Bethlehem, then there was no reason for Nolie to leave. He was supposed to stay right there and make it impossible for her to do the same, so she would run home and Marlene could be happy while everyone else in her world was miserable.

Damnation.

When a car started up the hill, he set the cereal down next to the beer, sat up, and swung his feet to the floor, prepared to disappear inside if it was Nolie—not likely in the middle of the afternoon. But, hey, unlikelier things had happened. He'd dumped her, hadn't he?

The car wasn't her old station wagon, though, or the Harpers' rental or Leanne's SUV. It was a Lincoln Town Car that drove right past Nolie's cabin and came to a stop in front of his. As the driver got out, Chase slowly got to his feet, his muscles taut.

It was his father.

Without a word, Earl walked around the car, climbed the steps, and faced him from ten feet away. His eyes hidden behind sunglasses, he swept his gaze slowly—insolently—over Chase before finally speaking. "You look like hell."

Chase couldn't argue that with him. He'd hadn't been sleeping, or eating regularly, and he hadn't shaved since Saturday. He was a far cry from Micahlyn's bogeyman, but give him a little time and he would get there again.

"I heard you'd come back." Earl's voice was carefully blank of emotion. "Seems like everybody in town's seen or talked to you, except for your mother and me."

"Yeah, well, I stay away from places where I'm not welcome."

"Your mother would be happy to see you."

But not you, old man. Some things never change. "I doubt that. She had plenty of chances to see me. College graduation. Law school graduation. My wedding."

Finally, when Earl removed the dark glasses, an emotion—just a flicker of guilt. "It would mean a lot to her to see you."

"What does it matter to you? I never could figure out why the two of you even got married in the first place, much less stayed together. The best I could figure was misery loves company."

Earl opened his mouth to speak, closed it again, then the muscles in his jaw clenched. "It doesn't matter to me. It matters to *her*."

"Yeah, right."

A long silence passed, then Earl gestured. "Where'd you get the scar?"

Chase automatically lifted his hand to the line across his ribs. When the laceration was healing and for a long time afterward, he'd been sharply aware of it—a physical reminder of an important lesson learned. In recent months he'd more or less forgotten about it, though the lesson was even more important now. "I got in someone's way and he didn't like it."

"In prison?"

The blunt question made him stiffen before he consciously forced himself to relax and return to the hammock. "Yeah. In prison." Then . . . "How'd you know about that?"

Earl shrugged. Keeping tabs on his wayward son? Chase wouldn't put it past him.

His father leaned against the post next to him and gazed toward Nolie's cabin. "Leanne told me you were probably gonna marry your neighbor, but the girl in question said you dumped her. Because of that hateful old mother-in-law of hers?"

Chase glared at him. "What do you know about Marlene Harper?"

"Marlene? Is that her name?" Earl rubbed his chin thoughtfully. "I would've pegged her for a Cruella or Vampira. Talk about misery loving company . . . that woman's not happy and she's not gonna be satisfied till *no one's* happy."

The apprehension twitching inside brought Chase to his feet again. "Answer my question, damn it. What do you know about Marlene?"

"I stopped by the feed store looking for you—I heard you've been spending your days there. This Marlene and her husband were there, and the old witch was telling Nolie all about your being in prison."

"Aw, hell." With the chill spreading through him, the best Chase could manage was a whisper. He'd thought Marlene's was an either/or proposition. Either he broke up with Nolie or Marlene would use his past against her in a custody battle. He'd thought if he broke up with her, the whole prison bit would stay between him and the Harpers. He'd hoped . . .

Of course Marlene wouldn't have kept his secret. She hated him for nothing more than being the man to take her son's place in Nolie's life, and she would use anything she could to boot him out of it. She'd coerced him into breaking up with Nolie, and now she'd done her best to turn Nolie against him.

"Damn it!" He kicked the beer can, sending it flying off the porch, trailing a stream of beer behind it. It hit the log at the edge of the yard with a solid *thunk*. "I should have known . . ." Forcing him to hurt Nolie hadn't been enough for her. Nothing would be, until she had Micahlyn back home in Arkansas with her, and to hell with anyone who got in her way.

Earl glanced at him before gazing out into the woods again. "She said you were innocent. Nolie, I mean. She read the newspaper articles, listened to that old woman, then insisted you were innocent. Not a doubt in her mind. She's got a lot of faith in you."

Faith he didn't deserve. Look how he'd repaid her—by telling her she'd been nothing more than a convenience. That he didn't want her anymore. By diminishing everything she felt for him and denying everything he felt for her. By bringing more heartache into a life that had already had far more than its share.

His father walked down the steps, then turned back. "You don't run into someone you love who loves you back every day. Don't give that up in some misguided effort to protect her." That said, Earl went to the car and opened the door, then called, "Think about going to see your mother."

Long after he'd driven out of sight, Chase remained unmoving, staring into the distance. *Was* his effort misguided? Probably. So damn much about his life was. But what choice did he have? He couldn't risk being the reason Nolie lost custody of Micahlyn.

But what if she didn't lose custody? What if, for once, justice was served? If Obie's dear old friend, the judge, recognized Marlene for the manipulative, domineering woman she was? If he agreed, as any rational person would, that Micahlyn was far better off with her mother than her scheming grandmother?

And what if he didn't?

What if, what if . . . Everything was a crapshoot. Life didn't come with guarantees, and justice sure as hell didn't. The risk in this particular instance was too big to take.

A soft sound from behind him—the rubbing of the hammock against the hooks that supported it—filtered into his mind an instant before a voice broke the silence. "I'd ask where you are, but I think I already know."

He spun around to find Sophy kicked back in the hammock, one foot on the floor to keep it swaying. She smiled brightly as if his scowl hadn't intimidated people bigger and meaner than her and waggled her fingers in greeting.

"You always go around sneaking up on people?" he asked sourly.

"I didn't sneak. You were preoccupied."

He couldn't argue with her. He had been a bit distracted the past few days. "What do you want?"

"Help."

"I'm out of the help-giving business."

"So you say. Actually, I meant to *offer* help."

He sat down on the step and leaned back until his head connected with the post. "Can you remake Marlene Harper into something resembling a human being?"

"I can't remake anyone. Everyone has to do that for themselves."

Not true. Nolie had remade him. When he'd come here, he'd been angry, bitter, and hostile, without much reason for going on. She'd eased all that, and given him plenty of reasons for going on . . . and Marlene had taken them away.

"You did that for yourself," Sophy said, and he wondered whether she was just continuing the thread of conversation she'd started or if, like before, she'd somehow read his thoughts. "You had to deal with the anger and the bitterness. Nolie helped by offering you things you need— friendship, affection, trust, faith—but you had to make the changes yourself."

"Yeah, well, Marlene doesn't want to change." And he *had* wanted to. Those things Nolie had offered had healed him and healing had made him want and wanting had led to . . . to exactly where he was now.

"Mrs. Harper is terrified."

He snorted. "*Terrifying* is more like it."

"Remember how you felt when you were arrested and you found out your wife was having an affair and she divorced you and you were convicted and got sent to prison? Angry, betrayed, cheated . . . and helpless. So very helpless. That's how Marlene feels. No parent should have to bury her own child, but Marlene had to. And no grandmother wants to watch her only grandbaby—her only link to her dead son—move halfway across the country, but Marlene did. And now there's another man in Nolie's life, one who's taking her son's place, who will soon be filling Jeff's place in Micahlyn's life, too. But what about *her* place?"

"It's back home in Arkansas," he retorted. "Where she belongs."

She gave him a chiding look. "Once Nolie remarries, she'll have a new husband and his family, and Micahlyn will have a new father and new grandparents. There won't be much left for the Harpers. Most courts don't place much value on grandparents."

He knew that was true—knew that many grandparents, following their child's divorce or death, were denied access to their grandchildren. He could only imagine how tough that would be . . . but it never would have happened with Nolie. Yes, she'd moved Micahlyn hundreds of miles away, but she'd been determined to keep the Harpers involved in their granddaughter's life. She never would have cut them off, and he never would have expected it.

"But they don't know that," Sophy said. Before he could consider the fact that he was *positive* he hadn't spoken aloud, she went on. "They were at the hospital when Micahlyn was born. They saw her every single day of her life for more than five years, and then suddenly she was gone. All they had were phone calls, and you can't get a hug or a kiss goodnight over the phone. Then *you* came into the picture with a sister, parents, and a nephew of your own, and you're right here, and your family's right here, where you can all be a regular part of Nolie's and Micahlyn's lives. Micahlyn's such a little girl. Who could blame her if she forgot the grandparents back in Arkansas in favor of the ones who live a few miles down the road?"

Scowling, Chase turned his back on her. "If they were afraid, they should have said something, damn it—not come in making demands and threats."

"The way you said something to Nolie about having been in prison? Or the way you said something to your father about all the years the two of you wasted? Or maybe the way you've said something to Nolie about how much you love her and want to marry her?" Then she smacked herself on the forehead. "Oh, wait, I forgot. You gave her the you're-not-my-type-you're-just-a-convenience speech instead."

Ashamed, he bowed his head. That speech, as she called it, had been the hardest words he'd ever said in his life. Seeing the hurt in Nolie's eyes, hearing it in her voice, and the tears . . . He'd hated Marlene, but even more, he'd hated himself.

"The Harpers need reassurance," Sophy went on. "They need to know they'll always have a place in Nolie's and Micahlyn's lives. Something binding, like a court decree. But if they have to take Nolie to court to get it, it's going to destroy their little family."

Something binding . . . like a contract. But it was a sorry thing when a family needed a contract in order to remain a family.

He shrugged as carelessly as he could manage. "You're talking to the wrong person. I'm out of this now. Marlene made sure of that."

Again with the chiding look. "She didn't force you out. She offered you a choice, and you made it. It was for the best of reasons, but it was still your choice."

"And what else could I have done?"

"You could have stood up to her, you and Nolie together. You could have had faith—in Nolie, in God, in the courts, in yourself. You could have found a compromise. You're a lawyer. Negotiating is one of your specialties." She eased to her feet, jumped from the porch to the ground, then walked backward to the road. "Think about it, Chase. You can give in and lose everything, or you can fight for what's right."

She waggled her fingers in another wave, twirled

around, then called over her shoulder, "It's your only *real* choice."

THE PHONE WAS RINGING WHEN THEY WALKED INTO the house that evening. Nolie's jaw tightened as she crossed the living room right on Micahlyn's heels, then reached over her daughter's head to answer.

It was Obie, sounding subdued and tired. "I hope it's not too soon to call."

"No, not at all," she said, making a face at the lie.

"I was wondering if I could take Mikey fishing tomorrow like I promised. I thought maybe in the morning, if that's all right with you, and then we could have a picnic lunch at the lake before we bring her back."

There was a plaintive note in his voice that made Nolie want to hide in a corner. This was the first time in Micahlyn's entire life that he'd been put in a position of having to ask anything. When they'd lived together, they'd just done things. If she'd had plans for Micahlyn, she had let them know, and everyone had worked around them, and vice versa. But he'd never had to humbly ask permission to spend a few hours with his grandbaby.

It wasn't her fault, she silently insisted—or, at least, if it was, it was only partly her fault. Marlene had threatened her. If Nolie hadn't stood up to her then, who knew when she would have found any backbone again?

"That's fine, Obie. What time do you want to pick her up?"

"How about eight? We can get her at the store, if that's okay."

"I'll have her dressed for wading."

He chuckled. "The little stinker still isn't convinced that fishing's best done from the bank, is she?" Then his humor faded. "Nolie, I'm really sorry about all this. I regret like hell— Well, I'll let you go. We'll see you in the morning."

Marlene must have come into the room, Nolie thought as she hung up. What a shame that he didn't feel he could have a casual conversation with his daughter-in-law when his wife was around.

And what a shame that *she* didn't want to have a casual conversation with either of them, unless it included the word good-bye.

She was still standing next to the wall when the phone rang again, startling her. This time it was Leanne. "I know it's last minute, but how about dinner at Chez Wilson? The service is excellent, the ambiance lovely, and the food has been awarded four stars by kids everywhere. Whaddya say?"

She should say no. The way she was feeling, she wasn't fit company this evening. But who would understand better than Leanne, and she *really* needed a few sympathetic words and a hug from someone who understood. "What time and what should I bring?"

"Seven, your child, my brother, and yourself. See you."

Leanne hung up before Nolie had a chance to tell her that she wouldn't be bringing Chase. Oh, well, some news was better broken in person . . . she guessed.

She hustled Micahlyn upstairs to change clothes, then went into her own room to do the same. Once they were both presentable, they headed back out to the car. "Where are we goin'?" Micahlyn asked as Nolie leaned across to buckle her seat belt.

"To Leanne's for dinner."

"Why isn't Chase goin'?"

Nolie straightened again and glanced toward the other cabin. The back end of his truck was just visible around the corner. For someone who'd been so eager to dump her and start a new life, he seemed to be spending even more time at home than he had before.

Maybe he wasn't spending it alone.

The pain that thought stirred was real, making her press one hand flat against her stomach to contain it. When she could take a breath, she did, and smiled vaguely at her daughter. "He's busy."

"Doing what?"

"I don't know, babe."

"Did you *ask* him?"

"No."

"Then how do you know—"

"Hey, Grandpa's taking you fishing tomorrow. Won't that be fun?"

Fortunately, Micahlyn rose to the bait and was off and running—or talking—about all the fish she'd caught in the past and might catch in the morning. Her chatter didn't wind down until they reached Leanne's.

Leanne answered the door, greeted them both fondly, then looked past them to the sidewalk. "Where's Chase?"

"He . . . uh, he's busy."

Dark eyes so like his fixed on her face for a long moment, then Leanne's features shifted to sympathy. "Oh, honey . . . tell me I'm wrong."

Smiling bleakly, Nolie shook her head.

"What happened?"

"Nothing, really," Nolie replied with a warning glance at Micahlyn. "We're anxious to see this great apartment of yours. Lead the way."

Though the stairs didn't thrill her—think of the exercise—Nolie loved the compact spaces, the colors, the whimsy, everything about the place. It was a wonderful idea, living above her business, she thought, and told Leanne so as they ended the tour back in the kitchen.

Micahlyn had remained in Danny's room, with the boy offering to show her all his toys.

"You've got a store of your own," Leanne pointed out.

"Yeah, but living above the feed store outside town isn't nearly as appealing as living above Small Wonders right on the town square. I'd fall asleep to the fragrant aroma of horse feed every night and probably wake up chewing on my pillow."

Leanne smiled faintly, glanced toward the hall, then said, "Okay. Tell Auntie Leanne what happened with my idiot brother. Do I need to go beat him up? I've done it a time or two in the past, you know."

"I don't think it'll help. He just likes . . . a different kind of woman. It's not his fault I'm too tall, too plump, too red-haired, too plain." She smiled hard as the damn tears started to gather again. She wasn't going to cry, not again, not with witnesses.

"You're none of those things," Leanne declared, "and I can't believe Chase said you were. A blind man could see that he was crazy about you!"

"Stir crazy, maybe. He was hiding out there at the cabin, never seeing anyone but Micahlyn and me, and he was bored and—and needy, and I—I was there. Food, companionship, and sex, all a two-minute stroll away. Who could blame him for taking advantage of such a convenience?"

Though to be strictly truthful, he could have found any number of women in Howland while he was still in hiding outside Bethlehem. And his self-imposed exile had ended the night *before* he'd made love to her for the first time, so he could have found any number of women in Bethlehem, as well.

Minor details. The bottom line was, she'd fallen in love . . . and he hadn't.

Leanne gave the spaghetti sauce a stir, put a loaf of buttered bread in the oven, then fisted her hands on her hips. Her eyes were flashing with anger, and there was an icy stillness about her. "He called you a *convenience?*"

"I— He didn't—" Heat flushed Nolie's face, and she covered it with her hands. "I shouldn't even be talking to you. You're his sister."

"And I'm your friend, and I'll make him damned sorry."

"Please don't. He feels badly enough about this. He didn't mean to hurt me."

"He called you a *convenience* and didn't think you'd be hurt? He's not stupid . . . though he *is* an idiot. Oh, Nolie . . . I'm so sorry."

Leanne came across the room, arms open, and Nolie took comfort in her embrace, even letting a few tears slide free before she willed them to stop. When she finally straightened, she sniffled, dried her cheeks, then grasped the first excuse to change the subject. "There seem to be more place settings than we have people. Does that mean the Jackson boys are coming?"

"Yes, ma'am. I so rarely cook, I like to take care of all my dinner paybacks at once."

"Is everything okay with you two?"

Raising her brows, Leanne gave an exaggerated shrug. "It seems to be. We're still spending all of our nights together. I haven't said the L word again, and he hasn't gotten that deer-in-headlights look again. So I guess we're fine."

Except for the facts that she'd *like* to say the L word again and she would really like to hear Cole say it back. It wasn't exactly Nolie's definition of *fine,* but it beat her own situation. At least Cole was still coming around.

The ring of the doorbell interrupted her thoughts and

brought a light to Leanne's eyes. "If the timer goes off, take the bread out of the oven, would you?"

Nolie nodded, then turned to survey the living room. The wicker table was set for four, with a centerpiece of fresh flowers and a lovely floral cloth draped over a solid skirt of midnight blue. A card table with three settings was situated in the middle of the room, its tablecloth vinyl for easy cleanup.

She deliberately removed one place setting from the wicker table, sliding the dishes into a corner on the kitchen cabinet as voices became audible in the hall.

Dinner was simple—spaghetti and meatballs with garlic bread, plus tiramisu for dessert—and as relaxing as it could be with three kids in attendance . . . and no Chase. Nolie assumed Leanne had filled Cole in downstairs, because he didn't mention Chase's absence. He was charming and attentive, almost gentle in his behavior and conversation.

Leanne was a lucky woman.

The evening was a badly needed balm to Nolie's spirit. The only interruption came when the meal was over, the dishes already taken to the kitchen, and the phone rang. Leanne took the call in the kitchen, then with a tight smile, picked up her keys from the counter. "I've got to run downstairs for a minute. I'll be right back." Directing her attention to the kids, she raised her voice. "Maybe while I'm gone, the dish fairies will guide the children into the kitchen and show them how to clean up."

"I wanna see the fairies," Danny piped up as Micahlyn chimed in, "Me, too."

Ryan snorted. "Dish fairies, my as—" At a sharp look from his father, he broke off, then rolled his eyes. "Why don't you just say, 'Ryan, it's your turn to do the dishes'?"

"Ryan, it's your turn to do the dishes," Cole parroted.

Nolie watched Leanne leave and the kids troop into the

kitchen, then fiddled with her napkin. She'd gotten so comfortable with Chase in the past weeks that she'd forgotten how tongue-tied she could be around a handsome man. At that moment she couldn't think of a thing to say to Cole, other than the usual, How's business? and how boring was that?

Then she remembered the check in her purse. Business in general? Yes, boring. Business involving her thirty-some-thousand dollars? Not boring at all.

"I read the stuff you sent—the investment stuff for Micahlyn's college money." Read it and didn't understand a word. "It sounded good to me, so . . ." She took the check from her wallet and slid it across the table.

He looked at it without touching it. "Are you sure you want to do this?"

She smiled faintly. "I've never heard of an investment counselor trying to talk someone out of an investment."

"I'm not. It's just . . . well, the market's pretty volatile, and as a general rule of thumb, you shouldn't invest anything you can't afford to lose."

"That's the point of diversifying, isn't it?" She knew that much, though if asked to explain the practice, she would have to fall back on a saying more familiar to a farm girl: Don't put all your eggs in the same basket.

"Yes, of course, but . . ."

"It's not everything," she said patiently. "That money's for Micahlyn. I have a little to fall back on if we have to." She wasn't rich by any means, but if the feed-store market dried up tomorrow, they wouldn't go hungry while she looked for another job.

"Okay," he said slowly, picking up the check. He folded it precisely in half, then slid it into his pocket. "I'll bring the paperwork by the store tomorrow."

When Leanne returned, they talked for a while in the living room. Before long, Micahlyn crawled up on the love seat with Nolie and dozed off. Catching herself swallowing her own yawn, Nolie smiled apologetically. "It's been a long day. We need to head home."

"I'm awfully glad you came," Leanne said.

"Me, too." Nolie stood up, then gazed at Micahlyn, now stretched out the entire length of the love seat. "Have you ever noticed how much bigger and heavier they get when they're asleep and have to be carried?"

"That's why my child walks—always," Leanne replied. "Carrying him would give me a hernia."

"I'll get her," Cole said. Before Nolie could protest, he scooped Micahlyn into his arms, then started toward the door.

Nolie turned to thank Leanne for dinner and found her watching Cole with her heart in her eyes. When she realized Nolie was watching *her,* she laughed, embarrassed. "Okay, so I'm a sucker for a big strong man who's tender with kids," she murmured. "What can I say?"

"No excuses needed. So am I." She'd been married to one such man, and had fallen in love with another, or so she'd thought. Too bad she'd been wrong about Chase.

While Ryan stayed behind with Danny, Nolie and Leanne followed Cole downstairs and outside into the warm evening. Her car was parked around the corner, and as they strolled in that direction, the door to Small Wonders opened . . . and Chase stepped out. He stopped abruptly, a folder in his hands, and stared at them.

For one painful moment, Nolie stared back. Then she forced herself to drag her gaze away and smile for Leanne. "Thanks for dinner."

"Thanks for coming."

Leanne hugged her once more, then Nolie caught up

with Cole. She wasn't sure, but behind them, she thought she heard the distinctive sound of a hand smacking against a solid arm. *Do I need to go beat him up?* Leanne had asked.

Nolie guessed some things were just too much for a sister to resist.

Chapter Seventeen

THE PAIN CHASE WAS FEELING HAD NOTHING to do with the punch Leanne had given him.

Nolie had looked at him as if he were a stranger.

No, that wasn't true. She'd looked at him as if he were someone she would rather never see again. Not the man she loved. Not the man who was trying really hard to make things right.

Of course, she didn't know anything about that.

Leanne hit him again. "You used her because she was *convenient*? What the hell kind of thing is that to tell a woman?"

"A lie," he murmured, staring after Nolie. When she'd driven out of sight and Jackson had returned, he refocused on his sister. "Not now, okay? I can't handle . . . Thanks for letting me use your computer, though you could have warned me she was upstairs."

"If I'd mentioned her at all when you came, I would have had to hurt you bad. And what would you have done if I'd told you? Hide like the coward you are?"

He couldn't find the energy to be insulted by her

question. Besides, he *was* a coward. He'd taken the easy way out of every problem that came along. But not anymore.

"Thanks," he said again, then moved around her and started toward his truck.

"Chase!" Leanne sounded as if she were on the verge of stamping her foot in a temper. "Why did you hurt her like that?"

He gazed back at her. "Ask her mother-in-law. She'll be happy to tell you."

Then he climbed into his truck and drove away. He still had plans to make and arguments to prepare.

The most important arguments of his life.

NOLIE WAS MAKING CHANGE FOR A CUSTOMER Wednesday afternoon when Chase walked in the door. Stunned by his appearance, she pressed the money she held into the customer's hand, murmured, "You're welcome," then stared down as he approached.

The older gentleman she'd waited on looked from the money to her to Chase, then back again. "Now look here, missy, the way it goes is I give you this money and you put it in the cash register and say, 'Thank you. Come again.' You can't give this stuff to me for free, else you'd be closing your doors before long, and for good this time."

"Wh-what?" Nolie asked blankly.

"Aw, hell." The man came around the counter, nudged her aside, and opened the cash register, dividing the bills and coins into their proper spaces. " 'Thank you, Stu.' 'Why, you're welcome, missy.' 'Come back and see us sometime.' 'I surely will.' " With a *harrumph,* he closed the register drawer, picked up his bag, and left.

She was only vaguely aware of his leaving, and all too aware that she was alone in the store now with Chase.

Chase, who didn't want her.

Abruptly, she turned away from the register, intending to . . . what? Hide in the storeroom? There was no lock on the door. He would follow. Instead, she made a wide sweep around him and began straightening a shelf that didn't need it.

"Nolie—"

She picked up a bottle of plant fertilizer and moved it to its proper shelf across the aisle. "Take whatever you need and go."

"You can't give stuff to me for free, else you'd be closing—"

She fixed a fierce stare on him, angry beyond words that he could come in teasing, and his words abruptly stopped. After a moment, he made an awkward gesture. "I'm not here to buy anything."

"Good. Get out."

"I can't do that. Not yet."

His answer annoyed her and made her knock over a display of insecticides. She straightened every last box, then glared at him. "Why didn't you tell me you'd been in prison?"

A tinge of red crept into his cheeks. "Because I was ashamed . . . and afraid."

"Of what?"

"That you would believe I was guilty."

"So you didn't even give me a chance."

He came a few steps closer. Clutched in one hand was the same folder he'd been carrying last night outside Small Wonders. She wondered what it was, and why he'd come to torment her, and why she couldn't be tiny and delicate and black-haired and exactly what he wanted.

"Okay," he said softly. "Here's your chance. Do you believe I stole that money?"

"Does it matter?" Her own voice was petulant, and she
didn't care. He had a lot of nerve, after the things he'd said
to her Sunday, to come here wanting her to prove her trust
in him.

"It matters like hell to me."

She studied him a moment, then returned to cleaning
the shelves, her movements less frantic. "No," she said at
last. "I don't believe you're guilty."

Of some things, at least.

"Why?"

Discovering a sudden need for every box on the shelf to
line up in perfect order, she focused on that for a moment.
Of course, it didn't make him forget his question . . . or
keep his distance. He came even closer.

"Why do you believe that? My wife didn't. My friends
didn't. My firm didn't. The jury damn sure didn't. Why
would you?"

Wishing for a customer who would require her attention, she gazed out the plate-glass window, but the only
cars in the parking lot were theirs, and not one of those
whizzing past on the highway showed any intention of
turning in. "Clearly you were set up."

"What makes you think so?"

She didn't want to talk about this—didn't want to talk
to him at all. But he was there and not planning to leave
without an answer, so the sooner she gave it, the sooner he
would go.

With a great sigh, she turned back to him. "Fiona was
having an affair with Darren Kennedy, wasn't she?"

He nodded.

"She filed for divorce as soon as you were arrested, and
you let her have virtually everything, which was an awful

lot, granted, but there was a legitimate source for all of it. Not even so much as a dime could have come from the $1.1 million. As soon as the divorce was settled, she married Darren Kennedy, who happened to have been the one to discover the missing money in the first place, along with every bit of evidence that pointed to you. And the money was never found. And"—the most important part—"I know you."

"Fiona and Darren . . . why? I would have given her a divorce if she'd asked."

Most important to *her,* at least. "Would you also have given her everything you owned except the money you needed to pay your lawyer? If she had come to you and said, 'I'm having an affair with the guy you work with and I want a divorce so I can marry him,' would you have said, 'Sure, honey, and while you're at it, here, come out of the marriage a rich woman and leave me broke'?"

"Probably not," he murmured.

"This way, you were preoccupied. You already had one battle to fight—to stay out of prison—so you didn't fight her. Plus they got that extra million dollars."

His gaze darkened and his mouth flattened in a thin line. "It seems I have a history of turning away from the wrong fights."

He looked so bleak that she wanted to go to him, wrap her arms around him, and tell him it wasn't true. He'd been facing the ruin of his career and reputation and the loss of his freedom. That had required all his attention.

But she couldn't go to him or wrap her arms around him, and because of that, all she wanted was for him to go. He'd made the decision to cut her out of his life, and as long as she was living with it, so should he.

"Look, I'm really not up to this," she said, needlessly rearranging a shelf. "If you would please just leave . . ."

"I can't. They're here."

The sound of a slamming car door drew her attention outside, where Obie was circling his rental to open Marlene's door for her. "Hell," she muttered. "What are they doing here, and where the hell is my daughter?"

"I asked them to come, and to drop off Micahlyn at day care on the way."

"You *what*?"

"You believed in me regarding the embezzlement charge. Trust me on this, too." He reached out as if to cup his palm to her cheek, then caught himself and let his hand fall. "Please, Nolie."

The annoying thing was, she couldn't refuse even if she wanted to. Unlike his feelings for her—whatever they were—she couldn't turn her trust on and off to suit her needs. She did trust him. Period.

The bell rang in warning as the Harpers came in, and Chase's first thought was surprise that Nolie had finally gotten it fixed. He hadn't heard it ring when he'd come inside, but then, he'd had more important things on his mind. Like the rest of his life.

Obie looked uncomfortable, Marlene antagonistic. At least she was there. That counted for something. She looked at him as if he were contagious, then fixed her gaze on Nolie. "I assume you had a reason for asking us here today."

"Actually, no, I didn't, because it wasn't my—"

"I'm the one who invited you," Chase interrupted, "and, yes, I had a reason for it." He flexed his fingers around the file he held, wondering whether to explain first or let them read for themselves. He'd gone over the words a dozen times, softening, strengthening, and he still wasn't satisfied with them, but they got the point across. They would do. "Let's go to the counter."

He stepped back so Nolie could precede him up the aisle, but for a long moment she refused to move. It was a hell of a time for her to develop a spine where her in-laws were concerned. Finally, though, she relented and led the way to the counter.

Chase detoured to the door, turning the OPEN sign so the BACK SOON message on the reverse showed, then he followed them. Obie and Marlene stood on the near side, Nolie opposite, all three of them pointedly ignoring the others. He went to stand beside Nolie, and she ignored him, too. He couldn't blame her.

He tapped the file folder on the countertop before setting it down. "You people have known one another forever. You were around when Nolie was born. You took her in when her parents died. You were there when she married your son and had his daughter, and you were there when she buried him. And now you can't carry on a civil conversation or even be in the same room with one another without getting angry."

Nolie gave him a less-than-agreeable look.

"I know," he said. "You think you have good reason to be angry with Marlene. And she thinks she has equally good reason to be angry with you."

"But she's wrong," Nolie said politely.

"You don't get to judge her perception as wrong. *You* see things *your* way. *She* sees them *her* way. You might not agree with her, but that doesn't make her wrong."

That polite, even tone didn't waver. "I disagree. Using my daughter to threaten me because she didn't like the man I was seeing was very wrong."

"That wasn't a threat," Marlene replied coolly. "It was a simple fact. I won't have Jeff's little girl exposed to—to trash like him."

"Marlene—"

She gave Obie a derisive glare. "Don't 'Marlene—' me. You were as concerned as I was when we found out our grandbaby was practically living with her mother's ex-con boyfriend!"

"Sure, I was concerned, and I agreed we should come here and make sure everything was okay, and it was . . . at least, until *we* arrived."

"Okay?" Marlene echoed, her voice little more than a whisper before it rose to a shriek. "*Okay? This* man, this-this thief, is trying to take Jeff's place in our family! He's sleeping with Nolie! He's reading bedtime stories to Mikey! She already talks about him as if-as if he's—" A strangled sob cut off her words. She dragged in a breath and her shoulders slumped before she found a new source of strength. "He's not her father, and he can't ever be! I won't allow it!"

"*You* won't allow it?" Obie looked as if he wanted to shake his wife, but his hands remained at his sides. "Who do you think you are? It's not your life, Marlene. It's Nolie's, and you have no say in how she lives it. As long as she's a good mother to Mikey—and you know she is— how she lives and who she chooses to live with are none of your business!"

Marlene drew up to her full height, the very picture of self-righteous anger. "We'll see if Harrison Clinton agrees with you. I've already spoken to Tommy Wilks, and he thinks Harrison will be very sympathetic to our case."

Wilks, Chase assumed, was their lawyer back home— and probably second cousin to the judge, with his luck.

"Our *case?*" Obie echoed. "What the hell are you talking about?"

"We're suing for custody of Mikey. Tommy will file the papers Monday," Marlene announced calmly, then flung a hand in Chase's direction. "I warned him. I gave him the chance to do the right thing, and he refused. Heavens, I gave Nolie the same chance, and she refused to see what was before her own eyes. 'Chase isn't a criminal, he's innocent,' " she mimicked, then made a disgusted sound. "They've left us no other choice. Jeff isn't here to protect his daughter, so we have to do it for him. Now . . . I've heard all I intend to listen to. Obie, we're leaving."

He stared at her, openmouthed, while Nolie gazed at Chase, a speculative look in her eyes. Before either of them could speak, Chase resorted to the voice he'd used with the most recalcitrant of his former clients. "Mrs. Harper, please come back here and hear me out."

There hadn't been a murderer or drug dealer in the bunch who'd refused him. For a long moment it looked as if Marlene would be the first, but finally she returned and stood scowling at him.

"First, I know you don't think much of me, but I am— I *was* a very good lawyer. If Tommy Wilks is any kind of lawyer, he'll tell you right upfront that you don't have a case against Nolie." It shouldn't have taken so long for him to arrive at that realization—back in Boston, he would have lambasted any lawyer so imperceptive—but at least he had the excuse that this situation could decide his entire future. A man could be excused for letting emotion rule.

"To get custody of your granddaughter, you'll have to prove that her mother's unfit. Living in a state other than Arkansas and dating a man you don't like doesn't make her unfit. Having a love life doesn't, and neither does having that life with an ex-con. I served my sentence. The state of Massachusetts has no further interest in me, and with regard to that aspect of my life, neither does any other jurisdiction. If you go into court, even in front of your good friend, Judge Clinton, with nothing more than that, you're going to be dismissed as a bitter, petulant, domineering woman."

Conveniently, he ignored the fact that injustices still occurred, that her good friend just might give her her heart's desire.

When she would have spoken, he raised one hand. "Worse than that, you're going to destroy this family—not just you and Nolie, but also you and Micahlyn. Do you think she's going to take kindly to the grandmother who's trying to destroy the mother she adores?"

Marlene didn't answer—just pursed her lips sourly. It was a good sign that she didn't try to argue the inarguable.

"Truth is, Mrs. Harper, you don't want to hurt this family anymore than it's already been hurt. You don't want to take Micahlyn away from her mother. I don't think you even care that much about getting rid of me." He didn't pause long enough for her to dispute that last statement. "You're afraid of losing Jeff's place in Nolie's and Micahlyn's lives. You're afraid Nolie will fall in love with another man, that Micahlyn will call him Daddy, that she'll call *his* parents Grandma and Grandpa. You're afraid of losing *your* place in their lives."

She continued to stare, her expression unrelenting, but her chin trembled just a bit.

"That's not going to happen," he went on quietly. "You've been in their house. There are pictures of Jeff in the living room, in Nolie's and Micahlyn's rooms. There are pictures of you and Mr. Harper. One of the first things Nolie ever told me was that she talked about Jeff a lot so Micahlyn would know what kind of man her father was and how much he loved her. That'll never change. Even if Micahlyn chooses someday to call another man Dad, it's not going to diminish Jeff's place in her life."

The silence dragged out, moment after moment. Finally, Marlene spoke, her tone still hostile, though subdued. "Is there a point to all of this?"

"Yes, there is. On the surface, it appears that you and Nolie have totally different desires. You want her and Micahlyn home, where you can take care of them and be a part of their lives. She wants to stay here, where she can live her own life. But in your heart, you want the same things. You want to be happy, you want to keep Jeff's memory alive, and you want Micahlyn to grow up safe and well-loved.

"If there's one thing I learned practicing law, it's that every problem can be resolved, usually by compromise. You each give a little and, ideally, you each get a lot. That's what I have here—a compromise. It ensures that you and Obie will always be a large part of your granddaughter's life, but it gives Nolie the right to live without undue interference from you. She gets all the responsibility of raising Micahlyn the best she can, and you get all the fun of being grandparents." He removed a stack of papers from the folder, then passed a copy to each of them. "Read it—and don't say anything until you do," he added when Marlene opened her mouth.

He had a copy for himself, but he didn't bother to look at it. He'd practically memorized the text while he worked on it in Leanne's office. It was written in the form of a contract and basically stated, though in more detail, what he'd already said. It covered major holidays, summer visits to the Harpers' farm, and the grandparents' right to spoil their granddaughter rotten, while granting Nolie the right to make all the decisions for herself and Micahlyn, from where they lived to whom they loved, without interference. It ended with a clause tying it all together. Everyone had to live up to his or her end of the bargain, or they all lost.

If they lost their family, they would lose big.

The heavy silence was finally broken by Obie. "You would agree to this?" he asked Nolie, hopefulness heavy in his voice. "Letting us spend Christmas with you? Letting Mikey spend a whole month in the summer with us?"

Beside Chase, Nolie remained silent, her skeptical gaze on the document. Out of sight of the Harpers, he nudged his foot against hers and she shifted a few inches away before looking up. "Having you here for Christmas would be great. And, yes, I'd love to let Micahlyn visit you during the summer, though I'd like to wait until she's a few years older before she goes away for a whole month."

There was another pause, then another question from Obie. "This is just an agreement between three people. What if Nolie changes her mind?"

"I wouldn't do that," Nolie replied. "It was never my intention to cut you out of Micahlyn's life. That wouldn't be fair to her, to you, to Jeff, or to me."

"But what if you—" Obie's mouth thinned, and he took a quick look at Chase before going on. "What if you remarry, and your new husband believes he has good reason to not like us? What if he tells you we can't see her anymore?"

Nolie's jaw tightened and her voice took on a sharp edge. "That would never happen. What would I want with a man who could dismiss your importance in Micahlyn's life?"

Chase wanted badly to volunteer that *he* understood the importance of family, though he hadn't always—to assure the Harpers that he would never interfere with their rightful place in Micahlyn's world. He remained silent, though. This was the more minor of his problems. No matter what happened here, he still had to make things right with Nolie, and so far, she hadn't given him much encouragement.

"They say at Harry's that Christmas is really something around here," Obie mused. "It might be a nice change from our last thirty Christmases."

"I think it would," Nolie agreed.

Marlene dropped her copy of the agreement and let it flutter to the floor. "I'm not spending Christmas here. And why should I settle for a month with Mikey when I can have her year-round?"

"You won't get her year-round." Chase's voice was firm, his conviction solid. "You might persuade Judge Clinton to grant custody of her to you, but Nolie will fight it, and I'll help her—and I warn you, Mrs. Harper, I don't fight fair."

"You're not a lawyer anymore," she said dismissively.

"No, I'm not. But I've still got all the knowledge, expertise, and experience that made me the best criminal defense lawyer in Boston. I can keep you and Tommy Wilks tied up in court until Mica's long past the age where custody is even an issue."

For a long still moment, he held her gaze. She wasn't backing down . . . but neither was he. This was one battle he wouldn't turn away from.

When Obie spoke, his voice was so calm, so reasonable, that it caught Chase off guard. "That won't be necessary," he said and he reached for the ink pen resting next to the cash register.

"You can't sign that!" Marlene shrieked.

"I *am* signing it, and what's more, so are you." He scrawled his name on his copy, took Nolie's and signed it, then retrieved Marlene's from the floor and signed it, too. Done, he slid all three copies to Marlene, then offered her the pen.

"I won't do it."

"You will."

With bright spots of color in her cheeks, Marlene shook her head. "I'm getting custody of my grandbaby. I'm calling Tommy as soon as we get back to the motel, and I'm telling him to file the papers immediately."

"I'm calling Tommy as soon as we get back to the motel, too, and I'm telling him that I will not pay any legal bills you run up. And then I'm calling Harrison, and I'm telling him he'd better not consider, for even a minute, helping you with this madness. And then I'm calling the airline and making reservations to go home as soon as possible. You can go with me, or not. It's up to you."

Clutching one hand to her throat, Marlene looked as if she might faint. It was probably the first time he'd ever denied her anything she wanted, Chase thought, and it had left her speechless. Probably the first time for that, too.

Obie slapped the ink pen down on the counter with a thud. "Sign the damned papers, Marlene."

She wanted to refuse—it was obvious in her expression—but some part of her was afraid he would make good on his threats. Some part of her was very afraid that the family she was about to destroy was her own.

Grudgingly she picked up the pen and wrote her name on each of the three copies. When she was done, Nolie did the same.

Chase handed a copy to Nolie, two to Obie. "This is pretty much a symbolic gesture, but if you want to make it binding, you can have it notarized and swear under oath to uphold the terms therein."

"We're family," Obie said stiffly. "Family doesn't have to swear under oath. Nolie . . . I am so sorry for all the trouble we've caused. Things will change. You have my word on that."

"Mine, too," she murmured.

"We'll be in touch later. Right now we have things to discuss." Taking the papers in one hand and Marlene's arm in the other, he turned her toward the door, and he didn't let go until he helped her into the car. She sat there, stiff and pinch-faced, as he backed out, then drove away.

Chase raised one hand to ease the tightness in his neck, exhaled loudly, then looked at Nolie. She was looking back, an intense, steady gaze that made him shift uncomfortably. The minor problem was out of the way. Now for the major one. . . .

"Thank you."

He wanted so much more from her than thanks, but he automatically replied, "You're welcome."

"After all that happened, I know it wasn't easy for you to step back into your lawyer persona and draw up those documents."

"Sometimes the law can be used for good instead of evil," he said with a wry smile. "I'd forgotten that."

Still speaking in a very polite tone, she said, "So I have Marlene to thank for the misery of the past few days."

"Marlene . . . and me. She didn't force me to make that choice, but . . . I'm sorry."

"You thought it was best for Micahlyn and me." She raised one hand to brush a speck of something from his shirt, then left it there, palm flat against his chest. "You were terribly wrong, but you had the best intentions."

"I couldn't be sure she wouldn't win a custody battle."

"So when you said she couldn't a while ago, you were lying?"

"We lawyers prefer to call it bluffing."

She smiled, a sweet, faint upturn of her mouth. "You bluff very well. You practically had me convinced I meant nothing to you."

Laying his hand over hers, he curled his fingers with hers. "Practically?"

"I had a little faith."

"You've had more faith in me than anyone else I've ever known. More than I've had in myself."

"So . . . are you going to tell me anytime soon that you love me?"

"Yes, I am." But not yet. Lifting her hand from his chest, he pressed a kiss to the back of it, then stroked one fingertip back and forth over the band on her fourth finger. It was slim, gold, marred by scratches and the hard knocks of life, but it hadn't lost its sparkle . . . or its meaning. He wanted that symbolism, wanted that meaning, for her, for himself, forever.

Looking up, he found her watching him with a tentative smile. He stroked the warm gold once again for courage, looked her in the eye, and asked, "If I give you a ring of my own, will you put that one away for Micahlyn?"

Her smile grew steadier, surer, brighter. "Yes," she replied simply. "I will."

T HE NEXT AFTERNOON, MARLENE AND OBIE LEFT for home. Nolie had offered to close up the store and go to the airport with them, but they'd preferred a private good-bye in Bethlehem over a crowd at an airport. Marlene unbent from her martyrdom enough to cry, and so did Micahlyn. While Nolie didn't get weepy herself, she *was* sorry to see them go—and a little relieved, too, without feeling the least bit guilty about it.

After they'd gone, Chase took Micahlyn to day care, then called the store. "Put up the CLOSED sign and meet me for lunch at Harry's."

"Umm, you tempt me."

"Oh, babe, that's not tempting. Tempting is when I . . ." His voice trailed to a whisper, his tone naughty, and raised her body temperature a few hundred degrees. Before she could respond—or simply sink weak-kneed to the floor—he laughed. "Come on. One hour. Lunch."

She really shouldn't. She would bet old Hiram hadn't ever shut the store down when it was supposed to be open, not when his wife left him, not even when his daughter ran away.

But she wasn't old Hiram. She had a life, and family, and more important things to do in the middle of the day than work—today, at least. "Okay. I'll be there in five."

It was closer to ten minutes when she parked off the square across from Harry's. By the time she got out of the car, Chase had crossed the street to meet her, casually kissing her mouth, then sliding his arm around her. "Walk with me."

She gave him a sidelong look. "If you're thinking to build up an appetite, I know better ways to do it, no special clothes, no equipment required. In fact, it works best without any clothes at all."

"Now *you're* tempting *me*." But he didn't lead her back to her car and head for home. Instead, they strolled across the street and into the square. The grass was lush, the flowers in bloom, and a few birds chirped overhead. How much more perfect could the center of town be?

At his urging, she followed him up the steps of the bandstand, where he backed her against the railing. "Did you know I got my first serious kiss here?"

She shook her head. "How old were you?"

"Fifteen. I also came to my first band concert here and sat on Santa's lap for the first time right over there. I smoked my first cigarette here, too, and got caught by the chief of police."

"A place for firsts," she said with a smile.

"Yeah." His dark gaze turned serious, and for a moment

he simply looked at her, as if memorizing the lines of her face. When he spoke again, his voice was low, throaty, his emotion intense. "I love you."

She knew that. Of course she knew it. How could she not? Oh, but it was sweet to be sure he knew it, too. She raised her left hand to touch his face. "What a coincidence. I love you, too."

"I was counting on that."

Catching her hand, he stroked the skin, worn smooth after seven years of the wedding band she had removed last night. She'd tucked it into a velvet box and slid it to the back of her lingerie drawer, along with the agreement signed by Marlene and Obie. She'd felt a moment's sadness, as if she was saying good-bye to Jeff all over again, then she'd glanced into the dresser mirror and seen Chase watching her from the bed. It wasn't good-bye. She'd loved Jeff dearly, and always would.

Just as she loved Chase dearly and always would.

Abruptly he let go of her hand, laid his hands on her shoulders, and turned her so her back was to him. "Choose a star and make a wish."

She laughed. "It's the middle of the day. The stars aren't out."

"They're out. You just can't see them."

"How can I make a wish on something I can't see?"

"You take it the same way you've taken me. On faith," he murmured, his mouth close enough to her ear to send a shiver through her. "Besides, you said yourself you close your eyes when you wish on stars. So close your eyes, pick a star, and make a wish with me."

Feeling foolish and not caring, she did as he said, envisioning a sky filled with stars, choosing the best and brightest one, and making the best and brightest wish. For a moment, the air around them seemed to shimmer with expectancy, making her skin tingle and her palms grow damp.

Or was that merely Chase's body pressed close against hers?

"Open your eyes," he commanded softly.

The day was just as bright, the breeze just as warm, the town just as normal, but her heart couldn't decide between beating double-time and not at all, and her breath was caught in a knot in her chest. She stared, wondering how his hand could be so steady when her entire being was shaky, but he was steady as a rock. The ring he held for her inspection didn't tremble at all.

"Oh, Chase, it's beautiful."

"It reminded me of you."

Nestled in a burgundy velvet box, the ring was antique gold filigree with one perfect pearl in the center. It was beautiful, warm, and lustrous, and would look lovely on her hand. She reached out to touch it, but he pulled it away.

"Not until you say the magic word."

Turning in the circle of his arms, she was about to ask what the magic word was, but she knew. She could see it in his eyes, could feel it in her heart. "Yes," she whispered.

Still he withheld the ring. "You'd better be sure, 'cause once I've got you, I'm never letting you go."

"Yes."

"You know, I come with baggage—a sister who's always getting her heart broken, a father I have a lot of unresolved issues with, and a mother I haven't seen in years."

"Yes."

"And there's the little matter of my background—"

Catching handfuls of his shirt, she yanked him to her and kissed him. Almost immediately, he took control, sliding his tongue into her mouth, taking his sweet, lazy time tasting her. Not that she minded. Oh, no, they could kiss like that all day and into the night . . . once she got one important matter out of the way.

"Ask me to marry you, Chase," she murmured.

"Will you marry me, Nolie?"

"*Yes.* Now give me the ring."

And he did.

A S NIGHT EASED INTO DAWN, COLE SLID OUT OF Leanne's bed, careful not to wake her. He dressed quickly, quietly, then stood for a time looking down at her. He'd tried to stay away from her, he really had, but it hadn't worked. Every morning he left, intending to end things with her once and for all, and every evening he found himself right back in her bed. He'd been born with a weakness for women in general, but he'd never had one for a particular woman . . . until now.

In his business, he couldn't afford a weakness.

He wanted to walk out without a look back. To strip down and crawl back into bed with her. To put off leaving until tomorrow. To already be gone.

He settled for touching her, just his fingers against her bare shoulder. She smiled in her sleep. He'd never been good at good-byes, mostly because he never stuck around long enough to say them. It seemed he was always leaving town in a hurry, either of his own will or with the cops on his tail. He rarely had the time or the inclination to prolong his departure with farewells.

But he'd never left anyone important behind before.

He touched her once more, for the last time, then left the room. Across the narrow hall, he went into Danny's room and crouched next to the bed. The kid had kicked off his covers, so Cole slid them back into place before turning his attention to Ryan, asleep on an inflatable bed.

Lamplight illuminated his face and kept the nightmares at bay, making him look like any normal twelve-year-old boy. No one would guess to look at him now that he'd been abandoned and betrayed by everyone in his life who should have cared. When he woke up in a few hours, he would lump Cole in with the others, but damn it, it wasn't a matter of caring. The kid needed a regular home and respectable parents who could raise him right. He needed things Cole couldn't give him, but someone in Bethlehem could.

Before he started second-guessing his decision, Cole got to his feet, moved stealthily down the hall and the stairs, then crossed the street to the Miller house. He didn't bother to shave or change clothes. He packed his bags, quickly and efficiently, and carried them along with his laptop computer to the Lexus. Within twenty minutes of leaving Leanne's bed, he was driving past the town limits sign, heading out of Bethlehem, out of the valley, and out of Leanne's and Ryan's lives.

Forever.

About the Author

Known for her intensely emotional stories, Marilyn Pappano is the author of nearly fifty books with more than six million copies in print. She has made regular appearances on bestseller lists and has received recognition with numerous awards for her work. Though her husband's Navy career took them across the United States, they now live in Oklahoma, high on a hill that overlooks her hometown. They have one son.

Follow the charming and spirited
adventures of Leanne and Cole in Marilyn
Pappano's next enchanting novel . . .

SMALL WONDERS

Coming in September 2003

Read on for a preview . . .

COLE SAT, STIFF AND SILENT, IN THE BACK seat of the SUV. His hands were cuffed in front of him, then attached to a chain around his waist, restricting any movement of more than a few inches. He wore leg irons, too, attached to a chain that passed through a steel loop bolted to the truck's floorboard, then again to the waist chain.

His muscles ached from holding the same position all day, but he had no one to blame but himself. He'd been more comfortable the day before—handcuffed, but otherwise free to move. He'd been so comfortable, in fact, that when they'd stopped that evening to gas up and hit the bathrooms, he'd tried to move right on out of Sergeant Bishop's custody. Obviously, he hadn't succeeded, and the chains and leg irons were the thanks he got for his effort.

He stared out the side window, barely noticing the woods and occasional house. They'd passed through Howland some time back. Soon they would start the descent into the valley where Bethlehem was located. Soon they would be there, and there wasn't a damn thing he could do about it.

From the moment the Savannah cops had turned him over to Bishop, Cole had wanted to ask about Ryan—where was he, was he all right, who was taking care of him—but had stubbornly refused to do so. The kid was better off without him. He needed a mother, a stable home, someone to teach him right from wrong. It hadn't escaped Ryan's notice or Cole's how hypocritical it was for Cole to try to do the teaching when he hadn't done an honest day's work in his life.

But he wanted Ryan to be a better man than him. That was why he'd left him behind. It didn't matter that it had been a lousy thing to do, or that Ryan would hate him for it. It had been best, and that was all that mattered.

Realizing that the road was curving steeply downward, he spoke for the first time all day. "How much longer?"

"Five, ten minutes."

Cole's gut knotted. It was a short walk from the parking lot outside the Bethlehem courthouse to the police department on the first floor and the jail in the basement. Was it too much to hope that he could make it without running into anyone he knew? Probably. But as long as he didn't see Ryan—or Leanne, a sly voice inside him whispered— he would be all right.

He'd had a whole lifetime of learning to be all right.

The church steeples came into view first, followed by rooftops. Long before he was ready, they were passing Hiram's Feed Store, owned by Nolie Harper. One Saturday night last spring he'd gone there with Leanne to take Nolie, suffering from a bad case of food poisoning, to the hospital. She'd been seeing Leanne's brother—probably still was—and had welcomed Cole into her home and trusted him with thirty grand and change that was earmarked for her daughter's education.

The next business, just barely within the town limits, was a gas station and garage. Leon, the owner, had contributed $5,000 to Cole's scheme. Melvin Fitzgerald at the hardware store on the right had chipped in another $5,000. Elena who owned the bookstore, Betty who worked there, Harry and Maeve at the diner, the Knights, the Graysons, the Winchester sisters, the pastors of most of the churches belonging to those steeples. . . . He'd been an equal opportunity cheat.

Bishop turned on the far side of the square, drove to the end of the block, and parked outside the courthouse. Cole did his best not to look in the direction of Small Wonders, Leanne's shop across the street, or the Miller mansion, which he'd shared with Ryan for his short residence in town. As usual when it came to good intentions, his best wasn't good enough.

The shop was closed and dark except for a few lights shining on the window displays and another one over the cash register. There were also lights showing through the apartment windows upstairs, though neither Leanne nor Danny came near the windows during the few moments he could see.

Bishop opened the rear door and unlocked the chains, then the leg irons, but he left the handcuffs in place. Cole slid to the ground, his joints creaking, a rush of pain shooting through his muscles at the sudden movement. He did his best to stretch, then, with a nudge from Bishop, he started toward the courthouse. Jillian Freeman—in to him for $7,500—was standing outside the house across the street that was home to both her and her law office, her expression less than friendly. An officer leaving the courthouse—in for $2,000—held the door for them and called Cole a thieving bastard when he passed.

He'd ripped off two of the three judges in town, both lawyers, and a fair number of cops. This was *not* a good place to come back to.

After he was booked, Bishop escorted him downstairs and past the first cell and the second, both empty, before locking him in the last cell. It was the only one with a window, set high in the wall and too small for even Ryan to wiggle through, and when Cole lay on his back on the cot and gazed out, all he could see was Leanne's apartment.

His punishment had already begun.

The first floor of the Bethlehem courthouse was taken up with the police department and the sheriff's office. On the second floor were administrative offices and the courtrooms, and on the third were more offices. There were only two courtrooms, and the one Cole was escorted into shortly before one P.M. was small. Three tall windows let in light, but the dimpled frosted glass blocked the view outside. The paneling, woodwork, and plaster were probably original to the room—such quality work would cost a fortune these days. A mural depicting blind justice covered most of one wall, and wooden benches, worn to a muted sheen by years of use, filled the back half of the room.

He kept his head up, shoulders back, and his gaze on the floor. He caught vague images of people sitting in the gallery but didn't look to see if he knew them. He would rather not see any more familiar faces. They made him feel guilty, which, of course, he was. He just wasn't used to *feeling* it.

The jailer, accompanied by a deputy, nudged him into a seat at the defense table. This time the older man hadn't handcuffed Cole, and he'd been allowed to wear his own clothes. It was an improvement over the times in the past when he'd been forced to appear handcuffed, shackled, and wearing an ugly orange jumpsuit.

His lawyer, Alex Thomas, already sat at the long oak table, looking none too friendly or hopeful. That was okay. The only thing Cole hoped for was to get out of Bethlehem as quickly as possible, and he didn't care where he had to go to do it—prison, hell. . . .

At precisely one o'clock, the judge came out of her chambers and took a seat on the bench. Cole tuned out the proceedings, fixing his gaze on the glossy wood floor where it met the wall, willing his mind to go blank. It was a state he usually achieved without much effort, but this afternoon it wouldn't happen. Words from the prosecutor's speech kept slithering in: *defrauded, stole, abandoned*. Unfamiliar emotions kept seeping to the surface. Regret. Guilt. Shame.

Every profession had its downside. Lawyers lost cases. Doctors lost patients. Teachers couldn't teach everyone.

This—arrest, a trial, jail—was the downside of his business. Avoiding it was the challenge that made his work fun. Accepting when it couldn't be avoided was the cost of doing business. It was a common setback, and it shouldn't make him feel so damn lousy. It never had before.

For the fact that this time it did, he blamed Bethlehem. Ryan. Leanne.

Thomas's chair scraped as he stood up, then he touched Cole's arm, gesturing for him to rise. Cole refocused his attention on the proceedings and his gaze on the judge, who was looking annoyed at obviously having to repeat herself.

"How do you plead, Mr. Jackson?"

You'd better think about your plea, Thomas had told him that morning, but when Cole had returned to his cell, instead he'd lain on the cot, stared at the windows of Leanne's apartment, and considered how completely he'd wasted his life. He was thirty years old, and he'd contributed *nothing* to society. He'd never made anyone happy, never helped anyone in need, had never done a damn thing that justified his continued existence. The world would be a better place without him in it.

That was one sorry epitaph.

The judge watched him, her mouth pursed in a thin line. If he tried to speak, he wasn't sure he could find his voice. The words he wanted to say, needed to say, didn't come easily to a man like him. From the time he was five years old, his father had taught him to always proclaim his innocence. To never admit guilt even if he was caught red-handed. To always lie, and once he'd found a lie that worked, stick with it no matter what.

Owen Jackson would box his ears for even thinking what he was thinking.

"Mr. Jackson," the judge prodded impatiently. "How do you plead?"

Thomas was looking at him. So was the prosecutor, the court reporter, the bailiff, and everyone in the gallery. He drew a breath, but his chest was tight and refused to accommodate more than a gasp. His voice was strong in spite of it, though his jaw was clenched so tightly that his mouth barely moved. A lifetime of learning could be difficult to overcome . . . but it *could* be overcome.

"Guilty."

The relief rushing through him was almost equal to the panic. No son of Owen Jackson's *ever* pled guilty. A jury might judge them so, but they always put up a fight. What the hell was he doing, rolling over without even trying?

He was accepting responsibility for what he'd done. No son of Owen Jackson's ever did that, either, and it felt damned scary but good. Now he would go to prison. He would leave Bethlehem for the last time, and this time it really would be the last time.

He would never see Ryan again, or Leanne.

That was also one of the downsides of his line of work.

The judge set a sentencing date for the following Thursday, which brought more relief. He knew from family experience that sentencing dates four weeks or more after a conviction or entering a plea weren't uncommon. If he was incredibly lucky, he could be out of town by Friday. He could stand four more days. As long as he didn't have to see anyone but the jailer or the officers who delivered his meals, he could stand anything.

The judge dismissed the court and the deputy signaled Cole to leave the courtroom. He circled the table and walked behind the jailer and in front of the deputy halfway to the door before some indefinable something jerked his gaze to the left. Standing there just inside the door was Leanne, and she was giving him a look of pure loathing.

The deputy gave him a push, and Cole realized he'd

stopped in his tracks. He started walking again, came abreast of her, gave her a cocky grin and a wink, and said, "Hey, sugar."

As if he hadn't stolen her money, or broken her heart, or left her with his son.

Her expression didn't change—not a flicker of surprise, not a hint of temper. She just watched him as if he were scum scraped from the bottom of somebody's shoe.

In that moment, that was exactly how he felt.

As if he didn't have a care in the world, he walked through the doorway, then followed the jailer to the stairwell. Didn't want to taint the decent people taking the elevator, he supposed.

A few minutes and three flights of stairs later, he was back in his cell with no place to go, no one to talk to, and nothing to do. He stretched out on the cot with his head at the end where he couldn't see out the window, used his clasped hands for a pillow, and tried to concentrate on his future. Not the years he would spend in prison, but after that. Where he would go. What he would do. How he would live.

But it was hard to think about all that when other images kept intruding. Dark hair and dark eyes, filled with condemnation, contempt, confusion. Hell, he couldn't even say exactly whose image he was seeing. Ryan, Leanne, and even her son, Danny, whom Cole had fallen so easily into the habit of calling *son,* all had identical dark hair, eyes, and skin.

And they all had good reason to hate him.

He closed his eyes, hoping that would chase away the vision. For a moment it worked, and the tension slowly started seeping from his muscles. Then he heard a sound— the soft scuff of a shoe on the concrete floor—and it came rushing back.

He opened his eyes, turned his head, and saw Leanne standing on the other side of the cell bars. He wished he could ignore her, pretend she wasn't there, make himself disappear. Of course he couldn't, so he sat up, grinned, and leaned back against the stone wall. "I'd invite you in, but I seem to have misplaced the key."

For a long stiff moment she stared at him, looking as if any expression at all would cause her face to crack. Then she stepped forward, slid a plastic bag through the bars, then let it drop. It landed with a particularly loud thump.

He looked from her to the bag, then back. "What's that?"

"Books. Ryan thought you might be bored."

"Then why didn't Ryan bring them?"

"Because he's hoping you'll rot here so he'll never have to see you again."

Pain slashed through Cole, making his chest tighten, forcing him to swallow hard. It had been too much to hope that Ryan would understand why Cole had left him behind. He was a kid, after all—just twelve years old and abandoned by everyone who'd owed him something better. When he got a little older, though, he would see that Cole had owed him better, too, and had done his best to see that he got it. A kid couldn't ask for a better place to grow up than Bethlehem, or better people to grow up with.

Cole shrugged callously as if he didn't give a damn about Ryan's hopes. "If that's all you wanted, you can leave now."

She didn't. Instead, she came closer to the bars, resting one hand on the crossbar. "I talked to the jailer, and to Alex, and to Nathan. You haven't even asked about Ryan."

He shrugged again. "He's not my problem anymore."

Her mouth worked, but no sound came out, and her

fingers tightened around the steel bar until they turned white. After a moment, she found her voice. "You worthless, lying, cold-hearted *bastard*. I hope you burn in hell!"

Spinning away, she stormed off toward the opposite end of the corridor, and he watched her go. Once the heavy steel door closed after her, his shoulders slumped and he bowed his head. Burning in hell sounded preferable to the mess his life had become. All he'd wanted was to do the right thing—for Ryan, for Leanne, even for Danny—but as usual, he'd screwed up. It was proof that he wasn't cut out for being decent, and he damn sure didn't deserve to care about anyone.

Leanne was mostly right. He was a worthless, lying bastard, and by God, he would learn to be cold-hearted . . . or he would die trying.

with *Marilyn Pappano*

sometimes miracles do happen . . . .

Some Enchanted Season
___0553-57982-7 $5.99/$7.99 in Canada

Father to Be
__0553-57985-1 $5.99/$8.99

First Kiss
__0553-58231-3 $5.99/$8.99

Getting Lucky
__0553-58232-1 $6.50/$9.99

Heaven on Earth
__0440-23714-9 $6.50/$9.99

Cabin Fever
__0440-24118-9 $6.50/$9.99

Please enclose check or money order only, no cash or CODs. Shipping & handling costs: $5.50 U.S. mail, $7.50 UPS. New York and Tennessee residents must remit applicable sales tax. Canadian residents must remit applicable GST and provincial taxes. Please allow 4 – 6 weeks for delivery. All orders are subject to availability. This offer subject to change without notice. Please call 1-800-726-0600 for further information.

Bantam Dell Publishing Group, Inc.
Attn: Customer Service
400 Hahn Road
Westminster, MD 21157

TOTAL AMT $_____

SHIPPING & HANDLING $_____

SALES TAX (NY, TN) $_____

TOTAL ENCLOSED $_____

Name _____

Address _____

City/State/Zip _____

Daytime Phone (_____) _____